GRAVITY

JOURNEY TO NYORFIAS, BOOK 2

TERRY ROY

A Zapstone Production

GRAVITY Journey to Nyorfias, Book Two

A Zapstone Production

3rd Paperback Edition

ISBN-10: 1937899810

ISBN-13: 978-1-937899-81-3

On Epnoce, heavier gravity, frequent earthquakes, extreme arctic conditions, and killer storms are the least of Rett's troubles...

THE MAJOR WAITED UNTIL EASY Force had gone before speaking again.

"What happened up there, Sergeant?" His voice was dangerously calm.

"I mistakenly assumed the demonstration wouldn't involve others, sir. I had to make some last minute adjustments."

"And the arm?"

"Nothing much, sir. Slipped a bit. It's icy up there."

"Nothing much?" He took a step closer. "Let's see." His strong fingers closed over her left shoulder.

She kept her face still, hoping he wasn't going to try much more pressure than what he exerted already...

"You call this nothing much?" He didn't let up as he reached for her wrist with his free hand. "Dislocated shoulder. Fractured wrist and forearm. Nothing much." The combined assault of pain almost buckled Rett's knees. "Rhozev!" Yidnar snapped the medtech's name like an electric spark. At the same time, he released his grip on her so abruptly Rett lost her balance and fell at his feet.

"Yes, sir?"

"Escort Sergeant Rett to Medical. She is suspended from all Battalion activities and will be barred from Battalion areas until I consult with you again. I'm sure you'll want to impose your own restrictions as well. Any questions, see me after you've dealt with her."

"Yes, sir," said Med.

Suspended...!

More Books by Terry Roy

~ ~ ~

Science Fiction/Action
Convergence – Journey to Nyorfias, Book 1
Gravity – Journey to Nyorfias, Book 2
Stratagem – Journey to Nyorfias, Book 3
Carakenne – Journey to Nyorfias, Book 4
Kyarta Girl – Journey to Nyorfias, Book 5

~ ~ ~ ~

Sff-Romance
Discovery – A Far Out Romance

~ ~ ~ ~

Romance
Fear of Flying (Romantic Suspense)

~ ~ ~ ~

Humor
as Terran Moffat
First Bass and Other Stories

Visit
https://teryvisions.wordpress.com/
for the latest news, updates, sneak previews, and more!

Contact the author!
terzap@gmail.com
Please write with any comments, concerns, or questions

CONTENTS

~oOo~
For my sisters, of birth and of soul,
who have inspired many of the qualities
of the characters in this book;

And for my one and only special big brother, Tim, without whom
I'd have never discovered
science fiction in the first place.

~oOo~

AUTHOR'S NOTE

This is the SECOND book in the Journey to Nyorfias storyline. The three installments make one epic story that is simply too long to put into one printed book. (Even cutting some parts out!) Like the first book, *Convergence*, this saga is composed in a series of connected episodes rather than conventional chapters. This story can stand alone, but please note: you will not understand quite how things got started if you skipped *Convergence*, and while there might be an episodic conclusion at the end of *Gravity*--it's not the close of the story arc.

I feel I need to point this out due to various reactions I've had from readers. So I'm putting it upfront.

Also part of the complete series, and containing important insights to the continuing saga, are the shorter novels *Carakenne* (the events take place during JTN2 *Gravity*) and *Kyarta Girl*, which should be read immediately after JTN3 *Stratagem*.

I highly recommend reading them in this order: *Convergence, Gravity, Carakenne, Stratagem,* and *Kyarta Girl*. So when you're done with this book, hop back to your favorite bookstore and check out a copy of *Carakenne* before reading JTN3 *Stratagem*!

I hope you are enjoying the adventure every bit as much as I enjoyed writing it!

GRAVITY
JOURNEY TO NYORFIAS, BOOK 2

TERRY ROY

"**H**OLD ON TO SOMETHING, SERGEANT!"
The force of acceleration slammed Rett into the padding of the seat so hard she had to wonder if holding on would even be an issue. She gripped the handle on the passenger side with her left hand, pushed her feet hard into the floor plating, and pressed her right arm over the precious carrier that sat on the console between them. "We have to get there alive, or timing it close isn't going to mean anything."

"Don't you trust me?"

"Sure I—"

A hard turn to the right nearly plastered Rett against the curved sidepanel. Before she could compensate, the rover dropped over an embankment to follow the steep path of a skid trail. A quick grab saved their delicate cargo from sliding free of its spot and slamming into the control panel. For a few weightless moments, she was sure her butt was somewhere close to her ears until her internal balance compensated and told her she was definitely descending...and straight toward a fast-moving river below.

Although they often crossed short expanses of water, most mountain rovers weren't meant as amphibious vehicles. She hoped the enclosed cockpit of this one was watertight, at least, because they were going to make a very large—

"Uhh!" A grunt was forced from her as the rover banked and the descent abruptly flattened into a horizontal attitude. The safety harness straps were going to leave bruises. She clamped the container between her inner arm and body.

"We'll be in the open in a few," said her companion as he guided the rover through a sunlit stand of young trees and brush. Rett couldn't identify much from the blur of vegetation going past, but she saw enough to guess the fire that made this slash through the older timber was at least a half-century past.

It took less than a minute to cover the area of younger growth before they plunged again into the shadows beneath the mature trees.

"Watch out for that—" She couldn't help it; she ducked as their rover slid beneath the low-hanging branch, the faintest squeak on the canopy material betraying they had touched it at all. The narrow space between the two longcones ahead, surely he didn't mean to try and go through it. Yet there was no other possible way to go, not at this speed.

What Rett intended to come out as another warning instead erupted as an exuberant *"Whooo-hoooo!"* as the rover banked like a fightercraft and shot through the narrow passage with room to spare. "Yeehaw!"

"Whooooo!" echoed her driver, laughing with glee as the rover emerged from the thick cover of timber. A sharp bank put them on the fire road toward Branch.

"Way to go, Zlotfyr!"

Damn it, Pam! Rett peeled the left side of her face from the clear canopy, where it had been plastered during that last hard turn. She released her grip on the seat long enough to pull away the harness that had embedded itself in her body. *Don't encourage him.*

~God, Rett, lighten up. He might be two hundred years old, but he knows what he's doing.~

He's not two hundred. He said he was a hundred and twenty-five. Which was, perhaps, cause enough for concern. But the hard forces of acceleration and sudden turns apparently didn't bother the silver-haired reservist piloting the rover at such glorious, reckless speed. Instead, he now looked twice as lively and energetic as when she first met him that morning.

Aloud, Rett said, "I had no idea a rover could do that. Or go this fast." Her heart rate was dropping back to normal, and yes, she had to admit the initial increase was more from adrenaline than nerves. She had never expected her easygoing, elderly guide to switch gears as well as personalities for their wild shortcut through the forest.

Her driver sent her a grin so huge she had to give one back. "Oh, they can't. I did a little fixing on this one. You try that in a normal rover, one that isn't weighted and balanced for it, we'd have been smeared on several trees back there already."

"So you're an engineer."

"Dabbled. I flew with the firewatch and the militia for sixty years, and did a lot of experimenting on my own time."

"Pilot." This time Rett leaned toward him, her interest sharpened.

"Once."

"Oh, I think you still have it. And if you haven't shared some of your rover modifications yet—you should think about that, too." She extracted the carrier she had tucked protectively beneath her arm and peeked inside .

"Everything survive?"

"Looks good. For a moment though, I thought it would be mashed fish and mushroom soup for our dinners."

Zlotfyr slowed the rover to a more sedate pace and called in to the gate as they neared the northernmost entrance of the huge military base on the outskirts of Branch town. "Canopy open."

The old man halted the rover at the marker and lifted both his hands, palms facing toward the gate. Rett didn't have to focus her energy sense very hard to discern the hard yellow glow of a powerful force field several lengths in front of them. She fished out the ID from around her neck. Leaving her finger in the lanyard loop so that the data storage unit was easily visible and ready for inspection, she mirrored the driver's position. Only then did the rover move forward, this time under the control of the base security.

Did you see it? she asked Pam silently. *The barrier, and the opening we just went through?*

~No. Maybe, for a second. But… no.~ Pam's thought was disgruntled. ~I'm still not getting it.~

I wasn't focusing on it much, Rett admitted then. *Maybe if I did next time. I mean, it's so strong a field I didn't even have to think about scoping it like I usually would. You wouldn't want to try going through it, even though it shouldn't kill you.*

~It shouldn't?~

3

No, the programming allows for adjustments: if the sensors detect anything living in the field, it's zapped out or paralyzed until someone comes and fishes it out. It hurts—then your nerves sort of buzz for days afterward.

~You got stuck in one?~

I almost did once, but that's a story for another time. Even so, training makes sure we know what it feels like to walk into one.

After they were through the gate, she slapped the release catches on her harness and straightened her clothing. Going out of uniform to a meeting with her commander felt strange, but it couldn't be helped.

~He did say come as you were, just get there on time because he had things scheduled,~ reminded Pam.

And almost as if he were synched to Pam's internal comment, Zlotfyr called Rett's attention to the chrono display on the instrument panel. "See there. Told you I'd get you here and with time to spare!" He laughed again in satisfaction, faded brown eyes sparkling.

"I never had the slightest doubt," Rett said truthfully.

~No, you just doubted if you'd arrive alive, or in one piece,~ came the interior voice of her alien companion.

No different from any combat mission, countered Rett.

~Rett, this was a fishing trip. And a bit of fungus gathering. It was supposed to be fun, not a life and death thing.~

Rett grinned inside and out, for Pam, for Zlotfyr, and slid from the rover. "Thanks for the company, and for the ride. That *was* fun. Let's do it again sometime."

2.0.1 2023RD CO'S OFFICE, MILITARYCENTRAL, BRANCH
0535.08.06 (LOCAL RECKONING)

"**T**HE BATTLE FOR EPNOCE IS going to be far different than most of us can imagine."

Rett accepted the mug of tea Major Yidnar handed her and waited while he moved around to the other side of his desk.

"It will," said her battalion commander, "go well beyond the matter of being indoors in buildings that contain more square lengths of habitable space than the entire city of Circle."

She covered her dismay at the prospect by lowering her face to her mug and taking a sniff at the aromatic vapor. She'd do whatever she had to, wherever she had to, with her bare hands if necessary. But being indoors all the time, fighting constantly between walls, floor, and ceiling? "Surely we'll be outdoors some of the time, sir. It's not as if we can access one complex from the next, they're too far apart."

Yidnar nodded. "Some of the time, yes, but not much. There's also no cover sufficient enough to base, deploy, or use ground troops the way we did here. As for the subsurface railtube system that connects many of the complexes to each other, we've written off securing any of it for our use. But since the enemy's come to depend on it, we'll definitely spend time spoiling the system for them."

"Even if the landscape wasn't an issue, the weather isn't going to help," Rett said.

"Or the quakes."

She didn't want to think about those. One of her juniors, H'tenneck, native to Epnoce, didn't think dealing with the earthquakes would be as much of an issue as adapting to the different air, gravity, and climate. Rett wasn't so sure. Lifting her mug, she finally took a sip of tea. The blend surprised her; it was a local mix similar to the favored morning tea from her native province and included fresh blue pine. From the extra tingle, it wasn't only fresh; it was the pale, whitish new growth that even now was frosting the deeper blue foliage of the mature trees. She wondered if Major Yidnar had made it with her preferences in mind.

When she glanced up at him, he raised his own mug, his dark blue eyes twinkling. "I've heard that in different proportions and with a few secret ingredients, this stuff is great for hangovers—of any type. That is, if you live long enough to get it down."

"I'll be very happy to make that version for your next hangover, sir," Rett said.

Yidnar's thick eyebrows formed a single line over his nose. "You've been on remote assignment away from Battalion for far too long, Sergeant. I've not known you to be so impertinent to ranking officers."

Pam, stop it. Rett grabbed the inside of her cheek with her teeth. She had to watch it. It was one thing to make such comebacks to her peers. It was another making them to her seniors. It was a good thing she knew the Major was amused by her remark; the bright sparkle of energy that rippled through him after she had spoken revealed that much.

~I'm not doing anything!~

6   *After those strange sounds you made me come out with on the ride over, I can't be so sure.*

~Okay, sure, I admit I helped with that, but don't try to put this one over on me. You've been lightening up all on your own, Rett. Stop blaming the dimwitted alien mindforce from Earth, okay? I thought we'd moved past that.~

"Now, where was I?"

"You're telling me this campaign on Epnoce is going to be pretty much run out of one main base, sir," Rett said. "At least at first."

The Major managed to give her an approving nod while taking another swig from his mug.

That isn't too reassuring, Rett thought to Pam, *considering the enemy holds nearly every complex on Epnoce at the moment.*

~And there you'll be with all your eggs in one basket, as we say on Earth,~ replied Pam.

For once, Rett didn't need her alien friend to explain one of her peculiar anecdotes. "The task force we have there now almost has that base secured for us." The Major leaned forward, crossing his forearms in front of him without regard to the arrangement of hardcopy reports, electronic notebooks, and file folders on the desk. "Tell me what concerns you."

She placed her mug carefully near the edge of Yidnar's desk. "I don't see where we're going to have *time* to train or acclimatize, sir," she said, perplexed. "The task force we sent wasn't that large, and what was left of our militia on Epnoce all those years was…" She scrambled for something a little less bleak than the truth but gave up. "We had no military left on Epnoce. There was only the civilian resistance. Even with the GTC Rangers and marines there now, what's going to keep the enemy from coming out of the other complexes and taking back the base—or leveling it—until we establish a better holding? Do we *have* that many personnel, with air and space support, to continue as defense and attack? Or did the Galactic Trade Commission manage to get even more support ships and troops in than we were told?"

Yidnar's grin was more a predatory display of teeth. "No. Not yet. But our Nyorfian-GTC task force isn't the *only* asset we have on Epnoce."

He cocked his head to the left in a peculiar manner, and when he again opened his mouth, she prepared to interpret the information he wasn't about to speak aloud. "We've been deploying personnel there for some time. Almost a third of the 2023rd is already there, as well as several infantry divisions and a full AirSpacefighter wing."

Rett was glad to be sitting down. "And is that what happened to the 10th, 16th, and… and the 21st?" she asked in the same manner, moving her lips without sound.

He indicated the affirmative with a slight nod.

~Isn't that your father's division? The 21st? I'm just asking—yes or no?~ Pam headed off any irritated response on Rett's part.

Yes.

Rett had never believed those three infantry divisions had been redeployed to the small, outlying continents off the shores of Main. Why waste such well-seasoned troops on guard duty to old Coalition bases? She hadn't questioned it, though. Unless it involved her platoon, it wasn't her place to judge troop deployment.

Evetez hinted there was some rumor about sneaking in a couple infantry divisions. But how in two worlds did we manage getting three of them to Epnoce without anyone finding out?

~Hmm,~ ventured Pam, ~my guess would be Jaq Pym, and a lot of help from the civilian resistance you've been telling me about. I mean, look at H'tenneck and the few others who managed to sneak off to bring information here.~

Maybe, Rett thought back, attention tight on Major Yidnar, *but he's not going to elaborate.* Just one look at him was enough to know that for sure. So Rett buried the new information along with her curiosity—and her relief. The subject was closed.

"Now," Yidnar said, "in the light of how we're going to conduct operations once we're there, I'm creating several new assault groups. We'll need to pack the biggest possible punch into a unit sized small enough to move easily, yet large and diverse enough to split into as many parts as needed. In the same manner our Nyorfian-GTC task force is opening the way for us to Epnoce, the Special Forces assault groups will need to open clear paths for the infantry units who will back them up and will, hopefully, provide the new defense for each complex we regain from the enemy."

Rett nodded, already getting a clearer idea of it.

"Not unlike the strategy you implemented for the Circle campaign," added the Major.

"Major, I—" *Can't take credit for the entire strategy* was shot down as her commander interrupted.

"You were in command of the entire initial strike. You would have taken responsibility had it failed—why not with its success as well? It was brilliant."

"Sir, I wasn't alone." There. At least got that out.

"Of course it was a team effort. But it started with you accepting that impossible assignment from Colonel Evard, and it went with others having confidence enough in you to do anything you asked."

"The odds weren't exactly in our favor, but impossible?"

Yidnar's left eyebrow rose, his gaze nailing her into silence. "Did you not—at first—refuse to volunteer F-troop to spearhead such an operation because of the circumstances?" At her reluctant nod, he continued. "You were well within your rights to do so. It *was* suicidal. MainCommand never expected the attack to succeed, no matter who commanded it."

"I did refuse, sir, but that was before I was told there had been Coalition troopships ready to lift off from Epnoce." An old, familiar turbulence started deep in her guts, and it wasn't a delayed reaction from her wild ride in to the base. She regretted having anything to eat that morning.

Yidnar nodded. "That was true. We needed to lock down the Circle spaceport as soon as possible. Of course they hoped the plan would succeed, but MainCommand had to face facts. The odds were impossible. So all wishing aside, all they had to realistically hope for was that the Wide River Gap Bridge and Circle attacks would focus Coalition attention long enough to redeploy our other forces for the next—hopefully successful—attack. That one would have been assisted by the GTC."

Rett lowered her head and stared at her knees for a moment. She could see the logic of the move, accepted the necessity, had known the risks. But to hear it had been so matter-of-factly *expected* that their effort would fail before it even started… well, that blew her off balance.

9

"I'm glad we pulled it off," she said, unable to put much energy in her voice. She reached for her mug, dragged it off the desk, and drained the last of her tea in one long gulp. Hangovers weren't the only malady blue pine helped settle.

"You wear that Freedom Star on your headband as proof."

Maybe to him she did, but she regarded it as her memorial to those who'd paid the ultimate price of their lives. "Did you expect us to fail, sir?" She forced her rebelling stomach to settle as she met his gaze, surprised to find his rugged features so charged with compassion. The chill that had gripped her heart warmed.

"I don't ever expect any of my people to fail. In anything. Why do you think I pushed Evard to put you in command of the operation? This brings me to the real reason I wanted to meet with you before things get really crazy."

~Take a breath and hold on to your headband, Rett,~ advised Pam, even as Rett's instincts went into defensive mode.

"Even at the expense of breaking up a top team like you and F-troop, I really would like you to reconsider your position on advancement. I really can use you in a larger capacity. You've proven beyond anyone's doubt that you're able and ready to handle it."

With a deliberate motion, she replaced the empty mug in the precise location it had occupied before. One of the few personal choices she had in her military life was the right to refuse advancement—to a point. This point.

She'd never given advancement much thought until she'd been given command of F-troop and had reached the highest non-officer rank the Nyorfian military had. After her last three reviews—each time turning down the rank upgrade due her—she knew damned well the next time she was asked, like now, that Major Yidnar would make it an issue. Especially with the way he mentioned Special Forces was going to be deployed on Epnoce.

"I'll give you forty more seconds to give me one *solid* reason this time." He steepled his fingers together and tapped his chin with them, almost as if he was counting off the seconds that way.

Rett knew that saying she liked exactly where she was and didn't want to leave F-troop wasn't what he wanted to hear.

"Experience handling people, in general, as well as their more personal problems, sir," Rett said. "I'm not that good at it."

"There's quite a few years' worth of personnel records and interviews from those under your command in my Omni right now that say otherwise."

"I can't take the credit for those," Rett said, twisting her hands together in her lap. "I've had help. Even with the help, it wipes me out. Every time I have to handle something out of the ordinary with them, my insides get into a huge mess over it. Managing the platoon's other business, materials, training—that's not a problem. With C-troop, all I had to worry about the first four years was my squad, until I was third-up. And even after that, if I couldn't help someone out, I just sent them up the chain of command.

"With F-troop, it's taken two years to get to the point where every personal decision and problem I handle with my platoon doesn't keep me awake all night worried if I made the right decisions or not, or if I was fair enough, or that I might have misunderstood. I can't imagine doing it on a larger scale without learning from someone who has the skills I lack."

Her fingers had twisted themselves into knots, and her insides felt the same way. Major Yidnar was one of the few people in who she could place the utmost personal confidence. If she wanted to, she could tell him anything, and everything. *Okay, so I made an exception not telling him about the ego-merge*, she thought in response to a little wiggle from Pam's corner.

~Then why not tell him?~

Because if I did, and someone found out, he'd be in trouble for keeping it secret, too. Bad enough Ariam knows.

"That was quite possibly one of the longest voluntary speeches I've ever heard from you all at once, Rett." The Major sat back in his chair, his hands lowered now, resting on the desk. His face could have been set in pourstone.

She didn't answer. Her lack of people skills and social awkwardness had been a concern to her for years, even before her military life. She was sure that Major Yidnar knew that already. He should know it better than almost anyone else, except perhaps for Ariam.

"All right, sport," he said at last. "You're safe—*this* time."

Her breath of relief was so strong it nearly sent her off her chair.

"There's a time limit on it, and you're still getting reassigned."

"Reassigned, sir?" Leave F-troop, even the half that was left? Her heart sank right to her boots.

"Yes, that's not contestable. And since your new assignment is going to be with someone who has the skills you need in abundance, I'll expect you to be his prize student. I'll also expect him to learn what you have to teach him in return."

"Yes, sir," Rett heard herself say, while thinking, *Ariam is ready to step up, Trebor and Worren will be great support for her.* "May I ask what this assignment will be?"

"You and F-troop, along with Sergeant Semage's B-troop, and R-troop under Sergeant Tris, are going to be part of the new assault group Easy Force under Lieutenant Evetez. Easy will include D- and S-troops, who are already on Epnoce as part of the initial strike team."

Her sinking feeling had reversed the instant she heard she was staying with her troop. "Are Atira and Mordell still up front on D- and S-troops?"

Yidnar nodded.

Deities! It was even better news than the recall to the 2023rd. *As you like to say, Pam, we are going to kick some major enemy butt!*

~Do you ever get the feeling Yidnar likes pushing your buttons as much as your sister does?~ Pam countered with the clearest impression of a mental eye-roll Rett ever experienced.

So clear, in fact, she started physically responding in kind. Rett froze every muscle in her face, but not quickly enough.

"Do you have a problem with that, Sergeant?"

"No, sir. Not at all."

"Good. Now about—" The faint triple-chirp of an incoming priority message sounded from somewhere beneath the jumble on Yidnar's desk. His rugged features twisted into a frown of concentration and a blunt, scarred hand dove into the pile and swam around before emerging with his personal Omni. "Well, Rett, our time's up. I'll let you get back to..." He hesitated, and Rett saw the shift in his energy aura she interpreted as a mixture of empathy and amusement. The tone of his voice confirmed it. "Your last few hours of leave. Are you sure two hours will be long enough for what you need to wrap up?"

She rose at the implicit dismissal, taking up her mug. "Yes, sir. Besides, I'm still *officially* on leave for the next twenty hours," she couldn't resist adding as she turned to deposit her mug on the counter near the tea carafe. "Not going to be doing much but lying around until then."

"Yes," said Yidnar ironically, "but lying around in Medical having bouts of chills and muscle spasms while that wayward metabolism of yours readjusts to your implants probably wasn't what you had in mind."

The Omni bleeped again, insistently, and her commander dismissed her with a gesture and the long-suffering look of a man who wished he had five more copies of himself to handle everything. Of course most of the 2023rd was on base, so he had plenty of staff, but everyone was busy with preparations to go to Epnoce.

And I've preparations of my own, Rett reminded Pam as she exited.

~Is this adjustment really going to be that bad?~ Pam asked. ~You're just about in knots over it.~

I suppose, on a scale of bad to worse, it's merely bad, Rett allowed.

-But aside from having a bad period, you came off them all right.-

Taking out an implant is one thing. Re-introducing a foreign body or substance into me with my metabolism? The one that either rejects or reacts badly to drugs or other things it needs to decide to accept or reject? That's different.

The sunshine and fresher air outside helped dispel the last of the unsettled sensations in her guts. *The adjustment's not going to kill me, or even hurt that much—in a manner of speaking. It's uncomfortable. I'm out of control, emotionally, physically... maybe a bit mentally as well, although I can control that part. Mostly.* Rett brightened. *And probably better since you came. So, maybe this time it won't be so bad.*

-I'm sure both of us can manage to distract each other, even if it is. After all, there's still a lot of stuff I want to know about you, and Nyorfias, and everything else.-

Rett's heart warmed. *Well, let's get going and get it over with.* She lengthened her stride as she headed toward the rover pool, hoping to find a ride available without having to call for one. She was glad to see Zlotfyr, his ice-white hair shining in the sun, as he sat chatting with several other reservists and volunteers old and young who made life a little easier for the Base personnel.

-Just look at him. You'd never expect such a daredevil to be lurking inside.-

It was a nice surprise.

"Ready to go back, then, darling?" the old man called as she drew near. He creaked to his feet with a huge smile.

"Yes—but not to fishing. Can I keep you for a couple hours, or do you have something scheduled?" She smiled a greeting at the others.

The old man shot her a glance. "*Keep* me? I'd like nothing better for you to take me and put me to work, full time, with that platoon of yours."

"We can use the help, that's for sure. Haven't you heard we're short on fighter pilots? I'm surprised AirSpacefighters hasn't solicited you."

Zlotfyr laughed as he led the way to his rover. "This is the closest I'll get, at my age. But what's your rush? You're not due back until tomorrow at third shift, so you said earlier."

13

Rett slid into the rover. "I need to be back here in two hours and have several errands to run across town before I go. Covering that much ground in time will take an experienced pilot like you."

The old man cackled, pleased with her comment. He pointed in the back, where now two insulated carriers rested instead of the original one. "Split up the fish and forage. I was going to drop yours off at your hostel, now you can just take it with you."

Rett shook her head. "Plans changed. You take charge of the lot."

He sent her a long glance, then nodded. "Then I'll see you get your errands done on time." He engaged the drive. The rover lifted on its cushion of air, banked like a fightercraft, and sped toward the town.

NEXT LEVEL
A PLACE OUTSIDE OF TIME

PHEASYCE WATCHED THE PLANETARY JEWELS that were Nyorfias and her sister Epnoce as they continued their dance around the sun that held them in such compelling thrall. Smaller and closer to the source of light, heat, and life, vivacious Nyorfias, clad only in swirls and wisps of cloud, flashed like a deep blue-violet and green gem as she flirted with her solar lover. Icy Epnoce, aloof and regal on her farther orbit, only glanced at the sun when she felt like it, sending a wink of frosty opalescence through thick furs of storm gray and chalk white.

Deep in the thoughts that were hidden and private, she lamented that below the beauty seen from above, her Players, her children of this two-planet system, were struggling for their lives.

Three bulky armored troopshuttles broke the upper levels of Nyorfian stratosphere and escaped into true space, where a shifting constellation of escort craft surrounded them.

And so the second level of this match begins.

"You know on this level *we* have the advantage for the opening moves with your champion and her peripheral Players." Condescension and gloating anticipation oozed from the dark voice that was the instrument of the Dark in this place.

"Yes, so you reminded me at our last meeting, Xonomer." Pheasyce acknowledged her opponent with a slight bow. *That is why I had to remove her spiritual companion.*

It was the second time Pheasyce had severed the merger between her key Player and the female mindforce from Earth. Both times Pheasyce regretted the abrupt terminations that whisked the alien consciousness back to her distant world and left Rett bereft of the presence she had at first met with such whole-souled rebellion. So much, in fact, that Pheasyce had initially been ready to send the borrowed mindforce back, rather than cause her Player any more stress. The Guardians of Balance never took choice away from their Players and to continue the merger any longer with Rett so unwilling would have been unconscionable.

But then the miracle had happened. Acceptance. Cooperation. Bonding. On a scope far greater than Pheasyce could ever have hoped. Especially after her first impressions of the woman that the Guardians of Earth had selected.

It was by the Earth Guardians, as well, that restrictions had been applied to Pheasyce's use of the borrowed mindforce. This had resulted in the first severance.

This current separation, however, was Pheasyce's own decision, one necessary to keep the secret of Rett's untouchable source of support. In this, the second level, Xonomer would be ascendant, able to make personal contact with all of Pheasyce's Players, and at strong advantage for the opening moves. With such allowances, the energetic mind of Pam, the woman from Earth, might very well be detected.

"Your Knight-Protector is very unhappy."

The speculation and pleasure in the voice of Xonomer wrenched at Pheasyce. Her opponent would take full advantage; it had already. Already in the short time the second level started, its dark and icy fingers had been raking the Nyorfian like the claws of a predator toying with a wounded animal.

"A Knight-Protector," said Pheasyce. "What an interesting choice of title." She clamped down on any other thoughts. Xonomer knew she had been seeking advice from other Guardians. It wouldn't do for her opponent to know advice wasn't the only help she had received.

"It is completely meaningless to you, is it? A Knight-Protector is the chosen warrior of a ruler, one specially selected to represent and protect the realm. For now, that ruler is you."

"My Players have free will. I do not rule them. The decisions they make, the actions they take, are their own."

"But I shall rule them. Not only that, I will turn your Knight. I told you before, your victory in the first match will not last long. Already her confidence has eroded. What she gained will soon be lost, and the next fall will be even harder. She will not recover so quickly this time."

Pheasyce didn't respond.

"Look to your champion!" Xonamer sneered. "So she has opened her heart and soul and revealed her own weakness."

And as wounded as her heart and soul have been and will yet become, it will be her heart and soul that is her strength.

"I have yet to look away," Pheasyce answered finally, softly.

Aboard the third Nyorfian troopshuttle, Pheasyce's key Player stared at her informational device without seeing it. She was quite alone, despite the presence of others. Her heart and mind were filled with lonely, unhappy thoughts.

Pheasyce had to fight not to react as Xonomer's insidious presence wrapped around her Player like a deadly mist.

"Watch closely, neophyte. We'll see how quickly your Knight-Protector's defenses fail when those closest to her are no longer so close. Her lover. Her friends. The very ones who brought her out and who are her support will be her downfall and her reason for turning to me." Leaving only the echoes of mocking, cruel laughter, Xonomer withdrew.

Helpless, Pheasyce remained still and silent, agonized in her help-lessness. *I can do nothing now or I forfeit the Game. All my children and these worlds I have labored to serve, protect, and nurture will be lost to the darkness.*

Once again Pheasyce doubted her readiness to ascend to the status of a full Guardian. She had the power to make a difference. By the rules of the Guardians, however, she couldn't use it, not even for something as simple as an act of soothing the hurt of a frightened, wounded child.

For a while longer, my daughter, this must be so. Perhaps, in time, I might make it clear to you. Your faith in yourself and those you love is and will continue to be sorely tested, but it is strong. Hold fast to it. My opponent has only a limited time to take action. It might seem endless, but truly, this trial will last only a short length of time as you know it. You must hold out.

As tempted as Pheasyce was to overstep limitations and extend a soothing touch, such an action could not be risked, or all would be lost. Even if Xonomer remained unaware, the Arbitrator would know, and the judgment would be cast in favor of the opposition.

But this much, she could do. A tendril of the nebulous energy that was Pheasyce reached out and made a small adjustment to the air quality aboard the troopshuttle.

As the troubled turbulence filling the mind of her key Player ebbed into sleep, Pheasyce withdrew.

REFUGE
TREETOP PROVINCE, NYORFIAS
522.07.32 LOCAL RECKONING

A N URGENT PATTERING ON THE hand Rett had flung over the edge of her bed brought her to sleepy awareness. "Tovadan. S'matter?" she murmured drowsily, reluctant to wake up.

"I'm scared."

"Mmm?" She blinked as a lightning flash startled her eyes awake. The smaller hand clutching hers trembled in response even before the resultant explosion of thunder. The lovely dream (in which she hadn't been much too tall, or inclined to stammer, or socially awkward) popped like a bubble.

"I'm *scared*, Rett."

A late summer storm. Drawing a soft breath and scooting over, Rett patted the open space. "C'mere." Where's Ari? she wondered as her brother slipped in next to her. He nestled in close, hiding his eyes against her shoulder as another lightning flash seared into the room. A squeaking sound escaped his throat.

Rett hugged his compact, wiry form to her body right before the boom and felt his sigh of relief. Just in time. A hard gust of wind sent icy raindrops through both windows. She felt some of them hit the arm she had around Tovadan.

"Bug screen off, and close," she said. The electronic field deterring insects from entering the open windows shut down, and the clear window panels slid from their recesses in the walls to form a more solid barrier to the elements raging outside.

Some of the hard shivers in his muscles relaxed as her warmth reached through his chill. "You're all right. You're here now." She combed her fingers through his tangled black-brown hair, adding another voice command to the central household control. That one would close the rest of the windows in the house and start the ventilation fans going instead.

Quivering a little, he turned his face so his nose was in open air and not jammed against her collarbone. "Will I always be afraid?" His muffled boyish alto broke into a deeper tone as it so often did lately. "What if I'm still afraid when I'm as old as you?"

"You're only two years younger than me. And there's nothing wrong with being afraid," Rett said, working her fingers through a particularly nasty tangle they encountered. "Who told you there was?" He mumbled it against her skin, but she knew what he meant. "Some of the other kids?"

He nodded. "You're never afraid. Like Dad and Mother."

She used to think her parents had no fear, too. *Now I know they're afraid lots of times, just like me.* "You know better than that," she admonished. "Remember when I thought I was going to have to leave for fighting with Bressim? And those times you and Ariam—"

"That's *different.*"

"Well, maybe. Maybe not. But I do get afraid, just not of thunderstorms," she answered. The storms had never bothered Rett, even as a much younger child. Why they affected Tova and Ari so badly was anyone's guess. Mother thought part of it was due to her own apprehension of violent storms. Maybe the other part came from the fact the children's young and untrained psi-talent just couldn't handle the undeniable surges of raw energy given off by the storms. "There's a lot of other things I'm still afraid of."

"You are? What?"

She didn't know exactly. She never remembered her own nightmares beyond the suffocating terror of being alone and helpless, unable to move or see. She couldn't finger any coherent thing as terrifying to her as storms were to her brother, so she pulled a handy item off a tall stack of things she worried about more than feared.

"Like you and Mother going away to Epnoce next winter. I'm afraid I'm going to get stuck with all your chores as well as hers. Dad's always getting called out to the yard or to the ranges, or to meetings with the militia—and Ariam's not yet strong enough to do everything you do. So that leaves me picking up the slack for everyone. I have an entire year and a half to worry about it. By the time you go, I'll be so terrified I won't be able to let you loose."

She squeezed her arm around him in demonstration, extracting a squeak of protest. "Mother and Dad and Rafe will have to bring their cutters and peaveys and skid rovers in here to pry me off you. Maybe they might have to use explosives like we do in a logjam."

When she relaxed her grip, he ducked his face back into the curve of her neck. He released a shaky sort of giggle there so the sound wouldn't carry, although the pounding rain made enough noise to cover their conversation.

"Oh, Rett." Tovadan laid his head on the pillow beside hers and lifted his right hand to her face. As he had since he was a baby, he traced his fingers lightly across her features. "You're worried about that? You're dark and sort of blotchy."

He wasn't talking about her complexion, although by either night or daylight, she was much darker than her siblings. And plagued by a handful of blotches, which her father assured her most teenagers had to deal with. She was lucky, Dad added, that she didn't have to deal with a face full of them, as he'd had to.

Tovadan was talking about her aura. He saw, as visible colors, the aura of people's feelings and personalities. It was an ability many children had during their early years and expressed most often in their artwork. The ability started fading in most children about age six or seven, until it faded, forgotten entirely.

Not so in Tovadan. Her brother's empathic talent perceived the emotional colors and patterns he saw around people as clearly as others saw the colors of their clothing or features. At eleven, his talent was growing, not receding, and touch enhanced it.

Rett had no idea how either of her siblings used their Talent, only that it happened. She accepted it as part of them; at the same time immensely relieved she didn't have a single measurable shred of psi.

Dad said while a lot of Nyorfians possessed small psi talents, hardly enough to register, those with stronger ones generally got them from outside influences. Like Ari's and Tova's. It came from Mother's side. And while Tonia, like her middle sister, possessed no measurable psi, her parents and her oldest sister were registered at GTC adept levels.

Their mother was born in a solar system far, far away from here. As far from GTC Central as Nyorfias was. The name of Tonia's homeworld was even more complex, and both words, almost all vowels, tangled Rett's tongue. From Tonia, they flowed like dreamy, exotic music. Even when Rett's mother spoke Standard, the notes of her homeplace colored her underlying accent. As much as her mother loved them and loved Nyorfias, Rett harbored a secret fear Tonia would want to go back home one day. Or else start to travel in space again. This trip to Epnoce just might spark the wanderlust that had brought her to Nyorfias in the first place! What if she decided to keep going and take Tova with her? What if a little while turned into a long time…or forever?

Abruptly Rett bit her lower lip and changed the track of her inner-most thoughts. As unlikely as the entire scenario was, lately she was forgetting all too often to account for the fact Tova and Ari were getting older and reading much deeper than the feelings and emotions on her surface.

Tova's hand became still and flattened against her cheek. "You *are* afraid of us going," he accused, "but not because you'll have to do everyone's chores."

Rett closed her eyes and sighed. "It's just…Epnoce is so far. We've never been that far apart. And for *three* months." Dad assured her the time would fly past, and like the steelhead, Tonia and Tovadan would return with the spring weather. Rett doubted the time would go quickly at all. It seemed like forever. "One hundred and twenty days. That's a long time."

"Ariam said that too," he whispered. "But Rett, I'll get to *fly*." The way he said it made her shiver, not with cold, but in the same secret delight that momentarily banished Tovadan's fear. "I'll fly in a shuttle, one of the new ones." The dim and cloudy light from the windows pooled in his charcoal dark eyes until they glowed with eagerness.

A dream they shared was one of flight, although Tovadan's interest delved far deeper into the actual science and mechanics of it. Starships, freighters, and short-range shuttlecraft breaking away from the atmosphere, heading into the unknown, covered the display areas on his bedroom walls and popped up on his school Omni at moments when he was supposed to be studying.

On the other hand, Rett's interest was on a smaller, faster, immediate scale. She just wanted to do it. Preferably close to home. Something small and nimble instead of big and bulky. Just as she preferred watching the antics of the short-winged raptors or the chewie birds, who moved with amazing speed and dexterity through the thick forest, over staring for hours at the high-flying carrion eaters who sometimes seemed to hang motionless in the sky. She'd take a firewatch jumper over an intrasystem shuttlecraft any day. For that fact, she didn't begrudge Tova his edge in being the first of them to have such an experience.

Tova's eager glow faded as soon as it appeared when the staccato ping of hailstones sounded on the roof and a sharp gust of wind pounded against the house like a giant fist. Then he pulled his hand away and flinched as another blue-white flash lit the room more brightly than any household light source ever could.

"I thought it was ending." Again, he hid his eyes against her.

"Sorry, sport. It's just getting started."

He pulled in a breath and cautiously turned his head enough to continue speaking. "I want to go, but I don't want to leave. I wish all of us could go. Maybe by next year, things will change and we'll go together."

Was he trying to convince her, or himself?

He sucked in a breath as thunder boomed and the entire house shook from foundation to roof. "Rett, what if there are bad lightning storms on Epnoce?"

She laughed a little and bent her neck enough to kiss the top of his head. He smelled clean from the bath he'd taken earlier, fresh as newly sawed blue pine. She wished he'd remembered to comb his hair before it dried. Her fingers were never going to escape this knot, much less eliminate it, without some tugging.

"Let's not worry about that any more right now, all right? Or I will be crazy by the time you go." She managed to free one finger and a thin strand of hair from the big knot. "You know, even Dad says you never stop being afraid, it's just that once you get over or can handle one fear, there's a new one right there waiting to take its place."

"Dad said that?" Tovadan digested that news a minute. She understood his doubt, since Reve had been the one to gently discourage the younger children from his and Tonia's bedroom when he thought both were old enough to know better.

"Yes, Dad said that. Mother says you and Ariam will grow out of this in your own time."

"You told her we come here? OW!" Tovadan forgot his fear long enough to sit up, yelping as his abrupt motion pulled her fingers through the last knotted length of his hair. He rubbed his scalp and stared at her. The dim light entering the window from the storm-tossed world outside was enough for her to see the expression on his narrow face.

"I didn't have to." Rett stretched her arm over the floor and shook his hair strands off her fingers. "She knew all along, from the first. Dad...he didn't know for a long time. Now he does, especially since the last storm got so bad he went around checking on us."

Tova's jaw dropped. "I don't remember that."

"That's because you and Ari are usually sound asleep five minutes after you get in bed with me. Even if the roof of the house blew off, you'd still sleep through it."

"He didn't make you take us back to our own beds?"

Rett shook her head. "He didn't say anything. I was worried for a moment he'd be tiffed, but he didn't say a word. He just looked for a minute with that funny little grin he gets—"

"Like you get, too. You grin like Dad, but you smile just like Mother."

"—and then patted my head and kissed everyone and tucked us in. I think Mother's convinced him to let it go."

Satisfied and relieved, Tovadan lay down again and plastered himself against her in his usual manner. His tremors had quieted, although he cringed with each flash and roar from outside. "Where's Ariam?"

"Rett," whispered a tremulous little voice on her left.

"And here's the one for my other side, not to be left behind." She smiled a welcome into the darkness and lifted the blanket for Ariam.

24

The mattress gave beneath them as the girl quickly scrambled up and snuggled close to Rett's side. Her right arm closed protectively around her small sister.

Tova's right hand reached across her body to clasp Ariam's left. Rett waited, feeling them draw currents of support from her and pass them through each other. The sensation of oneness this contact produced never ceased to amaze her. When they were like this, it was almost as if they could share more than emotions and feelings.

So Rett imagined the soft cool wind off the year-round snowpack on Cadie's Peak and the deep flickering shadows under the thickest branches of blue pine. Added the swift liquid murmur of the river and the way the sunlight dappled and flashed off the restless water.

After a minute, the trembling in the smaller figures on either side of her diminished. A gentle sigh from Tova was echoed by a sleepy yawn from Ari.

She tightened her arms around her brother and sister. "All snug?"

They were all together now. Safe. Now it was time to sleep. Tomorrow would be another day to wonder of future dreams in the daylight. Two nods and the sensations of happy security answered her query. Ariam wriggled around a little, her golden head on Rett's shoulder. Tova's position changed so his ear lay above her heart, his breath warm through the material of her sleeping shirt.

As sleepy as both of them were, they waited for her to complete what had become a ritual.

Her lips brushed Tova's finger-combed hair; Ari's pale forehead. "Sleep," she whispered. Alert now, Rett would stay awake and watch, as always, until they drifted off. "Sleep. I'll keep watching until you start dreaming good dreams. Just to make sure you get there…"

2.1.0 GRAVITY
2.1.1 TROOPSHUTTLE, ENROUTE TO EPNOCE
0535.08.10 (LOCAL RECKONING)

TWO LIGHT, QUICK, FINGER-TAPS ON her knee were enough to awaken Rett, tell her the situation was not an emergency, and to identify her awakener as friendly. *Wait a minute. I was sleeping? Again?*

"S'up," she mumbled thickly, her mind and larger muscle groups ready for movement before her tongue. Deities!

"You might want to change your position before we hit atmosphere, Sergeant."

The sharp, biting displeasure of that familiar voice was enough to banish her distorted sense of time. For some strange reason, she had thought she was home…there had been a bad storm, and her brother Tovadan and little sister Ariam had crept into her room and into bed with her.

"Unless you want me to give you this immunization in your ass, that is. Nullgravity aside, how you managed to make your body fold in such a manner will remain a mystery even to one of my medical experience."

Med was goading her, but she wasn't in the mood to make a comeback. In Rett's estimation, there wasn't anything all that unusual about her position, as long as she ignored the fact that when she looked around, she saw deck plating marked as the floor and the frameworks beneath rows of seats. Only the near-absence of gravity aboard the troopshuttle had made her current position a comfortable one. The medtech was right, if entry was imminent, she had to make some adjustments. She reached for the Omni that obediently floated near her head and tucked it into its belt pocket.

"I can't believe I fell asleep, just like that. *Again.*" Slapping the quick-release catches on her safety harness, she flipped into a sitting position relevant to her chair. "I can't seem to stay awake. Good thing we're not on alert. Glad you found something to do, Ariam." She nodded at her second in command, who accompanied Med. Then she yawned and brought a hand up to scrub over her face.

With an exasperated sound better suited to the parent of a toddler and a suffering look in his gray-green eyes, Med snatched an item from a container Sergeant Ariam carried between her left arm and body. The medtech intercepted Rett's hand before it made contact with her face and shoved something cold and damp into it.

"Use that," said Med. "Sleep, that's something you won't hear any complaints from me about. You can use a lot more of it, that's fact. Shoulder, please." The sandy-haired medtech indicated the handful of transdermal patches in Sergeant Ariam's other hand and the injector in his. "I expect you to put some effort into getting more of it once we arrive—"

She heard him go on, but the sight of the injector in the medtech's wiry hands was enough to temporarily freeze all her bodily functions. The patch has extra vitamins—no problem. And it was only an immunization. It wasn't going to bother her beyond some itching for a few minutes.

"—since no one newly arrived is expected to do, or is going to be doing, much of anything for the first shift or two. I expect this transfer to hit you harder than anyone."

As fleeting as her actual hesitation was, her medtech noticed anyway. Not much went past him. Thank all deities he was more than familiar with her medical peculiarities.

The short, slender man's scathing monologue and cantankerous expression disappeared just long enough to promote compassionate reassurance. "So, whenever you're ready, then."

Puffing out a breath and releasing most of her tension, she slid the fingers of her left hand beneath her collar on that side. She pulled the sturdy but giving material away and down enough to give Med access. "You had this discussion with me before we left," she pointed out, not wanting a repeat of it here and now. "But don't forget I just came off leave, and all I did for that entire time was rest. Mostly," she was quick to add.

He pressed the supplement patch firmly in place. "What you went through the night before last wiped most of that clean off your record," snapped the medtech, his acid level back to normal. "Besides, *resting* is one thing. *Sleeping* is another. It would take you years to catch up on all the good sleep you've missed just in the time I've known you."

As Med leaned closer, she automatically thought to warn Pam to go deep and quiet. Then she remembered that wasn't an issue. Pam was gone, her corner a cold, empty spot in Rett's mind.

"What's up with you?" Med caught her chin in his free hand and eyed her face intently.

She sat motionless, knowing better than to bother avoiding his inspection. She kept her thoughts on how she had slept, that she had dreamed, how thirsty she was starting to feel now she was awake. She shrugged.

"Hm. But you did catch some good sleep just now—dreamed, too, did you? Good."

He sounds like Pam. She was always on me to let go enough to dream... problem is that there are things I don't want to have dreams about. At least I had a good dream.

The injector hissed. Rett turned her shudder into a swallow and continued speaking. "As soon as I stepped on this shuttle I haven't been able to stay awake more than an hour at a stretch." She wrinkled her nose. "Too warm, or not enough air or something. It isn't normal."

Med closed his hand over her shoulder and the area he'd just injected. "Don't go rubbing at this as soon as my back is turned."

She made a face. He knew her too well.

"And try this thought," the medtech suggested. "It was a quiet trip. We were bored out of our minds. Not much to see between Nyorfias and here. *Everyone* slept, even me. I know you're dry, but don't have too much to drink. We've the atmospheric entry to get through first. What are we going to do as soon as we're checked through and sent to our section?"

Rett sighed. "Eat."

None of the Special Forces personnel aboard had eaten anything six hours prior to the trip. She guessed AirSpacefighters and Spacemarines wanted less chance of in-flight messes should the forces of gravity wreak havoc with internal plumbing. The troopshuttle didn't offer luxuries like acceleration seats and sported only the most rudimentary of inertial dampening systems.

"Eat," she repeated, making sure Med heard so he would go away. She was hungry, no worries there. The last time she'd eaten anything was before checking in for her implant adjustment.

Those few extra moments Med lingered were enough to kill her immediate urge to go after her shoulder. She watched Med take himself off to finish his immunizations. He moved with the enviable ease of one who'd experienced the space environment many times before. Sergeant Ariam followed him, throwing a smile over her shoulder.

Rett scrubbed the wipe hard over her face and neck to remove the last traces of sleep.

Thank all deities for Med. Despite the running battles they engaged in almost daily over various matters—which he usually won—and her personal griping and complaining about his griping and complaining, Rett never failed to be grateful for having him in F-troop. Especially for one simple fact: his preferred method of pain control didn't involve chemical drugs.

She had inherited many odd characteristics from her offworld mother. Some gave her an advantage, like her strength. Others were a problem. The same immune system and metabolism that kept her from getting infectious diseases rejected even some of the most commonly used substances. The smallest dose of a child-safe painkiller was enough to induce hallucinations. Most anything else was a medical emergency.

Med, however, was a master of alternative techniques. His formidable skill as a medtech and the empathic talent, which clued him to anyone's slightest ache or illness, were bonuses.

Feeling vastly refreshed, Rett tucked the material into the recyclables pocket of her utility belt. Amazing, the difference one little square of damp wipe made. Then she covered her mouth against a tremendous yawn that contracted every muscle she had into tight knots, brought out chillbumps on her body from ankles to nape, and finished off with a shiver. The spot on her shoulder prickled and itched. Scrunching deeper into her seat, she started to reach for it.

"Ah-ah-ah. Don't," said Med from somewhere aft.

Grumbling, she settled for stretching as much as it was possible for someone to stretch while remaining within the confines of a safety harness. It would have been nice to eliminate the harness altogether, but in case of attack, no more than three of them at any one time were allowed to move around untethered. The Spacemarines and shuttle crew certainly didn't need the extra hazard of a hundred and fifty unrestrained bodies tumbling around the inside of the ship during an emergency. So, any movement was limited to trips to the head, as the marines called it, and fifteen minutes of light exercise every four hours. The exercise was restricted to a small, enclosed area and supervised by one of the marines.

She was glad of the escort, within the troopshuttle as well as outside of it. If they needed to take action in nullgravity, she wouldn't be prepared. Not many Nyorfian ground troops had that sort of experience or training; there hadn't been much of a chance for it. But the AirSpacefighters and Spacemarines were experts in these conditions. In addition to her suspicions about the air aboard, Rett would be the first to admit that knowing they were on alert made it easier for her to give in to sleeping so much and so deeply.

She took a moment to look around. Stretches and yawns were occurring over the length and width of the troopshuttle. Med was right, it looked as if she hadn't been the only one sleeping more than expected. Well, with the exception of the shuttle crew and escort details.

"That's right, wake *UP!* Suck in some air. No fun hitting gravity all muddle-headed." The voice boomed through the passenger area, causing more than one newly awakened face to flinch and raising a few grumbles or comments about hearing loss. "Up! Last chance for the heads."

The source of the booming voice, a formidable armored figure in flat slate gray, stopped near Rett's seat. "Heya, Sergeant."

She offered a grin as she looked up to meet the affable greeting of one of the marines, noting the insignia denoting her rank and position: second in command of the detail aboard. "What's up, Lieutenant?"

From the glance the woman gave the insignia on her armor, Rett guessed that she'd been newly upgraded and was still surprised to be addressed with her current rank. Now that she thought about it, she hadn't heard many of the Spacemarines aboard address each other by rank.

The marine flashed her an appreciative and proud smile. "Quiet ride. Gotta admit, this group took it better than most. Not to have anyone get sick is amazing for dirtsiders like most of you."

"Go figure," Rett answered dryly. "Maybe because we were unconscious?"

The marine laughed and swept her flame-red fringe from a forehead lightly dewed with sweat. The rest of her fiery locks were shorn close to her scalp, like all the marines aboard. Given the fact Rett had learned the average Spacemarine spent one and a half shifts out of three (for a thirty hour Standard day) encased in his or her armored shell, it wasn't hard to understand the necessity of the hairstyle. But those cropped heads made them all look even more ridiculously out of proportion to the armor that served them as both protection and weapon. The helmets that would completely seal them inside their self-contained mechanized units hung in easy reach over left or right shoulders, whichever the individual preferred. A set of quick-release straps secured them.

"Troopshuttle's not like civvie transport, that's fact," the Spacemarine said "Just a fingertip over cargo. You'll notice what I mean when we hit atmosphere. We come in hot and fast, not cool and easy like the passenger shuttles before the war. Have to. Can't take chances Coalition won't sneak by and try to tag us while we're blind."

"Never a dull moment," Rett said. "Hey, I thought there was some sort of problem with the air a few times. I kept falling asleep. Was there?"

"May be right, Sarge. We thought some prob with the mix a couple times 'cause our external 'viro monitors pinged." The marine tapped a gauntleted hand on her armor to indicate the onboard systems. "But when we checked, no prob. Sleepies are always an issue on long trips though, good air or no. Anyway, good thing your med righted you up. Hitting full gravity with your head to the deck woulda dented you for sure. Not that we woulda let that happen."

"Appreciate that."

Leaning forward a little, the marine added with a grin, "Admired the view while it lasted."

"Nice to hear something positive about it." Rett sniffed and took a fast glance in Med's direction.

"Something to write home about." The marine's cheerful expression dimmed. "Once we're able to get messages through again, that is."

"Where's home?" Rett asked softly.

The marine gestured downward with her chin, indicating the planet they were approaching. "Northeast part of the main continent. Complex 63."

"Been a long time for you, hasn't it then?"

"Since it started. I was on a farm on Nyorfias doing a pre-qual internship when they took Epnoce. Didn't take me long to switch careers once I came of age. I've been on space duty ever since. My little twin brothers have never seen me—they were babies when I left. Not even sure they're still alive." The marine shrugged, a tiny motion that Rett nearly missed since most of it was inside her armor. "Sorry. Didn't mean to go off. We're all pretty much in the same situation."

"I didn't mind." Rett made a gesture that included the rest of the incoming troops on the craft. "Tell you what. We dirtsiders will see what we can do about it."

The lieutenant answered with a fierce show of teeth. "That's what we're hoping for. We'll keep 'em off your back from up here, and you grind them into the landscape down there. Who knows, maybe it might actually help the ecosystem recover. Later, Sarge." With a laugh, the lieutenant moved on to make sure everyone was awake, properly seated, and ready for entry. Her voice boomed out once more. "Ditch the sleepies, people. You have ten minutes! We're incoming and on a schedule—not like we can stop and wait for you!"

Glad it was Med who woke me. As cheerful and bright as the lieutenant's voice was, if that booming tone had been what slammed Rett out of a dead sleep, her awakening might have been more violent.

She was going to have to ask for the lieutenant's name, or get a scan on her armor's ident code next time she passed. If she had opportunity to get better information on the civilians in Complex 63 once they were down there, she'd pass it on. Any news would be better than not knowing.

She turned her attention forward. A bank of screens high on the compartment bulkhead displayed what was outside on all sides of the shuttlecraft.

Ariam returned and pulled herself into the seat alongside. "Hey, sleepy. Whew. I volunteered to help Med because I was so *bored* and wanted to move around a lot more than we did in that closet back there." She snapped the catch on her restraining harness and pushed back a stray wisp of golden hair. She took another huge breath, as if she'd emptied her lungs completely in both motion and greeting. Gesturing over her shoulder, she indicated the "closet" she'd meant was the exercise area toward the rear of the shuttle. "Won't be so quick for that next time. I really overcompensated. Now I know what a ricochet *feels* like."

"You weren't having too much trouble."

Ariam snorted, then slid Rett a sideways glance and sheepish laugh. "It's a big shuttle, and Med did everyone on the right side—"

"Starboard," supplied Rett, having been corrected herself when they'd first boarded.

"—this side of it. Med Shenyver from B-troop did the other side. You slept through everything."

"Wonder what else I missed," muttered Rett. She hadn't slept that hard in years, not even while on leave.

"I've decided if I have to float or make motions to swim, I would prefer to be in water. The only upside to low grav is if you drop something, you don't have to bend far to get it." She grinned wistfully, adjusting her safety harness. "Remember how excited Tova was about going into space?"

"He didn't stop talking about it from the time he was told he was going until the time we took him and Mother to the Circle spaceport." Rett was surprised the remembering came easier and didn't hurt as much as it had in the past.

Neither of them ever talked about Tovadan nor their mother very much. Seemed peculiar to talk about it now, especially since Rett was certain she'd been dreaming about her brother right before Med woke her. She glanced over, ready to inquire what had triggered Ariam's mentioning Tova. Seeing that her sister's attention was on something she held protectively in her hands, Rett hesitated.

As the object turned and caught the light, the full spectrum of blues, from white to deep blue violet, escaped in a spray of glittering color through Ariam's slender fingers.

Another shivery sensation of memory made Rett rub her arms. She'd dreamed about that recently, too. Pam had influenced her to sleep, and that time it had been about that day she'd given Tova and Ari the azurium crystal she'd found in perfect halves among the river rocks.

Ariam glanced over and away again, but not before Rett saw the expression on her face, the soft sheen of tears in her huge gray eyes. It wasn't hard to guess the crystal half her sister cradled was their brother's. No wonder. "Have yours?"

In reply, Ariam's left fist closed around the azurium crystal while her right hand reached into a belt pocket for its twin. "He asked me to keep it safe until he came back." Ariam spoke so softly Rett had to lean closer and strain to hear. "And I know better, Rett, but I can't help but think, once in a while, that I'll be able to give this back to him. I still think—dream sometimes—that he and Mother aren't really dead."

Ariam fitted the halves together for a moment, just as she had all those years ago…how many? Rett didn't want to think about that. She leaned closer and squeezed her hand tight over her sister's hands and the crystals within them. Meeting the younger woman's eyes, she whispered, "Sometimes I think that, too."

Rett pulled her hand back. Ariam put the crystals away. Nothing more was said.

Rett turned her attention to the viewscreens and watched as the fighter escort, which had accompanied the troop shuttle since its entry into space, peeled off in smart formation and arrowed toward a distant speck. Was that far-off carrier Nyorfian or GTC? Didn't matter. All that mattered was they were out there keeping this corridor open and safe between the planets during the transfer of troops and supplies between Nyorfias and Epnoce.

Rett wanted to think it was her imagination, but no, she was sitting deeper in her seat. Epnoce had them now. They weren't flying toward the planet as much as falling into it.

A deep flare of anticipation grew inside her as the Spacemarine detail leader ordered his people to strap in for entry.

"Here we go," said Rett.

"Here we go," Ariam echoed. "As one of the marines told me, this is the part where we make like a meteorite."

"That's not reassuring." But Rett had to laugh.

At first, the change was gradual. Sounds from outside the craft came first. Then the odd sensation of non-movement disappeared; the shuttle was definitely in motion. There was a hard lurch, a skip, and a flare of sound, followed by alarmingly strong shudders from nose to tail.

The outside monitors were awash in static for a few seconds before going blank. There wouldn't be anything to see for a few minutes anyway. Rett supposed she should have felt the slightest bit afraid, since "make like a meteorite" wasn't far from the truth. During atmospheric entry, a ship was in the greatest danger; either from attacks above or below or from a failure of the shielding and equipment. But instead of fear or anxiety, she felt oddly elated, curious, and more alert than she'd been since coming aboard. Going in blind, flaming hot, whatever happened, she wasn't going to miss a second of it.

The noise inside the craft increased, a deafening mix of roar, crackle, hiss, and ping. She laid a hand flat on the outer wall to her left, feeling the strain against the ship's exterior right through the layers of hull plating. The surface heated rapidly, but didn't get hot enough to make her pull away. What about the outer hull? she wondered. Was it really glowing hot, like they'd seen in vids? Her energy sense couldn't tell her much, just an intense yellow glow of appropriate brightness and size that was normal for any kind of generated energy from a lightning bolt to a spark. The heat beneath her fingers and hand made a sharp contrast to the frigidness she had felt earlier while in space.

Then, almost at once, the jolting and shuddering ceased; the hissing and pinging sounds stopped. Beneath her hand, the surface of the inner hull began to cool down. The growing sensation of motion and weight no longer grew—it crashed as solidly into her as an armored rover.

"Whew! What a ride. Most fun I've had for a while," Ariam said with a wicked little laugh.

Rett's feet felt firmly connected to the deck below, her bottom settled solidly in her seat. Gravity. It dragged on her from the inside out, and as the blood drained right to her feet, followed by all her internal organs, she experienced a moment of breathless vertigo until her body compensated.

"Good gods and deities," she muttered, blinking to clear her vision.

A new set of vibrations pulsed through the ship and those aboard: the roar of the powerful atmospheric engines. As the ship leveled off, some of the pressure she was feeling eased. Then the monitors cleared, showing a metallic sky with thick cloud below. Taking flanking positions around the shuttle were a new group of fightercraft. Their pale, frosty colors and distinctive markings identified them as one of the squadrons based on the icy planet they approached.

Rett tried to imagine what it would be like to insert herself into one of those sleek, fast ships and tear a hole in the sky like a bolt of lightning.

"All go over there? Good, good. Got a prob, shout out! Ears feel stuffed, clamp your back teeth together, swallow a few times." Another Spacemarine came up the aisle. "Good, good, good," Rett heard him mumbling in between giving advice as he went along the aisle.

A peculiar hum accompanied his every step. At first puzzled by it, Rett soon realized the sound came from the tiny motorized joints in his armor. Of course. Now they were in Epnoce's gravity, it would be almost impossible for these marines to move very well, if at all, without assistance. One of them had mentioned earlier that their armor, empty, was the equivalent in weight to two hefty adult Nyorfians. That was, under Nyorfias-normal gravity. On Epnoce, it would be equivalent to nearly two and a half hefty adults.

"E'v'rone all go, no prob, Sarge no prob. Not long," said the sweating Spacemarine cheerfully as he passed Rett's place.

"Thanks." She was beginning to associate their stilted, abbreviated manner of speaking while in a working mode as an affectation peculiar to their branch. Good thing it seemed to disappear to a more normal syntax in social conversation, or she would've had a harder time conversing with the Spacemarine lieutenant earlier.

"I thought I was glad enough we didn't have to deal with the armor the infantry wears. I can't even begin to imagine moving or fighting in something like that rig," Rett said softly to Ariam.

"Can you imagine if you lost power and couldn't move?" Ariam shook her head.

Rett's shudder wasn't forced. She didn't have to be encased in an armored shell three times her weight to know how that felt. "From what I understand, they still can move, just not very fast. I thought they had cooling systems built in, though."

"Blaze told me—"

"Who?"

Ariam clarified. "Lieutenant Kalenthi. The marine who came around checking when Med and I were making the rounds."

"Okay." Rett reached for her Omni and made a note. *Junior Lieutenant Kalenthi/Blaze, SMar. Complex 63, northeast main continent.*

"What's that for?"

"She has family there. If it ends up being one of our target areas, I might be able to get her some firsthand information."

Ariam nodded. "Blaze is also the one who very neatly caught me right before my third bounce off various surfaces and…people. I don't think old Dinnold is ever going to forgive me for detonating on him like a cruise missile." The younger woman chuckled, obviously still amused by her misadventure in low gravity.

"You smashed into Dinnold? And he let you live?" Rett couldn't help a laugh. The R-troop squadleader wasn't noted for his sense of humor, about anything.

"Saved by the laws of low gravity. I'm sure he'll get back somehow, in drill probably. Anyway, we were talking before, and Blaze told me that Spacemarines couldn't run their armor cooling systems efficiently unless they had helmets on, and they had to conserve that sort of output for when they really need it. She says you get used to it." Ariam shook her head.

"Blaze. How did she get tagged with that one?" Nicknames that weren't a shortened form of a personal name weren't common.

"The hair," explained Ariam.

"Oh." Rett chuckled. "It fits."

Again they settled back to wait. The view on the screens was obstructed, showing thick cloud and mist wrapping the shuttle in a bulky gray blanket.

At last, some coherency defined the limited view of the world outside. They were on a landing final and the runways and landing pads were becoming visible through dense mist. The Epnoce-based squadron that had picked them up immediately on entry and escorted them to the base broke off, leaving only two to see them completely to the ground. Rett watched the rest head off for their own landing area until they disappeared into the dense fog.

"You ever regret it, Rett?"

"What's that, Ari?"

Her sister smiled. "Not going to AirSpacefighters. I see that look you get every once in a while. I've seen it a lot on this trip, every time the fighters came on the screens."

"I don't think I consciously started thinking about it until a short while ago. Am I that obvious?"

"Only to me. Anyone else would guess you were thinking about Jaq."

Rett dug her elbow into her sister for that one. "Stop that."

But she hadn't ever considered how different her life might have been had she followed her longtime desire to fly instead of answering the challenge of the Special Forces. She doubted even Pam's imagination was up to the task.

So she simply answered Ariam's question. "Not really, I guess."

The troopshuttle came to ground, rolling smoothly at first, then jolting sharply as braking flaps were deployed. A ramp-rover appeared on the screen, disappearing as it came closer, into the range of the forward camera. Rett heard a metallic, hollow clank as the magnetic tow cable attached. The rover would tow the ship the rest of the way.

Painful silence replaced the deafening whine of the shuttle's engines.

Rett gave her attention to the side views on the external monitors. Epnoce had been beautiful from space, but now that they were down, she wasn't too impressed.

The terrain she'd glimpsed outside the shuttle appeared anything but imposing. The sky was gray; the clouds were gray; the ground was gray and flat as far as she could see, which wasn't very far thanks to the fog. Gray mist shrouded the gray buildings of the base. The entire landscape was drowning in a cold, gray, straight rain that gave every promise of turning to gray sleet before night settled.

Yuck. Was there any hope that something was wrong with the color control on the external cameras?

She hoped the insides of the buildings were a little more colorful. The working grays she and the other Special Forces personnel on the shuttle wore were positively vibrant compared to the landscape. Their combat uniforms would make it worse, since the light-bending and reflective properties of the material would take on the same color and quality of their surroundings. The prospect of being drowned in shades of gray thirty hours a day, for however long they would be on this planet, was too dreary a scenario to contemplate.

Maybe Pam would have found that thought amusing. Pam also would've thought up sixteen different ways to comment on it in the time it had taken Rett for the one. Despite all the people around her, one or two practically touching, a sensation of loneliness rose so strong and hard it nearly closed her throat. She pushed herself upright with relief—and a soft grunt—as the signal came for her section to prepare for exit procedure.

Pam would be happy that she had dreamed again—a good dream about her brother.

The unfamiliar tug of the heavier gravity only added to a gloomy sluggishness Rett couldn't quite shake. Sure, it had left her for a while on the voyage—as long as she was sleeping. Or actively involved in conversation. It was back now. She told herself it was the leftover effects of her hormone adjustment, and that activity would keep her focused. Funny. It did feel as if she was underwater, although without buoyancy of any kind. Every movement was met with weighty resistance.

Once outdoors, her attitude perked up a bit. In spite of the lack of color, this world was new to her, sparking her curiosity. The cold, damp air had a different and unique smell and feel to it. Her lungs tingled after taking a few deep breaths. Epnoce had more gravity, yes, but the atmosphere also contained a slightly higher percentage of oxygen.

As much as she desired activity to soothe herself, she was glad that she and her comrades-in-arms were not going to cover the two-mile distance between this terminal and the main hub of the massive building on foot, extra oxygen in the atmosphere or not. There were big rovers waiting; staffed by friendly civilian volunteers, most of them teenagers or able-bodied elders.

With formidable efficiency, gear was offloaded, checked, and sent off on cargo floaters. Rett and the other humanoid passengers were whisked into the rovers. Several of the civilians who hopped aboard with them offered advice on easing the adjustment to the heavier gravity of their world.

During the ride, she glimpsed big anti-aircraft guns and missile launchers with prepared artillery crews and alert MP and infantry patrols standing watches or making rounds in the cold rain. Maybe it wasn't the most interesting landscape, but she was starting to think that being outside in it might a better option than being stuck between walls, floor, and a ceiling for deities knew how long.

The rovers entered the main hub of the building via several huge bay doors and she had to suppress a shiver as the last glimpse of the outside world disappeared. The military check-in procedure demanded her attention then, but it went so rapidly that only the receding view of the checkstation was proof they'd actually been there.

Impressed with the organization and efficiency of the base and the civilian and military personnel running it, she found herself smiling by the time she and F-troop fell in to follow their gear to the section of the complex reserved for the 2023rd.

"I'm glad you're feeling a little better," said Ariam, who fell into step alongside as Rett came near. "It's going to end here, you know."

She sent a penetrating glance to her second in command. "Care to explain?"

Everything about the younger woman was calm and positive. Even that dull undertone Rett perceived in Ariam's normal body energy, left by Kraym's death, was gone. "These people know the war's reached a turning point. And now that we're here, they're finally able to see an end to it—in us. I'm surprised you're not scoping it. If it were any stronger, everyone would see it with their physical sight, just as Tovadan used to."

"You forget I'm not naturally Talented, Ariam. If I pulled enough personal effort to scope and interpret the energy auras of every individual I've walked past so far, I'd be flat out on a floater and headed to Medical," Rett answered dryly. "Are they looking at an end *in* us, or an end *to* us?"

OW! She nearly bit through her tongue in the effort to turn her surprised reaction to silence. Ariam's retaliatory smack had been entirely too close to the spot Med had injected earlier.

42 "An end to the war, upon which the Nyorfian system will be free of the Coalition, and," her sister hastened to add before Rett jumped on her omission, "with our remaining civilians and resources relatively intact and able to recover within a reasonable timeframe."

"I hope you're right, Ari," Rett said, rubbing the stinging spot on her shoulder. "I really do."

"These people are happy to see us—to see anyone from Nyorfias," Ariam pointed out. "Especially Special Forces. And you."

"I'm sure, Sergeant Ariam, that my presence isn't as significant as the GTC military units who finally made it out here to improve our chances." Rett pulled a tone of acidity worthy of Med at his finest. "And let's not forget those who came before us, liberated these people and this base, and made it possible for the rest of us to be here."

She had to wonder if Ariam knew their father and the 21st was on Epnoce somewhere, part of that very task force. The exact designations of all the units in that grouping hadn't yet been declassified. Rett had been allowed to tell F-troop about the GTC Rangers and the Special Forces' involvement, but the other details were still confidential. Not that she worried Ariam would sense their father's proximity and blurt out anything. Rett wasn't thrilled with the thought of running into him any time soon, in spite of needing to know if he was alive and well. Then again, Ariam would be the first to know if something was seriously wrong.

"I'm not forgetting them," Ariam was saying. "They're glad we're here, too! As a matter of fact, Blaze mentioned she heard 'Sergeant Killer' mentioned from one of the Rangers."

Rett swallowed her annoyance. Her notoriety from the enemy side didn't bother her as much as the admiration from people on her own side. And little thanks to the Nyorfian media for noticing the nickname and starting a trend for the average citizen to see her and immediately think "Sergeant Killer" instead of "Sergeant Rett". Worse yet was the way they presented the stories—giving an impression that Rett fought the entire Coalition without the slightest shred of help from anyone else.

"I'd like to meet a Ranger," she said in an attempt to change that topic. "I can't imagine how I would feel to actually talk to one of them." Just thinking about it gave her insides a flutter. The Rangers were legendary.

"Me too," Ariam said "Remember when we were kids and we actually saw two Rangers at the Circle spaceport?"

Her sister's warm hand squeezed Rett's forearm for a moment, and through the contact came soothing waves of calm. Gratefully, she allowed Ariam's empathic skill to quiet the remaining turbulence that had come to a simmer beneath her skin.

"I remember. I forget where Dad said those two were from. I remember how they looked, though. Alien. Huge. Big enough mouth to swallow you down in one chomp."

Ariam giggled. "I remember thinking they'd eat you in two chomps."

"I'd bet one of their kind, Ranger or not, could make one of those tentacled Unethi crap themselves. I should ask the Major sometime if he could tell us what species they were, since he served with the Rangers for a while."

"I still can't get over the fact the Rangers are comprised of a lot of different species, but they're all male," mused Ariam.

"Yeah, isn't that strange?" agreed Rett. "Then again, not all cultures and species are alike, and there's a lot of different people in the GTC we don't know about. I mean, look at the diverse species in the Coalition alone. Jaq says a lot of the non-humanoid people never leave the ships because they can't adapt to the same environment that supports us. So they usually serve as permanent crew. Only the species that can live without special adaptation get sent down to fight. "

"We've seen a lot of diversity, all right," agreed Ariam. "Including a few I don't want to think about. Speaking of diversity, though, where's our Jaq?"

That was a good question. Where was Jaq? The assigned seating on the troopshuttle hadn't given Rett any opportunity to speak with him except in passing, and now that they were in a loose file, it was unusual not to have him in a more direct line of sight.

Pushing forward with her energy sense, she tagged his familiar output quickly enough. She followed her impression forward, scanning the outlines of bodies so familiar she could identify each of them from any angle, in any light, sometimes from the shadow they cast. Even with her eyes closed, she'd know the unique energy auras that defined them as individuals.

There were fewer bodies than she had become used to seeing over the past few years. Not wanting to think about that, she fiercely redirected her thoughts to the task of locating Jaq.

There. There would never be any mistake identifying her Tech Advisor. That rampant gold crest was unmistakable. His wild-haired head, every shade of brown from red to gold on either side of the lighter central crest, was bent in conversation, yet rose above the other black-banded heads in their group. Easily the tallest of them, the ex-Coalition trooper from Zetinor Prime walked with Mikel, H'tenneck, Steffi, and Jessek. They were talking with great energy and animation about something undoubtedly technical, and as far over Rett's head as the vacuum of space.

Her mood lifted even more as soon as she spotted him. She hoped they would have some time alone together before things got too crazy.

"I know part of what's bugging you has to do with Pam being gone," Ariam said, her tone almost too low for Rett to hear.

"Yeah, who would have thought it would bother me so much?"

"She's been an...well...an intimate part of you. But don't backslide, Rett. You were doing so well. Others might put the credit to Jaq, but I know better. Pam put a lot of effort into you, and if you throw it away she'll be tiffed."

Rett kept her sigh inside, and even as she nodded to Ariam, her thoughts went to Pam and that strange planet called Earth. Maybe something terrible happened. From what Pam had told her, Earth sounded like it was always on the brink of destruction from its own inhabitants. Maybe it finally occurred.

Deities, I hope not, thought Rett. The thought brought the reminder that planetary devastation was still a very real possibility for Nyorfias and Epnoce, despite their fresh hopes for success. Her shiver came entirely from within, a moment of bleak terror coming so fast and so strong that another body up ahead stepped out of the file and turned to wait for her.

"What's up, Med?"

The medtech just shook his head. "I'm going to be watching you, Sarge."

"So you've told me."

"And—"

Rett was saved by a hail and the approach of two of their civilian assistants. Giving Med a nod and gesturing Ariam to follow her, she dismissed her uneasy thoughts and gratefully focused her attention on the present.

45

2.1.2 FARM, HUNTERDON COUNTY, NJ USA EARTH
CURRENT ERA

THE LATE AUGUST WEATHER WAS muggy and hot, and Pam tried hard to concentrate on the big Thoroughbred she was working. The horse was not long off the racetrack and everything was spooking him. Having over a thousand pounds of frolicsome horse on the end of a thirty-foot, inch-wide nylon line and trying to make that half-ton of nervous, living animal trot in a circle demanded close attention and infinite patience.

Today, "close attention" buzzed and darted around Pam with the same annoying frequency of biting flies, always just out of her reach.

I can't imagine a race of people not knowing where they came from or any of their history prior to their landing on a new world. I wish we had more time to explore that aspect…

The line jerked in her hands. Pam shook her head, fiercely directing her mind on the horse. She spoke softly to calm him; eventually his stride relaxed and evened out, the circles grew smoother and rounder. He still pulled hard, resisting the bit and limits of the line, but Pam automatically used the line to communicate to the horse that he'd better stay in his circle, settle down, and stop this nonsense, or else…

Or else we'll be doing this all night!

As soon as the horse went around in a proper circle, relaxed and calm on the bit and ready for her commands, they would stop. All this was communicated by gentle, but insistent vocal cues; the give and release of tension on the long rein, and guided by movements of the long training whip.

I wonder what Rett's doing right now? Did they get to Epnoce yet? How much time went by for them? Last time I was gone, it was only a few hours for her, but for me it was—

A light breeze stirred the cornstalks in the next field and the harsh, metallic cry of a pheasant exploded from the hedgerow just behind the arena. The frightened city horse—who would walk calmly past moving cars, racetrack crowds, and huffing tractor-trailers—lunged into a gallop. A good four feet of line jerked through Pam's hands as the horse's wild leap triggered her reflex to hang on. She gripped the line firmly, moving off with the now bucking and plunging animal, cursing herself for not paying attention and worried sick the big bay would take a bad step and tear the newly healed tendon in his left foreleg.

"Whoa, Doc, big guy—whoa!" Pam called. "Whoa, now! Easy, easy, easy." She pitched her voice low and soft to calm the horse. Nine months of work, thought Pam as she tried to regain control of the horse. Nine months of waiting and bandages and liniment—nine months and who knows how many dollars of hay and grain and stable rent and vet bills wasted if he bowed that tendon again!

And it would be my fault. But all the same I'm going to catch that bird and his cousins and make them into pheasant-salad sandwiches!

"What's wrong with you, Pam?" called her friend Jen from her perch on the arena fence. "I came to get some pointers for training my colt, and you can't even control your own horse!"

Pam finally managed to get next to her stallion's head, one hand closing firmly on the headstall, the other wrapping the length of the longe rein. He shook his head in anger and half-reared, Pam moving with him, her attention anything but diverted now. "Easy, easy, easy," she repeated like a mantra, her tone so low it hurt her throat. Finally she coaxed him into a walk, then a halt. The horse stood, sweating, trembling, blowing hard, his tail snapping in nervous agitation. 47

"Whoooaah, big guy. It's okay…okay, whoa." She scratched and petted him and hugged his wide-eyed, beautiful head. This action the horse understood. His blowing and snorting eased as he lowered his head, gave a great sigh, and pressed it tightly against her for reassurance.

"I'm just not with it, today, Jen." Pam loosened the horse's side reins and surcingle. "The heat's getting to me." Pam looked regretfully at her right palm, where the latest rope burn had abraded the tough layer of callused skin gained through her work. She wiped the blood on her palm onto her jeans. "I guess I got spoiled working in air-conditioning."

"I still can't believe you quit the store and got a job at the farm. I wish I was brave enough to take a chance on doing something I liked full time…even if it meant a lot less money."

"Bravery had nothing to do with it," Pam mumbled. "It was more like desperation." And a near miss with a nervous breakdown. She'd thought Rett had been pretty close to one before Colonel Evard made her go on leave—but Pam never realized she had been so close to a meltdown herself until a week or so after she'd awakened from her second merger with Rett.

Soon afterward, she'd found a new job and a new apartment instead of a rented bedroom in the house of a noisy, constantly fighting family. Life wasn't so ordered or predictable any more. Or easy.

But she was happier. All she needed at the moment was some energy.

"But it's not the heat distracting you, it's that story, isn't it?" Jen met Pam at the arena gate and held it open until Pam and the horse came through. "Ever since you had that weird dream last winter—boy oh boy, you've been in outer space for sure!"

Jen, you'll just never know how true that is, thought Pam, coiling up the long line.

"It doesn't seem like that long ago."

"Do you even sleep?"

"Yes, I do."

"Come on, I know how you get. As soon as you get home, you get on your computer and write. I don't think you even got to bed last night."

"Jen, I slept, all right?"

"In the same clothes you had on for the past two days."

Pam tightened her hand on the wad on nylon webbing. The sting of her new abrasions took the edge off the words that rose to her lips. "The horses don't care what I wear."

"I don't either. But I care about you. You get so obsessed with a project, you don't think of anything else until it's done to your liking. A story, mucking a stall, drawing a picture…it's the way you are." Jen patted her arm. "I'm not trying to get you mad."

"I know."

"Do you think you might do anything with this story when it's finished, or will it be another of the many that you won't let anyone see?"

"I'll let you see it if you want. I'm just having a lot of trouble trying to work out some of the background information." Pam sent a smile toward her friend. "Maybe you can give me some ideas."

"It's a good story, Pam. I like it a lot. But you know what works best when you're stuck on something. It's what you always tell me. Give it a rest, do something else, go off in a different direction." Jen scratched the horse's sweaty shoulder, a worried frown on her pretty face. "Shit, Pam. I hope you don't daydream off like this while you're handling those yearlings and stallions and crazy broodmares at the farm. You could get hurt real easily. Look at what just happened. Do you know how close you came to going under him?"

"I knew exactly where both of us were," Pam said, matter-of-fact. She was sure of that. She couldn't explain how, maybe she had picked something up from Rett.

"We both know accidents still happen. Then who'll take care of this place?" Jen shook her head, her long, platinum hair swinging.

Pam managed a smile for her friend. "Yes, you're right. Thanks for looking out for me, Jen."

"You think it was real. Even now."

"I don't know. All I know is that all of a sudden I knew this stuff. Had all these ideas. Felt like I knew a lot of new people. Even after a year the feelings haven't changed."

"You're scaring me, you know. But I wouldn't mind seeing the sketch you did of that hot guy with the weird Mohawk again."

This time Pam laughed. Sometimes she wasn't so sure if her…virtual? Temporal? Astral? journey to a place called Nyorfias had actually happened. She couldn't deny she knew and thought about things she never knew or thought about before. And had other thoughts, ones she couldn't focus upon. Those bothered her the most, staying just out of her reach, teasing her from a nebulous, out-of-focus grayness when she went to sleep. The rest of the time, the details were so sharp they practically leaped from her mind to paper like eager colts from a starting gate when she sketched or wrote.

Could she really discount that? Throw it out as results of her well-known overactive imagination?

"Earth to Pam!" Jen poked her friend in the arm. "Hey! You're doing it again. Are you listening to me at all?"

Pam came back with a start. "Sorry," she said in apology. It was time to get her friend's attention on something else. Jen had enough of her own problems. "How are things with Peter? Any better?"

49

Jen sighed. "Not really. We are talking again, but he wants a divorce. I don't want to talk about that right now."

"He's not scaring you or—"

"No. Not at all. No. I wouldn't still be in the same house with him, you know that."

"I was a bit concerned when you wanted me to come over and stay the past few weekends."

"You're good company…when you're not in outer space." Jen smiled, but there was no reflection of the expression showing in her dark blue eyes.

Pam nodded. Maybe later. In a companionable silence, she walked up the long hill with her horse and her friend. Pam poked at the glasses that slid down her sweaty nose and tiredly waved a pesky fly from her hot face. Even that little action made the nervous Thoroughbred shy and rear.

It's just not my day, Pam thought, calming the horse again. *Damned flies.*

Her thoughts went back to Nyorfias. How long had it been for Rett? Why was the passage of time so screwed up? *Rett doesn't even know I left the store and work now at a breeding and training farm for racehorses. She doesn't know I have a new horse. Shit, I don't even know if she made it through her implant adjustments. I got yanked out five minutes after she left Yidnar's office.*

They never did get the chance to talk about all those things they planned to ask each other. Maybe Nyorfias lost the war. Maybe the Coalition blew them into atoms.

Maybe it had all been a dream after all, and she'd never know what happened.

That thought disappointed Pam the most. So much, in fact, she forced herself to keep her mind on Jen and what she was doing at the large old barn she rented to keep her two horses and the other five boarders she cared for.

2.1.3 CORRIDOR, SECTION C, EPNOCE MAIN COMMAND
0535.08.11 (LOCAL RECKONING)

"Rett!!"

She stopped short, waiting for Jaq to catch up. "Yes, I'm on my way to get something to eat. You can tell Med no one had to drag me, all right?"

"And who put the stingfly in your pants? I was only going to talk to you."

She raked a hand thorough her hair and offered him an apologetic smile. "Sorry. You're starting to sound like a Nyorfian, Jaq."

He looked pleased at that. "You've been so busy running around the past two shifts that I was beginning to think I had to send a message to your Omni. If you're headed to the mess area, mind if I go along? I didn't think I'd be so sleepy on the trip over or after we were quartered…but I was. Hungry now."

"No…I don't mind. Not at all. I'll be glad for your company." She took a look at her chrono. Had they really been on Epnoce almost two entire days now? As the device on her wrist confirmed what her mind denied, the rest of her body caught up with it all and she felt an overwhelming rush of fatigue and hunger. *Fifteen minutes into third shift. Deities, I'm on free time until curfew.*

"We're both on free time now," Jaq said, sounding halfway between questioning and hopeful.

"Yeah." Rett hadn't been planning to go to the mess hall to actually eat: She had been hoping to run into Ariam or Trebor there or in the common area. She changed her mind as her stomach growled. "*Definitely* on my way there," she confirmed, glad her body decided to back up her words.

"That was you? Thought we were having a quake for a moment."

He chuckled as he fell into step with her, but Rett noticed that her initial flareup had affected him. She saw it in her mind as the pure blue gradient of his normal aura darkened and rippled with muddy streaks. "What is it you wanted to talk to me about, Jaq? Besides idle mealtime conversation, I mean."

"Something deep is bothering you. What's wrong? Can I help?"

51

Giving him a diverting smile, she leaned a little closer and slid her arm through his. He felt so good, and just being next to him brought her a feeling of contentment and comfort. He was always ready to support her. Suddenly she wasn't hungry for food any more. Or for rest.

Most of the others might have been taking it easy since their arrival, as they were told to do. But after seeing everyone settled and checking out the quarters she'd share with her second, Rett had been studying. No matter what Med said about sleeping, there was far too much new information to assimilate. They'd be getting some training lectures and presentations, but she'd never been more than scholastically average. And that was average only with extra study and hard work.

And today, after some medical tests, an exercise period, and a lecture on complex emergency procedures, she'd gone back to her studying. It was high time for a break, and some time alone with Jaq was exactly what she wanted. But where?

She had to again wonder if Zetinorians were capable of mindspeak because Jaq touched her arm and said, "If you'd prefer something else before dinner, I know where we can go."

"How do you know?"

"I was stationed here for a while when it was still held by the Coalition. I know all the serviceways and service areas in them, and how to make them invisible for just as long as needed, too. That is, unless things were changed since then. I told MainCommand about the blanking program—" Jaq stopped short.

Rett hugged his arm. She still felt deep amazement and respect for Jaq, who'd done so much behind the backs of the enemy to thwart their efforts and help the Nyorfian cause. She found out something new and different about him almost every day. Not from Jaq himself—he didn't talk about just how much or what it was he had done. At least, he'd never said anything to her, unless it came up directly.

And he got so...*appealing* when he was being modest about his more than dangerous exploits.

"Why would we bother to remove safeguards the enemy couldn't crack? Especially since you told MainCommand about them and how they work."

Even now as she pressed closer in a half-hug of appreciation, Jaq's already ruddy skin darkened. His defection—his *escape*, as Rett preferred to call it—to the Nyorfian side couldn't have been timed better, since he'd been close to being discovered more than once, and Zetinorians were already treated with dislike and suspicion by the Yixolryn Coalition.

"I don't think MainCommand expects me to use a blankout code just so I can get some quality time with you."

Jaq looked worried now, and she understood why. He was still on trial and bound by rules and restrictions both from his agreement to fully cooperate with the Nyorfian government, and his application process for citizenship. If he stepped outside of any of those rules, things wouldn't go well, especially with the war still going on.

"Well, I have a way around that." Rett leaned even closer. Inwardly, she smiled, thinking of a much younger version of herself back in Special Forces training, when they were told to do something—and all the loopholes and angles she and the other trainees would come up with to get the job done and still stay inside the restrictions they were given. "Did they say you couldn't tell *me* any of that?"

"No, as a matter of fact, I'm supposed to tell you anything you ask me to. It's part of why they agreed to assign me to your unit."

Rett let her smile show on the outside. "Good."

She glanced around. The side corridor they had drifted into was deserted: nothing but storage and emergency equipment. And, Rett noticed, the inevitable combination of service access, earthquake shelter, and escape routes the corridors in each complex had every hundred lengths.

"Then you'll tell me the code we need here, and I'll enter it, and we'll see if it still works. If it does, I blank it out, and no one will bother us."

"Rett—"

"Don't worry, Jaq. We're both on free time." Like other combat group leaders, Rett was given the master codes to any locked service door on any Epnocian complex. Still, she felt relieved when she didn't have to use it—the door was unlocked. Service doors were only locked if there was a safety or security issue involved.

53

"And no one inside—the indicators would be lit," Jaq said, pointing at the exact spot Rett was eyeing on the information display.

"Unless your program is active?"

He nodded.

"As soon as we get on the other side of the door, then, we'll try it out." In a moment she was ready to suit action to words. "All right, let's have the code." She tapped in the sequence of symbols as Jaq spoke them. At the same time she committed the sequence to memory, setting a mental reminder to have Jaq test her on them later. "How do we know it's working?"

"Look here." He tapped a smaller display panel just inside the space behind the door. "This should be reading two lifeforms standing right where we are, but it's showing blank space. Now, try to find yourself or me on your Omni."

54

"Well, I guess we know your program still works!" Rett tried to locate herself, but the readout remained the same. NOT AVAILABLE. Just to be sure, she told the Omni to find Ariam, who still lingered in the mess area. "Wow. Jaq—is this program in place only here, at MainCommand, or in every complex?" If his program was in place elsewhere, it could be a significant strategic advantage.

"I'm not sure. I gave the program to a few members of the civilian underground, and they might have managed to get the protocols in place at other locations. But I don't know, and there's no way to check until we get there and can test it like we just did."

Rett nodded and turned toward the corridor that led deeper into the secret places of the huge complex. The tiny vestibule seemed huge by comparison as she entered the narrow passage. Since Jaq followed her, she tried to keep her shiver inside. It wasn't one of tingly anticipation—it was fear. She hated tight spaces; being restricted in movement. The service corridors were tight, and she and the Zetinorian were by no means small people. Jaq had to hunch and sort of turn sideways, and Rett had to watch her head. Her shoulders brushed the walls on either side.

"I hope this doesn't get much smaller," she muttered.

"It doesn't. But if you think *this* is tight, you should try it in armor," Jaq said with good humor. "Even that partial armor your regular infantry wears would cause an issue with someone as big as me, even as big as you."

"I'm glad there'll be more room in the control bay." Rett angled her body in an attempt to give herself the illusion of more space.

"They've made them bigger?"

Jaq sounded surprised, and Rett turned her head to look at him. "Aren't they?"

"You've never been through one of these accessways before, have you?"

"We've not been here long. We don't have buildings like this on Nyorfias. All I've had time to review were access codes, images, where essential control and emergency areas are, and only part of the schematics." Any pleasant feeling inside Rett started draining. Going into a tight space because she had to was one thing. But not for the fun of it. Not even to be with Jaq. She tried to control her breathing and the sharp onrush of fear that filled her. "This is a bad idea. I can't—"

Jaq's warm hand closed over the top of her shoulder. "It'll be all right." His touch and calm, low voice soothed her. "There *is* more space. More than out here. There's the access, ahead."

Swallowing, Rett forced herself to move ahead. Her ardor had cooled, but she knew she had to continue and face down her weaknesses. At least Jaq was with her. She wasn't alone, she wasn't helpless, and she was making a choice to do this.

But it wouldn't hurt if Pam were here, too.

The air was thankfully fresh and as soon as Rett slipped inside, it started moving, proving the motion- and body-sensing life support system were indeed operational. The circulating air was cool and moist, emerging from a self-contained unit separate from the rest of the complex: one of the many backup systems should the complex be damaged in an earthquake or another disaster.

"You okay, Rett?"

"I can't believe that entire groups of people would hide in these rooms. For *days*." Rett prowled the small space with misgivings, scrubbing her hands up and down her arms. She felt cold, and it wasn't from the temperature. "Jaq, I'm—"

She found herself in his arms, against his large, hard body. At first she tensed, but as Jaq's soothing presence enveloped her, she relaxed. She rested her head on his shoulder and his hand smoothed the back of her head and neck. She burrowed closer, locking her arms around him, needing his warmth, his support. She didn't have to be Rett the platoon leader now. She could just be Rett, let herself lean on someone else, and feel safe.

Well, that was until he started making her feel other things.

His lips touched the exact right spot below her left ear. The feelings she thought had fled returned as his touch in that one spot ignited sensations in at least a hundred other places in her body. The hand that had been stroking her head and neck now drifted lightly down her spine, stopping short of her weapons belt.

Jaq could play a long and delightful game of getting her aroused to the point of mindless insanity before he even broke a sweat, but unfortunately, they didn't have that sort of time. Rett was rapidly learning firsthand about many Zetinorian peculiarities. Most of them she'd discovered recently, while on leave in Branch.

Just thinking about some of those times raised Rett's temperature a few more degrees. For someone who didn't have any previous consensual sexual experience, Jaq was amazing. Naturally gifted, Pam had said. Both of them had been skeptical of the Zetinorian's claim that males of his race didn't feel the need for their own fulfillment before his partner had experienced at least one climax.

But Jaq had erased that doubt, more than once. Rett heated still more, remembering, her arms no longer simply holding tight around Jaq's waist. Time to set some fires of her own. She lifted her head from its cozy support, and nipped along the Zetinorian's jaw. She was still surprised it was so naturally smooth. Sure, there were Nyorfian males who seemed to never have to shave or use facial hair suppressors, but Rett had never had intimate relations with them.

She was rewarded by his shiver and a soft growl. But of course, to keep her from doing it again, he claimed her mouth.

Jaq was an excellent kisser.

Definitely naturally gifted, thought Rett, and then stopped thinking about anything, except how giddy she was starting to feel.

In the time it took her to start getting more than pleasantly warm, Jaq had neatly discarded all the hardware between them. His hands were working their way up her ribcage as his lips traveled away from her mouth and down her throat.

Rett, meanwhile, was using her own skills, and another recent discovery. Now that she had the top half of Jaq's uniform and his inner shirt out of the way, she was able to play her fingers through the soft mane along his spine. There was one spot in particular that seemed particularly erogenous. She had discovered it the last time they had made love before leaving Branch, and he had already been fully aroused. She wanted to test it when they were just getting started, and now seemed like the perfect time.

So she gently stroked his mane from top to bottom, feathering her fingers through the sensitive strands. When she reached the spot she wanted, just about a handwidth above his hips, she gave it a little more attention. As their tongues twined and danced, so did her fingers in the chosen tract of mane.

Jaq's reaction to this was almost instantaneous. With a gasp, he pulled back, a hint of wildness and worry in his eyes. His pupils had dilated, giving them the darkness of twilight.

"Rett—" He sounded strained. Sweat beaded his forehead. His body vibrated.

She smiled in satisfaction and pressed closer, feeling his arousal through the clothing they both still wore on their lower bodies. Reaching down, she said: "Let's just not worry about that, Jaq."

"Re-eett—"

"This time is for you as much as for me. And I'm ready. I want you to be, too."

* * * * *

THEY CLEANED UP AND DRESSED quickly, since the air in the service access felt even chillier against bodies warmed by lovemaking. Then Jaq drew Rett against him and held her close, stroking her back. She seemed to like it, and he did, too. He especially liked it when she abandoned herself to the point of allowing him to support her completely, so that if he let her go, she'd have to either fall down or scramble to regain her balance.

He loved that feeling, actually. He felt strong and protective, something he never quite got to be to her in their daily life.

He always felt a little touch of anxiety, however, thinking about her absolute silence during lovemaking, a silence that reminded him all too much of the same stoic silence a Special Forces operative maintained during combat or under torture . At first he'd thought he might be doing something wrong, because, well...it was pretty much a given that there was usually some degree of vocalization. There certainly was on his part.

Then again, he hadn't been trained the same way she'd been. His training hadn't been much of anything, really, and most Coalition soldiers who earned the displeasure of ranking seniors learned that proving they were able to take pain in silence just earned them more of it.

But she left him no doubt she enjoyed what they did together. Her body language, her breathing, the expression in her space-dark eyes. The way the hard warrior body became soft and pliant and trusting when he touched her.

By the One, how he loved this woman.

Jaq turned his face into her hair, marveling at the slick, soft feel of it. He liked the way the short strands swam through his fingers, taunting him with the impossible task of taking hold. He liked the fact both of them had unusual hair. But aside from all that, he loved her, no matter what was on the outside.

He breathed, "I love you, Rett," into her ear before tucking her head beneath his chin and closing his eyes.

* * * *

THE HARD, SMOOTH POURSTONE BENEATH them suddenly bucked and heaved. Caught unprepared, Rett went backward into a corner with the dense Zetinorian's considerable weight pressing the air from her lungs. Before she could wheeze a protest he shifted, but the floor continued to move beneath them. She tried to get up, but Jaq prevented her from rising.

"Let me up!" She struggled, but gravity, Jaq's weight and leverage, and the pitching floor conspired against her. The shaking and undulations made her decidedly queasy. The wall at her back was vibrating. "It's not an explosion?"

"Quake. Stay down until the shaking stops."

Quake. *Quake.* This? It was like nothing she had ever experienced before. She'd felt quakes that made her stumble, and others that rumbled in the ground like thunder, and once had seen the side of a mountain fall into a ravine. But none of those times had been like this. She counted automatically in her head, but the seconds seemed more like hours. Finally it stopped. She wriggled out from beneath Jaq, took a breath, and got to her feet. "I think we—"

"Get down, Rett."

A percussive reverberation and another sharp heave from below sent her down again and rolling into the opposite wall. This time, she ended up on top of Jaq. It took her a moment or so to register her new position since her head had stopped short against the cover panel for an entire array of environmental routing controls. She knew that because she'd had a good, close-up view right before she saw shooting stars. And comets. Definitely a comet in there somewhere.

"Ow," she mumbled, blinking her vision clear.

The shakes subsided, at least on the outside. She rolled away from Jaq, pressing the heel of her hand against her forehead.

"Over here."

She didn't understand at first, because he wasn't headed in the direction she wanted to go: out. He instead pushed himself into an inside corner, wedging his big, dense body into the space. "Quickly, come on."

His tone was low and urgent, so she didn't resist and followed the directions of his hands to sit in the space between his legs and lean back

59

against him. He wrapped his limbs around her protectively. This time, they remained anchored in place when the next shock hit. Instead of up and down, the motion rolled back and forth. It felt like that time she tried to ride a log through the rapids at Freten's Knob.

The lights flickered and the walls undulated, and this time she not only felt sick, but dizzy. Her sense of balance was gone. She plastered herself into Jaq and wished she could stop the incessant trembling of her body. She cursed inwardly for being unable to dampen her fear and control her reactions.

"Easy," Jaq said. "Yes, it's a quake, a big one. Actually, this is the fourth one—so far. But we're safe here. These accessways aren't as shielded against the shaking as the main areas, but they are strongest since they're also the escape routes in case of structural damage. We're safe here," he repeated, gently fingering the spot where her head had made impact with the panel.

60 "Let's get out of here." Every sense she had was protesting the movement of what was supposed to be firm, stable, unmoving. Her fears of being immobilized, trapped, as the ceiling and walls crushed in on them, was so sharp she tasted blood from biting the inside of her cheek. She had to get into open space. She'd start screaming if she stayed here another minute. "Come on."

"Not yet," Jaq said. "We have to wait for the all clear. Quake safety briefing, remember? The one we got as soon as we checked in?"

Rett did remember, and of course he was right, but every instinct she had was against taking that advice. The tremors now were coming from her, not the planet. Damn it, she had to get a grip. Quakes were going to be routine now, and she had to get used to them. All the same, she'd prefer to be naked and unarmed against a direct assault from an enemy battalion. That she could handle.

Jaq's embrace shifted and she almost protested aloud, but then something cool pressed against her sore spot. A gelpack. It felt good.

She took a breath, forcing the remainder of her panic down into her protesting stomach. Amazed at how tightly her entire body had been clenched, she forced herself to relax. "I didn't even hear the alert. How are we supposed to hear a clear?"

"Indicator light."

The cool spot that soothed her bruised head went away only long enough so that Jaq could direct her glance toward the informational display, which flared the unmistakable orange background of a complex emergency situation. She didn't get much farther than that before another tremor—from outside again—started the walls vibrating. She knew at that point if she made herself try to read any of the other information she'd end up spewing, and in this small space that was the last thing she wanted to do.

Thankfully, the gelpack went back to her bruise, and Jaq's other arm and his legs exerted reassuring pressure around her. And then she realized the shaking had stopped. This time she didn't try to move anything but her eyes, and they focused on the display. Still orange. Data was scrolling across the screen, too. Reports coming in from the different sectors of the station: minor damages, minor injuries.

"I'm sorry," Rett mumbled.

"What for?"

"I don't usually..." She didn't know how to explain. "Go off like that." Not for a long, long time.

"I know. It's all right. I don't care what kind of training anyone's had, when the ground starts moving—it's going to affect them. The first bad one I experienced on this planet scared me so badly my hair was on end for a tenday. I felt sick, dizzy. So did a lot of others, humanoid and alien alike."

Rett had to laugh, imagining the already wild-haired Zetinorian with every living strand of his hair standing out straight, not only on his head, but all the way down his spine to his hips. "It must have hurt to keep your helmet or shirt on."

"I don't want to think about it." He sounded sour, but the movement of his chest against her back betrayed amusement. "Brace yourself," he said then, his limbs tightening around her. "Another hard jolt."

"How do you kn—"

Rett bit her lip as once more the room slipped sideways. Things she didn't want to think about creaked and groaned and screeched all around them.

"Jaq."

"Yes, Rett?"

"Next time I get the bright idea to have sex in a service access, punch me."

His chuckle warmed her. "Too bad the timing wasn't a little better. You could have thought it was me making the planet shift for you."

Rett twisted her upper body and reached around to give him a one-armed hug. "You do that already. But I don't walk away from you feeling like I have to throw up."

"Here. I have something for that." He let go long enough to reach to his utility belt.

He showed her a tiny green container. It was nothing she recognized, and had no medical mark. If it was something unique to Zetinorians, something they required for injury, Med should have informed her. No one ever carried anything in medical packs that hadn't been authorized by Med, disclosed to Rett, and subsequently made known to everyone else.

"What is it?"

"Med gave it to me." He flicked it open with his thumb. A tiny puff of mist escaped from the opening. "It's—"

"Shit, Jaq!" Rett's first impulse was to block his hand and recoil: she was as phobic about unknown chemicals and medicines as she was about small spaces and immobility. The tiny container hit the floor and rolled in a drunken arc.

"—mountain blue pine, longcone, and some other everbearing tree."

"Damn it. Med gave that to you for your kit and never told me? You know people aren't supposed to medicate me!"

"Well, he said it wasn't medicine, and it was in my personal item pocket. Not my medical pouch." Jaq sounded puzzled. "He said smelling it helps you feel better when you're tense. More relaxed."

Rett finally let out the breath she'd been holding, took one in, and let it out again with a sigh. It smelled like a summer afternoon at home, and while it eased her tension and settled her roiling stomach, it also brought a moment of homesickness.

"It does." She unknotted her muscles for the second time and leaned forward to retrieve the phial. "But *please* tell me what it is *first*, next time. Before you open it. Maybe before you even reach for it." Her heart was still racing in her chest. "I didn't break your hand or anything, did I?"

"It's numb, but it's fine. I'm sorry."

"It's all right." She angled her body more so she could kiss him. She'd never get tired of kissing him. It always made her feel better. Then she grimaced as Ariam's familiar voice came through her pcom.

"Sorry to interrupt your free time." Ariam didn't sound very sorry at all.

"Go ahead, Fang Two." Rett checked her chrono. She wasn't late—yet.

"Fang team is checked in and all go. Just wanted to let you know."

"Thanks. Fang Tech and I are all go."

A second voice joined the transmission. "FangMed says you've bashed your head and you need to report to Section C's med station."

Rett made a face. "It's only a bruise, it's fine. We've a gelpack on it."

"Actually, it's bleeding—" murmured Jaq, and Rett dug her elbow into him.

"That's all right, Fang Tech, I knew that already. Fang Lead, be here, five minutes, or I'll send someone to bring you in." Med signed off.

"Uhm, where are you, exactly?" continued Ariam. "I know you're not far, but no one can find your bio readings anywhere or get a lock on your locators."

Rett muted the pcom input, knowing it would be impossible to smother the chuckle that even now escaped her. "We'd better get out of here."

"Yes." Jaq entered the code to open the section on the touchpanel to the left of the information display, and then they started back along the way outside.

"Ahh, Fang two," she said, reopening the transmission, "we're in Section C, Area Four, Subsection Thirty-seven in emergency shelter."

"I'm not reading a shelter or any bio readings in that section—wait a moment, it just came up. Can you check that out?" Ariam's last remark was clearly to someone else.

"We were rattled around some over here," Rett said. "Our locators might have been damaged, we'll have them checked out."

"See that you do, I'll have Fang twenty-three standing by," Ariam said, and signed off, sounding both suspicious and amused.

"She'll sic H'tenneck on us as soon as we show up."

"He'll cover for you," Jaq said simply.

"He would. But I don't want him to. I'll come clean with Ariam so she doesn't have to strain herself next time. I was blocking her, too, and she doesn't like that."

"I don't get how you can block an empath like Ariam without any formal training."

Rett snorted. "Try growing up with *two* of them."

"Maybe I did. I don't remember."

She felt awful for forgetting he didn't have many recollections of his former life. Most Coalition troopers who were put in deepsleep mode for transport lost a lot of detail from their memories, retaining a vivid memory here, a nebulous impression there, knowing there was someone but never being able to recall a face, a voice, a name. Like Jaq, who knew he'd had parents and a few siblings, but couldn't remember anything else about them, except for the fact he'd seen them all killed before the Coalition dragged him off as a slave.

What was worse, he told her that he didn't even know exactly how long he was in stasis, or remember his birth year or the year he'd been taken. All he knew was his homeworld didn't exist anymore, not for over a hundred years of time as the GTC measured it.

"Jaq—"

He smiled down at her. "It's all right. I'm glad I remember they died, and they didn't have to go through what I did. It's really all right. Besides, Zetinorians as a race aren't psi-able, not like, say, the Kyarta. So any empaths in my family would have had to have offworld blood. And between what I remember and what I studied, my people didn't outbreed too often. But now that I'm being considered for citizenship here, I'd like to change that, one day." He bumped her with his hip.

"It would be interesting," Rett said noncommittally. She turned into the corridor and wondered what any children she might have with Jaq might look like. Then she threw him a sharp glance. "If you're not psi-able, how were you able to tell another shock was coming, and how come you're always speaking my mind?"

"Well, when I tune in, my hair can feel certain disturbances before they manifest fully, you know, like some animals can. The lighter part, especially."

Rett nodded. Okay, she'd take that. "That's why you said what you did about your hat in Branch. That night I took off and you came looking, and I jumped down and startled you."

"Yes. A hat, helmet, or too much clothing or armor is almost like putting a wall up."

"Do you remember how people dressed on Zetinor Prime?"

"Hm. I haven't thought about that. What people wore. I just tried to remember who they were. I'll think about it and let you know. As for you, I simply think we're on the same track all those times. I mean, you've done the same thing with me, too. Look, there's Med. And I'll tell him right away we're headed to the mess area afterward."

Rett grimaced. She felt fine now, but the quake had erased her appetite and left her feeling edgy and distracted. *I have to eat, though. At least make a public appearance.*

* * * * *

SHE WAS GRATEFUL THE VISIT with Med didn't take long, and he spared her any of his usual griping. There were enough people with minor injuries from the quake walking in and out from the Medical annex to distract him. Rett couldn't help wondering what casualties might have been like if the building hadn't been specifically engineered to withstand the shaking.

She shivered. *This is what we're going to have to work with—and through.*

"Something else is bothering you," Jaq said as they continued toward mess.

"I'm just feeling a little wiped out, Jaq. Deities, I'm glad we're not going to be doing much for a day or so."

The small sound of assent he made told Rett he wasn't about to be put off that easily. If Jaq had been about to say anything else, it probably went right out of him with his exhale as they turned into the mess area and found themselves in the middle of a sea of black-banded heads, which seemed to bob and drift around the room without benefit of bodies.

"Lords of mercy!"

Rett grinned as she looked around. "Welcome to the 2023rd, Jaq. Ready to dive in?"

The color and light reflecting properties of the Special Forces combat uniform was in full effect here. In the off-white room, with off-white tables and chairs, and overhead, neutral lighting, portions of people covered by uniform disappeared, leaving only their shadows.

"This is scary. I've never noticed this effect before, and I've seen you people combat-garbed in groups more than once. Especially the past few tendays."

Her grin widened as Jaq glanced down at his feet as if to make sure they were still on the floor, and then felt his head to see if it was firmly attached to his shoulders. She'd seen that exact same reaction before. She'd experienced it herself.

"This is weird," he said.

"You'll never find a Special Forces area that's monochromatic, that's why. Give us a few days. I'm sure we'll redecorate. In the meanwhile, don't try to look head on. Go a bit to one side or another. Like you would in the dark. That helps."

She saw him try it and nod in agreement.

"I have to admit I forgot what this can be like with so large a group," she admitted. "In a few days, though, we'll be used to it. In a couple more, we'll probably be wearing half our other gear to mess and meetings, so there'll be a little more breakup, too."

They hadn't taken five steps deeper into the room when a voice called out: "Yo, hey, Rett! Rett!"

"Good gods and deities!" She turned to her right to match that long-unheard voice to the face she remembered, and was not disappointed. "Sergeant Wreagor!"

Grinning up at her was none other than her old trainee unit instructor. His seamed and wrinkled face threatened to split with pleasure. Rett automatically started to salute, but the grizzled old veteran opened his arms for a hug.

Wow, I never expected to ever hug Wreagor. But she was so happy to see him now that she easily made the transition to the more personal greeting. The heavier gravity didn't stop her from lifting the old TI right off his feet.

He pounded her on the back in greeting as much as protest. "Damn it all, girl, put me down!"

When she released him, he stepped back a pace, face flushed a little. "The *least* you might have done was make it look as if you exerted some effort," he grumbled. "Let me look at you, Rett."

Gnarled hands gripping her shoulders, bright eyes missing nothing, Wreagor inspected her from boots to hair. "What happened?"

"Quake damage," answered Rett with a droll glance ceilingward.

"Ah. You're not the only one. But good to go, that's what matters. You look great. Stronger than ever." Wreagor squeezed her shoulders. "Heard life's been rough on you. Glad to see you're still going despite that. Gods, but I really miss that long hair you used to have. I'll never understand why you chopped it off."

"Didn't have time for long hair," she told him, flushing as she smiled. "Still don't." She tried something she never would have dared back in training. "How come no one's made you retire yet?"

Wreagor chuckled, and she relaxed, trying to get used to the shift in their relationship. Deities, it was strange to have him treating her like an equal instead of the naive, green trainee he'd seemed to enjoy calling out, finding fault with, and putting on the spot every chance he'd had.

"I'll be with this battalion in some capacity until I can't move, you know that. Everything's moved here for the duration, even training ops."

"Wow. And Lieutenant Vanfreiss? Captain Jelenek?"

"That's *Major* Jelenek now. And Captain Vanfreiss."

"I've been out of touch for a while."

"We know that. You're not the only one. Introduce me." The old man's gaze went to the Zetinorian.

"My tech advisor, Jaq Pym. Jaq, Sergeant Wreagor, the best TI in Special Forces."

"Welcome to Special Forces. Heard all about the great work you're doing for us." Wreagor appraised the Zetinorian candidly. "You're big enough, aren't you?"

"Nice to meet you, Sergeant. Call me Jaq. What's this about Rett and long hair?" Jaq, his eyes twinkling, covered the upturned palm Wreagor offered in greeting with his big ruddy hand.

"Nothing," Rett said, hoping to divert the topic.

But Wreagor had other ideas. "Hair, you've certainly plenty of it now, Jaq, hey? You'll not be getting lost in this bunch any time soon." He stared with unabashed curiosity at Jaq's wild head. Rett could almost see the questions rising to the surface, one right after another, in a queue as close and tight as chain ammo for a heavy machine gun. "Does it really have nerves? Does that middle part react to your emotions? Does it grow to only one length, or keep growing? How far down does that white part go? Doesn't wearing close-fitting clothing on your back or a helmet bother you?"

She had heard Jaq answer the same questions countless times for curious Nyorfians ever since coming over. He cheerfully answered them again, firing off his replies in the same manner the questions were asked. "Yes, at least sort of; yes; each strand has its own set length; down to hip level; sometimes, and only if it doesn't fit right."

Wreagor abruptly gestured toward Rett, getting around to answering Jaq's original query. "Hers was to her shoulders and her fringe came right down to her eyes. Dark as space and thick, couldn't get a hand around it." He held open a gnarled, scarred hand, making a circle with his thumb and fingers in demonstration. "Plenty tried, since hair is a good handle in a fight. Not hers. Just slides out of your fingers like water. Got that from her mother, I guess, she came from offworld. As short as it is now, you've probably noticed that peculiarity about her hair."

She shot her old TI a sharp glance of inquiry. And why would he think Jaq noticed that?

In answer to her silent query, Wreagor smiled. A serene expression of innocence in his eyes vied for dominance over one of outright mischief. "I always had to wonder how you kept hair ties and safety helmets on. Or, for that matter, your headband."

"They're not warm-blooded or covered by some kind of skin," supplied Jaq before she could remind Wreagor he knew those answers.

Wreagor laughed, a wicked delight growing. "So, Jaq Pym, you've done some research."

Of course that was what he wanted. A better picture of what Jaq knew about her that most wouldn't. And although she knew better, she couldn't quite shake off the old suspicion she used to have back in training: that Wreagor was Talented. Deities, that meant he knew exactly what she and Jaq had been doing before coming here.

"Want to see her before she cropped that hair? I've some images of her from training. Quite a few of them."

"Aw, deities, Sarge, please don't—" said Rett. She'd sooner forget about a few of those he'd managed to get.

Too late. Wreagor had his personal Omni in hand and was showing Jaq a few from his collection. She couldn't blame him for wanting to share his images. The 2023rd was his only family, as it had been since its beginnings almost thirteen years before. Before that, Wreagor had spent fifteen years full time with the planetary militia as a trainer; and before that, twenty years as a GTC Ranger. He had images from those days, too.

"And that's who?" Jaq asked. "Evetez? Yes, we met briefly in Branch… what's with the feathers stuck all over him?"

"A training exercise," Wreagor answered.

"I've heard Special Forces training is different, but feathers? What, do you camouflage yourselves as birds? Wow, that fish is huge. Who got eaten?" Jaq wanted to know a moment later.

"Deities. Not *those*." Rett groaned.

"That'd be Rett."

"I thought those feet looked familiar."

"She wasn't *in* the fish, she was beneath it." The old man shook with barely contained glee. "That day was one of the high points of the first half of the training period."

"Looks like it. And that's Sergeant Semage…" Jaq laughed, but it sounded forced and a bit sad. "They all look like kids." He looked up. Catching Rett's gaze, he sent her one of his special smiles before returning his attention to the viewer.

"They were," said Wreagor softly. Someone else in the crowd hailed him. "I'll catch up with you later, Rett." He retrieved his viewer and gave her a parting clout on the shoulder. To Jaq, he gave a nod and "We appreciate your helping us out. I hope to be seeing more of you sometime."

Jaq watched the older man go, feeling a little wistful as he tried to remember who Wreagor reminded him of. "I like him," he told Rett after Wreagor had disappeared. "I think I had an uncle like him once.

"I'm sorry you can't remember much about your life, and your family."

He shrugged and shook his head. It really seemed to bother her. He supposed it should have bothered him more, too, but he'd had a lot of time and distractions to get past it. There was nothing he could do to get back what he'd lost, so it seemed more practical to move forward. "Thanks."

He noted her silence after that but didn't comment on it until they gathered some dinner and settled at a far table. He took several moments to examine her present expression, wondering again what she was thinking. What troubled her so deeply? He'd sensed the change in her even before they had departed from Nyorfias. No matter what she said before, he knew there was more to it.

"What is it? Please tell me what's wrong."

"You are, Jaq."

"Me? It's me now, is it? What did I do?" He kept his tone light and took a casual bite of the vegetable on his fork.

"Oh, nothing much. Nothing at all. Except the entire Free Army seems to think you and I are the match of the century. Good thing you're being kept away from the media or I'm sure the entire GTC would know by now."

He took another bite of the steamed vegetables on his plate and chewed. As he watched her push her own dinner around without attempting to eat it, he considered her words, hearing the confusion and frustration beneath them.

"Are they coming up with any more suggestions for the name of our firstborn yet?" he asked casually. "I liked Jemrett a lot. It has elements from both my names and your name as well. It would do for a girl or a boy. Actually, I think twins would be nice. Does your family's genetic history include any twins? Maybe we can have one of each. Jemrett and Tejaq. Or Jaquet. Haven't you given the least bit of thought to this?"

Rett's startled gaze leapt from the uneaten food on her plate to his face. "What?"

He had to fight to keep his expression bland. "Our children, Rett." He pretended to take a sip from his mug of tea, not daring to let any of the liquid past his lips. The laughter was just too close to the surface to risk it.

Where was that old man with his Omni full of candid moments? Jaq gave up any pretense of drinking. He gave his complete attention to her face as her expression phased from shocked surprise, disbelief, dismay, wistful speculation, and back again. Then she looked as if she were unable to breathe. She gasped, almost choking. Propping her elbows on the table, she dropped her face in her hands. A long, wet sort of snorting sound escaped and her strong shoulders shook.

"Hey," he said uneasily, his amusement vanishing. "Rett? I'm—"

Her head came up, dark eyes shining with tears, lips quivering. She gulped in a breath and howled with laughter.

"—kidding," he lied. He had said it to lighten the mood, but he still thought it was a great idea. He smiled in a lame fashion at those seated around them, who in turn raised eyebrows, grinned, or chuckled before going back to their own conversations.

Fortunately, she gained control of herself after a minute, swiping at her watering eyes with a wipe from the dispenser on the table. "I'm sorry, Jaq." She sucked in another breath and pressed the fingers of her right hand to her lips for a moment, sparkling merriment lighting the dark eyes that had been so introspective and sad before.

His lips twitched. "It wasn't *that* funny," he grumbled, stabbing a cube of baked knotroot.

"No," Rett said, her face and voice under control again; most of the newly kindled radiance vanishing.

He cursed himself for a fool, remembering that she'd mentioned to him, once and very briefly, that she used to dream of having a life partner, children of her own, and a family life. And that she didn't dare think of it now, she simply couldn't afford to speculate. Not until the war ended and she lived to see that end. What he said hit all too close to that fragile dream of hers. He was such an idiot. Damn it! Why didn't he think before he just came out with that?

"I'm sorry."

She shook her head. "Don't be. I needed that. I think I found it so funny because not too much shocks me anymore. That did, coming out of nowhere like that." She looked away for a second. "It's not a bad thought," she added so softly that Jaq wasn't sure if she wanted him to hear. So he pretended not to.

"Hardly nowhere," said Jaq, thinking how very much he was getting to like knotroot. He eyed the untouched serving on Rett's tray, leaned over and speared one of the golden brown cubes. "F-troop's been speculating on how many kids, when the first would arrive, what sex they'd be and what we would name them ever since I arrived."

She grinned. "I hope they've invested those credits. It might be a long time before they see who wins."

"Hopefully not." He swiped another one of her vegetables and then nudged her plate closer to her. "Eat."

* * * * *

RETT PICKED UP HER FORK, and stabbed one of her now-cold knotroot cubes before Jaq ate all of them. For a moment longer she held her grin and eye contact while she chewed, but soon lowered her gaze to the tabletop again, with the excuse of making another selection from her plate.

I thought I would feel better after sharing some time with him, quake or no quake. She pushed a section of yellowstem through a congealing slick of juice from the meat she had yet to touch. How she wished she could confide in him about Pam. Or find words to explain the confusion and uncertainty she felt when she tried to decide exactly what she felt for him. Instead, she put down her fork, reached across the table and clasped one of his hands tightly for a moment. "Jaq, have I told you lately how much I appreciate you?"

"Sure," he answered. "Just now."

She felt better as a smile lit his beautiful eyes and sent warmth deep inside to touch the cold void of doubt inside her. His fingers tightened in hers.

"Now, you don't need Med on your back, so keep eating. You'll need the energy just to handle this gravity for a while. We all do."

She obeyed his subtle threat and had a few more bites. All too easily her mind wandered again. His voice lulled her as he carried on a conversation about the similarities in gravity between Epnoce and Zetinor Prime that soon blended into background noise with every other conversation going on in the room around her.

What was Pam doing right now? Was the entire five tendays of their second merger just one night's sleep for her, like the very first merge was? That one had been slightly less than two days long. How was it possible that, for Pam, it had happened in six or eight hours? Was the second time the same?

Damn it. Pam, where are you? Don't pass out or anything, but I really need to talk.

No answer.

Maybe the ego-merge had been imagined. Maybe Rett was the one dreaming. One day she'd wake up, find out she'd collapsed from fatigue, and the past two, three months of her life had been nothing more than the fevered hallucinations of a broken mind.

She actually itched to be on a combat assignment so she would have no time to think about anything, only her mission.

You have to stop running. Pam's words echoed in her head. Deities, had that been less than three tendays ago? It seemed like a lifetime.

A cold, creeping blackness gripped her inside and out. Terror closed her throat, drove a sharp pain through her guts. A new dread grew from it. Suddenly, she felt trapped, driven, hazed in the same manner a wounded dunos was run to the ground by a growtu pack.

Her leg muscles twitched and tensed. She had to force herself to remain in place, to continue the appearance she was eating and listening to Jaq. Yes, she had to stop running and needed to stand and fight whatever hounded her. But she couldn't, not yet. Not yet. She couldn't stop running until she found a place to make a stand.

And, of course, it would help to know what was making her run in the first place.

2.14 FARM, HUNTERDON COUNTY, NJ USA EARTH
CURRENT ERA

PAM SLID FROM HER SEAT and slammed the door of the Ford pickup with unnecessary force. She needed to quit thinking about this damned ego-merge...dream...story. Whatever it was. Maybe Jen was right to tell her she was obsessed. She made a face and kicked a dandelion, exploding its fuzzy head into a puff of fairy parachutes.

She was depressed, too. The continued hot weather didn't help; it was nearly the end of September now and still felt like August. She never liked the hot weather, not even when all it meant was summer vacation. Her thoughts had been on anything but her driving this evening, so much that on the way from work to her own barn and horses, she'd run a red light on the highway—right in front of a police car, too—and got caught. That was the reason for slamming the truck's door harder than necessary.

Pam kicked a clod from her path and trudged around the silo to go inside the old barn. Not only did she get a ticket for the red light, she also got one for overdue inspection; another for presenting an expired registration. The cop had threatened to have her truck towed off, even grumbled that he shouldn't be letting her drive it. In fact, he was deciding whether or not to give her a ticket for not wearing a seat belt, either, when he relented and let her off with the three tickets and the warning to get things caught up, or else!

Lucky she kept up with the insurance, or she'd really be in trouble. Damn it, two nights of her life. Just two nights, a bit more than a year ago. Hard to believe two nights of her life had made her so crazy. Shaking her head, she stomped to the stall where she kept a ready supply of hay and the bagged wood shavings she used for the horses' bedding.

She reached overhead and gave a practiced yank to the bale of her choice, then had to stagger back a step when she didn't get the weight she expected. In less than a second, she realized there was nothing but broken baling twine in both fists. Then disaster struck in an avalanche of tightly wadded flakes of billions of slender greenish-gold strands.

"Son of a—!" She got an arm up to protect her eyes as the bale disintegrated on her head, scattering to the ground around her. She spat stems of timothy and orchard grass from her mouth, tried to rake it from her hair, felt it down her shirt and hell, everywhere. "Damn cats—you're here to kill the damned rats, not let them chew the flipping damned strings on the bales!"

She was sunburned, hot, and cranky. Earlier that afternoon, a yearling she'd been holding for the blacksmith went airborne and kicked her. The kick hadn't been serious, just enough to knock her glasses off, bruise her jaw, and cut her lip on her teeth. But it hurt. She wished she was trained, like Rett, to overlook discomforts, but she wasn't, and couldn't. Pam could take getting injured, that happened almost every day working with so many horses. But going over a certain level of pain only made her a solid-gold bitch.

And she was over her limit now, for sure.

Has to be hormonal or something, Pam thought, de-haying herself as thoroughly as she could. She'd regret it later if she didn't. Every sliver, splinter, prickle, burr, seed, or itchy thing imaginable usually announced itself loudly from the most unlikely places if left ignored. Often at the most inopportune moments.

Be careful, she cautioned herself. She had a tendency to get really stupid a few days before her period. Plus, the moon was full, which exaggerated any mood or temper she was in even more. She drew a breath, determined to stay on top of herself and enjoy her evening routine, often the most pleasant part of her day. She should be unwinding, relaxing, taking pleasure in what she did now, and not flying off into a rage. That was the last thing anyone needed to do when working with animals.

Despite the self-given pep talk, she performed her evening routine mechanically, fluffing up bedding in the stalls, preparing the grain and hay. She went to whistle up the horses from the field. That gave her some pleasure, and she had to grin at their usual wild race up the hill, even the oldest of them bucking and acting like a colt. No matter how peaceful or sleepy the horses looked at pasture, at Pam's feeding-time whistle and "Come on, boys!" they came alert with comical speed.

As usual, they crowded at the big sliding door, waiting for her to step aside and let them in. Each animal would file into the barn, go directly to its own stall, and from there Pam would come around closing doors behind them. Today, however, a fight blew up among the six animals on who was going to be first. There were squeals, kicks, and that unmistakable sound large teeth made taking a swipe and missing. The pecking order had changed recently and the new boss of this small herd was still undecided. Pam's Appaloosa gelding, Ming, had always been the first one in, and now he was gone.

She'd learned horse signals over the years; knew them more than ever now since working with the field-kept horses at the breeding farm. Walking into a group of fifty-plus hungry brood mares with a sack of grain over one shoulder—usually getting boots mud-sucked off at the same time—invited the same sort of attention Rett received from Coalition troopers. Pam had learned fast to take control or get trampled. Her body language now was of the boss-horse, head low, teeth bared, dealing out hard smacks and low, harsh words. She wasn't worried about injuring one of them—smacking a horse hard with one's hand usually broke human bones before even bruising a horse. When she was present, Pam was dominant horse of this herd, and her discipline came from an equine level. She pushed back one animal and swatted another forward, straightening out the equine tangle.

The procession bottlenecked again as Jen's gray colt challenged her by shaking his head and striking with a forefoot. Pam squealed like an angry mare, lunging at him and snapping her teeth, sending the half-Arab three-year-old skittering to one side. The rest of the horses backed off, then queued up meek and calm as milking cows to file through the door and into their stalls without further ado.

She took a deep breath and leaned against a wall for a moment. Playing boss horse always left her feeling a little weak in the knees. *Close*, she thought, grinning a little. Again she found herself thinking about Rett. She'd have to remember to tell her about comparing the broodmares in the field to Coalition troopers—if she ever went back.

"Will you just stop?" she ordered herself aloud.

She went around quickly with the grain, closing stall doors behind her. She almost brought grain and hay to the now-empty stall where

Ming used to be. She stopped short, gave the hay to another horse and left the grain bucket on the floor to dump back in the bin later. She took the hose around and topped up water buckets, once again almost stopping at Ming's empty stall.

Tears burned into her eyes. No wonder she was extra-depressed. It was still hard to face the reality Ming was dead, gone…she would never see him again. The long, hot summer had proven too much for her old gelding to handle. In that same spot she had parked her truck, just last week, his life had ended, all in a matter of seconds.

She coiled the hose slowly. She thought she'd felt awful enough taking responsibility for Skipper after the truck hit him. That had been just months before she merged with Rett. Skipper hadn't been her horse; he belonged to the family who owned the place where she rented a room. They had been away that day to a show with another one of their horses—leaving a gate unlatched.

By the time Pam and the other young woman who rented a room 77 in the house realized the whinny that should have come from the back of the house came instead from the direction of the driveway, it was too late. The driver of the vehicle had walked away, but that wasn't the case for poor Skipper.

She shuddered, thinking of the horse all bloody in the road, with two broken legs, one almost severed. Pam had to sit on his head to keep him still, as the horse, terrified, kept trying to get up, to run away from the pain it didn't understand. She almost got in trouble with a cop that day, too, screaming at him to shoot the horse and not make the suffering animal wait for the vet. She'd even tried to make him give her his gun.

She grabbed a broom and started attacking the cracked concrete aisles, sweeping in hard strokes. That was the reason she'd been able to relate with how Rett felt when the sergeant had to give mercy to one of F-Troop. Gerrale hadn't been a horse, though. She had been a person, part of a band of soldiers that were so together they regarded each other as family. And through Rett, Pam felt that fierce deep love turn to a pain just as intense.

Pam had loved Skipper, but he hadn't been her horse. But, like Gerrale, he was strong and in his prime. What happened to them both was violent and horrible. Pam couldn't find words or thoughts to describe what Rett had been feeling, and she would never try. But she knew that Gerrale had been lucky. She didn't have to struggle and thrash while people stood around arguing who was going to be sued before ending her pain.

Ming hadn't been in pain like Skipper—or Gerrale. He was old and sick, but she loved him, and he was her best friend. Pam had told her horse secrets she wouldn't dare tell anyone else, not even Jen.

Her Thoroughbred, Doc, was blowing loud, unhappy snorts and moving in restless, nervous circles in his stall. She realized he was sensing her distress, and when she finished with the other horses, Pam went inside with him. She stifled her own emotion long enough to comfort the bay, hugging his head next to her body, kissing his velvety muzzle and speaking softly.

Doc reacted as he usually did, pressing his big head to her chest for comfort, snorting in softer tones as she hugged him. Her words and actions were enough to fool the animal and calm the wild look in his large eyes. As usual, Doc's displays of trust and affection nudged her into a good mood.

If anything, she felt the big ex-racehorse really loved her. Even if it was only for the grain and hay and grooming, his favors weren't lightly bestowed. She'd never known him to come to anyone else for the physical closeness he seemed to give her. His former grooms and exercise riders at the track thought him a terror and horribly spoiled. They'd been glad to see him go, and would've been even gladder if he'd been going to dog food instead of Pam.

"At least I have you, big guy." Pam gave him another hug. "Eat your hay. I'll see you in the morning."

Doc followed her to the door, whuffing in protest as she closed it behind her. *Stay with me,* he seemed to plead.

"Sorry, big guy. Tomorrow. It should be cooler and we'll go for a ride."

On her way out, she stopped and filled the food dish for the cats. "Just try to get some rats. I don't have time to shoot them any more." The cats settled around the dish, a furry circle emanating satisfied purrs.

Feeling better now, she gave everything another check and went outside. Pam looked over the beautiful sweep of farm and forestland surrounding that small area of Hunterdon County, glad this was one place in New Jersey the developers hadn't invaded—yet.

Then she looked up at the sky.

"God," Pam said, "if you can put a good word in with those entities who do the merging, let them know it's been long enough, all right? Or else, at least let me not be so obsessed all the time! Please?"

2.1.5 MESS AREA, SECTION C, EPNOCE MAIN COMMAND
0535.08.11 (LOCAL RECKONING)

"I say, Rett, have you been listening to me at all?"

She came alert with a jerk. "No," she replied honestly. "I wasn't. Sorry, Jaq. My mind is elsewhere."

"I wish you'd talk to me," Jaq said gently. "You know you can tell me anything."

She looked away, wishing again she could confide in him about Pam and the ego-merge—but she couldn't tell him any more than she could tell Major Yidnar. It was enough that Ariam knew.

"I told you what it was."

"Maybe you should talk to Med."

"I don't need to see Med. I saw enough of Med before we left, and on the shuttle, and barely thirty minutes ago, and I imagine I'll be seeing him daily whether I want to or not, thank you very much."

"Then maybe you should go straight to your billet and sleep. You look a bit off."

"Good deities, the last thing I need is more sleep!" She barely managed to keep her voice light and her flash of irritation checked. "I appreciate your concern, and how much you care, and how you're so willing to support me. I really do. But I don't need you deciding, planning, and executing what you think is best for me."

"Rett—"

She felt bad now for her inattention to him when all he'd been trying to do, as usual, was make her feel better. The panicked, trapped sensation was returning in force, sweeping in an icy wave from her toes to chest.

Taking a deep breath, she shrugged and looked up. "Never mind. I'm fine." Breathe. Breathing was good. And then a strategic withdrawal before she did or said anything else.

She stood, picked up her tray in one hand. With the other, she reached to caress the strong line of his jaw. "I'm really glad we had that time together—and afterward. But right now I need space. I need to be alone. I'll see you in the morning."

She paused a moment longer before leaving, trying to interpret the subtle shifts in his energy. She couldn't. Her guts started to cramp. Nausea rose. The jumpy, bone-deep urge to get out, into the open, was blocking all other processes. "I have to go. I'm sorry."

He nodded, gave her a smile. "That's all right, *kelani*. I'll be around. You know where to find me."

Rett managed a dignified exit, even a few nods and casual waves at those who called out as she went by. As soon as she was in the corridor, most of her anxiety faded, but the turbulence in her innards didn't. Recognizing an additional symbol over a service access, she turned into it, ducking into a lavatory.

For a long minute she thought she was going to be sick, but it passed. She relieved herself and went to the sink, splashing water on her face, letting it run over her hands and wrists. Damn it, where had that come from? She hadn't a panic attack like that in years. The yet-unfamiliar gravity dragged at her, but her muscles begged for a run, some form of hard exercise, her usual remedy for personal distress.

She didn't need to trigger Med or attract attention by running. Walking, then. A walk wouldn't hurt. It would help her unwind and help her to sleep. But where? Not here, not in their area.

She slipped out of the lav and headed in the general direction of the section set up for all aircraft operations. It would be interesting to have a look at the modified assault troopjumpers designed for Epnoce. A close-up peek at the sleek fightercraft that had escorted the troopshuttle to the base when they arrived would be nice, too. Maybe concentrating on something so different would be exactly what she needed. The process of coming to a decision on her destination, and validating a reason for it, soothed the twitchy urges in her limbs.

It was a long hike from Section C to the hangar area. Rett didn't mind. With all this security at the base, she could also semi-relax her constant, alert attention to danger.

Damn it, she was lonely.

81

Her fault. Her own choice. She could talk to Ariam, talk to Jaq, anyone in her platoon was as ready to listen to her as she to them. Talking wasn't what she needed. Sex wasn't what she needed, either. Even though being with Jaq was far beyond a physical thing. He made her feel warm, loved, safe, beautiful. Under other circumstances, she would have been content if after mess they had just gone to the common area and sat together, breathing the same air, until it was time to sleep.

Deities, she was tired. And not because she was lacking sleep.

It was the war. All her long-repressed longing for home, her own family, a loving partner, came back in a rush so hard she almost gasped aloud from it.

"Our children, Rett."

She heard his voice so clearly she had to glance around to make sure he hadn't followed her. Doing so made her realize just how far she'd come, and that she was getting out of breath. Whether that had to do with exercise or the unsettling direction her thoughts were taking, she wasn't sure.

Rett slowed her stride and looked for a place to take a breather without being noticed.

There. More than glad of the uniform she wore and its camouflaging properties, she slipped neatly into the semidarkness of a utility passage. She leaned on the wall, then slid into a crouch.

Please, no quakes. At least not right now. She puffed out a breath. *Ugh. I'm going to feel this in the morning. Maybe sooner.* Pressing her back against the cool wall, she scrubbed her hands along her thighs and calves.

Going for a walk was supposed to have calmed her down. Instead, she'd let her thoughts overcome any benefits. Well, time for a reality check. It was back to the war now and wishful thinking had no place. Taking deep, slow breaths, she waited until her heart rate normalized again before standing up, ready to continue her walk. A glance at the chrono as she slipped into the corridor told her she had just less than three hours left.

Long enough to look and start back. She lengthened her stride.

In spite of all the other things Rett had to think about, her thoughts returned to Jaq. She didn't know if she'd ever truly feel the same way about Jaq as he did about her. And this whole Zetinorian "curse" thing unsettled her—the convenient nickname that was given to the Zetinorian peculiarity that tied them to a lifemate, sometimes just by seeing an image. Like Jaq claimed he'd known from the first image he'd seen of her.

She couldn't deny they had a mutual attraction, but she couldn't wrap her head around his claim that his feelings for his had started from seeing a murky security camera image of her, from the back.

Growling, she shoved those thoughts aside. She packed them off into Pam's empty corner. The only thing she had to wrap her head around was adapting herself and her people to Epnoce and getting on with their job. She was glad they hadn't been sent into combat right away. Had they been, and she felt like this, she'd relieve herself of command, take herself to Med and ask him to lock her away so her attitude and wandering attention wouldn't get people killed.

She ordered herself to keep that in mind.

Twenty lengths more, and she stopped at the checkpoint outside of the flight operations section. 114th AirSpacefighter Wing. They had an interesting design below the standard AirSpacefighter logo. She had to look twice, having never seen anything like it. Someone had put the short wings and tail of a forest falcon on the stylized form of a leaping growtu. The strange figure was in white against a gradient that went from purple-white to black.

Tearing her eyes from the symbol, Rett extracted her ID as an MP came forward to scan it. After studying his Omni for a while, he simply stepped aside and allowed her access.

Well, that was a relief. She hadn't been told they were restricted from any area. Helped to know that was true, at least for here.

Fifteen, twenty steps in and through a wide blast door, she entered what had to be the most massive unbroken expanse of interior space she'd ever seen. The dim, slightly tinted white lighting gave the impression of infinity to the shadowed areas of the space. Moving glows here and there marked technicians and crew with head-mounted lights that gave them additional illumination for the work they needed to do.

Fresh air. Oh, how she needed to see the sky—dark, cloudy, didn't matter. She just wanted to look up and know a roof of some kind wasn't in the way.

She wasn't trying to go unnoticed, but reflex and the properties of her uniform made stealth automatic. While watching the activity around her with interest, she moved slowly, kept close to walls or shadows. Soon, she found a corner near one of the huge outer doors: out of the way, yet offering a good view of the hangar and all the activity. Even better, she had an excellent view of one of the same type of fighters that had been on escort detail.

Oh, it was tempting. Tempting enough to change her mind about slipping outdoors for the moment. Four steps more and she could touch it. Resisting the urge, since most likely the craft had an alarm system, she settled into a relaxed stance and let the wall hold her upright. She'd cool down before going outside.

Her exercise, and the turbulent stream of consciousness that had accompanied it, had been beneficial. She was calm now. Leaning her back against a cool, smooth wall, she admired the beautiful, deadly silhouettes of the fighters, like so many sleeping raptors waiting to awaken and take flight. For a few minutes, she was isolated in a safe haven of solitude, the sounds and voices in the area providing a background of white noise punctuated every so often by the whine and rumble of engines. Even the sharp odor of lubricants and propellants didn't seem as bad as she usually thought they were. They belonged here. She took those minutes to immerse herself in the new environment and enjoy it.

The worry reasserted itself. She had to get her issues under control. What was going on? What was causing her to panic, to keep zoning out? It was more than Pam being gone. She shook her head at the irony of it all. Here she was, her main problem acute loneliness. So, what did she do? Leave the people she regarded as friends and family. Walk away from the only person who made her feel vibrant and beautiful. Right. Good response. She went off so she could be alone more and more alone. Great.

She pushed away from the wall, determined to deal with her mood. She'd get a glimpse of the sky, a few lungfuls of air that didn't come through a filtration system, head back, and find Jaq. She didn't take two steps away from the wall before the internal war with her conscience started again. She didn't want to use him. Going to him now would be using him, wouldn't it?

She raked a hand through her hair as her aura of calm and purpose shattered like thin ice under impact.

Good gods and deities, stop being stupid and sorry for yourself. Get over it. Jaq doesn't mind, are you crazy? Go find him before lights out.

Her combat senses sharpening, Rett turned her attention to the left. Someone was coming. The energy aura she scoped emitted no threat, so she flattened to the wall again and remained motionless, curious.

A man's voice called softly: "Hello? Who's there?" as he moved boldly into view. "I'm showing your readings, but I can't see you." One hand was ready on the grip of a small stunner.

"I mean no harm, Citizen," responded Rett in just as quiet a tone.

"Lights up thirty," said the man in a brisk tone. The barely glowing lights immediately overhead brightened. She nodded slightly as they made eye contact and held her position. His weapon was aimed straight at her head and she didn't want to invite him to use it.

The newcomer appeared a little confused, and she remembered he must only see her head, since her uniform made it appear as if the rest of her disappeared into the wall. She shifted just enough to also let him notice she cast a definite shadow.

A bright grin broke the darkness of his face. "You're one of those Special Forces people that arrived. Deities, am I glad everyone doesn't wear those uniforms. I'd go completely ballistic. Hello." He sounded the greeting out with a shameless charm that brought instant heat to her cheeks. Relaxing his ready stance, he tucked his weapon back into its holster while giving her an appraising look, one that didn't linger enough to take as an offense, but enough to let her know he was interested in what he saw. "We're glad you're here, we can use all the help we can get. I just wish they'd send us some more pilots. What's your name, Sergeant?"

The man was dark of skin, compact, slender…good-looking, added the part of Rett that was female and appreciative of male beauty. The quality of the lighting couldn't hide that, or the pilot's insignia followed by a fighter group leader's patch on the sleeves of his flightsuit.

"I'm not purple or have green stripes or have turned into some other species, have I?" he asked, pushing back the sleeve of his flightsuit to check for himself.

Realizing she was staring, Rett scrambled for something to say even as her eyes sought rank insignia. Why did she feel as if someone had just punched her in the stomach? "Sergeant Rett, Captain." She was pleased that nothing shifted in his face or energy, the response people had sometimes when they recognized her name and immediately associated it with "Killer".

Maybe, Rett thought with sudden hope, *he's never heard of Killer at all. It might be nice to talk for a while to someone who didn't have any preconceived notions of me.*

The captain held out a lean hand, palm up. "I'm Etron. Nice to meet you. And now I need to ask what you're doing here. Admiring my machine?"

Rett's palm covered his upturned one and their hands closed firmly in greeting, a normal, businesslike exchange quite at odds with a few of the sensations the pilot had invoked in her. Just an anomaly. Rett dismissed her reaction in favor of something that really sent her pulse racing: the fightercraft. "Yes, sir. I had every intention of spending a few minutes outside. But then I started admiring it. And thinking."

"Nothing wrong with that. Although it's a bit cold and wet to go outside right now without being geared up for it. So, like it?"

"It's beautiful, sir." She meant that, and already had left off watching the pilot to return her gaze to the aircraft and the sharp, sweet sweep of fuselage and wings.

"Ever been up before?"

"Not in fightercraft," Rett said wistfully. "Maybe one day."

"How about right now?"

Rett laughed and shook her head. She needed a diversion. But was it the pilot, or his offer? Didn't matter.

"You're kidding with me, sir. I'd take you up on that if I thought you were serious."

"Kidding? I don't know that word. Serious? Definitely. You want a glimpse of sky, some space around you, I can do that. Want to fly a patrol with me? Nothing hot, just routine, and I'd like the company." He sounded serious. Not in the least flirty like he was before.

Rett studied him, pulled in hard on her ability to sense and interpret his body energy. If this was a come-on, he was good. Evetez never tried this sort of angle with anyone, she'd bet her last credit on it. Not that many would take someone up on, *"Hey, gorgeous, want to go on a ground survey behind enemy lines with me? Maybe get shot at a few times?"*

She scoped nothing that offered her a clue he was being deceptive or had an ulterior motive. She remained cautious. "I have to admit this isn't an offer I hear every day."

"I should hope not." The pilot's teasing, flirting tone came back and skated right around the edges of his sober-faced reply. "This isn't the sort of offer I make every day, either. Not to people outside my own branch, anyway."

Rett's gaze left him again for the aircraft, desire shooting as keen as pain through her. "Is something like this legal, sir?" She tried to quell her longing to give in to such an outrageous temptation. Every regulation she knew flashed through her mind at that moment. As hard and deep as she pulled them into focus, she recalled nothing that prohibited such an action on free time.

Of course, maybe there wasn't a rule, since what Etron proposed was so extreme no one would expect anyone to dare think of it.

"This isn't a combat mission, or I'd never suggest it, Sergeant Rett. I won't be flying over any hotspots, just doing some high altitude patrol-recon, and since the enemy's running out of fuel and supplies, they've stopped bothering our high patrols. Of course, there's always a risk of something happening, but if it does, we won't have to worry about either one of us getting in trouble, would we? It won't take long—" He cocked his head to one side, smiling at her with a knowing gleam in his eyes. "And anyone who looks at a fightercraft like you are shouldn't pass up an opportunity like this."

She felt fresh heat flood her face and tore her eyes off the fighter. "That still doesn't justify—"

"Can you run reconnaissance scanners?"

"Yes—"

"You've had training in taking over troopjumpers for emergencies, like most Special Forces?"

"I can, but—" *But that was a long time ago,* never made it out of her mouth. He was already speaking.

"Then it's justified. We're shorthanded; we re-purpose people constantly." He frowned just a bit. "What happened to your head?"

"Quake damage," Rett said with a grimace. "From earlier."

"That was a pretty good shake. But you're not concussed? No headache now?"

"No, just a bruise and a little cut."

"And when did you eat last? Or relieve yourself?"

"Captain—" Before she could ask why he needed to know, he explained.

"If you're not used to the gravity yet, there might be some complications on takeoff, maybe even in flight."

So she told him.

"You sound all right to go, but I do have to warn you, since you're not used to the gravity, there's still the chance you may black out for a short time on takeoff. But that's normal for the first two or three flights, even for people who've acclimated. It never lasts more than a minute or two. Still up for it?"

Rett took a breath; let it out slowly. Think about it, she cautioned herself. She did, for two seconds. "I'd love to, sir."

"Want to knock off the honorifics? I'm not partial to formal modes of address, especially from people I'm flying with. Etron will do just fine. May I call you Rett?"

Oh, why not? Might as well have both their military careers go down together on a personal name basis. "Sure." *You can still back out, you know,* she told herself.

"Well then, Rett, I'll go get you some gear. I'll be right back."

I should go. She'd get out, vanish before he returned. With luck, he'd think he dreamt the entire encounter. She was sure there might be a more amenable time when someone—maybe even him—would be able to do something like this when they both had free time, in a trainer or simulator or something.

"You know what, Rett," she said aloud, her eyes drawn to the aircraft in front of her, "you've done entirely too much thinking in the past few hours. Just stop. And shut up."

* * * * *

IN THE UPPER REACHES OF Epnoce's stratosphere, the sky was clear and the stars were cold, untwinkling points of fire. The three little moons reminded Rett of the bellies of three women in late stages of pregnancy, waddling low on the horizon. She laughed to herself, reminded of what Jaq had said earlier. No one had ever named those moons in a non-scientific manner, so she did in that moment, and would forever think of them as Jaquet, Jemrett, and Tejaq.

Jacy, Jem and Teja for short.

Below the craft, the cloud tops, fantastically lit by the triple moon-light, boiled in turbulent patterns. It was breathtaking and Rett felt a wonderful sense of freedom. She'd experienced only a slight grayness around the edges when the fighter took off, no sickness at all; the truth was, what she felt was closer to sexual pleasure.

She wanted to laugh aloud. Ariam, Pam, and others had told her she should let loose and be spontaneous once in a while. Well, this took the prize!

"Okay back there, Rett? Your bio signs look good."

"Fine. Everything's fine." She could have had this. But for one small notice on a message board, she would have gone to AirSpacefighters ten years ago—it had been her first choice. She had no regrets. But she had to again wonder how her life would be right now if things had been different.

"You can start up those scanners any time you're ready," Etron said.

"Yes, right." She tore her fascinated gaze from the view outside the cockpit and looked over the instrument panels surrounding her. She touched several switches she recognized and computer screens lit up. "Where's your regular backseater, anyway?"

Etron's reply was dryly amused. "What regular backseater? Although the GTC's here now, we haven't done any redeployment. Only half of the wing came from Nyorfias, the rest came in here and there from space service. Most AirSpacefighter pilots are still on space duty, actually.

MainCommand's working on getting more of them insystem, but the big thing now is to keep more enemy reinforcements from getting close. We're waiting for more from Nyorfias, too. It's going to take a while."

"AirSpacefighters is doing a damned fine job despite that," Rett said. "If it wasn't for your guys and the Spacemarines, we would have been overcome years ago."

"We're all in this together. And don't forget that timely assist from the GTC."

His reminder made Rett smile. He sounded like she did, when she had to remind others that she hadn't taken Circle on her own. It was so unexpected, a nice surprise. He was so self-confident and forward she'd had the impression there wasn't a modest bone in his body.

"The GTC didn't hold out alone, against all odds, for almost twelve years," she countered lightly, and then by some unspoken mutual agreement, they both fell silent for a time.

90   The fighter banked, then started into a shallow dive. "Surveillance scanners recording?"

"Yes, sir." She hit several more switches; glad now of the extra training that she'd never thought to actually use. It had been for emergencies: in case anything happened to jumper crew or pilots on a combat mission. But Major Yidnar also had the ambition for as many Special Forces operatives as possible be trained to operate any land, sea, or flying craft the Free Army had.

The only problem was taking time off from fighting the Coalition to do it.

"Just keep one eye on the warning lights and sing out if anything spots up. Shouldn't. I usually run all that from up here, but—"

"Don't worry. I like it. It's different. Must get pretty hectic sometimes trying to run everything at once."

"Believe it or not, this thing runs smoothly no matter what, which is good because I get lazy once in a while." A quiet chuckle followed. "And when things do heat up outside it helps to have most of the systems on automatic or voice so I can concentrate on fragmenting enemy ships!"

For a few minutes afterward, the only sounds in the fightercraft were soft multi toned hums and occasional pings or clicks from the scanning and tracking computers. Rett wondered again what it would be like to actually fly one of these, her own hands on the controls. Just thinking about it was enough to bring back the pleasant, visceral ache she associated with desire.

"Yours is one of those small splinter assault groups, isn't it? Noticed your diamond. Which unit do you lead, Rett?"

"F-troop," she said after a second of hesitation.

"I also noticed your Freedom Star," Etron said with interest. "Seen a few others, and we've a good troopjumper pilot who's received it twice. But one doesn't see so many that one doesn't notice right away."

"No." She kept her eyes on the readouts. "Most of those who get it are dead. Or off Active duty permanently."

She didn't think about hers at all unless someone brought it up. Rather she thought about Gerrale and all the others from F-troop who had died taking the Wide River Gap Bridge and the city of Circle. Of course the Freedom Star meant nothing to the dead, but it meant a great deal to the surviving families and friends. *You're sinking back—get off that tangent.*

With a little shiver she went on. "That troopjumper pilot you just mentioned—his name is Deeclar."

"You know of him?"

Rett smiled then. Know of him? Deeclar had been well known throughout the logging and mountain communities all over Main long before the war. He was one of her personal heroes as a teenager. She had an ulterior motive for taking her track as well: she hoped to keep Etron diverted from making an association between her, her platoon leader's diamond, and her Freedom Star.

"Yes. I met him once when I was a kid. I always hoped that if I ever passed my jumper quals I'd get to train with him. He's from northern Branch. He flew search-and-rescue as well as smokejumpers and firefighters in and out of the Skyraker foothills and central Branch Range for years. In any condition you can think of. Storm, fire, anything that anyone else said was impossible. He said 'as long as someone is alive, nothing is impossible'. If he's here at the base, I hope I get a chance to see him again."

91

"He's here, all right. I'll see what I can do about it." Etron was quiet again for a few moments, then a soft, startled exclamation came over the headspeakers.

She looked over the readings anxiously. "What is it? Screens read clear."

"It's not that. I can't believe how dumb...I mean—" He blew out a breath, it sounded like a dull boom in her headspeakers. "Right, Etron, pull your head out of your ass. I just didn't connect the evidence with the face, that's all. I just now realized who you are!" He sounded amazed.

Rett muted the audio pickup in her helmet and sighed very, very loudly. She was hoping the pilot had never heard of her. No such luck. Oh, well. She glanced around the interior of the fightercraft and smiled. *For this, I can't complain.*

Except for Etron's conversations with FlightControl, nothing more was said. Rett almost protested aloud when she realized they were getting ready to land—they hadn't been gone long enough for a full patrol, had they? Then she had to remind herself that an aerial patrol was a lot faster than the patrolling she was used to doing.

And it's back to reality, she thought as the fighter taxied back to the hangar area. She heard Etron talking to his crew over the com, and made a face as she realized he was sending them on a mission so they wouldn't be around until she was well clear of the fightercraft. He probably did something similar prior to the flight, as well. Shorthanded or not, Rett had seen enough AirSpacefighter operations to know the pilot simply didn't show up, hop in, and take off without other people being involved.

No matter what he said about borrowing people, he was likely to get in trouble for this. Wonderful.

Once things were shut down, Etron jumped out. He reached for Rett's hand to help her down from the rear cockpit.

"You're a recent arrival," he reminded at her hesitation. "Jump now and you'll think your toes blew right out the ends of your boots. I'm stronger than I look."

"I'm heavier than I look," countered Rett.

"I know that. I had to factor my backseater into my fuel consumption."

So his fighter weighed me? Wait a minute...he's going to have to account for extra fuel burn because—

He didn't give her time to think about it further. "Come on, that little detour I sent my ground crew on has a time limit. And if I've overestimated myself, I'll just end up between you and the deck. And that would be very interesting."

"Which might be fatal," she flipped back, "and not exactly what you hoped to die from."

She accepted his assistance. Rett's descent resulted in more of a slither down the length of him. During the process, both his hands transferred to her hips, braking her drop between his body and the smooth skin of the aircraft.

She imagined he braked a lot more than he had to. By the time her feet touched the hangar floor, a hot flush heated her from toenails to hair. She didn't trust herself to speak. Between the wing, the fuselage, and the man, Rett had nowhere to go.

"I hope to die from old age, but if you would have flattened me just now, at least I would've died with a smile," he said, whisper soft.

What was she doing? Such a position, with no easy access to open space, wasn't ever a situation in which she put herself voluntarily. Yet she saw it coming, and could have avoided it. Then it occurred to her she hadn't wanted to avoid a closer contact with him. Maybe she'd even been hoping for it. Why was she thinking at all? She needed to concentrate on breathing.

"Is it really you? Has to be. Freedom Star and all." He chuckled softly, lifted the helmet from her head, and tossed it into a corner, where it landed on some polishing cloths with a soft thump. "All those stories. None of them mention how attractive you are."

Reality check. "All right, Captain Etron." Enough was enough. "Thanks for taking me up, but we're both going to be in enough trouble without—"

"You have the most amazing eyes," he said.

"What?" She barely heard her own voice.

"Your eyes," he repeated slowly in a voice like fragrant smoke, "are like space. Dark, but full of little points of light. Deep, and full of secrets."

Some part of her noted he stood shorter than she by a fingerlength. The greater part of her started to tingle under his intent, serious regard. She swallowed. Why was she still standing there? Maybe because she wasn't sure where her feet were. Or maybe it was that flight had left her more than aroused: from the combination of possible trouble they both might get in; from the always present hazard of personal risk, and her own lifetime longing to fly. And she couldn't forget the attractive man watching her with such obvious interest.

No, all things considered, this was an unusual predicament. This couldn't be happening. Less than three hours ago, she was with Jaq. Now here she was, having thoughts about someone she just met. She closed her eyes for a count of five, breaking the near trance into which she'd slipped. "Captain, I'd better go."

"I suppose I must, as well."

"Thanks a lot. It was great. Almost like I dreamed."

"Almost?"

"I wasn't the one doing the flying."

"Then we'll have to do it again sometime, and see that you do." He stepped back a little.

"Maybe." She shrugged, a tiny movement of one shoulder. She wanted to know what color his eyes were in a brighter light. Brown or black? All she knew for sure was there were lighter colored circles around the outside edges of his irises. "I guess I'll be going, then."

Etron nodded, but didn't move, since she made no motion to leave.

"Uh, did I say thanks for taking me up?" Vaguely Rett wondered again why her feet weren't moving. Maybe the gravity had become stronger or something.

"Yes, you did," Etron replied, if possible his voice darker and softer than before. His right forefinger traced over her lips, leaving behind a tantalizing, burning tickle. "Good night then. And welcome to Epnoce. You can leave the flightsuit over in the corner. May I?" She must have given some sign of assent, because then he leaned forward a little to kiss her cheek.

Rett didn't even think twice. Her arms went around him, she tilted her face so he missed her cheek and caught her lips. From his eager response, he didn't mind in the least. The metal skin of the fightercraft pressed hard against her back. But she didn't care. If she hadn't been in his arms, against the fightercraft, her fingers entwined in his curling hair, she would have slid right to the hangar floor and taken him with her.

Etron came up for breath, his eyes darker than before. Trying without success to control her breathing, she settled for gathering her scattered wits.

"Sure you have to go now?" he asked. "In about ten minutes, I'm on free time. Maybe we can talk. Or not. I'm easy to get along with."

Did she have time? Lifting her left arm, she glanced at her chrono. Shit. Reality flooded back completely, from her head right down to her feet. "I'm really sorry. I didn't mean for that to happen at all, much less let it get as far it did."

"I didn't mind. Did you hear me tell you to stop?"

"I have to go."

He turned her loose instantly, a disappointed flash flickering in his eyes. "Let me guess, while my free time is coming up, yours is ending."

"Yes. And I've only five minutes to make it back to my section, since I have to check that everyone else is where they're supposed to be. It took me forty minutes to walk here. Any ideas? I'll have to go on report for being late, even if I call in."

The pilot laughed. "I like you, Rett. Come on, I'll take you back, and you'll even have a minute to spare. Jump out of that flightsuit first."

She did, shedding the garment that had gone on over her regular uniform; becoming a floating disembodied head again beneath the lighting. Etron bundled the flightsuit around the helmet in the corner. Then he guided her to another section of the hangar.

"We keep a pair of shortrangers at various stations, always ready to go. Anyone qualified for them has free access. Never know when we're going to have to hop from one side of the complex to the other. As shorthanded as we are, being able to cut down on time spent traveling through the base corridors comes in handy."

"Evening, Captain Etron," greeted the technician near one of the craft. "Take that one, sir." A speckled silver head nodded to the craft on the left. "Twenty-six there," his nod went to the other ship, "wants a bit of adjustment." A smile grew on his face as he looked at Rett.

She smiled back, but inwardly, she cringed and waited to hear the expected "Sergeant Killer" she hated so much.

"Sergeant. I heard the rest of Special Forces came in the other day." As he stepped aside for them, he saluted her. "Glad to have you and your people here. Now we'll finish getting those Coalition jerks off Epnoce!"

* * * * *

ETRON LANDED NEAR A ROOF accessway over Section C. "Two levels down. You've two minutes."

"Thanks." Deities, when he said access to the little jumpers cut down on travel time, he wasn't kidding. Rett studied him for a moment before getting out. In the bright light from the building she saw what color his eyes really were. A gray-green border was responsible for the lighter circles around them. And they were brown, as brown as spicebush bark, the same lovely rich color as his skin.

She felt weak in the knees, and not because of all the walking she had done. Time for a strategic withdrawal. "Look, if you get in trouble, don't try to cover for me, okay? I—"

He pressed a finger lightly to her lips, amusement increasing the curvature of his smile. "Understood. My CO will call your CO, all right? Can I see you again?"

"I'm not sure what my schedule's going to be like. But you can contact me." She slid out of the craft, again checking the time. "Thanks for the lift."

2.1.6 BILLET, SECTION C, EPNOCE MAIN COMMAND
0535.08.11 (LOCAL RECKONING)

ARIAM WAITED FOR RETT IN THE small barracks room they shared as platoon leader and second. The rest of the platoon was four per room and she wondered if they felt as peculiar about it as she did. This had to be the first time they all had so much private space since F-troop first came together. Even back at the Circle spaceport, their quarters, while roomy, shared the same walls, floor, and ceiling.

Ariam had made sure the rest of F-troop was settled for the rest period and was starting to enjoy the silence—and just starting to worry where Rett was—when her sister entered and closed the door quietly behind her.

She closed her mouth on a comment, their empathic connection triggering a heightened awareness. Deities, she already guessed something out of the ordinary had happened, but with Rett this close, there was no doubt. She waited without probing as the older woman keyed her code into the panel near the door, checking in as well as acknowledging to Battalion that F-troop was all present, accounted for, and where they belonged.

Then the sergeant turned, and one look at her face was enough to confirm Ariam's feelings. She knew that expression. She didn't see it on Rett too often. As a matter of fact, she didn't recall ever seeing it on her sister at all. The heightened color blooming through her warm brown skin, the deep fire in her eyes, had nothing to do with embarrassment.

For a moment, the rent left in Ariam's heart after Kraym's death throbbed with fresh pain. Seeing the flush on her sister's face had just triggered an entire series of memories that had left a similar heat in her own cheeks in the past. For a moment she closed her eyes. Kraym would always have a special place in her heart and would always have her love. But they had promised each other that they would go on, move forward, if either of them died. It was hard, but at least she was in a better mindset with it now.

Then realization dawned, and Ariam sat straight up. Rett hadn't been with Jaq. *What happened?* "You just made it," she said as a soft tone chimed over the companel on the wall.

"Uh-huh," Rett said.

"Did Jaq find you? He was asking after you. He's worried."

"No, he was looking for me?"

Ariam stared hard at her sister. "You were with Jaq before the quake—and during, right?"

"Yes. Turns out he developed a nice little code that blanks out certain spots when needed. Which is why you couldn't find us."

"All right. I'm glad. You can tell me more about *that* later. Jaq said you had dinner together, but you left before you finished. And that you were upset or stressed over something. What happened?"

Rett sat on her bunk and began to remove her boots. "I needed some space, so I took a walk to the hangar area."

Ariam arranged herself comfortably and waited. "Well?" she prompted, seeing Rett wasn't going to continue on her own.

"In the hangars, I met this pilot and he asked me to fly a patrol sweep with him. I did and it was really intense and that's what happened. It was great—flying in a fightercraft was something I've always wanted to do. Okay?"

"No. Keep going. And I know it's something you wanted to do from the time we were kids, but I'm sure just flying a patrol sweep wasn't intense enough to leave this much of a flush on your face."

Rett shot her a look. "I had to check everyone else and make curfew," she retorted.

"*I'm* on watch duty today, you *know* I would have accounted for everyone but you already. Go on. I know it was more than that. Tell me!" She followed Rett to the tiny lavatory and planted herself at the door.

Her sister didn't pause in her preparations for sleep. Ariam bared her teeth as she felt Rett's shields slam into place inside and out. Rett then proceeded to ignore her as she relieved herself, washed, and cleaned her teeth.

"Re-ettt!" Ariam's voice went down in volume, but up an octave into the range she'd had as a little girl.

Rett frowned and poked at the bandage on her forehead, then pushed past her without a word or a glance.

Ariam knew damned well that her sister wasn't above deliberately prolonging her agony, considering it payback for all the times Ariam took teasing to the extreme. At the same time, a lifetime of Rett and her peculiarities also clued Ariam to the fact that she wouldn't talk about some things at all unless harassed into it. So she followed her sister as close as she dared.

"Come on, *talk* to me."

"Look, do I demand all the details of *your* personal life?" demanded Rett with a snarl.

"No," Ariam said, "but then again, I tell you most of them whether you ask or not."

"Unless you want to wear this shirt with me, I suggest you back off."

Ariam backed off a handspan or so. "Tell me. You know I won't leave you alone unless you do."

99

"You've hit the target there," grumbled Rett as she slipped into the thigh-length shirt of soft slate-gray. "You'd find more ways to make me suffer for not telling than even Pam has—had the imagination for."

"You need to talk to me anyway. You know what happens when you keep things locked up. I'll pull my prerogative as second in command. You can start off with this pilot, and work your way backward."

"Deities, little sisters are such a pain."

Despite Rett's snarl, Ariam sensed her surrender and relief.

"Okay, we kissed," the sergeant admitted, using intense concentration to arrange her discarded uniform neatly on a wall rail. She tossed a set of fatigue bottoms toward the door, where they landed next to the pair Ariam had set out, handy and quick to grab for emergencies. They were ready to roll in any state of dress or undress, but it was too cold here to leave a lot of skin exposed and become a liability instead of an asset during an emergency situation.

"Don't stop there. And…"

Rett looked up, all pretense of evasion gone. "Ari, if we didn't have this curfew, I might still be with him. I don't know what got into me. I'm not sure if it was his fighter, or him, or both."

"One thing for sure," Ariam put in with a lightness she didn't feel inside, "you'd not have been there kissing a fightercraft."

Rett groaned and rubbed at her eyes with the heel of her right hand. "The thing is, I was with Jaq, and kissing Etron a few hours later. It isn't me. And it's not Pam, either, even if she were here."

"What's the big deal? It was just a kiss, right?"

Rett sat cross-legged on her bunk. For a moment she didn't say anything. "Yes…that's all it was."

"You're worried how Jaq would feel about it."

"I guess. It's more than that." Rett raked her fingers through her hair in sudden agitation, a gesture she'd used since childhood. It was a gesture their mother had used as well. Then she slid to a sitting position on the floor and reached for her weapons and utility belts. Ariam didn't worry that this was another attempt at changing the topic, not at all. Completely opposite. With her hands occupied in familiar tasks, Rett was more inclined to relax and talk. Her nimble brown fingers started to check each pocket and its contents.

"More than what?" By association, Ariam imagined each shape and contour her sister assessed: the order of the routine was so familiar that only something damaged, missing, or out of place would disrupt it.

"Ever since Pam's been gone, nothing's felt right." Rett's sidearm was soon in fifteen pieces on the floor; just as quickly together again and back in its holster. "Part of me is glad we're not on combat alert yet, the way I've been feeling. What happened just before mucks up everything I'm already confused about into more of a mess."

"Everything?" Ariam stretched out on her bunk once more and put her legs up against the wall. Her bones and joints had protested the impact of the new gravity with deep, dull achy pangs she hadn't felt in years. Wiggling her toes inside their warm liners, she enjoyed the sensation of relief her new position brought.

"Legs hurt?"

Ariam smiled at the ceiling at the sudden concern in her sister's voice. "A little. Nothing I won't get used to in a few days. Med's on it. Please, go on, Rett." If she let Rett go off worrying about her sore joints, they'd never get back to this.

"Well, first, there was the ego merge. And everything that happened since then, from the ambush at the Gap bridge, until now. You know—"

"I know," Ariam said gently. "Go on." She wished with all her heart she might have the ability to ease some aspect of her sister's life, so she gave her entire self to listening.

"I barely got used to having Pam in my head—and learning how to interact with her without letting on to anyone else that I was actually having an ego-merge. Then came Jaq…and I'm still trying to sort out all that."

"Simple attraction, true love, or gratitude for what he's done in the past?"

"Yes, exactly. Then Captain Etron comes along and…" Rett paused, struggled for a concept. "And sweeps me off my feet."

"That's an interesting way to put it."

"One of Pam's sayings that actually makes sense," Rett admitted. "Anyway, as far as I know, at this rate, by the end of the tenday there might be fifteen other men asking me what we're going to name our firstborn." She groaned. "Deities! What a nightmare! Forget I said that. I just might make it happen."

"Having kids? You love kids."

"Of course I do, I didn't mean that. I meant the fifteen men who want to father them."

Ariam tried not to laugh. Rett often accused her of being dramatic, but her older sister had her own way of blowing things out of proportion. "You sound as if both worlds are going to end tonight."

"Ari, I don't know what to do. I'm not ready to jump into anything with Etron—that moment's passed. But he's in a job that I might have had. It might be a good thing, having him for a friend, casually, at least. At the same time, I don't want to make Jaq—"

Ariam's feet came off the wall. Rett didn't need this on top of everything else. She turned on the side facing her sister. "Rett, it was only a kiss. I know Jaq has been having a hard time understanding the relationship dynamics we have in our society, but one kiss shouldn't throw him into a tiff."

Rett laid aside her utility belt and pulled her knees to her chest, wrapping her long, muscular brown arms around them. "I can't believe

I agreed to go up with Etron in the first place. Maybe it wasn't written down anywhere not to do it, but I did. And he'll most likely get in trouble."

"I wouldn't worry about that either," Ariam said easily. "I mean, remember that time me and Worren—"

"The time I had to bail you both out from an MP lockup for making base security think the place was under attack?" Rett's eyes narrowed.

"Exactly. We were zoned, it was a stupid idea, it was definitely wrong, but we're still here."

"And who's going to cover *my* ass, Ariam?"

"Your friend Evetez, of course. Or did I misunderstand he was our new CO, and you're his second? You can't tell me he hasn't pulled a stunt like that a time or two. Or more. The point is, that I seriously doubt you're going to get in trouble. Now had you been *late*, that would've been a different scenario. Rett, I'm not going to deny there's something deep bothering you—but it has nothing to do with Jaq, or this Etron, or anyone else. You had a wonderful experience—flying, I mean—it made you feel alive and happy. I'm glad it happened. And, I have to admit I'm glad you enjoyed being spontaneous. It's always fun, and not worth a guilt trip. You're not planning on seeing him again, are you?"

"He asked if he could call, but no, I'm not planning on it."

Uh-oh. Ariam knew that look. When Rett started to frown that way, it was a signal Ariam had pulled the wrong trigger.

"But why should it bother you if I were?" asked Rett. "Haven't you, of everyone, been on my back most especially these past two years to 'get out more'? Have a social life when I could, *outside* the platoon? So, now, all of a sudden that's wrong? Because of Jaq."

Ariam sucked in a breath. "I—"

"It's sort of hypocritical, isn't it? You and Kraym made a promise once things grew deeper between you. I have strong feelings for Jaq, yes. But I've not made any promises. I can't. I won't. Not now, and maybe not even for a while after I can."

"Rett—"

Rett waved her hand. "Forget it. I'm just pointing that out. You know me. There was a time when having more than one friendly intimate relationship at a time wasn't a problem. I've changed since then. And, since the time I was so…injured, I never thought it possible for me to actually want to…"

"Make love again," supplied Ariam as her sister faltered.

"Yes. Much less have someone interested once he took a good look."

"I know that. And then came Jaq. And he got you over that ridiculous idea that no lover would ever want to see or touch such revolting scars. And now there's potentially another. It's never been an issue before, from what you told me."

"No, it wasn't an issue. But I'm not like you. And I've not come close to the number of lovers you used to rotate through before you started getting serious with Kraym."

The glance Rett sent her: part amazed, part exasperated, and part ready to apologize, made Ariam respond with a wicked, delighted laugh of agreement. "I wonder how I ever found the time."

"Don't think you broke any records. Lieutenant Evetez and a few other notable friends of mine have left entire battalions weak in the knees."

"Thanks for keeping me humble." Ariam smothered another giggle with her hand.

Rett, however, wasn't laughing. "I know you have strong ties to Jaq, Ariam. And you're hoping something permanent between me and him comes of it. Like others in the platoon, shit, in the entire Battalion. But don't push it. Don't push me. I need to know you have my back, as platoon second and as my sister."

"I'm sorry. And I do. Look, no matter what you decide, make sure you talk to Jaq."

"I will, I have been, but I don't think he'd blow it off as easily as we would. In spite of his promises to adapt himself into our culture, he has this little issue of having himself all fixed up with me in his mind from the start."

Ariam made a face. "He's trying to understand, but it's hard for him. He doesn't understand the openness we have until we commit."

Rett snorted. "You're telling me. He almost shit himself when he found out that we might choose to lifemate with more than one partner. If he's any example, Zetinorians seem to be as territorial as growtus. You should have seen him around Evetez and Semage at first. Not to mention anyone else I might be on hugging terms with. Although he didn't seem to think old Sergeant Wreagor was a threat."

"Wreagor? You and Wreagor are on *hugging* terms?"

Rett chuckled. "As of earlier this evening, we are. And I didn't make the first move—he did." Her abrupt change in position brought a responding one from Ariam.

"What is it?"

"Just a cramp, Ari," Rett managed to say through clenched teeth.

"That hole in your right leg again?"

"Yeah." Rett levered herself from the floor to the bed, stretched her right leg straight along the mattress, and let the left leg dangle. "Guess that long walk aggravated it a bit."

Ariam settled back as Rett went at the sore spot with the heel of her hand. "Just make sure you talk to Jaq. As many times as it—" Then she sat up again. "Something's happening. Something's wrong."

"What is it, Ari?"

In the next second Ariam was on her feet, trying to trace what had triggered her into alert mode. She closed her eyes and pushed her awareness out as far as she was able. She didn't like to rely on those flashes of premonition, but she was unable to touch any living minds. "Rett, we're—"

Then an alarm sound they hadn't heard before wailed from the communications panel, yellow and orange alert bars pulsed. The lighting went from normal to emergency mode, only faintly glowing strips in the floor, marking emergency routes, were active in their room.

The Base was under attack.

Rett, who was already in fatigues, weapons belt with sidearm slung over one shoulder, snatched up her headband and was consulting her Omni on her way into the corridor. It was barely illuminated, but brighter than their quarters. "Come on, officer of the watch, I'll stand this one with you. Let's make sure the kids stay in their bunks. We're nonessential personnel right now, we're to sit tight."

"That sucks." Ariam caught up, jamming her headband over her loose hair before hopping into fatigue bottoms. As much as she sensed things first, she'd never be as fast as her sister. Then again, Rett reacted the moment Ariam had said something instead of sitting still, trying to identify what it was. "Sitting tight while others fight. It doesn't feel right."

Through the thick walls, she could hear the sounds of antiaircraft batteries, of energy and missile type, as they fired at the aerial attackers.

"It doesn't feel right at all," Rett agreed.

Multiple rising screams from outside ended in huge whumping crunches. The building shuddered with the explosion. It had sounded nearby, but they were told how sounds echoed through these complexes and, had it been that close, they definitely would have known. It was a different vibration from anything Ariam had felt during the earthquake: shorter, more direct, more concentrated. She didn't like it. They'd been through bombardments from air and artillery before, but always in the open.

"Deities, I hate being inside," mumbled Rett. "Ariam, you take the station, I'll make the rounds."

Ariam went ahead to the end of the corridor to take her place at the watchstation. "Com connect Battalion OD, this is Fang Two, on station with Fang Lead."

She pulled her legs up, heels to butt, and wrapped her arms around them. An explosion from above crashed like thunder, making her shiver and remember the storms that had so frightened her as a child. She hoped whatever that was had been something that bounced off the complex's shields instead of something that might have taken out one of the rooftop defense batteries.

Adjusting her pcom to the shared command frequencies, she listened in for some clue of what AirSpacefighters and the complex defense garrison were going through. It was going to be a long night.

2.1.7 DRILL AREA, EPNOCE MAINCOMMAND
0534.08.17 (LOCAL RECKONING)

WRITHING, GLOWING FINGERS OF ENERGY lanced down the stairs and corridor, ricocheting off glass and polished stone. Rett and her team pressed flat against one corridor wall as the streams sliced past, too close for comfort. She watched carefully for interruptions in the shots and tried to find a pattern to the firing. They had to get through, and quickly.

Years ago, back in training, Sergeant Wreagor had told her that no matter what, there was always a pattern. "It may not be something you could time out, but it's always there. Your gut and heart tell you when to go, so pay attention. You usually won't get a second chance to make a mistake."

Without taking her eyes off the path ahead, Rett motioned to two of her people. In pairs, she sent them through the concentrated SMG fire. All they had to rely on was their own speed and skill. And her judgment.

Her turn, now. It seemed to Rett the pattern changed, as if they knew she was now running the obstacle set up for her unit. A few times she felt hot lines of energy make fleeting contact, although not enough to count or bring her down. Reach the stairwell. Grab the rail, jump. Three lengths down.

Ow! Flex more next time. Two on the right have me targeted, jump left and go down. The shots passed overhead.

Reaching the cross-corridor, she noted with dismay it seemed to be a solid mass of energy beams. She didn't see anyone down, so the others made it through all right. But how in two worlds was she going to—ah. There.

She threw herself flat into the corridor, letting her speed and momentum skid her beneath the lines of energy. She didn't know what felt warmer for those few seconds: the part of her creating extreme friction with the floor, or the portions closer to the SMG fire.

"That's what I call tight." Trebor, F-troop's third-up, waited for her with a handful of others.

"Let's go, we're on the chrono!"

"Cargo area'll be rougher this time." said Trebor.

"Thanks for the reminder. Get moving! Watch your speed, be ready for the guys at the bottom. Watch it, H'tenneck—go, go, go!"

Waiting for them at the bottom of the solid-sided stairway leading into the cargo bay was a group of MP combat specialists, acting as Coalition troopers. Seeing most of her platoon was out of the way below, Rett didn't wait. She remembered to adjust her speed and force and jumped from the middle of the flight to land with stunning impact against three MPs.

* * * * *

ARIAM AND THE OTHERS WHO'D finished the drill course enjoyed the opportunity to watch their platoon leader in action. When she felt someone next to her, she didn't look around, feeling no threat. Her eyes were on Rett.

"Is that two-length blur over there Sergeant Rett?"

She glanced quickly to the speaker, straightened automatically in deference to his rank, and then took a longer, second look. He was worth a second look. His face was strongly molded, nose proud, jaw wide and square. Curly brown hair tumbled around his head like ocean waves. Deep-set under nice eyebrows, tilted oval eyes of the same silky brown as martun fur glimmered at her. The rest of his body was lean and clad in AirSpacefighter's blue-violet and black.

"Yes, sir, that's right. And you must be Captain Etron."

"I am, but how—"

Ariam's attention returned to her sister. Wow. No wonder Rett had been burning brighter than a magnesium flare nearly a tenday ago! Outwardly, she made sure she showed nothing more than the polite, social smile expected of them when interacting with officers from outside their branch. Angling her gaze sideways, she said, "We know everything, sir, haven't you heard that?"

An amused chuckle rewarded her effort. In turn he nodded at the half-diamond of the platoon second on her uniform. "She must have told you about me."

"Yes, sir." Recalling the conversation she'd had with Rett six days ago, Ariam felt relief that Jaq Pym had been called out of drill early because Major Yidnar needed his technical expertise elsewhere. As much as the Zetinorian tried to keep his territorial instincts under control—and mostly hidden from Rett—to Ariam they had been apparent from the very beginning.

Oh, she knew that Rett had told Jaq she couldn't make him promises. Ariam had tried to explain their culture and customs to him. In his turn, Jaq had told her what he remembered about his own culture and customs. She had to wonder if Jaq was ever completely frank with Rett on the extent of his instincts, whether they were truly biological to Zetinorians or simply what Jaq believed to be true. Ariam was sure he'd been clear to Rett about his feelings toward her, but she had serious doubts he'd mentioned the action he might be compelled to take if she rejected him completely for someone else.

She felt a slight nudge of worry, a shiver of clairvoyance. She hated that intermittent aspect of her Talent, but try as she might, she couldn't deny those flashes when they came. She always ended up regretting those instances she ignored her insights. But efforts to mediate anything between her sister and Jaq would have to wait.

Rett's current biggest problem had taken a surprising turn—into Lieutenant Evetez. And since personal issues weren't a priority, Ariam had to concentrate her efforts on her duty as Rett's second in command. Jaq was going to have to trust Rett, suck it in, and deal with it—after a heads-up. She decided to let Rett know it was time to give him one, and then she'd stay out of it.

"Is there something I can help you with, sir?"

"I'm here to observe," the captain said. "Is this a bad time? I was farther back with the other observers, but it looked as if things were winding down and I wanted to get a better view. No one stopped me—is it a problem?"

"Not at all, sir. I'm Sergeant Ariam. We should be finishing here shortly."

He said nothing more, only nodded. Was he being level with her? Outwardly, she'd have to say yes. But many were skilled at hiding their true intentions. Ariam sent a tentative probe to his mind, testing. No duplicity, no lie, he was here, he was observing. If he had any attraction to Rett, it was buried beneath the fact that he was here in an official capability, not a personal one. She liked that. And had to admit she liked her first impression of him, as well. It was in a comfortable silence that they watched the rest of the drill, which concluded when the last MP hit the floor.

* * * * *

"F-TROOP! REPORT!"

Hissing a breath through her teeth, Rett reported. The lieutenant stood off to one side, a timer in one hand, a notepad under his left arm, and his Omni in his left hand. He was scowling at two of the three devices. No doubt had he another arm, or eye, the notepad would be getting a glare as well.

"Sir?"

Lieutenant Evetez regarded her for a moment. Then his gaze fell back to the timer.

"Thirty-one seconds overtime, Fang Lead. You'll have to do it again." 109

"What?" She barely kept her answer from exploding with the same thunderous report as a full power energy beam. They'd done the course twice already. And to think, she'd been so looking forward to this assignment with Evetez and the others. She didn't know what was going wrong—but things hadn't gone right since they started training together. Glancing at her chrono, she shook her head. "I don't think so, sir. I know we were close, but we didn't go over."

"Six minutes, thirty-one seconds, plus eight grazes, four serious but still mobile and slow. And one killed."

Even with the added time that incurred, the total was well within the tolerance zone discussed before the drill session began. "Maybe we should recheck the parameters, Lieutenant," she suggested, trying to push down her temper. "I think you're running the scenario for what it would take for a dry run, in Nyorfian gravity, without weapons fire. Or else you've loaded data for a Tac-Survey scout unit running only a handful of people." She took the notepad Evetez held out, but never looked at the display.

Unperturbed, Evetez retrieved his notepad. His blue eyes were cool as they leveled with hers. "You'll really enjoy it this time, Sergeant. You're the one who was overtime, so you're going solo. Since it is supposed to take six minutes for the entire platoon, and you'll have no one to look out for except yourself, you should be back here in four minutes flat. Or you'll run it again until you do."

"Yes, sir, that's fine. But can we talk about t—"

"Yes. We can talk about this. But we shouldn't have to." A challenging edge came to his voice. "You should know firsthand that if your timing is off on a mission, it could mean life or death! Better start moving. Mark! Three, two, one—go!"

Rett snarled under her breath as she took off. As she passed the rest of her platoon she searched for Bhayorn, finding his familiar bristling, thickset figure in the company of Med. But not, this time, in his usual role of med assistant. This time he was the patient. Bhayorn had fallen a good five lengths down a stairwell after catching that stun. He was one of the heaviest people in her unit, and getting him out had incurred time faults, but leaving him behind hadn't been an option, drill or real.

Seeing the big man on his feet again was reassuring. The significant nod Med sent her as their glances met reassured her even more.

Good thing this was drill. Bhayorn would have been dead for real had this been a live operation.

Rett spotted Ariam at the end of the group, and sent her second in command an exasperated look: *Can you believe this?*

"Good gods and deities!" Bewilderment replaced frustration as she noticed Captain Etron, someone she'd completely dismissed from conscious thought, standing right next to her second in command. He waved.

So meeting him hadn't been some sort of dream. He was even better-looking in regular lighting. Thank all deities she was well over that goofy reaction she'd had. All she felt now was the need to know what he was doing there standing next to—

Then the captain flashed her a grin so hot she swore it left a contrail between his eyes and hers. Having failed to factor in a defense against gorgeous pilots with lethal grins into her current mode, Rett nearly stumbled.

"Damn it," she muttered, and ran on.

2.1.8 DRILL AREA, EPNOCE MAIN COMMAND
0535.08.21 (LOCAL RECKONING)

AFTER FOUR MORE DAYS, RETT had just about all she was going to tolerate. As Lieutenant Evetez called down drill that afternoon, she decided it was time to talk.

Whatever it is, we have to fix this before S- and D-troops come off their break and we really get serious. I'm supposed to be his second. So far, that's just been in our planning sessions and postdrill reports. Rett lifted off her headband and pushed her fingers through her hair before settling the material in place again. She should have been the one over there with him now instead of R-troop's Sergeant Tris. But Evetez had decided Tris, as Easy Force third-up, needed to switch with Rett today. She didn't really mind. But it didn't help to see the lieutenant and the short man with the silver hair were getting along just fine.

She had to admit that, overall, everyone was improving, individually and as a unit. Easy Force was coming together, and Evetez was definitely an able commander. He encouraged, challenged, pushed if he had to, and demanded more. Told them he was pleased.

Pleased with everyone but her.

Oh, everything was fine on the administrative end. She was learning a lot there, and as long as they were working, they were in complete synch. But, in drill, nothing she did was right, or good enough, or in his allotted time. The more she gave him, the more fault he found. More often than not she—with or without F-troop or any other team she was drilling with—had to make up for her errors with three times the amount of physical work anyone else was doing.

The fact they had been close friends and trained together didn't enter the equation—from her side. But did it from his? She didn't think it was possible.

On the job, Evetez didn't lose his innately friendly personality, but neither did he let personal feelings get in his way. She'd learned that during the Azurebay campaign years ago, when she was platoon second for C-troop. So they hadn't been commander and junior then, but she'd seen how Evetez had handled his tactical scouting unit—and how

111

they, in turn, regarded him. Going on survey well behind enemy lines demanded a close-knit unit that could think, move, or act in accord even if they were miles apart. His training now as he brought them together offered some surprising new concepts; his record of handling people was perfect. Except for her.

What am I doing wrong? Why has Evetez singled me out? Major Yidnar said we were supposed to be learning from each other. And so we are. But I don't think this is what he had in mind. She honestly wouldn't have a problem with it if she understood what Evetez wanted from her. Easy Force was supposed to be a top team, and that took hard work. She expected it, and as far as she knew, she was giving him everything she had.

However, she hadn't spent almost a decade in active combat to be hazed the same way she'd been in training. That was the Coalition's job now. Not his.

"Maybe this is our lucky day," muttered Jessek as the seconds ticked by and Evetez didn't call out with his usual "F-troop, report!", a phrase all of them had come to dread.

"Maybe." Frowning, Rett stood on her left foot, caught her right in one hand, and examined the bottom of her boot. Either something had become lodged in the sole or the material was starting to split.

I'm beginning to feel as burned out as I did when Mott and Shamos were running us ragged. At least this time I get some time to sleep. Although most of her sleep period lately—when not interrupted by Coalition aerial raids—was spent wide awake worrying about how to solve this latest, and most puzzling, problem. Sleep seemed to come a minute and a half before wakeup. And their days were busy, busy, busy.

Once they'd had a handful of days for an initial adjustment, all the new arrivals had been put to work. When not performing routine duties, they were assisting with incoming casualties, loading up supplies, testing weapons, working on tech, performing repairs and maintenance. Until they were pronounced ready to engage the enemy in combat, Rett and the others recently arrived from Nyorhas gave their wholehearted effort to the war in alternate ways.

Rett didn't mind that work and was actually glad of it. The extra duty also freed up other personnel, military and civilian, for critical jobs better suited to those fully acclimated and conditioned to Epnoce. She was also happy that since F-troop and the other Special Forces units had now grown more acclimatized to their new base, they had true standby duties during the Coalition's regular attacks on the Base. Standing by for damage and fire control duty was better than being told to sit and wait it out.

She scowled at the sole of her boot, taking a pensive nibble or two on the inside of her lower lip. But Evetez…if he kept after her like this, she doubted if she could continue to make clean runs on the drills. Much less coordinate F-troop through the courses. She had to talk to him, but the problem was, every time she came close enough, he had something else scheduled, or was making her do something over again. *Maybe I should write a note?* She snorted softly. *Likely he'll send it back, with corrections.*

113

Ah, there it was. A sliver of metal. It wasn't a big problem, just annoying, since it seemed to scrape against the floor once in a while depending on how her foot came down. She'd take care of that problem right now.

"Look out, Sarge!"

Still bent forward and standing on one foot, Rett had barely let go her boot when a several armored bodies impacted with hers. She went down, cursing silently for letting down her guard. Barely in time, she twisted to avoid someone locking an arm around her throat. Another sharp lunge, twist, and thrust with both legs shot her from a second attempted locking hold and onto her feet again. Something stung her eyes as it whisked across her face, and blinded, she went into full combat mode.

Seconds later, she realized there was no one left to fight. She blinked her vision clear, a cold lump growing in her belly. "Oh, no." She turned, swiping her forearm over her streaming eyes. The bodies of five MPs were sprawled on the floor, against the wall, or entangled with a few Special Forces personnel who had moved to intercept them and break their falls.

Horrified, Rett slid to her knees alongside the closest of them, focusing her energy sense on him even as she reached for a physical reassurance he lived. "You all right?"

The man gasped and coughed. "Yeah."

He struggled to sit up and she was quick to assist, removing his protective helmet and face guard. The armor over his chest and left side was dented in enough to make her wince. She triggered the emergency release buckles on the reflective material and loosened the protective padding.

"That's better," he wheezed.

"I'm sorry, Vinzk. Anything broken?"

He shrugged slightly and managed a grin. "Know how you got that nickname firsthand, now." He patted the padding. "I'm all right. Thank all deities for this stuff."

She glanced over her shoulder to the spot Med knelt next to a still figure on the floor. Her energy sense, at least, told her the man was still alive, but that was all she could tell. "Can you stand?"

Vinzk nodded, so she helped him up, her anxiety rising as she sought out her other victims. H'tenneck was helping another up and sent Rett a signal that the MP was just fine, only a little dazed. B-troop's Corporal Rimms was supporting a third while a med assistant examined the man's shoulder. The discarded armor on the floor near their feet was dented and cracked.

And there was Lieutenant Wilkath against the wall. The leader of the team who took on the role of "enemy" in their drills. Rett took a step toward her, but Wilkath was already getting up, signaling she was all right. A quick sidestep and supportive grip of a nearby R-troop member as she staggered showed that maybe the detail leader was more shaken than she realized.

Rett went over to Med and the man still flat on the floor, her guts churning. "Med?"

He spared her a brief glance. She couldn't interpret the expression in her medtech's gray-green eyes, and his face was set. But his "He'll be all right in three days or so" was both good and disheartening.

"F-troop!"

Here it comes, she thought. Turning toward Evetez as he closed the distance between them, Rett schooled her features into an expression she usually reserved for undergoing interrogation by the enemy and her voice to the one required of a trainee to a senior of any rank. "Yes, sir!"

"Sergeant, what happened?"

What happened? You know damned well what happened. Her hands clenched into fists at her sides. "I was off guard and lost control, sir. I have no excuse. Sir." *Even after the drill was already called down, sir,* she added in her thoughts.

Her tone of voice had some effect: for a split-second, there was a crack in the lieutenant's composure, revealing surprise. Then his eyes tightened and he was a stranger again.

Good, she had his attention at least. Maybe they could talk about whatever it was he had a problem with. There was absolutely nothing wrong with F-troop's performance. Or hers. At least not until a few minutes ago.

"We need to talk, Lieutenant." Rett made her voice normal again, but kept it pitched at a volume that didn't go beyond the two of them.

"You're right." He turned to the rest of her platoon, who waited with B- and R-troops. "Sergeant Tris, please give me an update on injuries as soon as possible. Lieutenant Wilkath, are you operational? Good, if I can keep your people still on stations in the course a few more minutes? Thank you. The rest of you are dismissed." He turned back to Rett. "Sure, Sergeant, we'll talk. In about five minutes."

So much for that. And imagine, it had been only last tenday when Ariam said he'd be the first one to step up and get her out of trouble. "Just give me the mark, Lieutenant Evetez, sir," Rett advised him pleasantly. "If you say anything else at this point, sir, I might knock you on your ass."

2.1.9 2023RD MESS, MAINCOMMAND, EPNOCE
0535.08.25 (LOCAL RECKONING)

RETT WATCHED HER PLATE MOVE closer to her. What was doing that? No quake alarms had gone off, and nothing else was shaking. Maybe it was—

The freckled fingers and hand that came into view, on the far edge of her tray, broke her musing. Semage.

"If you don't start eating this on your own instead of staring at it, kid, Jaq and I will have to hold you down while Ariam shoves this stuff into your mouth." Semage's tone was half-teasing, half-serious.

Rett threw a guilty glance first to Ariam, who looked aggrieved, and then to Jaq, who frowned at her. No doubt he and Ariam had maneuvered her into sitting with their present company for this very reason.

"Stop calling me kid." Especially since, right now, she felt as if she were a hundred and sixty years old. At least.

"I mean it," Semage warned. "There are enough of us here to handle you. I'll give you two seconds to get started."

"You sound like Evetez." The sarcasm Rett intended didn't quite come out, since she was too tired to add much inflection to her voice. "Will you put a finishing time on this as well?"

"If that'll be what it takes," he said. "One second down already."

First, I was too moody to even feel hungry. Now I'm hungry, but I'm too tired to eat, she groused, but picked up her fork and searched out a target on her plate.

"I must be getting old." Spearing a chunk of meat half-heartedly, she chewed without tasting. She could have been eating a plate full of stewed wood chips and not notice the difference.

"That's not it and you know it. He's pushing all of us hard, yes, but Evetez is pushing you to do five times what anyone in top physical condition should be doing."

Just thinking about shrugging her shoulders in response was too much of an effort. She wondered if the floor was as soft as if looked. Maybe it wouldn't be such a bad thing to be flat on her back, letting them do all the work, as Semage had threatened.

"What's going on between you two?" Semage demanded.

"Damned if I know."

"Funny. That's exactly what Evetez told me." Semage's frustrated exhale made Rett look at him again.

"I'm sorry, 'Mage. I really don't understand."

"Jaq," said the B-troop leader, "back in Branch, did you notice any strain between us? Between Rett and Evetez, I mean? And when you were on the Base with us as a group, did you get any clue there might be a problem? I know you spent some one-on-one time talking with him." He appealed to the Zetinorian who sat by so silently.

A shadow crossed Jaq's face. "No. From the first time I saw the three of you together, I knew you were the very best of friends. Our other conversations were primarily on the topics of Coalition technology and tactics."

"I used to think I knew him," Semage said.

"Yeah. So did I." Rett planted an elbow on the table and used her fist to hold her head up. "Everything changes, I guess."

"It goes beyond that, Rett. I think you know what I mean."

She had to agree. It wasn't anything she knew how to explain. If she could explain it, she wouldn't be so miserable about it.

"Have you tried to talk to him in those meetings you have?" Semage swirled the tea in his mug. "You're supposed to be combat team leader. And his second in command. You two should be talking all the time."

"Oh, yes. I've tried. The last attempt," she said, managing to get another chunk of something on her fork, "was on Firstday. After he called down drill and threw those MPs at me."

"The MPs you almost killed?"

She shot Ariam a glare. "Yes," she said through her teeth. She wasn't about to forget about that. "Those."

"That was four days ago," Semage said. "Have you tried again?"

"I've been waiting for another opening." Rett stared at her plate again. "Either I'm missing them or I'm not getting any. Our free time, of course, never seems to coincide, since one of us always has to be on." She wondered if she could lift her mug of tea if she used both hands. No, wait. If she used the hand holding her face off the table, she'd be in trouble.

Jaq nudged her, and she glanced sideways to see his worried expression. She straightened, giving him what she hoped was a convincing, reassuring smile. To prove she was eating, she managed to get the food on her utensil into her mouth.

He angled his head slightly in the familiar signal the Special Forces used to indicate someone was going to speak without sound. *This time I'm taking you straight to bed as soon as you're done.*

Promise? She sent her answer back in the same silent manner. Jaq was determined to gain the lip-reading skills most of them had, and learning fast, but she let the expression in her eyes back up her reply.

His worry faded into a grin that promptly disappeared behind his tea mug.

"I looked at our drill reports," Ariam was saying. "Every one of them is well within tolerance."

Rett's brief moment of lighter spirit dimmed. "Obviously not according to the Lieutenant's standard."

She poked her utensil into an overly-steamed vegetable and stared at it for a moment. It looked as look as limp as she felt. A sensation of kinship and sympathy for the pathetic morsel arose inside her.

Ariam set her mug down and leaned forward, reaching for the tea carafe. "I know we've been here well over a tenday, but maybe Evetez is still having problems with the transition—like quite a few others. I'm going to get a refill. Be right back."

The meaningful glance Rett fielded before Ariam departed for the refill was from her second in command, not her sister. No effort was required to interpret that cold, stabbing glare of metallic gray. Ariam was going to get straight and dirty with her on certain topics later, no doubt. *Oh, joy.*

"Ari may be right," said Semage. "About 'Vetez having extra issues adapting."

The soft vegetable fell off Rett's fork as she sat up a little straighter. Evetez and his issues had nothing to do with the sudden warm surge of hope and energy that flowed into her tired body and eased some of the sore tightness in her muscles. "Ari?"

A twitch of Semage's lips and a slight deepening of his natural color told Rett enough. She sent her longtime friend a smile and mouthed: *'Mage. I think that's great.*

He shrugged. *We're talking, that's all,* he answered in the same silent manner.

"Usually a good way to start," Rett said aloud, but kept her voice down so the words stayed between them. Warmth filled her. It had been tendays since Ariam had talked to anyone outside the platoon—not normal for her naturally social, talkative younger sister. Ariam would always love Kraym, but she had made her peace with his death. When she was ready to move on, a closer friendship with Semage would be perfect for her. Rett hoped so, anyway.

"If she has the right idea with these problems being related to the adjustment," Semage went on after clearing his throat and acknowledging Rett's acceptance, "it will pass. I hope. And soon. Atira and Mordell's platoons are supposed to start training with us in two more days."

119

Rett nodded. She didn't know Mordell from S-troop by anything but reputation, but she'd met the D-troop leader, Atira, six years ago and looked forward to renewing their acquaintance. Atira was also Easy fourth in command and secondary team leader.

Semage took a sip from his mug. "Then again, he might simply be going all out to show he isn't playing favorites, but he's overdoing it. And overdoing you, Rett."

"Easy Force is supposed to be as topnotch as Evetez can make us. We know S- and D-troops are used to working as a group, but our three platoons never did. If we get over that before plugging in Mordell and Atira's platoons—things will be better. And there's no reason why I shouldn't be able to meet all his standards. Everyone else is, so I need the work. Let's forget it, okay?" Rett found another item that didn't require a lot of effort to eat and concentrated on the simple actions of chewing and swallowing.

Ariam returned, setting a new mug in front of Rett and whisking the other aside. "Compliments of Med."

From the undertone in Ariam's voice, Rett decided any comment on her part would not be prudent.

"These indoor live-fire drills are really a pain," grumbled Semage.

Rett glanced at him, knowing his statement came from more than a need to change the topic. He pushed back his own barely touched meal with a grimace. Semage had caught a full-power SMG stun at close range right in the stomach that morning, effectively killing him in drill terminology. He was injured enough to earn a two-day break from any drill activity from Medical. He still looked pale and a bit green around the edges.

Knowing from personal experience how he must feel, Rett took a sip of tea, swallowed, and grinned at him. "At least stun beams don't leave you with permanent holes. They're not very pretty, Semage. I'll show you mine if you want."

The B-troop leader chuckled. "Maybe we should compare them, since I've more than a couple of those myself."

"I'm glad it was a drill," Rett said with feeling. "Now where did Ariam go?"

"Here I am," replied Ariam for herself, returning to the table with the refilled carafe in her left hand and another new mug in the right. "Med Shenyver and our Med thought you might like this." Ariam placed the mug in front of Semage. "They're over there with the other Easy medtechs brewing up…well, tea. Med said there were so many drill casualties today it was a good time to experiment. They're going over all sorts of moss, leaves, seeds, lichens, and other stuff we can find growing in the area, as long as ice or snow doesn't cover them. And even if it does, I heard the snow in some areas has edible lichens and algae that grow in it. And there are icefields with zooplanktons that might be useful."

The momentary brightening of Semage's personal energy was sharp enough to attract more of Rett's attention. Her friend had just been fully qualified as a marine biologist before his enlistment. Maybe she could get them off her back by changing the topic.

"Can't those be harmful sometimes, too?" Rett asked. "I mean, you're the one who told us back in training that some blue pond scum was safe to eat, but some of us were running for a tenday from it."

"I also said that some people had to build up a tolerance for it. You know as well as I do there are risks when people try new things, but we'll worry about that another time. Let's get back to a bigger problem, shall we?" Semage nudged her tray again.

"I'm glad you know when she's pulling a divert and decoy as well as the rest of us do," Ariam said to Semage.

"She's the one who taught me," said Semage. "She'd go on in training about how some animals would put a predator off by faking something or creating a diversion. So I learned to spot it coming. Eat up, Rett."

"One good thing," Rett said morosely, flipping over a slice of something on her plate, "is that Evetez couldn't penalize anyone from F-troop for getting killed, disabled, or going overtime today."

"Or you for almost killing anyone, for real, again," muttered Ariam into Rett's ear she resumed her seat.

Rett chose to ignore that on the outside, but the reminder stung hard. Learning to control her strength had been a lifetime struggle, almost as much of one as her social awkwardness and her inclination to stammer—something she still found herself slipping with during times of great stress. "And that drill today was just about as nasty as any real fight I've been in."

121

She noticed a stirring in the room and angled herself to follow the direction the heads of those around her were turning toward. A figure in AirSpacefighter uniform was speaking to a civilian volunteer. The volunteer turned, and pointed straight at Rett.

Good gods and deities. Captain Etron. What is he doing here? She swiftly adjusted her expression before any of her comrades took notice, but she couldn't stop her pulse from racing and she was positive her keen-eared friends could hear the sudden thudding of her heart. Was it guilt over that questionable flight she took with him and anyone finding out about it, or something else? Or both? Whatever it was, she cursed her luck and his timing.

"Hello, Sergeant Rett, Sergeant Ariam," greeted Etron. "No formalities to me," he added, a swift gesture halting anyone's motion to show some deference to his rank and outside status. "This is your territory and I'm just a visitor."

"Captain Etron, this is Sergeant Semage, B-troop; and this is my technical advisor, Jaq Pym." Completely alert now, Rett made the introductions for the rest of those at the table. What did he want?

"Grab a seat, Captain," Semage offered. "Some tea? Didn't I notice you watching our drills the past tenday or so? Thinking of transferring over?"

The pilot chuckled as he pulled an empty chair over and sat down. "Just watching you Special Forces get put through your paces exhausts me. I wouldn't last thirty seconds in one of those drills!" He accepted the mug of tea Ariam slid over. "Thanks. Oh, call me Etron—no sirs or Captain, please."

"You'll have to excuse us if we let one slip, sir," Ariam said.

Rett didn't miss Ariam's saucy wink to the newcomer, which hinted at familiarity. So just how many times had Ariam run into him during their drills? Rett had only seen him standing alongside her for a few brief seconds that one time.

"All right, then. I know you're wondering what I'm doing here, so I'll get to it. Believe it or not, watching your drills was my CO's idea. She has some pretty far-reaching ones." Etron gazed into his tea for a moment and shook his head, a faint smile on his lips. "I mentioned I'd met Sergeant Rett on Thirdday last and the Colonel just took off on this big, strange tangent about how we should really get with Major Yidnar's people on a few things."

Rett didn't change her outward expression, but inside, she was thinking Etron's glib explanation sounded pretty far-reaching in itself. She slid Ariam a quick, sideways glance, a minute lift to her left eyebrow.

Ariam responded with a barely perceptible shrug. *Truth.*

Well, that was a relief. Rett looked toward Jaq. Although a pleasant, sociable smile was on his handsome face, he watched Etron with dark, brooding eyes.

"How can you apply what we do in drill to piloting aircraft?" Semage's friendly overture changed to keen interest.

"That's just it. The 'old' pilots," Etron used the label with respect, "always tell us our fighters are extensions of our bodies. And there's a point where you do feel that way. It's great when you do," he said, getting a faraway look in his eyes for a moment.

"Colonel said keep this in mind and pay attention to the close combat one-on-one, and one-to more. And you know what? Once I got used to just how to watch—you guys have a tendency to disappear into the landscape, you know—damned if she didn't have a valid theory. You don't spend all that much time on the ground at all. I ended up planning an entire new series of maneuvers for the squadron. We're going to be testing out a few later."

* * * * *

ARIAM'S ATTENTION WAS DRAWN TO Jaq Pym. She focused her talent on him as his measuring glance went from the new arrival to Rett and back again. Whatever he had been fighting to keep buried broke loose. The central gold crest in Jaq's wild red-brown hair lifted straight up all at once, the incredible blue of his eyes darkened to a dangerous gray-black, and his nostrils flared. His flare of defensive jealousy was so hard and strong Ariam was nearly breathless with it.

The Zetinorian had never appeared so alien to Ariam until that moment. She almost expected a flash of teeth and a growl to come next. She waited for a reaction from Rett, but other than a small shiver as if something gave her a chill, her sister didn't move. *Oh, this is it,* she thought, her tiff rising. *She's far too tired, and this is the last night for it! Even without focusing her energy sense, she should have been about blown off her chair by that!*

Quickly she shifted in her seat and gave Jaq a sharp nudge with her foot. Maybe being a Zetinorian gave him some advantages over other humanoids in a lot of ways—but not now. The force that had bound him to her sister left no room for any rivals, even completely amiable ones.

"Easy, Jaq," she said for his ears alone. "Calm down. The situation with Evetez has her under enough pressure."

* * * * *

JAQ SWALLOWED HIS ZETINORIAN INSTINCTS, forcing himself to participate in pleasant conversation with Etron and the others. He thanked the One for Ariam's quick intervention. Bad enough he had trouble controlling his outward feelings for Rett when other men spoke to her. Especially those she had close friendships with, even the easygoing Sergeant Semage. From what he was seeing, she was attracted to this newcomer in more than friendly way, and in turn the pilot didn't try to hide his own attraction for her.

Why should he? I didn't.

123

The presence of the group helped him stay in focus. The topic attracted a few more people from Easy Force to their table, further diluting the tension in Jaq, since everyone's attention—Rett's and the captain's in particular—turned to the discussion at hand. He shook his head a little, his own interest and zest for a good technical discussion growing.

The fighter pilot illustrated his animated speech with his hands, his enthusiasm and energy genuine. Despite seeing him as a rival for Rett's attentions, Jaq couldn't help liking the Nyorfian, and had to admit the AirSpacefighter officer really knew the gives-and-takes necessary for good communication. The captain stopped readily when someone broke in with a question or another idea and paid attention to what they had to say.

And soon, with the enthusiasm Jaq had come to expect from these Nyorfians, tea mugs and water bottles were pushed aside in favor of Omnis. Those with notepads, which had larger screens for drawing, brought them out as well. References were checked. Data called up. Diagrams and illustrations rapidly sketched, discussed, and just as quickly altered.

Jaq's wish to be elsewhere—preferably alone with Rett—dissolved as he was sucked right into the center of the discussion.

"Our Jaq Pym's the local authority on a lot of Coalition combat techniques as well as technology," someone in the group told Etron.

"Our" Jaq. He liked that almost as much as he liked Rett saying "my technical advisor" instead of "F-troop's technical advisor." F-troop had taken possession of him in that way from the beginning. He didn't mind. The addition of the possessive pronouns never failed to warm him, even now, when it drew him the close scrutiny of the dark-skinned fighter pilot.

"Great! Because that factor's missing, and we can use a point of view from someone who knows that angle." Etron beckoned. "Come on over here, Jaq. Take a look at this."

It didn't take long for Jaq had to admit he was interested. This was fun, and an enjoyable way to pass time. That was, at least as he didn't think about Rett and Etron's initial reaction to each other.

* * * * *

Rᴇᴛᴛ's ᴛɪʀᴇᴅɴᴇss ᴀɴᴅ ᴛᴇɴsɪᴏɴ ꜰᴀᴅᴇᴅ in the light of the fascinating discussion. Her mind wasn't on Jaq or Etron, her attraction to both of them, or her worry about a need to put Jaq's mind at ease about the situation. It was totally involved in the application of the movements of human bodies to aircraft. It was hard for her to grasp some of hard science and tech that was flying around her as thick and fast as the simulated enemy fire of that day's drill session. Determined not to feel stupid and follow along, she locked out everything else and paid fierce attention.

She nearly jumped from her seat when a tone sounded on her pcom. Converting her reaction into the full movement of getting up and stepping aside, she opened the non-combat battalion frequency with a voice command.

"Rett," she responded, barely remembering to use her name and not her combat call sign.

"Mahrhys," said a quiet tenor voice. Although she hadn't heard it 125 in some time—years actually—Rett would have identified him even without the introduction. Senior Captain Mahrhys was the 2023rd's Exec, direct second in command to the Major.

It's probably strange for them to be within shouting distance of each other too, Rett thought fleetingly. On Nyorfias, the Major and his juniors had been spread out all over the planet, coordinating and checking in with the widely scattered, two hundred-and-some small units that comprised the battalion. She hadn't seen Mahrhys for…deities, at least six years. Back then, she was C-troop third-up . "What's up?"

"Please report to Yidnar's office as soon as possible."

"On my way," confirmed Rett. The conversation around her table stalled as she turned back to face the others. "Sorry. Guess I'm in trouble again. I have to go. Boss wants to see me. I'll catch up with you guys later."

"I'll walk with you, Rett," offered Ariam quickly, before Jaq or Etron could speak up.

Rett smiled thanks, but she shook her head. "Don't need to have anyone else hear me getting yelled at. Stay here and fill in my end of the conversation, Ariam." *Stay here and keep the peace* was the silent message Rett added at the same time.

2.1.10 2023RD CO'S OFFICE, EPNOCE MAIN COMMAND
0534.08.25 (LOCAL RECKONING)

MAJOY YIDNAR WAS PREPARED FOR his visitor. The instant she came through the door, he headed off any action on her part with a quick signal and a nod to one of the chairs in front of his desk. "Sit down."

He sharpened his focus on her. The greeting alone should have produced a reaction. And so it did, but only in the slight hesitation as she redirected the muscles and limbs already preparing for one motion to change to the one he asked for.

He ground his teeth as he factored in her appearance, the already sharp angles of her face more deeply shadowed, the evidence she was in pain. The unconsciously careful way she turned to sidestep between the narrow gap between the chairs; the way she sat. She hid things well, all right, but not from him.

"Having any problems, Rett?"

"Not that I'm aware of, sir."

He expected the denial. That she even tried to lie—when she and quite a few others knew she wasn't any good at it—just added to his concern. "If there wasn't a problem I wouldn't have called you."

She had started to take a seat, but froze, her hand tightening on the back of the chair hard enough to make the material squeak in protest.

"Look, sport. Sit back and relax, don't hold back. Talk to me. What's with Evetez reporting F-troop, especially you, are having problems in the drills?"

The expression of polite inquiry on her face vanished, her features hardening to stone as she let go of the chair back and sat. She didn't answer, a fair indication of her present level of internal conflict.

"Let's hear it. Any way it comes out, I don't care. For some reason, it's obvious you can't talk to Evetez and work things out. But talk to me. If it helps—" He lifted his right hand toward his black headband, so they could talk as comrades instead of commander and junior.

"That's not necessary, sir." She took a deep breath. Most of it expelled in a near-silent rush, but the last of it brought words along. "I'm working my ass off in drill. I don't understand what Evetez wants from me. I give him everything he asks for—but it's never right, or good enough, or fast enough. If I ask questions, I get treated like a clueless trainee. I only slipped up one time that I know of. It was my fault. He made sure I paid hard credit for that."

Her struggle to keep her anger and confusion in perspective tugged at his sympathy. "Semage tells me he has you running drills over twice or better."

"Semage is in on this too, huh? I thought it was mostly Ariam and the rest of F-troop."

"Actually, it's just about everyone in Easy Force," Yidnar said dryly. "But Ariam's already been in to see me, yes. As well as Tris. Plus Atira and Mordell."

Her expression of surprise at the mention of the last two platoon leaders, currently on leave, would have made him laugh in another situation, but not this one.

"Atira and Mordell might be on leave, but that doesn't mean they don't stay informed about everything going on," he explained. "And, by the added virtue of being a personal friend of yours, Semage acted as the representative for the personal feelings from the rest of the group. So you can say I've heard from everyone. Except you."

"I was handling it just fine, sir." She crossed her arms over her breasts and made a good pretense of sitting back and looking unconcerned.

"That's not what I heard—or hear now. Nor is it what I see sitting in front of me. You can't keep going on adrenaline, or someone is going get seriously hurt or killed because you lost control. That situation you made reference to? I understand you very nearly caused five serious casualties, one of them just today released from Medical."

"Yes, sir, that would the one." Her long fingers tightened over her upper arms and her gaze dropped to the edge of his desk.

"Damn it, Rett. You never ask for anything, which is why I step way out for you. But this has gone too far. When we start punching live targets in another three tendays or so, I need you in peak form—not dead tired." He leaned back in his chair. "What makes matters worse is that I'm getting conflicting reports. I wanted to get your side of this before trying to get to the bottom of things with Evetez. That's why you're here. You don't know why he's leaning on so hard?"

She shook her head.

"You didn't have a disagreement?"

"No, sir."

He regarded her thoughtfully. "He's having problems yet adjusting, both to Epnoce and his new position. Why he's leaning so hard on you, I have no idea." He scratched his jaw with a forefinger before leaning forward, both arms crossed in front of him on the desk. "Remember how competitive you three used to be? I mean you were the best of friends off duty, the greatest team when you worked together, but always tried to outdo each other in everything else.

"Now Evetez outranks you, but your experience and performance record leaves his in the dust. Not to say Evetez hasn't been right up there. He wouldn't be in his position right now if I didn't have complete confidence in him. You know that."

"Yes, sir. I can't fault him as a team leader. He's pulled us together brilliantly through some of the toughest training courses I've ever had to complete. I've learned a lot from him, in drill, and with administration and planning."

Now that he was glad to hear, but he still watched her closely as she spoke. Rett's attempts at deliberate lies were rare, because she simply wasn't good at it. Which presented a perplexing conundrum, since she was an expert at most other methods of deception. Or as they called it, divert and decoy.

But she wasn't trying to deceive or disarm this time, not like when she came in. She meant what she said, every word. But what wasn't she saying? "Evetez also knows damned well you were my first choice for his position, as lead for Easy Force." Yidnar's eyes never left her. "Do you think anything like that might be bothering him?"

A scowl deepened the shadows in her face. "I'd hate to think that of Evetez, Major. Stuff like that never bothered him before. We had time for a talk or two before we even got started in with drills, and things were fine between us. Fine. We were both satisfied with our posting, and looking forward to working together." Her dark gaze lifted, the frustrated bewilderment in her eyes a plea for help. "This just isn't like him, sir. If he had a problem, he always came right out with it. I—" Her voice fell, stopped. Her strong shoulders rose in a shrug. "I don't know what to do."

"He might be too focused to see how hard he's being, Rett. Everyone knows you two trained together and are good friends. Semage thinks someone might have made a comment about that and suspects Evetez is going overboard not to show any favoritism—so far as to go the opposite way. The opinions of others, combined with the reputation of the teams in Easy Force, especially yours and F-troop's, are enough to stagger any junior officer in his position."

"Damn it, Major, I'm proud of F-troop, and our reputation. But I'm sick and tired of being singled out, and if my being friends with someone is going to make trouble for them—" Her right hand raked through her hair, a sure sign of agitation.

Yidnar laughed. "I caught that…er…interview you gave in Branch. Meant to comment on it at our last meeting."

129

"You were busy, sir. Was it wrong—?"

He was quick to reassure her. "Not at all. I was just going to mention how surprised I was, knowing how difficult that can be for you. I'm glad you did."

She made a rude sound. "My personal issues with public speaking aside, I had to set the record straight. Especially after hearing people were giving me and F-troop, mostly me, all the credit for single-handedly taking back the Wide River Gap Bridge and Circle." Now, a flare of indignant tiff lifted some of the dull tiredness from her face. "We all do our best, sir. Every single one of us!"

"You're right. Yet there are those who push a little harder, find a way to do something that no one else would think of, provide inspiration and example for others, and come through time after time, no matter how impossible the task seems to be. Those people are our heroes, and our people need them—just as the enemy does. For many reasons. Unfortunately, it's harder on you and other who get the attention from both sides, but it's doing good for the whole."

Her posture slumped and her gaze fell again.

"I can't do anything about what goes on outside the 2023rd, but you've just made your last payment as far as this Battalion is concerned, sport. I can't have a situation like this in one of my main strike forces. Everyone has to be able to think and act as one person. Especially the leader and second."

"Yes, sir."

"If things go any farther with this rift between you and Evetez—"

She looked up, surprised.

"Did you think I was reassigning either of you?"

"It would be the logical thing, sir. If I'm the only one in the group not getting along with—"

To avoid reaching for his hair and tugging it in the same manner to which Rett was prone, Yidnar made a pretense of scratching the day's worth of whiskers on the left side of his face. *Will I ever get her to stop taking blame she doesn't deserve?*

"Rett." Yidnar's right hand mirrored the actions of the left. "No one wants you to leave. I'm fairly certain not even Evetez wants you to go—he would have said so already. There must be something more to this, something we're missing. Med Rhozev is starting to think so, too, and he's going to have a sharp eye on you. I'll also have Evetez in for tests again, but I find it hard to imagine his problem is physiological. I'll speak to him. One way or another, I'll get this cleared up."

"Don't do that, sir," she said. "I mean—you probably want to talk to him, and deities know it's your prerogative. But I'd rather you didn't try to clear things up yourself."

Frowning, Yidnar leaned back, crossing his arms over his chest. "Can you give me a valid reason why I shouldn't?"

"Only a personal one, sir. Please, Major, Evetez is still my friend, I think, and I want to keep that. If your intervention goes over a certain degree it may be impossible for us to get back to where we were before this all started."

"I don't want you worn to nothing in the process. The last time I've seen you this tired and sore was after the battle for Circle. And you've lost more weight in the past tenday—"

The raw pleading on her face made Yidnar reconsider.

The effectiveness of his people depended so much on cooperation and respect. He couldn't have any one of his command unhappy with another and still expect them to work together in the full cohesion and intimate, absolute trust necessary for complete teamwork. He also had a responsibility not to allow things like Rett's situation to get out of hand.

But she was right, to an extent. She and Evetez had to get back to terms on their own. He based the entire structure of Easy Force on the past ability of critical team leaders to work smoothly together. But could he afford to wait for them?

Not if it was going to take too much time. He needed Rett. In full working order. He needed Evetez and his undeniable skills to lead and manage. It was Yidnar's job to step into these situations and help resolve them: as even it had been his job in civilian life to negotiate treaties and trade agreements when normal procedure failed.

Yidnar chewed the inside of his cheek for a moment. He had the feeling he was going to regret giving in to Rett, but it was so rare she ever asked any favors for herself. So rare, in fact, that he couldn't recall a single instance where she had ever asked for one.

131

"Okay, sport, I'll make you a deal. Just remember, I'm stepping way out for you. If this situation doesn't clear up by this time tomorrow, I take over. If, in the interim, I see anything I don't like, I also take over. I want you to talk to Evetez before this gets any worse. If you're bottoming out, tell him. Do you understand?"

"Yes, sir."

"If I have to take over, Rett..." He left the threat hanging unsaid, saw her swallow.

"Understood, sir."

"Then do we have a deal?"

"Not much of one, but I'll take it, Major."

"He calls you out in front of everyone, huh?"

"Keeps me humble, sir. I'm not perfect. It's time more people realized that."

He didn't respond to her attempt at humor. "If I have to call either one of you out, it'll be for a lot more than to preserve humility. That's how serious this is. Clear it up."

"Yes, sir," she said with feeling. "Thank you, sir."

* * * * *

RETT EXPECTED ARIAM TO POUNCE on her as soon as she came into their billet, and wasn't disappointed. The door barely had time to slide closed behind her when Ariam's "What happened?" nailed Rett so hard she almost tripped over it.

"Give me half a minute here," protested Rett, checking herself in and acknowledging all of F-troop was accounted for and where they belonged.

The surge of energy that had kept her going between Captain Etron's arrival in the mess hall and her meeting with Major Yidnar was melting as fast as snow in summer sunlight, and she hoped she would hold out the few more minutes necessary to prepare for sleep and perform her gear check.

"Nothing much happened. Pretty much the same conversation we had in the mess hall before Etron showed up," Rett said in what she hoped was a careless manner. "Apparently, Evetez told Major Yidnar I wasn't pulling my weight in drill. You and Semage, and deities know who else—"

"Everyone else."

"—are telling him another story altogether. The Major just wanted my side." She shrugged.

"Oh, I can imagine the side you must have tried to give him. 'Nothing's wrong, sir'," said the younger woman, deepening her voice slightly in imitation of Rett. "What do you mean, he just wanted your side? He's not going to stop you from killing yourself—or one of our drill assistants?" Ariam threw herself onto her bunk, her disbelief and displeasure thick as smoke between them. "I thought he'd clear this up himself. It's up to me, I guess."

Rett threw her boots at Ariam, following the trajectory of her foot-gear with her own body. "You can do whatever you want. But don't interfere with me and Evetez." Rett gave her sister a warning shake.

"Okay, okay! I'm just worried. Don't shake me. Come on—ow!"

"You look too full of yourself about something, little sister," growled Rett, tightening her hold. "What happened after I left?"

"Well, the flying talk sort of wound down, and since Captain Etron's going to be observing a while longer, everyone agreed to pick it up where we left off some other night. After that, Semage, Jaq, and I had a nice, social kind of chat with Etron."

"Jaq?"

"I think he didn't quite trust himself to move, or else he was really scoping out his competition."

"This isn't funny."

"I'm not laughing. You completely missed how he reacted to Etron. His eyes went all dark and weird and his hair practically stood on end. I thought he was going to jump Etron and rip his throat open with his teeth. It's not something I'm likely to forget."

"Go on."

"Well, it was about nothing, really. You know, asking each other things like where we're from, what we did before, that sort of thing. And then Semage—he's really observant—took Jaq off to look at some Coalition gizmo or another one of his platoon had confiscated a while back. I stayed to talk with Etron. Ow, take it easy! I need that arm."

"First Major Yidnar, then Etron. And just what did this private conversation involve?" demanded Rett. Sweat broke out on Ariam's smooth forehead when Rett's grip tightened a fraction more. "Tell me."

"All right. The captain is really attracted to you. Jaq's upset over it. Etron understood right away that Jaq has strong feelings for you. He doesn't mind, of course, he was just curious. He asked me about Jaq after he left and I had to explain some Zetinorian peculiarities, you know, like Jaq's every instinct claiming you as his—"

Rett leaned harder on the body pinned beneath hers, causing Ariam to yelp softly.

"Ow! Okay, maybe not in those words, but he had no idea about, uh, the 'curse', for lack of better terms. And that it is sometimes one-sided. I didn't tell him much else. Let go, Rett."

She released her hold on Ariam and sat on the edge of her sister's bunk, dropping her chin into her hands. Ariam sat up, rubbing her arm from wrist to shoulder. "That's not the end of your problems."

133

"I didn't think so, after that look you gave me earlier. Well, tell me about them." Rett sat up straighter, hands going to her knees. "That's part of your job, after all. Or would you like more encouragement?"

"I'll talk."

"I'm listening." Rett rubbed her palms against her knees briefly, then stood up and began to undress.

"Besides all the problems with adjusting, and having two men madly in love with you, and besides having Lieutenant Evetez ride your butt, and Major Yidnar—"

"Ariam," warned Rett, stepping into the lavatory, "get to the point."

"It's Med. You're losing too much weight and condition. He's come to me and reminded me that as your second in command, I'd better get really serious about doing something about it. Or he's going straight to Major Yidnar and pulling you off Active."

Rett came out in time for the last remark, a cold lump sitting heavily in her stomach, which was giving hard, clear threats of rebellion despite the fact it was empty. Major Yidnar had mentioned Med, but he hadn't mentioned this. "You've already been—"

Ariam, seated on the edge of her bunk, crossed her arms and fixed her sternest glare on her. She didn't let Rett finish. "After you? Oh, yes, me and everyone else in F-troop! So you've noticed? Shit, Rett! Why must you be so flaming logheaded over cooperating, then? What's up with that? You've never been like this, ever, not even when the ego-merge started. It might be part of the settling-in problems a lot of people are having here, but it's the parts that aren't related to settling-in that worry me. Do you think I don't notice you slipping back into not eating at all—or losing what you do eat? I grew up with you. I don't have to be with you or see you to know. Don't let me stop you if you want to throw up now."

Rett's hands clenched into fists at her sides. "Ariam—"

"I don't want to hear your excuses. I'd already decided tonight was your last chance. And when Med came to me, I almost asked him to go right ahead, since just like when you had to be ordered to go on leave, a drastic move like pulling you off Active would be about the only thing that would jerk your head out of your ass!"

"Great." Pulling on a sleeping shirt, Rett dropped onto her bed and yanked a blanket around her shoulders. She wished she had some answers. As much as she tried to fight it, she was losing control of herself. Deities, she might even suspect another sort of ego-merge, something more subtle and sinister than Pam's.

She shivered and pushed the heel of her right hand against the knot of tension between her eyes. No, it couldn't be. Ariam would know if there were another mindforce in her. She was sure of it, as sure as she was that Med would have already sidelined her if it was a medical issue.

Rett made a face. It was about to become a medical issue.

"What do you want me to do?"

"Let me tell you what F-troop and I want."

Rett lifted her head at the gentler note in Ariam's voice.

"We love you. We don't want to go into combat with anyone else. I love you, and I truly don't want to be in the position of relieving you of command. Much less let this go on long enough for Med or Major Yidnar to do it. I'd get called out for failing in my duty to you, to the platoon. And then there'd be two of us gone, under the worst sort of circumstances—worse than anyone finding out about the ego-merge. Is that what you truly want?"

"You know I don't." Rett hunched under her blanket.

"Then damn it, don't let it happen." Ariam sat next to her and hugged her fiercely.

"Ariam," Rett said, almost choking in an effort not to sound so desperate, "can you check and make sure there's no one else in my head but me?"

"I already have." Her sister's slender, sinewy arms tightened even more. "I've felt a wrongness on and off from you, like nothing I've felt before, but I'm sure it's just you in there, Rett. I don't know what's causing you to act like this. But it has to stop. You have to let us help you if you can't do it yourself. You know that. It's part of being a team."

"I know that." Rett leaned into Ariam's embrace. "Things will work out. I'm going to give it everything I have."

"And you'll let us help you?"

"Yes."

"Promise? You'll eat everything in sight without threats? And keep it down? You'll spend your free time relaxing instead of studying so much, or going to the gym and killing yourself above and beyond what you do in drill? And you'll talk to Evetez tomorrow no matter what?"

Rett hesitated, and Ariam's grip started getting painful instead of supportive. "F-troop and I are prepared to get aggressive to keep you, Rett, but you have to cooperate. Promise me! You have to settle things with Evetez if anything else—even your personal problems—is going to work out."

"That's what I want to do."

"I know he's running you harder than anyone else." Ariam released her embrace long enough to fuss with the blanket. "But he's not going to penalize you for being honest about your limitations—even ours. He needs to know what they are, how far you can be pushed. You and everyone else in Easy's chain of command. Promise me."

Hearing it from Ariam reminded Rett that deep down, she knew that. Why then, had she not kept it in focus? Ari was right. Everything she said was right. Rett's entire life was about to blow up in her face if she didn't take control for herself. "Promise, Ariam. I'll be good."

"Glad to hear it. You can start right now. Come with me."

It was only then Rett realized what Ariam had done with her blanket: created a strategic advantage. When the younger woman stood up and tugged, she knew better than to resist.

With an inward groan and roll of her eyes, Rett allowed Ariam to lead her to the worktable. "What's up, Ariam?"

"I've arranged a little snack. Sit down and eat it. Right now."

Rett sat and rearranged her blanket. Her tired tolerance quickly turned into dismay as Ariam produced several thermal containers and set them in front of her.

"You must be joking." Rett pressed her forearms into her stomach, telling it to behave.

"Trust me, I'm not. That's hunger that's hurting you now, not nausea. And if you tell me you're not hungry, I'll yell for Med so loud half the 2023rd will be right behind him."

With some apprehension, Rett watched Ariam open the first container. "Jaq—" she started.

"We're not going to discuss Jaq tonight." Ariam thrust a utensil at Rett as if it were a weapon; she barely got a hand out of her blanket in time to intercept it.

As cold as it sounded, she knew her sister was right. *I still have to talk to him. Tomorrow morning before we get started.* Rearranging herself on the chair, she stared morosely at the food in front of her. *How am I going to eat any of this, much less all of it?*

Then the tantalizing odor of roasted mushrooms and spiced grains reached her nose. Rett didn't have to pretend anymore. The uneasy turbulence in her innards became a loud rumble, but it wasn't something that meant she was about to spew. She was starving.

"Are you going to stare at me or sit down and keep me company?" She took a bite, then gestured to the second container where a couple of fruit rolls nested in with the plain ones. "You know you're the one who likes those. This is pretty good." She shoved in another bite of another bite of the mushroom pilaf, then snatched one of the fruit rolls and chucked it at her sister. As much as she had a weakness for mushrooms, Ariam would do almost anything for a spiced fruit roll.

The younger woman snatched the baked missile neatly, sat down on the edge of the worktable, and started by picking out the fruit bits first. "You'd better start getting used to snacking before going to sleep. And I'll warn you now, expect it all day long starting tomorrow. You don't want me or anyone else to directly interfere between you and Evetez, that's fine. But I've already briefed the platoon, and we're going to make damned sure you've the energy to handle what he's throwing at you."

"I'm supposed to talk with him tomorrow," mumbled Rett around another spoonful of food.

"Good. That's a start."

Trying to swallow her apprehension with her food, Rett only hoped it wasn't too late.

2.1.11 CORRIDOR, SECTION C, EPNOCE MAIN COMMAND
0534.08.26 (LOCAL RECKONING)

"Jaq." Rett stretched her stride to catch up with him. "A minute?"

He stopped to wait for her. He didn't turn more than his head, and that only partially. He didn't have to. His body language made it clear to Rett that he wasn't in the best of moods.

"About last night—"

He pulled away from the hand she was about to put on his arm. The movement was small, but the significance of it rocked Rett back on her heels.

"Last night?" he repeated, his voice as chill as the wind outside the complex. "What about nearly a tenday and a half ago? Or was last night when that was to come up?"

This time when Rett reached for him, she closed her grip before he could sidestep again. She pulled him to one side of the corridor. "What's that supposed to mean?"

"If you were going to meet one of your old lovers, you could have told me instead of telling me you were going off to be alone." Jaq sent her an oblique glance, his face set, blue eyes hard and dark. "It was fairly obvious something happened between you two. I suppose you'll now feel justified in telling me I have the choice of spending my time with anyone else, too."

It took her a moment to comprehend, another to make sure that when she spoke, that she kept her tone low and quiet. "First of all, I never in my life met Captain Etron before that night a tenday and a half ago. Secondly, I've had no contact with him since then, unless you count catching sight of him once at one of our drills. I understand he's been there more than a few times, but you should know I'm not paying attention to any of the observers. And last night, when he showed up? That was completely unexpected. Thirdly, had I been planning to meet somcone when I took my leave of you that first night, whatever the reason was, I would have told you."

Her hopes for a quick, reasonable exchange had vanished along with the time in which she had to make it. "What happened between me and Etron, Jaq, was nothing remotely close to the magnitude you are making of it."

"If it was no big deal, why couldn't you tell me?"

"Because it was no big deal is precisely why I dismissed it so easily until now! Look, I want to talk with you about this later. After drill. After I talk to Lieutenant Evetez. All right?"

"Fine." He hadn't softened. Even his gold crest reflected his attitude, bristling at odd, stiff angles.

Deities, she didn't need this on top of everything else! "Whatever problem we have is between us, no one else. I hope we can keep it that way until we can resolve it," Rett said.

He checked his chrono, the exaggerated motion most likely to remind her—as if she needed it—that they were on a duty schedule even as they spoke. "What problem was that, Sergeant?" He stepped back, away from the grip she had on his arm, and went ahead to the mess area.

Rett stood in place for a moment before following. Great. Not only was the Evetez she used to know turned completely on her, now it was happening to Jaq. She expected a disconcerted reaction on his part, of course, but not this. She also expected that he'd give her a chance to explain. And explain what? That meeting Etron had been an accident? It didn't change anything she felt for Jaq in the least.

She pushed it inside as she took her place with Ariam, Trebor, her squadleaders, and Jaq, since platoon business was generally discussed over the morning meal. But there were many watchful pairs of eyes on her, and aware of them all, Rett started in on her meal despite the building turbulence and hard ache in her guts.

Neither Ariam nor Jaq revealed one glimmer of stress, and Rett was grateful for it. Only for that fact was she able to make it past her first few bites without bringing back up what she swallowed. And after that, normal physical hunger reasserted itself, which was a good thing, because at least three different people brought her extras.

The mug of tea Med brought by and deposited at her elbow went down without even a second glance, although she really had to work to keep her reaction to the overly bitter stuff from showing on her face. Keeping her smile in place and blinking a few times, she swallowed hard, casually reached for a water bottle, and flushed the rest of the stuff down before it completely closed her throat. She went on with the plan to put some of the more junior members in squadleader positions for the first half of that morning's sessions as if she hadn't been in danger of choking to death a few seconds before. She was determined to remain upbeat and cheerful in front of her platoon even if it killed her.

Or, until more of Med's potions killed her. Because as soon as she finished the first mug, he produced a second, something different and sharp-scented enough for Trebor, on her left, to wrinkle his nose and angle his seat away. Med waited to make sure she drank that one. The vapor made her eyes water, but Rett tossed it back without a protest.

It wasn't tea, it was liquid propellant. It hit her belly and incinerated every particle of food she'd ingested. Thankfully the sensation lasted only a few seconds, and when her vision cleared, Rett was surprised that she felt pretty good—at least digestively.

So, aside from lingering fatigue and sore muscles, she was ready to go for the first half of the day's exercises. After yesterday's drill, which would have been a successful (although tragic) assault in realtime, to see everyone who hadn't been sidelined on a Medical disability for a day or so in such a good mood was heartening. Rett was pleased that Lieutenant Evetez took into consideration the fact most everyone was physically stressed, so his agenda for the day was simple exercise and practice on basic skills.

No live fire drill for a day—what a welcome relief. Despite the lighter workload, whenever there were a few moments between events, one or another of her platoon always managed to slide some sort of snack or a fruit drink or a water bottle into Rett's grasp. Even Jaq had handed her a protein bar at one point and stood by to make sure she ate it.

As this went on and Rett tried to protest to her third-up, Trebor, he simply broke off half the fruit bar he was munching on and popped it right in her mouth, effectively stopping her words. A warning look from Ariam kept it there.

Rett kept the sigh inside and started chewing. She noticed everyone in F-troop was snacking more than usual. Whether that was to keep their personal energy high or to encourage her, she didn't care. The love she felt for them fueled her spirit. After that, she simply accepted any offered tidbits. As a result, her energy was high despite the bone-deep aches in her body. But since that was the norm for almost every day of the past nine or ten years of her life, she was able to shrug it off. In her estimation, the best cure for that was to work harder.

The temperature outside the base building was downright chilly as a light rain fell.

"Get used to it," Evetez said to the group. "This is normal summer on this part of the continent. We're in the tropical zone of the planet. That's why most of the complexes were built in this latitude. Yep, this is the South Point of Epnoce, folks. Just be happy we're not having the lightning and ice that's been happening most of the tenday."

"And be happy we're not having quakes," someone else said. Rett recognized Corporal Rimms, from B-troop.

She was grateful for that much, too. They'd had to work through several temblors during a few of their drills since arriving. Which was fine: as long as she had a mission, the quakes were something she could deal with, merely another obstacle to work around to her goal. "Oh, good deities!" she muttered as the ground gave a defiant wiggle beneath her boots.

"Spoke too soon, Rimms," called someone else.

At least the weather was relatively calm. Since their arrival, Rett had heard of massive ice storms that left anything exposed to the freezing rain encased in a frozen, steel-strong shell anywhere from a fingerwidth to a handspan thickness. Or sleet so heavy it covered the ground knee deep in a matter of an hour. The lightning that accompanied some of the bigger storms was so intense it drove everyone to safety and suspended any activity outside the protection of a habitat, even for the enemy. The energy disruptions from these storms were also powerful enough to interfere with even well-shielded power sources, communications, and equipment.

Thinking about that made Rett appreciate the mist and drizzle. She thought for a moment about the accounts they heard from the locals.

It was all too easy to imagine Easy getting caught out in such a storm, all of them flash fried by a lightning strike. Or becoming coated in ice, locked into place, and slowly suffocating to death before the cold had a chance to kill them. A deep shiver ran up her spine, causing an outward reaction visible enough to earn her a penetrating glance from Med. Deities! Flashing him a grin, she shoved the track of her thoughts back to the present.

She kept her eyes open for an opportunity to talk with Evetez, who was in a great mood and didn't find fault with anything. At a poke from Ariam during one of the breaks, Rett went over to him.

"Lieutenant, I need to talk with you." She didn't understand why she suddenly felt so nervous. This was Evetez. So he'd been off his usual style for a while; so had she.

He nodded, his lips twisting for a moment into one of those appealing expressions he used so well. "I've not been making much time for you. We do need to talk, about a lot of things. Do you feel we have to discuss right this minute? I can have Semage and Tris manage."

Rett hesitated. A sharp pain in her left kidney was from Ariam, who had followed a few discreet steps behind her. "We're just about done here, right?"

"The weather's going bad, so I was going to try one more exercise and call it down. One I was hoping you'd help me with. "

This time, the pain came from Rett's right heel. Damn it, Ariam was asking for trouble later.

"What sort of exercise?" Rett wanted to know.

This time, her second in command didn't need to touch her physically to express displeasure. It was being projected with such force that Rett had to scramble to get what mental shields she could into place to keep her brain from blistering. "Excuse me just a moment, sir. Sergeant Ariam needs to tell me something."

Evetez nodded, and turned to confer with one of the MP drill assistants, who'd been standing nearby.

"Ariam?" Rett said through her teeth. "Do you mind?"

"Yes, I do. Don't blow this chance, Rett. Talk to him." Ariam's face would give nothing away to a casual observer, but her voice was fierce.

Tired of being pushed, Rett balked. "I don't want it to be interrupted by anything between now and the end of drill. You know how that goes."

"Rett."

"Dismissed."

"Sergeant."

She turned with a shiver from the ice-hard eyes of her second, back to Evetez as he swung back toward her.

"So?" asked the lieutenant, "Now? Or before, during, or after dinner?"

Forcing down the sensations of impending doom Ariam was pushing at her, Rett made herself smile at Evetez. The old familiar grin and the sparkle in his eyes did more to energize her than any amount of food or rest.

"Before dinner. The very moment drill's over, actually."

So she was cutting it close, and Ariam wasn't happy, but Rett wanted to keep whatever conversation she had with Evetez between them. And the very minute she was finished with the lieutenant, she was determined to grab Jaq—by the hair if she had to—and sit him down for a talk.

"Are you all right? Is it anything I should know right away? Your second didn't look very happy just now. You did eat today, right?"

"Yes."

Part of her was grateful that he remembered she had issues with food under certain circumstances, and part of her resented he was going to be riding her for that along with everyone else.

"And everything's fine for the moment, sir," Rett said with complete truth. "But it won't be if you back out on me. So clear your schedule to make sure."

He spoke to his Omni, then held it up for her inspection so that she could witness there was nothing in that particular time slot. He put her name there in the next second. "Now it's official. Ready to get back to work?"

"What was it you wanted me to do?"

143

"Something you're really good at, and like, especially since you grew up climbing trees and mountains and things." He nodded at a building section farther down. "Think you can show us how you go up a wall?"

Happy and hopeful that whatever problem Evetez had with her was going to be a thing of the past, Rett dismissed the nagging possibility he was asking too much of her at this point in time, and considered his request.

Six lengths! she thought. That was right at her present limit in this gravity. She wasn't loaded down with gear as they were during combat drill: something that was getting better with time, but still a concern for all.

"Are you up for it? You don't have to—there are a few others in the group who can do it. Not exactly the way I've seen you do it, though. You didn't seem to have any problems on the other walls."

She studied the wall and thought hard. She could do it. Plus, as soon as she did, he'd call down drill and they could have their talk. Which was good on two counts: she didn't have much time left on Major Yidnar's deadline, and, if she put what energy she had left into this ascent, she wouldn't be able to do it again without a break.

"I can leave it for another time," continued Evetez. "But who knows when the weather'll be this good again?"

He was right, of course. And the more people they could get to pick up on how it was done, the more advantage they would have. So she nodded in agreement. "I'll do it, sir."

"You're sure? That's great. Let's wrap this up, then." With a sharp whistle for attention Evetez soon had the entire group relocating to the building section he had pointed out to Rett.

"Taking shorter walls quickly, without climbing aids, is a specialty of Sergeant Rett's," Evetez told them. "Like this one." He pointed to the six-length building section in back of him.

"You call that short?" someone from R-troop asked with a whistle.

Rett was having second thoughts, which she soon dismissed. Thinking was giving her a headache.

"All right, so it's not exactly short," admitted Evetez. "But you people really ought to see how she does this. Fastest way to take off vertically short of launching a fighter. I'm hoping a few of us can pick up on it, since it can be used to our advantage. I've asked Sergeant Rett to demonstrate."

She started backing off, shedding peripheral gear as she went, handing it off to whatever helpful hand offered to take it from her. *Up, over, and done with it,* she thought as she tugged the half-gloves she wore to make sure they were snug. She calculated her approach. She'd be cutting it close, but no big deal.

"Sarge." Her second in command edged in to stand alongside her.

"Sergeant?" Rett dismissed any surprise she felt at Ariam's sudden appearance to the fact she still had all her mental blocks firmly in place. She checked her boots and make sure no mud slicked the soles.

"I'm not going to talk you out of doing this. But I've an odd feeling, aside from anything else you already know my feelings on," Ariam said. "Something's not right."

"What do you mean? Everything's been going great today. Is it me?" Without taking her main focus off the roof, she diverted attention to her sister. It was more than the concern that she would be overextending herself: Ariam's normal green energy aura was shot through with gray and dull orange. "Is it Evetez?"

"No, I'm not getting any off feeling from either of you," Ariam said. "And it's not a storm, at least I don't think so. There's nothing on the met forecast for the next few hours, I just checked."

Rett spared the younger woman a glance. Ariam always had a sensitivity to lightning storms. So had her brother. The charged atmospheric conditions messed with their Talent, creating static and mental turbulence in them just as it did in the air. "Nothing specific?"

Ariam shook her head. "Are you sure this is a good idea? It looks as if it's getting icy toward the top."

"Thanks, Ari. I see that. I'll be careful." Rett then set herself in a mode of total concentration. Deep breathing sent extra oxygen racing to energize her tired muscles as she began her approach.

* * * * *

Ariam stepped back, only part of her attention on what Evetez was telling the others about what to look for and to notice how Rett would arrive on the roof ready for anything.

Deities! Ariam gasped softly as the lieutenant's words sank in. Ready for anything! He'd put drill assistants on the roof to simulate enemy troopers? And he didn't tell Rett?

"Damn it, why couldn't I be a mindspeaker instead of an empath?" Although any projections she was currently making to Rett were being blocked, she added an extra sense of urgency and caution to them and quickly threaded her way to Evetez. "Lieutenant, you should have told her you put people up there."

"I'm sure she's figured that out already, Sergeant Ariam. I told her it was a demonstration. She did these all the time back in training. As soon as her foot hits that wall she'll know—she always did."

"Sir, that's still true, normally—" But at the stirring of surprise around her, Ariam stopped short.

Rett had started her run. Her sister had that effect on a lot of people, how she could go from absolutely motionless into full speed. Even those who expected it were often caught by surprise. Ariam overheard a few wonder aloud if the sergeant planned to go through the wall instead of up it, for as she drew closer her speed didn't falter.

"—but right now, that would be only if they're intent on deadly harm. She doesn't have the energy to scope anything more than that." Telling Evetez that wasn't interfering, she decided, it was important. "And she's blocking me."

Evetez tore his gaze away from Rett long enough for Ariam to see the comprehension dawn on his face. He took a breath, but Ariam grabbed his arm.

"Not now, sir, it's too late. Let's just hope for the best."

Even before Ariam had finished speaking, Rett's strong legs had turned into springs. Her leading foot landed head-height on the wall and the trailing leg pushed up with enormous impulsion. It appeared as if she ran straight up.

Of course this is a lot easier to do on a big tree, or a rough rock wall, thought Ariam. *I don't think she went up such a smooth surface as this before.* She caught a breath as Rett's third step slipped back a bit on the rain-wet wall, but her sister's upward momentum never stopped. With the next giant step the body that had been nearly perpendicular to the wall on the first step went parallel, almost home.

* * * * *

ONE MORE, RETT TOLD HERSELF, *reach up—Damn! Too short!* She redirected all the energy she had, mental and physical, into compensating for it. Her knee automatically pushed against the wall to give the extra assist needed to make up those three fingerlengths she lost. Her hands gripped the roof ledge, slipped on a light film of ice, but held.

The cautionary prickling at her consciousness she knew was from Ariam flared into full combat alert as she prepared to pull herself over the roof edge.

The greater part of her good mood vanished in an instant. Why hadn't she listened to Ariam? Why hadn't Evetez mentioned this was more than a wall climbing demonstration? An oversight on his part?

A bad assumption on hers, definitely. She should have asked, or should have made her ascent in a combat-ready mode in the first place.

Was his niceness today something meant to take her off guard so he could slip her up again? She was glad they had scheduled that conversation. Gladder still everyone else would be back inside when they had it.

Pushing off the wall with her legs, Rett varied her planned chin-up into a back flip intended to land her on the roof boots first. Her aim was true and she didn't worry about impact speed, since she'd lost speed making up that extra height. Maybe, she thought, she lost too much speed. The lack of thrust and the extra drag of Epnocian gravity really slowed the rotation of her body.

To make matters worse, her left hand touched the rooftop a lot sooner than she expected and slid out on a patch of ice. This drove her forward; her feet connected with the two MP drill aides and the ice patch ended. Her arm twisted and buckled under her. Landing hard on that shoulder, she swallowed a curse and clamped her teeth hard.

"I suppose by now we should have expected you boots first!" gasped a voice Rett knew. Lieutenant Wilkath. The drill detail leader and one of the handful of MPs she'd engaged with deadly force in the cargo bay a handful of days ago.

"And we even wore extra padding for this," said Vinzk, his familiar face appearing from beneath the Coalition style helmet and visor. He managed a breathless sort of chuckle.

"I'm glad of that." Rolling off her injured shoulder and getting to her feet, she angled the left side of her body away from him and offered her right hand to assist his ascension. "Soonjei—you all right, too?" Rett asked the third member of the team. As always, she felt relief at the confirmation.

Lieutenant Wilkath removed her headgear and goggles and nodded toward Rett's shoulder. "You went pretty hard on that ice, Sergeant. I thought I heard something crack. Are you——

Then a voice from below called: "Come on down, Sergeant!"

A tone Rett couldn't interpret was in his voice. It irritated her, and her temper flared. So she wasn't expecting the ambush, but she hadn't done a single thing wrong. She gave a demonstration. What was his problem with it?

"Are you all right?" Wilkath asked.

"Yes, sir. I'm fine." Rett saw right away the lieutenant or drill assistants in earshot weren't buying that. Stupid of her to even try. She should have kept her mouth shut, just nodded or diverted Wilcath's attention to the problems Soonjei seemed to be having with one of his harness straps.

"Sergeant, I distinctly heard—"

Rett flashed a smile she didn't feel at the MP lieutenant regarding her with such quizzical concern. "Have to go." She turned away before Wilkath could say anything else and went over the edge of the roof, hung her length from her good right arm, and let herself drop.

The jolt of the landing, no matter how her legs absorbed the most of it, nearly blinded her, bringing sharp nausea with the partial blackness. Only her level of tiff kept her upright.

She wasn't going to wait for the end of drill, she was going to have this out with Evetez right now. When the sick gray fog cleared from her vision, she swung to face him. First she'd push his Omni right up his skinny ass. Then the notepad.

* * * * *

"Oh, no." Ariam felt sick as one very strong emanation overwhelmed all the others she was filtering. Rett: hurt and angry enough to do something thoughtless.

Of course no one else around her was aware anything had gone wrong. To them, the entire maneuver had been one smooth, fast motion. It looked as if Rett had been completely prepared, just as Evetez had said. Evetez, also unaware of the sergeant's injury, was relieved.

"Wow, so that's how it's done. Now I finally know how she pulled that disappearing act on me in Branch."

During Rett's run, Jaq had moved to stand closer to Ariam. She spared him a glance. Beneath the admiration in his voice was a degree of the attitude she had witnessed him giving the sergeant in the hall that morning.

"Something happened, she's hurt," Ariam said.

"Huh?"

"Make a hole." Med brushed past them, the small man's narrow face wearing an expression as cold and flat as the landscape around them.

"She's hurt," Ariam said a little more forcefully.

"What? But I didn't see—" Jaq's attitude turned to concern in a flash. "Everything looked so smooth. Are you sure?"

"Oh, yes. And it's going to get worse." Biting her lower lip in worry, Ariam grabbed the Zetinorian's left arm and pulled him a few steps forward with her. "Deities, she's tiffed. Come with me Jaq, look at her eyes. I think she's going to kill him. I—"

Ariam's movement halted as Major Yidnar stepped into view, seemingly out of the damp mist. He was between Lieutenant Evetez and Sergeant Rett before either one took a deep breath. "Hold it, Evetez. You too, Sergeant. Dismiss your units, Lieutenant. Drill is complete for this day."

"Things just got worse," Ariam muttered, feeling faint but letting go of Jaq anyway. She wanted to avoid Yidnar's keen eyes but forced herself to seek them out, knowing without a shred of doubt what he was going to signal to her.

When Ariam turned to go on with the rest of them, it was as F-troop's leader.

She hoped it wasn't permanent.

* * * * *

PUSHING HER RIGHT HAND ACROSS her rain and sweat dampened face, Rett tried to change her combative expression to one more casual even as her heart sank. Major Yidnar never missed a thing. His present mien would have stopped one of the frequent quakes that shook the continent in mid-rumble.

She should have expected him to keeping a close eye, too. He'd said as much. Why hadn't she insisted on talking to Evetez during the break?

"Med Rhozev—stay."

Yidnar's terse order halted Med in his tracks. Rett didn't have to look at the medtech. She felt his eyes burning into her like twin energy beams.

The Major waited until Easy Force had gone before speaking again. "What happened up there, Sergeant?" His voice was dangerously calm.

"I mistakenly assumed the demonstration wouldn't involve others, sir. I had to make some last minute adjustments."

"And the arm?"

"Nothing much, sir. Slipped a bit. It's icy up there."

"Nothing much?" He took a step closer. "Let's see." His strong fingers closed over her left shoulder.

She kept her face still, hoping he wasn't going to try much more pressure than what he exerted already.

"You didn't talk to him yet, did you?"

She swallowed. "Actually—"

He didn't give her a chance to finish. "I thought you had more sense than this. I thought I did too, since I had a feeling something like this was going to happen." Yidnar's voice was low, furious, and meant only for her to hear.

"Yes, sir." He was right, and Rett felt sick to have failed his confidence. Not only his; she'd chosen to ignore Ariam, too. She'd failed both of them, and in turn, her platoon.

She should have simply given Evetez an overview of her problem earlier, even before they started drill, or missing that, definitely at the break. The detail could have come later. Either Evetez would have accepted that in the same good-natured mood he'd shown, or given her a clue that he was going to give her a hard time.

"I gave you your chance, Sergeant. You blew it."

"Yes, si-sir." Completely unprepared for the sudden increase in pressure that added physical emphasis on his anger, Rett's barely completed her reply before her vision went gray.

"You call this nothing much?" He didn't let up as he reached for her wrist with his free hand. "Dislocated shoulder. Fractured wrist and forearm. Nothing much." The combined assault of pain almost buckled Rett's knees. "Rhozev!" Yidnar snapped the medtech's name like an electric spark. At the same time, he released his grip on her so abruptly Rett lost her balance and fell at his feet.

"Yes, sir?"

"Escort Sergeant Rett to Medical. She is suspended from all Battalion activities and will be barred from Battalion areas until I consult with you again. I'm sure you'll want to impose your own restrictions as well. Any questions, see me after you've dealt with her."

"Yes, sir," said Med.

Suspended!

Stunned, Rett hardly realized Med was urging her to her feet. She fixed her face into the cool façade of emotionlessness demanded by formal situations, only to discover that, somehow, she'd kept the expression in place all along.

"Understood, Sergeant?"

"Yes, sir." Her right hand automatically went to her headband, pulled it off. It might have been someone else's arm stretching out before her, putting in the Major's hand. She felt nothing, the brush of his fingers against hers as he took the headband, the pain of her injuries, nothing. She was numb.

151

Giving Rett a final, icy glare, Yidnar turned to Lieutenant Evetez, who looked like someone just awakened from a bad dream to find out it was true.

"I want to see you in my office, Lieutenant. Now."

"This wasn't his fault," she wanted to say, but the words stuck in her throat. Her entire body was like that, stuck into position.

"Move it," urged Med, his steady touch breaking the spell. "You're in enough trouble. Don't add to it."

2.1.12 OUTSIDE MEDICAL, EPNOCE MAIN COMMAND
0535.08.26 (LOCAL RECKONING)

THREE HOURS LATER, RETT SAT SLUMPED on a bench outside the medical section. Her left arm had been immobilized from fingers to shoulder blade and fixed in a sling. The procedure hadn't gone well. The fractures in her forearm and wrist, along with old scar tissue and some thickening of her joints and tendons from repeated injuries, had complicated matters.

So, throughout the entire horrible session she'd sat there desperately wishing herself unconscious while listening to Med tiff and snarl that if she managed to stay alive to turn her third decade she'd more than likely need artificial replacements for seventy percent of the bones and joints in her body. There was nothing usual or comforting in his scathing tirade, either.

As if in punishment for her offense, Med hadn't offered to nerve block her in that absolutely marvelous pressure-point technique he used. Rett, in turn, was too upset to ask him, and since the pain was the only thing keeping her from wiping out completely, she focused on it rather than on what had happened.

She paid double for it now. Her arm felt as if it was going to blow off her body, she had a stress headache that threatened to liquefy her brain, and the rest of her was too sore to even think about. Somewhere else in the back of her mind, she realized she felt too cold sitting out here wearing nothing more on her upper half than the remnants of her inner shirt, a sling, and her bandages. At this point, however, she didn't care.

Somewhere in the background, she heard a quake warning siren, but she didn't react to it. It didn't matter.

I've been suspended. Not only grounded on Medical disability, but suspended. Sergeants Ariam and Trebor were in charge of F-troop now; R-troop's Sergeant Tris would take whatever place she had as Easy second and CTL. Rett was completely factored out of the equation until Med and Major Yidnar said she could return.

If they ever said she could.

153

Vaguely she noticed the building was vibrating slightly. She didn't care, not even when a sharper jolt a few seconds later sent her right off the bench and onto the floor.

Suspended. Cast out. Exiled. She wasn't allowed to contact anyone in the 2023rd for the duration. In turn, from the 2023rd only Med, Lieutenant Evetez, or Major Yidnar would be allowed to contact her, and then only if they thought it was absolutely necessary.

That meant she couldn't talk to Jaq. She couldn't talk to Evetez. Well, maybe Evetez, but he would have to come to her, and it would have to be authorized.

She pulled herself into a sitting position on the floor, leaning into the wall with her uninjured side. The rumbling and vibration ceased. Now the sounds were coming from her belly, and they weren't queasy, unsettled sounds: they were hungry sounds. How could her stomach possibly be hungry when eating was the last thing she wanted to do?

"Stop that," she snarled under her breath. Instead of eating, she wanted to find a deep, dark hole and cry herself into unconsciousness.

"Stop what? I haven't even started yet."

Huh? Deities, Etron's sitting right next to me and I never noticed him come. I guess I shouldn't have been surprised. After all, I didn't scope those MPs until the last second.

Rett was too tired and miserable to do more than glance at the pilot and mumble a greeting severely lacking in enthusiasm. "Go away."

"Can't. Quake. Stay where you are, get down low, no moving about, and all that. Medical stations are always in a sheltered section, so I'm staying where I am until the all clear."

"Great."

"I saw what happened outside. That Lieutenant Evetez of yours is—"

Rett cut him short with sudden viciousness. "Stop right there, Captain," she warned. "Lieutenant Evetez didn't make me get hurt. *I* did. This is the result of my own lack of foresight and bad judgment. I should have talked to him days ago." All clear or not, she pushed herself up and returned to the bench. At least her spot was still warm. "I don't want to talk to you, sir."

He ignored her, and also relocated from floor to bench, to Rett's annoyance. "I've been watching on and off for a while now. You know that. He's been pushing you harder than anyone. I agree that if you were having problems, you should have mentioned it earlier. I can also put together a valid reason why you didn't." He settled into a more comfortable position, which only raised Rett's ire.

"Despite that," he went on, flicking his fingers as if his preamble was of no consequence, "his asking you to take a tough wall like that, in this weather, with people waiting to take you out, barely two tendays into Epnocian gravity? It seemed a bit extreme. Even for Special Forces."

"We are drilling for actual Coalition encounters, under all conditions, Captain. If one of us can't handle a tough job, it's better to know it right now. Not when lives depend on it being done successfully!"

Etron didn't even blink in response to her angry outburst. Instead, he simply nodded and with sympathetic calm remarked, "You must be hurting pretty bad. Couldn't they give you anything for that?"

"There's the all clear. Go *away*, Captain." She turned sideways on the bench, putting her back to him. Pulling her knees up to her chest as much as her sling allowed, she proceeded to ignore the pilot.

He didn't move. "Is that thing about you being allergic to painkillers true?"

Rett hissed in disbelief. "Damn it! What hasn't the entire universe heard about me?" She suddenly wished she'd never met the fighter pilot. "Don't you get it? Leave me *alone*. Go away." She closed her eyes and rested her head in her hand.

Then she felt warm, firm fingers at the back of her neck, right in the knot that tension had tied there. When those fingers began to move, her eyes opened wide at the pilot's daring. Before she could decide whether she wanted to slug him or to get up and walk away, a feeling of relief began to spread, chasing the stiff chill that had settled. Reconsidering quickly, she decided that slugging him was a bad idea, since pilots were in short supply. As for walking away…well, maybe in another minute or two.

The captain easily avoided any movements that would aggravate her injury as his kneading went lower. His fingers and the heel of his hand worked down the column of her neck to the spot between her shoulder blades, and the screaming tautness of her overworked body and mind started to ease. Gradually, Rett relaxed.

"I'm sorry," she mumbled.

155

"Forget it."

"You're very skilled."

"Thanks. We get a lot of neck, shoulder, and upper back strain, so it helps to learn these techniques. It's amazing how it works on so many levels." His calm, matter-of-fact tone, as if he discussed the weather, was as soothing as his touch. "Are you all right now?"

"No. I wouldn't be here if I was all right."

"This is some landscape you have back here," he said then, softly. The slightest of shivers vibrated through his fingers and the heel of his hand. Since his contact remained firm and didn't avoid anything but the left side of her neck, shoulder, and back, he wasn't repulsed by what he saw or felt. Or, if he was, he did an excellent job hiding it.

"Been around."

"This doesn't aggravate any of them, does it?"

"No." She changed the topic abruptly. "I'm curious to know your interpretation of my reasoning. Or as you said, the 'valid reason why you didn't' in regard to speaking up before anything happened. Obviously, I haven't a clue."

"All right. Here's my basic take on it." He continued to work as he spoke. "For the past double handful of years, you—and whatever unit you were with at the time—had to keep going, no matter what. The enemy isn't going to stop for something as inconsequential as a sore muscle, let alone over two hundred sore muscles. And the levels keep building. You keep going. I guess after all that time, after all that moving forward no matter what, now it's pretty hard to separate drill from reality in certain aspects. Especially the way I've seen your people train."

She became very still, and for a moment his kneading stilled as well. She turned her head to the right just enough to catch a glimpse of him from the corner of her vision. "That makes a lot of sense. I'll have to think on it for a while."

"I know you're tired, but from what I'm hearing, you need to eat something."

Rett made a face, silently cursing her telltale stomach.

"So, how about an early dinner? I'm starving." His fingers started working their magic again.

"I guess I'm a bit peckish," she admitted.

"Peckish? After doing enough physical exercise, by yourself, to exhaust our entire squadron? Good deities, just the way you went up that wall would use an entire tenday's worth of calories."

Another loud growl from her belly refuted any attempt at denial. "Ravenous," she amended. "Right this minute, however, I'd rather starve than to have you stop what you're doing."

He chuckled. "No deal. I can do this any time, and if you don't refuel soon, you're going down. Let's go, then."

"It'll either have to be the main common area for the complex, or your section." The misery she felt from her banishment from Battalion stung her eyes and threatened to spill over, and she was glad she faced away from him. She angrily swiped at her face with her forearm. More than anything, that separation cut Rett deeply, more so than any wound she'd ever taken. "I'm not up to walking very far."

"Transport's not a problem. Where are you supposed to bunk?"

"Transient quarters. Main common area." This time she couldn't erase the dreary note of unhappiness from her voice. "Supposedly my kit was dropped there already. I can clean up a bit first."

Etron's warm hand moved from her neck to pat her good shoulder in understanding. "Let's just go right to my section. You need a change of scenery."

"I don't think I can. Even if I had the energy, I'm supposed to stay close to my quarters for the next two days, if not longer."

"Don't hate me, but I already asked and received permission to take you elsewhere for a couple hours." He held up his Omni to show he had been duly authorized by Med to see that she ate and had a chance to settle down. Two hours. After that, she was to return to her temporary quarters and sleep. "And maybe this suspension has a small positive side. For me."

Rett shot him a narrow-eyed glance. "Oh?"

"It's my digestion," he said in an aggrieved tone that was so affected she had to smile in spite of herself. He placed a surprisingly broad hand flat on his stomach. "You see," he explained, "if I was to have lunch with you in your section with all those floating heads, I think I'd start getting motion sickness. And in my job, that's not good."

157

2.1.13 SECTION V, 114TH AIRSPACEFIGHTERS
MAIN COMMAND, EPNOCE
0535.08.26

RETT DIDN'T REFUSE THE TECHNICIAN who came alongside the shortranger to offer assistance getting out as Etron finished the shutdown. She wondered if he'd arranged it, or if the technician had simply noticed she'd been out of sorts on the landing. She wasn't quite sure herself if she'd been unconscious or asleep.

She sat on a handy ledge nearby to wait for Etron. The captain wasn't long and soon she was being guided into the main corridor of the AirSpacefighter's section. It looked the same as any other part of the building; the only big differences were the insignia on doors or message boards and the predominant color of the uniforms.

No one looked at all surprised to see her with Etron. Rett was struck with the realization these people looked very clean. They flew things, after all, she reminded herself. Or serviced things that flew. Even if they didn't fly, not many of them at this base had to go out and fall down in the mud and slush.

Not that all AirSpacefighters had it so nice. She'd seen some horrendous temporary bases on Nyorfias: ships, pilots, and crew living in and operating under the most primal of conditions right along with the infantry units they were stationed with. Just as her unit had done.

To her surprise and dismay, Etron didn't take her to a regular mess area. Instead they went to the squadron's common lounge. Like Section C's lounge, the place was made to look like a comfortable, homey public house, such as one would find in almost any town on Nyorfias. Epnoce MainCommand didn't spare any effort when it came to realizing the value of having off-duty areas where people could relax in a homelike atmosphere.

She pulled up short, suddenly very much aware of just how disheveled she was. "Deities, Etron! Not in here."

She gestured at the mud that was splashed and dotted over her clothing and body. In addition, she was barely half-dressed. Repairs to her shoulder had left her torso clad only in bandages, sling and her sleeveless inner shirt. The top half of her uniform was rolled and tucked up into her utility belt. There were a few spots of blood on her bandages, and sweat stains on the slate gray inner shirt, which Med had cut up one side and closed again with a simple knot.

"Shit. I'm a mess. You might have let me get changed." She balked when he gestured her on. "*Look* at me. I don't know about your section, but we have appearance codes for ours."

Etron gave her a critical inspection from boots to hair. "You're wearing a shirt and you have your boots on. You're fine." He smiled, whipped out a comb and smoothed her hair. That motion only reminded her she wasn't wearing her headband, which made her feel even worse. With the careful delicacy of one handling live explosives, Etron made a minute adjustment to her sling. Then he neatened the untidy roll of material at her waist and flicked some dried mud from her legs.

A corner of Rett's mouth quirked. His efficiency was familiar. She'd seen its like hundreds of times. "From a large family?"

"I have six younger siblings, three of each. Does it show?"

"Just a little. Am I presentable now?" She doubted it. "We can go elsewhere—"

"You look beautiful. Don't worry about it. Worrying wastes time. Smile." He demonstrated, grimacing in such an exaggerated manner she had to give in. "There. Anyone looks, just smile. That's all they'll see. Come on."

He placed a hand lightly on her back to urge her inside, where he found a cozy corner table. The sight of the comfortable chairs flanking it made Rett's tired muscles wobble and she gratefully sank into the nearest of them. Just the short walk from the little jumper had burned up any temporary energy she had.

"Sergeant Ariam tells me you're fond of mushrooms…well, today is Mushroom Day at this base."

"Is it?" Come to think of it, she'd had the same mushroom pilaf for breakfast as Ariam produced last night. And there was a different sort of mushroom dish at lunch. Probably why she didn't have much trouble getting it down.

"Every Fourthday is. You've been here a while and haven't noticed? You have been busy."

159

She had noticed. At the same time, she'd had so much else on her mind she hadn't taken the time to notice it the way she should have. She realized now that Fourthdays had been perhaps the only days on which she'd actually taken more than that superficial interest in her food.

"We have a cook who can do things with mushrooms that would leave your mouth weeping with joy. Still want to leave?"

"Here is fine. Besides, I don't think I can move. I hope you have time to fly me back."

"I will. Right to your door, where a med assistant will be waiting to clean you up and tuck you in."

"Great." Rett settled back. "Just great." Of course she expected Med to have an entire array of assistants on call. He'd have her bedded down in the medical facility otherwise.

Etron went off to get them something to drink.

So here I am with Etron when I should be talking to Jaq. Only I can't, because I'm suspended. I can't even ask someone else to give him a message. What a mess. I wish Pam were here.

The pilot returned with a carafe of tea and a mug in one hand, a full beaker in the other. A basket of nibbles was clamped between two fingers, and a ridiculously pleased smile was plastered across his dark face.

"Brought you a little something from home." He presented the beaker with a flourish. "Just came in a handful of days ago. If I wasn't flying later, I'd be lifting a glass with you."

She stared at the familiar ruddy hue of the beverage before lifting the glass for a sniff. "Treetop bitter," she said with surprise. *One advantage of knowing how much time I have off. The one-off limit doesn't apply. I can go all out and have two.*

A mental roll of her eyes followed that thought. Not today. As tired and rundown as she was, she'd better stick to one, and have most of it with her meal.

Taking a tentative sip, she grinned her approval at Etron. All at once, she felt sixteen again, having her first brew served in a Treetop public house without benefit of being accompanied by one of her parents. It tasted like home. "Thank you."

He pushed the basket of small, spiced snacks closer. "It won't be long until the food is ready, but have some of these while we wait."

She made a selection from the assortment and bit experimentally into one of the round, flat wafers of roughly ground, toasted grains. The combination of spices was unusual to her palate, slightly hot. "These are good."

Etron popped a ball of something coated in seeds in his mouth and busied himself with his tea. "Tell me something," he said after swallowing his crunchy nibble. "How come you went to Special Forces instead of AirSpacefighters? Didn't your basic training unit recommend you? Your reaction speed is just short of miraculous, even when you're tired."

"You know, ever since I knew I was enlisting, I wanted to end up in AirSpacefighters. It was my goal all through Basic. I even thought about it before the war started, as my militia service," she admitted. "Then when Basic was over and it was time to choose secondary training, I saw the Special Forces notice and just couldn't pass it up. It was a dare, and at the time, I needed one. I really expected Special Forces to reject me during the evaluation. But...as you can see, they didn't, and my plans changed."

Smiling a little wistfully, she remembered the incredible joy she'd felt in the cockpit of Etron's fighter. "But, deities, I'd sure like to fly. I always wanted to. Like I told you, I had a dream of it. Not just sitting there, but in control."

"You would?" asked Etron, his brown eyes alight. His hand stopped halfway to the dispenser of sweetener. "*Really* would?"

Rett picked up her drink, suddenly very interested in the deep copper color of the brew. "Etron, it was just a wild thought. Why do you ask? Are you recruiting?"

"Maybe." Etron put his forearms flat on the table and leaned forward. "Why does it have to be a wild thought? It doesn't have to be a dream, either. You won't be doing anything for a while. You'd get mighty bored doing nothing, and you've heard me talk about my CO. She'd break your other arm in a second if that would keep you over here."

Not sure what he was getting at, she sidetracked a little. "You told her about that night, didn't you? You got in trouble for it."

"Of course I did. Colonel's like your sister—she's an empath, and just a tick below Adept level at that. She can smell a guilt trip before it's on a landing final. So it's best to just come clean right away."

"I didn't hear anything about it."

"That's because you didn't do anything that was against *your* operational procedures. Skated close, but didn't go over. Don't be surprised if the rules get changed in a couple months."

He went after the sweetener again and carefully added a few drops of the concentrated syrup of spicebush root into his tea. "Anyway, the Colonel ranted and raved at me for all of fifteen minutes, suspended me for five days, and then hatched that bright idea about me watching you guys in drill."

"She suspended you." Rett winced.

He shrugged as he stirred his tea. "Nothing more than I expected."

Was he insane? He knew he'd get suspended for flying her? "But pilots are in short supply."

"It wasn't as bad as yours seems to be." He waved his hand. "I would have been allowed to fly combat missions if necessary."

"And your CO had to have talked to Major Yidnar to get you clearance to be in otherwise restricted areas."

"She did, and I was there for most of it, so I know it had to do with her bright idea of watching the moves you people make and applying them to flight. She didn't mention to him at all that I was…grounded, just that I would be on a special assignment."

"That was nice of her."

"Of course my CO would have taken things a bit farther if I hadn't learned anything from the experience."

"And you did."

He nodded. "On more than one level. And I still am, or I wouldn't be continuing to show up four times a tenday. As much as I'd like to say you were the only attraction."

It was a clear opening to flirt. What would Ariam do right now? Probably pout a bit and make a comeback.

But I'm glad I wasn't the main reason he was there, and I'm not Ariam, she reminded herself, adding the hard fact that she felt not in the least flirtatious. Just hungry, tired, and in the need for diversion. Getting suspended on a disciplinary action wasn't something that inspired her, either. How could he shrug his off like that? Was he really that blasé?

"You can learn something useful from your situation, too." He wasn't flirting now. Some idea or another was percolating behind his luscious brown eyes.

"I'm under orders to do nothing." Rett tried to focus her tired mind on his aura for a clue, but the effort was beyond her present capabilities. She settled for watching him closely instead.

"With your Battalion," he reminded, and selected another snack from the basket. "Try this one." He handed it to her and chose another for himself.

She chewed the nibble without tasting it, thinking hard. Did she dare hope for rescue from the deadly dullness her exile presented? Or, somewhere beneath the thoughtful exterior of the pilot, was there someone who lived to get in trouble and never mind who went with him? She had to find out what he was up to. *But don't get yourself sucked into anything, because you're in enough trouble.*

"Med told me this would be off in two days." She picked at the sling. "The bones are already set, I'd only have to be careful about falling down until they finish with me in therapy."

"Well then. What are we waiting for?"

"Dinner." Rett wasn't going to yield on her mushrooms unless the building was attacked by the enemy. And from the enticing aroma that was beginning to waft toward them, she'd have to think twice about it even then.

"And you need to rest." He frowned at her. "No wonder you got into such a state, the way you've learned to hide exactly how tired you are." The pilot leaned forward again. "Give it the two days. You're at rock bottom. Don't deny it," he ordered, his eyebrows making a bridge over his proud nose. "So rest, eat, catch up on yourself a bit, and see what your medtech says two days from now. We can do the ground-work while you're still limited, only mental activity and some manual input involved there."

"I don't want to do anything that's going to get either one of us in more trouble." As tempting as it was.

163

"Studying is going to get you in trouble?"

"It already has," she mumbled. Her need to understand the situations her unit would face on Epnoce had led to all that self-imposed extra studying during her rest periods. "I'm not that quick when it comes to scholastic matters. I especially don't have much of a head for tech."

"Rett. Don't kill this off before giving it a chance. You've told me already you like a challenge. Let's see what might have happened if you had gone to AirSpacefighters all those years ago."

"Why? Do you have time? Don't you have to fly missions and practice maneuvers and things? Not to mention watch Easy Force drill four times a tenday?"

Captain Etron stared at her, any lightness in his face and voice replaced by an expression both wistful and serious. "I wish you might have seen your own face when you were looking at my ship that night. It was that expression that moved me to take you up, even though I knew the cost. And that look is why I'm making such an offer now." The tip of his forefinger skated around the rim of his mug. "The personal attraction I feel for you has very little to do with any of that."

"One would almost think," she said carefully, "that it would have everything to do with it."

He shook his head. "No. If all we had was a physical attraction, I doubt we'd be sitting here right now. You see, I would have said something charming, and went on with my mission. You would have gone back to your section. And that might have been the end of it right there. The look on your face changed everything. Deities help the man you might ever look at the same way."

Rett didn't know what to say to that, so she settled for taking another sip from her glass.

He shook his head a little and started to smile. "As far as having time to teach you, a couple hours here and there when our free time might overlap is easy to manage. And I won't deny that I hope to take advantage of the serendipity that brought us together for more personal reasons…since if you decide to take me up on my offer, I'd also get to spend more time alone with you in the bargain. That is, if there's time after lessons. Or am I wrong in thinking we had a mutual attraction for something more than fightercraft?"

"No. You weren't wrong. But that moment in the hangar was unusual. I'm not usually so…spontaneous."

At some unseen signal in the direction of the bar, he nodded. "Food's ready, be right back with it." Standing, he leaned toward her, reaching to touch her face with gentle fingers. "I'll take what you said into serious consideration. I also understand that you're in no condition for anything but some companionship and conversation, which I would be delighted to provide. But later, I hope you don't mind if I try to change your mind about being spontaneous again."

Rett almost forgot to breathe in the next moment, for the intense expression that darkened his gaze and caught her by surprise had nothing to do with flirting, or flying.

2.1.14 MEDICAL SECTION, EPNOCE MAIN COMMAND
0535.08.28 (LOCAL RECKONING)

RETT SAT PATIENTLY WHILE MED removed the rigid splints and tape that had secured her injured arm and shoulder. He probed; he prodded, his eyes never leaving her face. Any evidence of pain, no matter how slight, never escaped Med.

"Don't lift your arm, but rotate the shoulder, easily."

She obeyed. To herself she admitted it was still sore, but nothing she couldn't handle. *If I had to.* She knew now that she didn't want to try lifting her arm just yet, though.

Med just made a "hmm" sound and gestured her over to the scan unit. He arranged her forearm over the lower surface, brought the top unit down, and studied the video displays. Each screen showed something different, but she only paid attention to those she was able to interpret.

"All right," grunted Med, pushing aside the diagnostic unit. "You're on the mend, but it's still going to be a few days."

"Okay, Med."

"However, I've taken precautions. I know you too well." There was no grumbling, sour, tiffing-off air about Med as he faced her.

Awarding the medtech her undivided attention, Rett waited for him to continue.

"First shift, you can go wherever you like, except in areas occupied by the 2023rd, or where we may be training. Second shift, you're restricted to the main common area. Third is to be spent in your quarters in said area, preferably sleeping. If Easy Force's shift schedule changes, I'll let you know so you can make the same adjustments."

Rett nodded, trying not to look too hopeful or grateful for that concession.

"Every MP and security person on this base is under strict orders that all gym and drill areas are off limits to you. And until I clear you for more activity, anyone who sees you involved in any form of physical exertion—aside from walking, eating, or other normal biological functions—is instructed to stop you in any manner necessary, up to and including extreme force, and personally escort you to me or Major Yidnar. Conscious or unconscious."

"I'll be good, Med," she promised, her penitence unforced. "I want to go back to Active soon, so I won't screw up this recovery, don't worry."

"I am worried. And you should be, too. You're under my orders now, and I mean what I say. If you don't catch up with yourself, I can permanently suspend you from any combat active military duty. Or any military duty altogether."

"You wouldn't."

"Try me." The little medtech crossed his arms over his chest and regarded her with narrowed eyes. "MainCommand may argue against my decision, but they wouldn't be able to change it."

"Med, you know my word is good! I'll eat, I'll sleep, I'll—"

"I want results. If you want to go on combat active again, I want results!"

167

"Yes, Med." Every bit as stung and hurt as she'd felt after Major Yidnar walked away from her, she looked down at her hands.

The medtech wrapped her forearm and shoulder with a light, elastic bandage to help support the still-healing injuries, his face set in his usual sour expression. This time he wasn't muttering under his breath in the monologue so familiar to any of them who were injured. The silence put a distance between them that even numbed the firm contact of his hands.

"I want you here every day without fail at start of second shift, whether I'm here or not. Someone will be waiting for you, and deities help you if you're late. You're definitely having some chemical imbalances, but it's nothing I've seen before. Given that odd metabolism of yours, who knows where it's coming from. I'll want to get samples daily until I figure it out. I've noticed a change in how you feel to me, too. Ariam's in agreement, you've felt off in her opinion, too."

"I know that. I asked her to check me. I don't know what was making me feel strange since we left Nyorfias." Rett decided she had nothing to lose by admitting that much.

"I've felt something even before then, but different than what it's been lately. Is there anything you want to tell me?"

"No, sir," she mumbled. All Med needed to know was that she had harbored an alien in her head and managed to hide it from him. She'd really be in trouble then.

"Questions?"

"I really need to talk to Jaq." She knew that would be denied, but the words came out anyway.

"As of right now, I'm the only contact you're going to have with anyone in this Battalion until further notice."

She bit the inside of her bottom lip for a moment. "Can I use this hand and arm at all?"

"Not flaming likely. And if you're thinking of trying I'll block you so well you won't even be able to blink for a tenday."

"Med—"

"I mean it," he snapped. "You want me to go ahead? There's room for you here. I'll have you all hooked up in a matter of minutes." He reached for her arm, his slim, steely fingers closing over her wrist.

Feeling lightheaded in the face of his threat, which he was fully capable of carrying out, Rett licked her lips and took a breath, forcing herself to remain still. Med knew exactly what hurt her the most.

"I just wanted to know if it was okay to use my Omni, a notepad, or a work terminal for manual input." The small, resigned tone in her own voice surprised her and she didn't even bother to control the tremor on the last few words.

Med considered that, loosening his grip. "All right, as long as the arm is supported. Wear this. I've sent a few more to your billet." He handed an overshirt to her. "Your messaging and mail access to anyone in the 2023rd are cut off, you know."

She nodded, her throat hurting. "Yes." She knew that would be the case and hadn't even bothered to check. She wasn't sure she could handle seeing the "access denied" message. "Thanks, Med." Cautiously, she stuck her left arm into the sleeve of the overlarge shirt he'd handed her.

"What have you planned, then?"

"Read, study, log some notes. Nothing much else I can do," she mumbled.

"Besides eating—and keeping it down—and sleeping?" he reminded pointedly. "We see how it goes for a few days. Then I may clear you for some light volunteer duty for a few hours each day." He helped her get the shirt on the rest of the way. "Keep it there," he ordered, settling her arm in the sling. "Need more bottoms like that?" He nodded to the faded old fatigues she wore.

She held back her temptation for a sarcastic answer. Besides these old fatigues, which she usually wore to work out in, she didn't have a single stitch of clothing that wasn't a uniform of some kind, and he damn well knew it. "Yes, I suppose I will need more."

"I'll take care of that, too. And since you're not going to move much faster than a walk for a while—an easy one—you won't need to wear any breast support. Don't even try to get into one."

"Yes, Med."

"The sling and support bandage had better stay on: shower, sleep, sex, whatever you do. If I could lock them on you, I would," he muttered under his breath. "I'll pull the scheduled assistants, but let me know right now if you're planning on struggling alone with one arm in matters of bathing, dressing or whatever else is going to be difficult. I'll make alternate billeting arrangements." He gave a meaningful nod in the direction of the patient annex.

I'm down and he's going for the kill. Starting with the very instant Etron had returned her to her quarters two days earlier, assorted med assistants had shown up at regular intervals. Whenever she'd stuck her nose out the door between those times there had always seemed to be a handful of people right outside all but falling over each other to fulfill her slightest need.

For a second she considered things might be a lot more private and peaceful if she stayed here. Only for a second. As many as there seemed to be, at least the assistants were inclined to be in a cheerful mood. "I'll ask for help. Can I go now?"

"Rett, I'm not kidding. Remember that."

"I'm not likely to forget."

He gestured wearily. "Get out of here. I'll see you again tomorrow."

Etron waited outside. "Well?"

"Everything is wonderful. I'm still suspended, I'm on disability, Med has me under surveillance, and he's just waiting to put the whole of me into a sling if I don't settle down." Her voice was as sour as the medtech's. "With a lock," she added.

"Yes." Etron held up his Omni. "Looks like the entire base is on alert."

"Aww…shit." The entire base? She wished she could disappear.

"Don't worry. People care about you. You got hurt. You need time to recover. That's how they are going to look at it, not that you did something wrong."

Easy for him to say. She stood perfectly still, muscles clenched the length of her body, her breath hissing through her teeth. Why didn't she just turn right around and ask Med to render her unconscious for a month or so?

"Unless you're counting being too dedicated to your job in this incident, you really didn't do anything wrong."

Rett turned on him, disbelief closing her throat. How could anyone say that? Of course she had done something wrong; as a result she'd been injured. She could have prevented the whole situation if she had simply opened her mouth. Had her injury happened under any other circumstances, she wouldn't have been suspended but merely placed on disability. And she had no illusions about being irreplaceable, as platoon leader or soldier. F-troop would continue with or without her, as would everything else. But it was for the life and death of Nyorfias they all fought. How is it possible to be "too dedicated" to ending the threat of a Coalition takeover?

Etron stood his ground and cut her off before she found words. "I think you know what I mean. The separating drill from reality situation?"

Finally, she had to nod, releasing her breath in a long, slow exhale.

"Hey. Don't worry."

"I have to."

"Well then, let's see if I can take a note from your operating manual and cause a diversion. Did you ask about manual input?"

"As long as I don't have to throw a notebook or control pad at anyone, it's fine. But I really don't think it's a good idea right now."

She was having second thoughts about this. Not only about the entire learning to fly thing; she didn't want to start going off with Etron without talking to Jaq.

Etron sighed. "Think about it on the way over, but let's go, even if it's only for lunch. I can see you need to be away from here and I've the jumper outside."

"Excuse me, Captain," interrupted a familiar voice in a very unfamiliar tone, "but if you don't mind my delaying anything you had plans for, sir, I need to have a word with Sergeant Rett."

Evetez.

Now what?

"Schedule's flexible," said the captain matter-of-factly. "Don't mind a bit."

"Sergeant?" inquired Evetez.

The familiar, sick ache rose so quickly Rett's vision started to blur. Gritting her teeth, she swallowed back bile and hoped the clammy sweat that had broken out in response would be credited as a leftover from her meeting with Med. When she turned to face the lieutenant, she made sure her face was blank, composed. She ordered her stomach to behave.

"We never had a chance to talk the other day," said Evetez, his face and demeanor as blank as she hoped hers was. "Will you give me a few minutes now, Sergeant?"

It was clearly a request with opportunity for her to refuse. For a moment she considered taking that option, making him suffer for every time he'd tormented her from the first moment they'd met. Just as quickly she dispelled the notion.

All she wanted was to have her friend back. If she could still salvage that much, almost everything that happened would be worth her present condition. So she nodded and followed him when he signaled they should move a few steps farther down the corridor.

"I'm glad I caught you," Evetez said. "The Major sent me for some tests, probably knew you'd still be here. He cleared me to talk with you. Do you need to sit down?"

"No, thanks. I'm fine."

"You're sure this time?"

She nodded. "Yes, sir."

"Forget that." He reached up and pulled off his headband, then the junior lieutenant's filled circle and group leader's open diamond from his shoulders. "I would like to talk with you as Evetez."

"All right."

His face was troubled, making it look longer and older than it usually did. "I don't know what got into me since we started here. Almost as if…" He shrugged, at once a gesture of impatience and apology for sidetracking. "I don't know how to say this."

"Look," Rett said, "the point is, we've both been off normal since the transfer. Not to mention stupid."

He winced slightly, but didn't deny it.

Rett dropped all her barriers and put her heart and soul into her words. "As for what to say, you know me. Simple and short's the best."

Evetez leaned against the wall, the old, merry, deities-may-care expression coming into in his blue eyes. A grin tugged at the corners of his wide mouth.

"Simple and short. Back to the old, laconic Rett? I thought 'Mage and I managed to sophisticate that backwoods mountain kid." He hesitated, dismissing the moment of levity from his face and voice. "I apologize."

She would have accepted it at that, but he needed to continue.

"But it's not that simple. No matter what might have triggered it, I've had my head up my ass lately—and in front of the entire damned Battalion."

"Quite a feat for a bubblehead," Rett said lightly.

"Isn't it though? Must be the stress of being in command." He rolled his eyes. "It should have been you. I told him that when he offered it to me. He said you turned it down. You didn't think you were ready. But you are. You were."

Rett shook her head. "No way."

"I didn't come to argue. Did you know I was suspended since then as well, at least until about an hour ago?"

"No, I didn't. I'm so—"

He pressed a lean finger to her lips. "No, just listen. Simple and short isn't going to work, and it'll take longer if you interrupt. I've already given the others an apology. I thought things were going back to normal the other day. I was glad when you wanted to talk me, because I wanted to talk to you, too. To get matters sorted out, and get things with the unit sorted out. It all seemed so right, until... well."

For a moment he looked away, a flush of color staining his cheeks. "I just can't believe I was treating you that way since we started work. In some ways it was as if...as if I was watching a stranger take over my body. I saw exactly what the problem was, but instead of fixing it, instead of talking to you, asking what your limitations were, I got tiffed because you wouldn't tell me first. Then I tried to justify it by thinking that since you kept going, nothing was wrong."

She shivered at his words. He was feeling manipulated and out of control, too?

"You were absolutely right about my parameters, on a lot of levels," Evetez said. "They left out some important factors." He slowly reached toward her to finger the edge of her sling, a deep pain in his gaze. "And look what happened. I hurt one of the best friends I've ever had, inside and out. Can you forgive me?"   173

"I'm every bit as much at fault in this. Don't forget that," Rett said. "And as well-trained as we're supposed to be, we're still human, and we screw up. So let's stop blaming ourselves and each other and just get on with fighting something that's really worthwhile."

Evetez let out a breath. "You're right, b—"

This time it was her finger that pressed against his lips. "Please. You've said enough." She wanted to remember the consequences of letting things get out of control, but she wanted, at the same time, to forget it ever happened. "You're my friend. Of course I forgive you."

"May I explain?"

"Will it make what happened any different? Or make you feel better?"

He had to think about it. "No. Not really."

"So we would try to justify our actions all day long without getting to the point." She smiled. "What would make you feel better?"

"If you and I pick up where we left off in Branch as far as personal relationships go, and pick up when we worked so well together before that. You?"

"That's what I want, too."

Evetez curled his fingers around her wrist and lowered her hand from his face. "No holding back. On any count. If I start going off again, you tell me. And if anything I'm asking is too much and it's not a life and death situation, you tell me too. Promise?"

"Yes." She twined her fingers with his and squeezed gently. "I promise."

He pulled her into an embrace, being careful of her injured arm and shoulder.

Rett leaned close, tightening her hand in his. Likewise, Evetez leaned into her just enough to balance them equally. The familiarity of the gesture touched her deeply. For a moment, her eyes blurred, then she smiled into his shoulder and let out a long, soft, sigh. "Good to have you back, 'Vetez."

At last something was right again. That was all that mattered.

After a few quiet moments, Evetez said, "Thanks, Rett."

She lifted her head, her spirits lifting with it. "You and Semage are my best friends. Nothing can change that. But I have to admit, things got so screwed up I was worried."

He agreed with a roll of his eyes. "Speaking of screwing up, you'd better not do anything to screw up your recovery. I need you. Doesn't look good on my command record to have you suspended before you've even really started."

Feeling lighter and happier than she had in a long time, Rett laughed at his portentous frown. "How about the commander being suspended on his own command record?"

He snorted. "Yeah. Well. There's that, as well." The grin that had started to form reverted to a frown again, this one regretful. "Our time's up. I'm sorry."

"I understand." So it was back to exile, and no matter how much she wanted to, she couldn't ask him for any favors, or even speak to him again unless he asked her a direct question.

"Get going. And don't screw up your recovery, we need you. I need you." Evetez leaned in to kiss her cheek, then after a nod to Etron, turned and disappeared through the main doors of the medical section.

2.1.15 TRAINING AREA, SECTION V, EPNOCE MAIN COMMAND
0535.08.31 (LOCAL RECKONING)

THREE DAYS LATER, RETT WAS finding out exactly what it was like in the front half of a fighter's cockpit. She thought the previous two days of study had been hard. First all the reading. Then the vids, which helped make sense of what she had read. Each day, there was a fairly simple test on what she'd absorbed for that day, but simple or not, she sweated through them and wondered just what in two worlds she was getting herself into.

She had to wonder again as she sat deep in the pilot's seat of a flight simulator pod, comparing two Omnis and two notepads full of notes and schematics with the bewildering array of instruments, video displays, and controls.

She didn't bother to keep track of hours or minutes, not even counting off the time in her head as she did by rote while working or on a combat assignment. Etron hadn't given her any time limits, saying only that he'd check back on her later. When the simulator pod rocked slightly, she figured it had to be later.

"It's just me. Look at you, you're absolutely drenched. What were you doing, trying to lift this thing?" Etron's curly head came into view on her left. He took another step up the footrail in the side of the simulator pod.

"I think running drill is easier," she grumbled. "I haven't had to memorize so much in a long, long time." She pushed her fingers through her hair. Although she was exhausted, the arrangement finally made sense and she had a new sense of confidence in what she'd studied.

"Tell me about this machine."

Of course she expected him to ask. She told him what she knew.

The simulator pod, inside and out, was an exact replica of the Zen G-series dual-duty atmospheric/space fightercraft currently being flown on Epnoce. She had been surprised to learn that the very same Filania Zen, after whom that big glacier and forestry district in Branch was named, had been an aerospace engineer. The current design hadn't changed much at all—structurally—from the patrol craft the original settlers had used. As a matter of fact, Zen's design for the frame of the craft had been adapted by several other GTC member worlds; even GTC Central spacefighters used a slightly modified version of it.

"Very good. Ready to get out of here?"

Rett checked her chrono. "More than ready, but has it been three hours already? You're early."

"Every once in a while that happens."

She let her head go back—not too far, since the headpad behind it hadn't been activated to react to the pilot's motions. The degree of stiff soreness in her neck and shoulders amazed her, especially the left. Just from sitting! It wasn't hard to guess how and why Etron had acquired his skill in relieving neck, shoulder and back tension.

The captain reached in and snatched up the Omnis and the larger notepads, either dropping them to the floor or handing them off to someone. The latter, probably, since Rett didn't hear anything fall and there was a technician on duty in the simulator area.

She shifted, ready to get out, stretch, and make a trip to the lavatory. Etron shook his head. "Not so fast. This isn't any different from a straight book lesson. Before we go, I need to give you a test."

"Wasn't that what you just did?"

"Well, it's nice to know the history of the simulator and the fighter-craft, sure, but we're more interested in what you've learned about the cockpit and all these lovely controls and instruments."

She groaned. "You're evil. My brain's ready to implode already."

"Don't psych yourself out. You can do this." He started pointing. "What's that?"

"Navigational center: nav computer and nav aides, for atmosphere and spaceflight." There. That wasn't so bad. She puffed out a breath.

"This?"

"Engine systems center: fuel, engine temperature, external structures, outboard jet systems for both atmospheric and spaceflight."

For fifteen minutes he fired off one question after another, each one getting more complicated and coming faster than the last. Rett had a headache by the time he finished.

"You're quick enough, and have a clear head under pressure," Etron said with approval and encouragement. "Once you actually start interacting with the ship, it'll get easier. You'll be able to locate everything with your eyes closed, identify it by touch, just as you can with your own gear."

"You're not going to make me break down the engines on this thing and put them back together by touch, are you?"

He chuckled. "No."

"That's good."

"Just the instrument panels in front of you. For starters."

"Shit."

"You can't get out and repair your engines in flight, but if one of these gizmos goes out on you, and you take care of everything else you can, the craft is flying well, and you have time to do something about it, knowing what to look for can make the difference in an infinite variety of situations. Besides, it'll help you better understand how they operate. We've models of them all. In a few days, when you get to that point, you can take them with you to work on."

"That'll help." Rett twisted her shoulders a little, grimacing. "If Med sees me, he's never going to believe I've been sitting almost perfectly still."

"He won't see you, or even get close enough to trigger off that talent of his. My spies are everywhere."

Rett grunted. He wasn't kidding. Although they pretended to be oblivious, the entire squadron, from the freshest arrival out of training right up to the CO, was aware she was Etron's "project".

Knowing Etron wasn't going to get in trouble and that she didn't have to skulk around the 114th's area was a good thing. Her daily schedule for the past few days had worked out well. She came over to the AirSpacefighter's section at the start of her free time, catching a ride with one of the various personnel who ran errands in complex rovers. Since Etron was on duty, she simply went to the study area and started in on the assignment he'd given her the day before. Someone was always around in case she had questions. When his duty shift ended, halfway into her free time, he came and quizzed her on what she'd studied. Afterward, they went to get lunch. By that time Rett had to leave for her daily appointment with Med.

If Etron had a moment, he went over what she was to study until his free time, which now occurred halfway into first shift. He always arranged that if he was on a mission or occupied elsewhere, someone else would be on hand in case she needed help.

"You'll have the basics down in no time. And with all you already know about the weather, we just have to get you up to speed on Epnocian atmospheric patterns and how everything affects your aircraft.

"And then, of course, some hands-on experience." He leaned into the cockpit to help her out. "Come on, this lesson is over."

Soon she stood on the floor, glorying in the simple gift of being able to stretch. Her stomach rumbled.

"Thought that thing was starting up for a second there." Etron grinned, nodding toward the simulator pod from which she'd just alighted. "It's early, but I'm on empty too."

Rett carefully worked her healing shoulder with her fingers. "Ow. Damn. I'm for home and a wash, as soon as we've had lunch."

"You're not put off, are you?"

"I'm a bit…scared of all that book and classroom stuff, but I'm trying not to think too far ahead. But put off? Deities, no."

"That's good, since I've managed to get you scheduled in the simulator for the next five days. Captain Teague and Technician Brent volunteered a few hours of their free time those days to help you out, since they're my days to watch Easy Force in drill, so I won't be around at all. Someone will take you back over afterward, too."

Rett wondered for a moment if AirSpacefighters had some sort of bet running on whether or not Etron would manage to make a pilot of her. Before she could ask, Etron stepped closer, his brown eyes twinkling.

"Here's the best part." He paused for effect, letting her know he had some great secret and was going to make her stand there and speculate about it. "If you're still available and on the same rotation, you'll be starting some jumper ground training with Major Deeclar as soon as you've learned the fighter's instrument panel. He'll give you an hour and a half on odd days. When you're cleared medically, he's willing to take it farther."

Rett had to take two steps backward to keep her balance. "Deeclar?"

"He asked if you were a tall, skinny kid who didn't talk much and tried to hide a pair of big, dark eyes under a black fringe halfway down your nose."

Her mouth opened a little more. *And he remembers me?*

"I said I couldn't confirm anything but the height and eyes, but once I got going on those, he said he remembered you. Apparently you were eyeing up his smokejumper the same way you were looking at my fightercraft. Of course, he'd like to meet with you before you start working with him, and he wanted me to ask if it was all right if he joined you for lunch tomorrow, since I won't be around."

"Me? H-he wants to h-have lunch with *me?*" Not only did her voice crack, but the dreaded stammer of her youth crept back. She swallowed, took a deep breath, and cleared her throat. "Why?"

"I guess he needs to see that your hair isn't covering your eyes. Not a good thing for a pilot, you know," teased Etron.

179

When he handed over her Omni, Rett drew him closer with her right arm and kissed him. She intended the kiss to be a friendly gesture of thanks. Instead, like a heat-seeking missile, it detonated on contact.

This time, she kept a firm control of her sense of time and place while allowing herself to enjoy Etron's response. As a result the moment was short, but intense enough to drench Rett with sweat all over again.

He stepped back the same moment she did, his brown eyes nearly black. "Want to skip lunch? I'll guarantee you won't put any strain on the arm."

Etron...he was so very tempting. She felt comfortable around him and from what she'd seen from the beginning, he was patient and generous. For a long moment she looked back at him, torn between her need for time and the need to sample the delights the melting depths of his brown eyes promised her.

What about Jaq? her heart asked. *How would he feel about it?* She was worried about the coolness he'd shown since Etron showed up. She had a disquieting thought that no matter what she did, Jaq was going to take it in the worst possible way—he already had. *You talked about that with Ariam.*

Of course, Ariam had also said Rett had a right to do as she pleased. Jaq knew full well Nyorfians had different social habits. She wasn't going to hold back her life because it would hurt his feelings, was she? Damn it.

"I can see this isn't the right time," Etron said then, his face and eyes returning to normal. He smiled at her. "Answering such a question shouldn't be an ordeal."

"I need more time."

"And you're starving and tired. Do the transient quarters have those bathing tanks with the jets, or only those communal pools in the gym—which is off limits to you?"

"Med made sure I've the amenities," Rett said, feeling stupidly grateful she didn't have to make a decision yet.

"Next time I ask," he said in that voice as hypnotizing as sweet woodsmoke, "I'll try to get the whole of first shift off, and we'll skip the flight lesson altogether. And bring lunch with us."

She managed a nod. *Why does this have to be so difficult? Damn it!* There wasn't anything she could do about Jaq right now unless she broke the terms of her suspension.

But no matter what, the truth remained: she was sore and tired, physically and mentally. No matter who was tempting her, Etron with his silky brown eyes or Jaq with one of his incredible smiles, the last thing she was up to was sex.

2.1.16 A PLACE OUTSIDE OF TIME

"It was wise to have so many other Players ready to counteract Xonomer's manipulations of those closest to her."

"Thank you, Speaker." Pheasyce bowed before the Speaker of her Order. Explaining how it happened was of no consequence, but it hadn't been a matter of having her Players ready at all. They had free will, and were reliably unpredictable. She had merely tried to cover as many angles as possible. Chance played a major role, and some indirect suggestions at various times enhanced it.

She had not been in the Speaker's presence since first being assigned the Nyorfian system and given the wandering ship full of sleepers to populate it. She wasn't quite sure if this visitation was an honor or merely routine.

"Remain on guard," warned the Speaker. "Xonomer does the most damage in subtle ways. It is not over so easily."

"I am aware of this," Pheasyce said. "I fear what Xonomer has already done will cause permanent damage to my Player's bond with the Zetinorian."

"Have the Zetinorians, such as who are left, not yet been released to choose between you and your opponent?"

She was surprised that the Speaker was not aware of this, but only for a moment. "Tianorius clings to them even as the universe absorbs the last of his physical presence on this level."

"It is difficult for some to let go," said the Speaker gravely. "Small wonder that Xonomer fears and hates what is left of the Zetinorian Players. Tianorius' remaining grasp keeps them from being conquered completely. I fear that tenaciousness will prove the end of the remaining Zetinorians, since if Tianorius does not let go, Xonomer will have them by default when the last of his essence disperses."

"I have tried to convince Tianorius of this, Speaker. That if they so choose, the Zetinorians will be welcomed to add their unique stamp to those I live to protect." Pheasyce dimmed her energy out of respect and sympathy for the one who had struggled so hard to maintain

181

Balance on Zetinor Prime. "But, I also expected Jaq Pym's loyalty to remain with my key Player instead of to the beliefs of his dead world, even under the direct manipulation of my opponent. I fear in this I have made a grave error."

"Xonomer and those of the Dark can be very persuasive," the Speaker said. "And perhaps Tianorius hesitates because you are in the midst of your proving battle. They will be no safer with you if you fail."

"It is not too late to speak to Tianorius. Xonomer will use the fading grasp of Tianorius as a weapon."

Pheasyce bowed and reached out again in entreaty to the dissolving lifeforce of the Zetinorian Guardian. *Tianorius! I have learned from you to beware of walking too long in the Light as in the Dark. Will you not let me give what is left of your people a second chance?"*

But they are my children! mourned the shreds of feeble energy that were all that remained of the defeated Guardian.

A surge of genuine anger rose in Pheasyce. *"We are not given our Players to possess and use, but to guide and assist us in the course of our Game. Yet you would possess them, hold them fast even as you fall out of this existence, only to finally let the darkness take them. It would be kinder to have the minions of the Dark slay them as they did the others! You have walked too close to the Light; you are blind. Let go of those that are left. You cannot help them. That power was taken from you. Neophyte though I be, I can at least give them more time freely choose the fate of their souls."*

She felt the presence of the Speaker with her, although the elder made no comment. Leaving the Zetinorian deity to consider, Pheasyce withdrew. "I feel strongly that Tianorius will free the Zetinorians, and most of them will choose to live free. But in Jaq Pym I fear Xonomer has made a wound so deep it might not be healed."

The Speaker turned toward Pheasyce. "Your involvement must not become more personal, neophyte. Already you have gone too far."

Pheasyce dared to disagree. "In that matter, Speaker, I choose to differ. I am as much part of those planets and everything on them. We are individual and unique, yet at the same time, we are extensions of each other. We will ultimately live or die as one."

The Speaker remained silent for so long that Pheasyce felt her confidence erode. But then he said, "The paths you choose are dangerous. Yet they are none upon which any of the others have dared tread. Perhaps it is time we elders of this Order learn from our students. We are watching." The elder sounded speculative. "I wish you well."

And with that, the Speaker was gone.

2.1.17 BILLET AREA, SECTION C, EPNOCE
MAINCOMMAND
0535.09.07 (LOCAL RECKONING)

He must have become so attuned to her that he knew the instant her footsteps passed right through the thick wall that separated his billet from the corridor. Toeing off his other boot so he wouldn't walk lopsided, Jaq stood and went to the door of the space he shared with Worren, H'tenneck, and Ewayn.

"What's up?" asked Worren, whose head of damp, spiky brown hair had just popped out from the neck opening of a sleeping shirt.

H'tenneck charged out of the bathing alcove, his thin, sinewy body naked, shining black, and wet. He waved one of his innumerable half-finished devices. It shed water droplets and sparks in equal measure. "Deities—*ow!* The Sarge is back!"

"Shit! What in two worlds do you think you're trying to do with that?" Worren knocked the spluttering gadget aside and threw his own damp towel at the young squad second. "Deities! At least have the decency to dry off before you go flying outside! What's got you so charged up?"

Ewayn, his loosened black hair hanging halfway down his broad back, squeezed his thickset body past Jaq and fisted the door control. "He said the Sarge is back."

Jaq remained in place as the others went out to see if this was really true. Since most of F-troop was in the corridor in various states of undress, he assumed it was. It surprised him that he was used to this flare of unreserved love the platoon had, as individuals and as a unit, for their leader. It was a love that was fully reciprocated to them by Rett. It had been so hard for him to get used to, to feel as if he could share, endure, become one of many when all he wanted was to somehow keep her love for himself, and give her his alone.

He'd quickly come to understand the nature of the feelings between F-troop and the platoon sergeant, like most relationships between many in the 2023rd, were those of a closeknit family. He'd come to enjoy that special camaraderie, even becoming a part of it himself. It made

184

the completely non-brotherly love he had for Rett more special, more precious. The friendships she had with others outside the platoon had been harder to understand, the bonds so deep and strong he was unable to tell just what they involved, in the past or in the present.

"Does it matter what was involved?" Ariam had asked him once during one of the many long talks he had shared with her after F-troop had returned to the larger family of Battalion. *"Does she look at any of them the same way she looks at you?"*

He had to say no. So while his Zetinorian instincts remained wary, they'd never gone to battle stations the way they had the night Etron had walked up to their table. As they had that moment he'd sensed Rett's interest in the pilot as something other than a comrade-in-arms.

His conscience, the deep, loyal part of his soul, gave him a stern lecture.

You told her you would accept their ways. You told her whatever she decided to do, you would go along with it. You know she can't promise you, and why. And you saw in her eyes that she would have. You felt how her dreams changed to include you in them. You know, in a heartbeat, had she fulfilled the oath she'd sworn to uphold, she would commit her body, heart, and soul to you forever.

She betrayed your trust, argued his pride.

I didn't ask her to love only me, argued Jaq with the other parts of himself. *I knew I was taking a chance. I can't change her culture, her beliefs, just as she can't change mine. Yet I was the one who said I would accept their ways and become one of them.*

Besides, what opportunity had she to decide if I was the right life partner for her, as I know she is for me?

He stepped into the corridor, watching as the others made a tight cluster around Rett's tall figure. The lighting gleamed from her sleek dark hair, which had already grown out a half-fingerlength since they had left Nyorfias. The added length softened the sharp angularity of her face. He remembered the amazing slick feel of that hair in his fingers. The incredulity and fascination he felt every time he tried to take a hold, even with his fingertips, of the shorter length of it. The way those strands swam through his grasp, leaving only the pleasant sensation of softness and the fragrance of her on his fingers.

How he longed to touch it again, to touch her again.

The sleeveless inner shirt she wore left her shoulders and long, muscular arms exposed. He intimately knew every bit of that golden-brown skin, every scar. He admired the way the light made it glow or mapped the relief of her muscles as she exchanged greetings. Her pleasure at coming home was obvious in the soft blush of color that added drama to her high cheekbones, the deep sparkle in her space-dark eyes.

"We're glad you're back," Ariam was saying. "*I'm* glad you're back. You know how anxious I am to be platoon sergeant," she said so dryly that everyone laughed.

"Oh, I'm not back. I just dropped by to tell you that you're in command." Rett took her kitbag from Georg, one of the newer members who had joined them in Branch, and returned it to her shoulder. "I'm getting transferred to Seacorps. Apparently they need someone who knows how to split logs to crack the ice for them so their ships can move."

"Give it up, Sarge." Trebor yanked her kitbag away and tossed it to someone else. "Put that where it belongs!" said F-troop's third-up.

"Yeah, you couldn't lie your way out of an open door even if you were standing in it," said Bhayorn, shaking his shaggy, bearded head.

"You should know better than to even try," Ariam said, giving the taller woman a shove. Immediately, the platoon second followed the shove by throwing her arms around her sister's upper body. "I'm turning over command as of this minute."

"Then why are you breaking my ribs?" Rett's voice emerged as a breathless squeak. Ariam let her go, laughing. "All right, then," said the sergeant. "Before we all get in trouble, I suggest everyone go back to what they were doing, since we've only a handful of minutes left before check-in. Tomorrow's another day. Where's Jaq?"

The warmth he'd felt watching them slowly began to grow cold. *So,* said the voice that was the bruised pride of Jaq, *now that she's not going to have free access to her newest interest, she's looking for you. Probably to make some lame excuse.*

He stepped back, but not before her beautiful eyes found him, the sparkle there turning into the warm glow of afternoon sunlight.

The expression that started to transform her face, the slow smile that reached across the distance they stood, made Jaq want to push those bodies between them aside to take her in his arms and never let her go.

"Jaq."

By the One, that voice floated to him and took his breath away. How he'd missed hearing it, in whatever tone she spoke, as commander, friend, or lover.

How can you doubt what she feels for you? The truth of it is right there. So she spent time with someone else, but did you expect her to stay miserable and alone the entire time she was cut off from the people she loves as family and friends? She would have died. Her spirit would have died, and the rest of her with it.

And as if by magic the others withdrew, leaving them alone in the corridor.

"Jaq, can I have a word with you?"

It's about her pilot. She owes you an explanation. Maybe she'll even tell you the truth instead of that story she gave about meeting him by chance that night she left you, telling you she wanted to be alone. And never mentioned it since.

That's right, she wasn't going to tell you at all. And there she is, after twenty-two whole days of his company, probably going to expect you to simply accept the fact she's going from his arms to yours and back again in whatever frequency she chooses. And for you to accept that.

He stood in place, letting her come to him. Already her face was changing, a puzzled wariness growing that his inner voice claimed was guilt. Jaq crossed his arms over his chest, and she halted instantly in response to his physical warning to keep her distance.

"Hi, Rett."

"I missed you, Jaq. I never had a chance to talk to you before th—"

"How's your arm?" He borrowed the same distant and polite attitude as the one the commandos displayed toward ranking seniors of other military branches.

The soft breath that escaped between her lips might have been a sound of pain. "It's fine."

And just what do you think you're doing? Why didn't you just haul off and punch her in the face? It might not have hurt as much as that! His conscience, his soul, was aghast, so stunned he barely heard that voice of reason over the others.

"Missed me? I would think your Captain Etron would have more than made up for that."

The light drained from her eyes, like liquid from a cracked container, like blood from a wound. Although she was tall, nearly as tall as he was, she seemed to shrink, or he seemed to grow, until he towered over her and she cringed under his stare even as she tried to stand up to it.

Guilty, said his pride.

"Etron isn't you," she said.

"Oh, you were looking for a surrogate me? One to pass the time with until you got back to the real thing? I suppose that explains everything." He turned aside, in his mind's eye seeing his words and his actions like the motions of a knife twisting into her chest. *Yes, make her hurt, more than you did. She deserves it.* What did these Nyorfians with their backward colonial attitudes know what it was like to be a Zetinorian, a culture that had endured for thousands of years? They didn't even have any structured religion, not really any religion at all, although they called upon deities often enough. No wonder they had the breeding and courtship habits of lower lifeforms.

"I'm glad you're back, Rett. Excuse me, I'm tired."

She didn't seem able to speak, but her lips moved, and finally words emerged. "Jaq, don't cut me off like this."

"Oh, so it's fine for you, but not for me?"

She stared at him. "Since we became friends, when have I ever cut you off?"

"The second full day we were here. That night you went off to be with your new lover."

"I cut you off? I'm sorry you took it that way. I thought I was upfront about it when I took my leave of you. What happened afterward...I already told you it was unexpected."

With a fingertip he scratched delicately at an itch near his left eye before returning his arm to its position, crossed against his chest with its partner. "And you didn't even mention it to me afterward."

She raked a hand through her hair and blew a hard breath from between her teeth. "Look, I told you the why of that already, too. My friendship with Etron changes nothing about how I feel for you. Deities, Jaq, there wasn't one day, not one waking hour of any day, when I didn't think of you. When I didn't wish you were there."

"I see."

"No, I don't think you do."

"You missed me and wished I was there, even while you made love with him?"

She closed her eyes for a moment, but not before he saw the sudden flash of light on the tears that sprang into existence there. Her entire body clenched like a tight fist, too late to defend herself from his thrust. *And a very accurate one,* congratulated the surface voice that spoke as his pride. *See? Guilty!*

Somewhere in the background, from the very depths of his being, one of the other voices was screaming at him, the thin, wailing screams of one near death. Although it was vaguely familiar, he ignored that weak little voice, the one that spoke of truth and love with such whispery, fading tones.

The other spoke again. *You need to put them in their place, you know. Hurt them until they do what you want. Then you can reward them. But they'll always need reminding…that's the only way they learn.*

Jaq watched Rett's long eyelashes sweep up as she opened her eyes, the thick length of them shadowing the deepset depths even more than usual. The happy flush of color beneath her skin had faded completely. "Is this really happening? Or is it a bad dream?"

He wasn't sure if she whispered it aloud, or if it was somehow transmitted from her mind to his. *Since neither of us has telepathic ability,* he reasoned, *she must have spoken.*

"Jaq, I di—"

He interrupted. "Could we continue this at another time? It's getting late, and I don't think a violation of curfew will look good for you—or the unit—so soon after getting off suspension."

Sergeant Rett, the emotionless Nyorfian commando, not the woman he'd come to love, nor the cringing, guilt-ridden female trying to squirm her way back into his favor, now stood before him. "Sure, Jaq.

We will continue this at another time. Soon. When you're not so tired. Sleep well." With a cool nod, Rett turned on one heel and went to start her check.

As if from a distance Jaq saw his own face, but it wasn't his; it was Iheolon's, cruel, alien, brutish. A horrible, gloating smile spread on it as he watched her walk away, back straight, head up. That wouldn't last long. It would just be a matter of time before she came back to him. *And then,* said the persuasive voice, *she'll be ready to hand you her bleeding heart and soul and beg you for forgiveness.*

"Hey, Jaq."

H'tenneck's soft voice spilled from a bright crack of light into the corridor that was now dimmed for the duration of the rest period. It shattered the spell around Jaq, released a sensation of horror so deep he was nearly blinded with it.

What have I done? He pulled in a breath and started to call to her, but his voice stuck in his throat, the breath emerged instead with the same sound as a derisive "hah!"

The door to his billet opened wider, H'tenneck's ebony features and wiry form wreathed in the brighter light. "Jaq, time. Come on. What's wrong?"

Numbly he went inside, conscious yet heedless of the curious glances from his bunkmates, which soon turned into concern. If any of them spoke to him, he didn't hear them. He automatically finished his preparations for sleep, his mind blank, the voices of earlier silenced, leaving him hearing nothing but echoes of horribly familiar, cruel laughter.

2.1.18 UNDETERMINED AIRSPACE, EPNOCE
0535.09.10

THE SLEEK FIGHTERCRAFT STREAKED LOW over the icy, barren steppes of Aurora continent, leaving contrails as straight as young longcones in the cold atmosphere. Rett took a moment to let the view settle into her mind and memory, something she could pull out and use later. The stars, so large and close; the colors of the nebula too beautiful for description. Two of the three moons of Epnoce hung low in the sky, the third and outermost showing only a dull sliver behind the curve of the horizon.

"Sending you new figures for heading, flight level, and airspeed." Etron's calm voice in her ears brought her full attention back on flying.

She read them back aloud as they displayed on her monitor. There was a lot more talking involved with flying that she had ever expected. Not only was there the communication from pilot-to-pilot and pilot-to ground control, but vocal communication with the fightercraft itself. Plus a lot of extra repetition, since everything Etron or anyone else acting as instructor told her had to be repeated back, verbatim, every time. She was used to it now, and understood the necessity, but it still seemed a bit much.

"Manually configure the main airfoil spread for the new speed and approve changes via keyed input with FlightControl. Please verbalize your actions as you perform them."

"Airfoils adjusted manually to three seven point four six degrees, sir. Course adjustment to flight level three-four Echo and heading of four-eight is plotted and confirmed with FlightControl. FlightControl approves and recommends maintaining speed at factor six to stay ahead of the weather that's coming in."

She waited for Etron to acknowledge before she turned the fighter-craft loose on the new figures.

"Good. Let's go."

Her gloved hand pushed up the throttles and the fighter leaped forward, taking her along with it. In the rear view display she saw the peculiar burst clouds form as they climbed into the sky at six times the speed of sound.

"Why don't you alter course fifteen degrees east? We'll go that way for a while. Maybe we'll wake up some action for you."

She was well aware the diversion would take their craft toward the edge of the safety zone and the big Coalition weapons batteries along the coast. He was testing her, seeing if she remembered the intelligence they'd studied earlier.

"At this speed, that will take us over the safety zone in less than six minutes, sir. Are you trying to get me in more trouble?"

"When we leave the safety zone, I'll take over."

"Sir, we're not cleared to go out of the safety zone."

The cockpit was silent for a time, save for the soft noises of the computers and the well-muffled engine roar. "Then I suggest you arrange with FlightControl for another course alteration per the new figures I'm sending you." His tone of voice, the same calm, level tone he used while instructing, didn't offer any clues, but from the bright sparkles she could perceive in his body energy, Rett knew he was pleased.

She scanned the course and altitude adjustments he'd sent. None needed to be cleared with FlightControl, as they were still in the tolerance zone for the designated training area. She cleared them anyway and reported finally, "Heading three-zero-two, flight level three-six Cobalt, confirmed."

"Let's head home."

"I was beginning to think you forgot about my schedule," she commented.

Etron laughed. "No chance. We'll make it in plenty of time."

And it's back to reality. She took a final moment to appreciate the view before focusing her complete attention on a safe and expeditious return to Epnoce MainCommand.

* * * * *

SHE WAITED FOR THE ALL clear signal before dismounting the fightercraft. Etron made a big production of making sure no one was in sight distance, inventing on errand after another for his flight crew to do "right now, I can handle the shutdown" as soon as he taxied into the hangar.

Strip off flight suit, bundle it up with helmet and other gear, hand off to Etron. She slipped off to the side, smoothing her hair, settling her headband back into place. And another transformation was made: she was no longer the semi-unofficial student fighter pilot, but Sergeant Rett of F-troop, her uniform reflecting the colors around her.

She leaned idly against the hangar wall as the technicians arrived to service the recently landed craft, pretending not to see her and not doing a very good job of it. There was always a glance, a smile, sometimes a chuckle that slipped out. The entire 114th seemed to enjoy the arrangement of faking their complete ignorance of what Etron was doing. One of the ground controllers had told Rett earlier they even hoped for someone who was not of their squadron to show up and test the setup just for the added element of danger.

"You people have to get out more. Spend a tenday with us if you want some danger," Rett had told him.

She answered one of those furtive smiles with one of her own now. She held on to the sensation of lightness and freedom she'd felt while airborne. Up there she didn't have any problems, any worries. They lost their ever-present grip on her with the first rumble of the fighter's atmospheric engines. They were left behind as soon as the landing gear left the surface. All too soon she would have them back, have to turn and deal with them the best she could.

No matter how they hurt.

Etron joined her after a word with the crew chief.

"So, how'd I do?" she demanded. "And don't even think of giving me a test, I don't have the time."

Etron smiled at her. "There's always time for a test. But I'll let you off by saying that under any other circumstances I'd be sending you to solo tomorrow and discussing setting you up to train with a wingpartner."

A sensation pleasurable as orgasm caught her at the prospect. Deities! No matter what, she could actually say she made one of her lifetime dreams come true. Even if she never soloed. I *wish I could tell Pam. I wish I could tell anyone. Just like I wish I could tell others besides Ariam about Pam.*

"You've an hour and a half to get back. I go on duty in a half hour, but that's plenty of time to fly you over. Not that I'd have to any more—under other circumstances."

"What do you mean?"

"Major Deeclar told me as of last tenday that you definitely qualify to take yourself."

"And you're just *now* telling me? What is it with you, Etron? Do you like saving these surprises of yours up to hit me with all at once?" She hugged him. After another horrible day of Jaq doing everything in his power to avoid her, treating her as if she was some kind of disease, she needed good news.

"There's a reason for it," he said wickedly, "as I've come to learn you tend to become more spontaneous that way. Do I get a kiss with this?" He slid his arms around her waist. "Ow! Good deities! Not used to you wearing all this hardware."

Rett kissed his lips lightly and let him go. "That'll have to do. I'll be off. Easy Force called a seniors' meeting at 2330. I'll just make it if I run."

"Now, Rett—" He raised a reminding and admonishing finger at her.

"It's okay, did you forget Med passed me to full active this afternoon?"

"I'm sure he's still put a limit on how much you exert yourself."

"Don't worry, Dad."

"Dad!" Outraged, he swatted at her with his helmet as she started off.

2.1.19 CONFERENCE ROOM, SECTION C
MAINCOMMAND EPNOCE
0535.09.10(LOCAL RECKONING)

RETT SLIPPED INTO THE CONFERENCE room. Easy Force's other platoon leaders were there already, standing behind their chairs, awaiting the arrival of the officers. Despite rigid control of her breathing, the fact she'd been in a rush was evident.

Sergeant Semage tossed her a wink. Atira, from D-troop, simply gave her a smile and made a small head motion to indicate the empty place on her left. S-troop's Sergeant Mordell mimicked wiping the sweat from his forehead, a gesture with a double meaning.

Agreeing that she was glad to have made it just in time, Rett swiped her right forearm across her face quickly, checked the lay of her hair around her headband, and took a position behind a seat next to Atira. 195 A breath later Major Yidnar, Captain Mahrhys, Lieutenant Evetez, and Sergeant Tris came in from another door.

Rett had been back on conditional standby for only three days, and allowed to drill with the unit. Tris was still standing in for her as Combat Team Leader, and in drill, Ariam was in command of F-troop. Despite the fact Med had passed her that morning, her extra activity was indeed under strict limitations.

Good thing Med isn't included in this meeting.

Major Yidnar returned their salutes and his dark blue gaze turned stern and questioning as it settled on Rett's flushed face. "Hasn't Lieutenant Evetez been giving you enough exercise in drill, Sergeant?" he asked. Everyone laughed, including Rett and Evetez.

"It's only been three days, sir. And Med's had me eating so much and taking things easy for so long I've been feeling seriously out of shape."

The Major's grin flashed. Captain Mahrhys, alongside him, raised his eyebrows, the stone gray eyes beneath them amused.

"After two tendays of restriction, I suppose I can let this pass," the Major allowed. "This time. But there will not be a next time."

"Understood. Thank you, sir."

They all took their seats and Yidnar opened the meeting. "I said I'd keep this short, so I'll get right to the point. You all know our transfer and exchange lottery is next tenday. Any changes of personnel must be accomplished well in advance of our combat operations here on Epnoce.

"We'll be having a new option this time, which is what this meeting is about. Normally we'd have just posted Omni notes to everyone about this, but Epnoce MainCommand, for security purposes, has suspended military Omni activities as of ten minutes ago."

"I thought the atmospheric anomalies from the storms were subsiding with the seasonal change, sir," said Atira, leaning forward with a puzzled frown.

"It's a bit more than that. We've recently confirmed a security breach with our wireless signals and databases. They've managed to break through our latest protocols."

"Shamos," muttered Rett under her breath.

"It may be," agreed the Major. "He's on Epnoce somewhere, and knows our systems firsthand. We thought we blocked him out after his exposure as a Coalition agent but, we were wrong. In any case, this means that until we can get a completely new and secure system in place, we must stop using our Omnis for much more than making notes to ourselves or accessing data stored on our personal units."

"Shit and bother," growled Tris.

No one else said anything, but Rett had no doubts the thoughts of the other platoon leaders mirrored hers. *No access to the Omni networks? What a pain in the ass this is going to be!*

"I'm not happy about it either, but we'll endure. The main networks are secure, we'll make do. Captain Mahrhys—" Major Yidnar indicated the 2023rd's quiet XO, "has hardcopy handouts on the new reporting and mail procedure, so let me just get to my topic for the meeting."

He looked tired, his normal blue and gold energy dull and gray around the edges. Rett found herself wondering when the Major's last vacation was. She had the distinct feeling he was getting pulled in seventeen additional directions more than the usual two handfuls. Glancing toward the slender man with the iron gray eyes and hair on Yidnar's left, she wondered if Mahihys had to nag him into remembering to rest, eat and sleep the same way Med, Ariam and the rest of F-troop did with her.

Then again, like the rest of the 2023rd, the command staff had been scattered, hardly ever in the same place at the same time for the past few years. Until now.

"That topic is our biennial transfer lottery. As well as the usual open exchange, you can arrange exchanges between specific units, with the agreement of all personnel involved—and mine, of course. What I want to say is, you do have your pick from the entire 2023rd for replacements, but any exchanges of Easy Force people I'd like to keep in Easy Force. Same is going for the other four assault groups."

Makes sense.

"Are there any disagreements? Questions? Okay, those of you with questions can see me now. The rest of you can obtain a procedure from Mahrhys and are dismissed. Thanks."

⁕ ⁕ ⁕ ⁕ ⁕

Semage fell in step with Rett as she headed off toward the quartering area. "How are things going, Rett?"

"Good. Getting back into things. Sometimes I feel as if I were gone a lot longer than two tendays, other times, it's as if no time passed at all." She shrugged. "Making any exchanges, Semage?"

"Not for exchange, no one's asked to trade out yet. But I've a few openings for incoming transfers. I'm still lacking three people."

"Mmm. No one's asked me yet, either." Rett flipped through the procedure manual in her hands as they walked. "Before we came over from Nyorfias, the Major sent me five people from other units, but I'm still short fourteen of a full platoon."

Semage swallowed. He'd taken his share of heavy casualties with B-troop, but not as hard as losing fully half his people in less than the span of a Standard day. Rett's mention of actual numbers focused on those empty ranks with harsh clarity.

Strange. He never thought of F-troop as lacking in personnel when he saw them as a group; even when they worked together. As pleased and proud as he was with his own people, he couldn't help a momentary envy that even at half-strength, F-troop easily did the work of five times their number. *It's a reflection on her that they do.* He watched his friend from the corner of his vision as they went along. *Because that's simply the way she is.*

Rett closed the manual, chewing her lower lip. "Ariam and I'll have to look over the lists again tomorrow. Picking fourteen is going to be a bother if we have to crawl through hardcopy and use the main network." She gave him a questioning smile. "Why are you staring at me?"

"I was thinking about a certain seventeen year old kid I met once."

"She's long gone, 'Mage."

He would have disagreed, but the way her eyes became shadowed and the lift of her shoulders was a sure sign her mood had changed. Semage scratched the back of his neck, changing his mind about asking Rett his question. "Well, guess I'll see you tomorrow morning, Rett."

"Good night, Semage. Was there something you wanted to ask me?"

"Yes, there is. But it'll keep until tomorrow."

"Are you sure? I don't want a repeat of what happened two tendays ago."

"I'm sure. It's been a long day and I'd like to talk when we're both fresh. All right?"

"All right. Find me."

"I will. Good night, Rett."

2.1.20 COMMON AREA SECTION C, EPNOCE MAINCOMMAND
0535.09.11 (LOCAL RECKONING)

AFTER SIX HOURS OF DRILL the next day, Rett was now four hours deep in busywork. She flipped through files and reports while Ariam regarded the computer display as if it were a Coalition target to be destroyed. Ariam's frustration painted dark, smoky streaks in her usual clear green aura. It had to be more than this busywork that bothered her.

I don't think it's me this time. I've been good, I've been eating, sleeping, and being cheerful even when I don't feel like it...I'm keeping whatever is going on with me and Jaq away from our work. I wonder if she's having a tiff with Semage. Maybe that's why he wanted to talk.

"That's the last," Ariam said finally, as she entered the final replace- 199 ment choice into the computer. "Twenty-two of them. Any more?"

"No, that's it. I really hope we get our first picks. There are some excellent people here I'd like to have in F-troop."

"Hope so, too." Ariam tapped her fingers as she waited for the machine to save and print their choices along with the regular reports.

Not being able to use their Omnis for this was even more of a pain than Rett had expected. The new procedure involved using a mix of the complex's workstations, hardcopy files, which had to be checked out and back in to the battalion clerk, printouts filed with the battalion clerk or recycled if a worksheet, and data storage units. And all DSUs had to be hand delivered to the battalion clerk personally by each unit's senior member.

It meant a lot of extra work for them. But she hoped the Major had at least a platoon's worth of help for the poor battalion clerks.

Tossing the last personnel file on top of the pile of hardcopies, she leaned forward to pop the data storage unit from its bay on Ariam's computer. "Thanks, Ari. Put up these files for me, all right?"

Ariam nodded. "Okay. What are you up to?"

"I have to drop this off, then I'm on free time. I was supposed to go to Supply and put in a few hours volunteer time, but there's something I need to do first and I'm not sure how long it's going to take. Page me out if anything comes up."

"You're going to see Etron."

Rett stood up. *Where have I heard that exact tone of accusation lately?* "As a matter of fact, I'm not. But does it matter if I was, Ari? You're the one that told me I shouldn't deny myself personal pleasures."

"So you are making love with him."

Rett had to struggle to keep her face still and her emotions firmly blocked. "And if I told you I wasn't? And haven't?"

"I'd believe you."

"Without trying to probe me for the truth?" Rett threw that out as she felt a tentative push from her sister.

"You're starting to block me, Rett. You're being evasive. You go off to spend time with him, but you never tell me what you do. Why, unless you're hiding something?"

"I am not on intimate terms with Etron. Do you believe me, or not?"

"I do," Ariam said after a minute. "But others might not. Like Jaq."

So this is part of it.

Rett turned back and resumed her seat, letting every bit of her frustration on that subject come to the surface. "I did *not* spend my entire suspension period in Etron's company. Nor am I now spending all of my unallocated free time with him. Contrary to anyone's opinion. You know that." Rett reached an upturned hand toward her sister in entreaty. "Tell me you know that."

Ariam made a motion so small that if Rett blinked at the wrong time, she would have missed it. "So you've told me."

Deities, not Ariam, too! "Ariam, I think you'd better tell me what Jaq's told you."

"I never thought Etron's interest in you would affect him so badly," admitted Ariam. "I mean, he's taken it way out of context. And it just got worse while you were gone. He asked me yesterday if he was eligible for exchange, since he's part of F-troop and Easy Force, yet he's also on special operative status as tech advisor."

"He did?" Rett stared at her sister. *So it's coming down to this?* she thought, a bleak chill shivering her heart.

"Yes."

"What did you tell him?"

"The truth. I don't know. I told him I'd ask you. Is he?"

"If Major Yidnar approves his application."

"What about your approval, Rett?"

Rett stood up again. "I usually don't stand in anyone's way, Ariam. If Jaq, or anyone else, really wants to leave F-troop, if they feel they're stagnating or unhappy here, who am I to tell them they can't? I can't expect good performance from people who would prefer to be assigned elsewhere."

Ariam didn't answer right away. She bent over the pile of printouts, forming them into orderly stacks. Her sudden evasion of eye contact raised more alarm in Rett's bruised heart.

"Ariam, what is it?"

"Nothing."

"Don't say 'nothing' when you can't look me in the eyes and say it. Please. I know I'm not that great at handling people, I never was. But I've tried hard. I'm trying hard. I've always had you, Kraym, others to help me. And Evetez now, I couldn't have done it otherwise."

"Rett, you handled me, the business, and ran our house without any help for two years. Of course you worked your butt off to do it, but you did it. Even the adults looked up to you, just like they did to Dad."

"Dad? Who told me I'd always be a failure? Let's not bring Dad into this."

"All right. I won't." Ariam continued organizing the files.

"At least answer me this, Ari. Has there been a time when I didn't listen to anyone in F-troop if they were unhappy with something or needed a change? Have I held anyone back? Made anyone feel like they couldn't ask me anything or tell me anything, anything at all? Am I doing it now? I have to know."

"Never." The conviction rang strong in Ariam's voice even though she kept her eyes on the work her hands were doing. "If anything, you go completely out of your own way and overlooked your own needs to make sure we have whatever we want. Within reason, of course." Ariam glanced up. "No one could say you're not a good leader. Better than you think you are. And more than fair."

"What about you? What aren't you telling me?"

Ariam became very intent on her hands once more. "I—I can't talk about it right now."

"Ariam, that's twice in less than half a day someone's put off discussing an issue with me. I'm having enough problems with Jaq. And I do *not* want a repeat of the situation I had with Evetez from you, Semage, or anyone else."

"There's something I'm thinking of doing, and I want to talk about it with you. But I still have to think about it some more first."

Rett decided she'd better walk away before saying anything in response. She tucked the DSU into a pocket, accepted the reports that Ariam handed over without raising her head. Grinding her teeth together, she turned on her heel and headed for the door. "See you later, then—I'll be around. And if you see Jaq, don't tell him I'm looking for him. It'll just give him a reason to hide."

Deeply troubled, Rett started for the battalion clerical office.

Jaq wanted out.

She knew why. There was no sense in even asking herself. Ever since the night Etron had shown up, Jaq had taken the art of backing down to entirely new levels.

And Semage had neatly avoided something he obviously needed to bring up last night.

Now Ariam was being evasive.

Why me? Rett thought. *Where's Pam when I really need her?* She gritted her teeth and lengthened her stride. Well, she wasn't about to let this go any longer, as she had with Evetez. *I'm going to drop this off, then turn around and find them, starting with Jaq. I'll make the three of them tell me what they need to before—*

"Hey, Rett. Have a minute?"

She stopped without turning around, waiting for Jaq Pym to catch up with her. She wasn't sure what she would see in his eyes today. More distance? More of that cold, mocking contempt he'd hit her with the night she came back? Rett focused on his aura before daring to turn her face to him. It seemed fairly normal, if showing some orange stress around the edges.

Ah. So he is in a reasonable mood. Before I sail right in with an "I heard", I'll hang on to him for a few minutes and see if he mentions it first, she told herself firmly, turning to face him with what she hoped was a friendly, open expression. *Maybe he was just curious. Maybe he's changed his mind. Either way, we're going to discuss this, even if I have to take a death grip on his hair.* "What can I do for you, Jaq?"

The big Zetinorian looked down at her with a smile on his lips, but there was no reflection of it in his beautiful eyes. "Rett, I've been out of sorts for a while, and I'm sorry I took it out on you. Can we talk?"

She wanted to shout *Yes!* and throw her arms around him. She settled for giving him a big smile. "Of course, Jaq. I was hoping to find you with some time. We've both been busy. This is perfect. Just let me run into the office with this and we'll go grab a corner of the complex."

Jaq's expression was tinged with relief. "Okay. I'll wait out here."

"Don't go anywhere." Feeling happier than she had in three tendays, Rett went inside and handed over her reports. "Any messages for me?" she asked the battalion clerk on duty. She noted with satisfaction that there were plenty of assistants: a mix of various military branches, even a few civilians.

"None that I know of, Sergeant Rett, but I just came on shift. Let me check." He coded his computer and waited for a readout. "No messages, Sergeant."

"I'd like to leave one then. Anyone outside of the Battalion calls for me, I won't be available until further notice, and can you call Supply and tell them something came up that can't wait, so I won't be coming later?"

"Got it, Sergeant Rett."

She rejoined Jaq outside. "I'm clear. Do we need to find a spot—" *where we can speak without interruption* never emerged. She tried not to look hurt when he shook his head and spoke before she finished her query.

"Feel up to an ale?" He checked his chrono. "We've time for one, as long as it's in the next two hours."

Rett made the best of it. "Sure. And they have Treetop bitter here. Are you buying?"

Jaq made a good show of rolling his eyes and looking pained. "I suppose I can, this time. You pull five times the credit I do and you're always making me buy."

"I have to replace my personal gear and weapons when they get lost or destroyed," she retorted. "So as far as numbers in a credit readout go, you probably have a lot more than I do."

"With all you've had to get replaced over the years, you're likely funding the entire Nyorfian war effort single-handed," agreed Jaq. This time, it was with genuine good humor. "And today is—"

"Fourthday," supplied Rett. "Mushrooms. Do you have time for lunch, too?"

"I do," agreed Jaq. "I've developed a fondness for those marvelous fungi myself."

* * * * *

By the One, her eager, beautiful smile and the bright shine of hope in her dark eyes had almost killed him. He knew he hadn't been helping matters for either of them by avoiding her, by deliberately hurting her.

Not knowing how to explain or how to begin, he kept up a light conversation over lunch. He liked the ale and took satisfaction in watching her, for the first time he could remember since her leave, eat a complete meal and enjoy it. As time went on and he kept turning the subject whenever she came too close, the brightness in her began fading and her smiles showed some strain.

It wasn't until they finally sat back over steaming mugs of spicebush tea that Jaq finally felt as if he had enough nerve.

"I guess you heard from Ariam I was thinking of applying for transfer."

* * * * *

Rett nodded and said nothing, just traced idle designs in a damp ring on the table. She wished again for the supporting presence of Pam. Her face was now carefully devoid of personal expression. Her heart sank right down to her heels and stayed there, quivering.

"I wanted to stay with Special Forces because of you," he said. "Your Planetary Council and officers wanted me to do straight technological development with MainCommand, but they gave me a choice. Actually, it was Major Yidnar who made sure I knew I had a choice. I love you, I always will. Nothing can change that."

Words rose inside her, hurting, bitter words, but she held them back. It was his time to speak, and he wasn't yet finished.

He took a sip of his tea. "I'd hoped your feelings for me were just as strong, but now I'm not sure. I guess I just can't understand Nyorfians that well yet. I've always felt I couldn't share anyone I really cared about. I've tried—"

No, you haven't. The words leaped into her surface thoughts with a savage rush of fury. *You haven't tried anything except avoiding me ever since Etron showed up in the mess area that night. You just turned me off and avoided me. Not like he ever came looking for me or asked me for my free time, either, until after I was hurt.*

205

Her flare subsided before it reached any visible levels, but it left a hard ache behind.

"—to. And I can't expect you to be with me and no one else, we never made that sort of commitment."

"No," Rett managed, her voice one notch above a whisper. Her throat was so sore and tight she didn't think even that much would come out of it. She was regretting her lunch with every advancing second.

"I'm still amazed we had anything together."

"Had?" she repeated.

He laughed shortly. "I mean, me having been part of the Coalition, having this stupid fantasy about giving you one magical kiss, fixing everything that was wrong, having you forever. When that seemed to happen—sort of—it was like some wonderful dream."

Oh Jaq, you did fix a lot that was wrong. And you have part of me forever, Rett wanted to say, but this time, although her lips moved, no sound came out.

He shook his head. "I can't believe how stupid that was. Etron's a nice guy. I like him, as much as I'd like to hate him. He really is decent. You're seeing a lot of him, I guess."

"You guess? Are you forgetting that a few nights ago you practically accused me of spending the duration of my suspension, some six hundred and sixty hours, in his company?" She took a sip from her tea, which had gone as cold as the inside of her body felt.

"I was…not myself, Rett." He looked away and then back, still not quite meeting her eyes.

That's not enough! She almost shouted it aloud, but she had to consider the sudden strong flare of sickly green-gray terror that leapt into his aura for a moment or two, the color that desaturated the ruddy red overtones of his skin. Rett's throat went completely dry in response, and she quickly took another sip of her tea, which at least was wet.

By that time, Jaq was in control of himself, but she was left unsettled and closed her fingers hard over her mug to hide the tremble that ran through them.

"Are you in love with him?"

There it was again, not fear this time, but the same dark shadow she'd perceived the last time. The same darkness she'd sensed in Evetez.

The same she had felt clouding her own reason since she'd left Nyorfias.

The shadow crept through Jaq's aura like an infectious disease. It flickered through and disappeared as if swallowed, leaving her uncertain if she'd seen it with her ability or merely imagined she did.

She cleared her throat. "No. I'm not in love with him. I'm not going to deny that I find him attractive. Or that I enjoy being around him. But Etron never was and never will be a replacement for you." Unable to find a simple way to explain anything, she raked her fingers through her hair.

He reached across the table, taking her hand. "I said some awful things, didn't I?"

"Yes, Jaq," she said evenly. "You did. I'm sorry for not thinking ahead enough to simply have told you what happened that night in the hangar. Maybe we could have avoided a lot of misunderstanding."

"It's not your fault, Rett."

"What?"

"I mean, things are happening too fast for you."

"What do you mean?"

Inside, that was exactly what she felt. Things were happening too fast. The pattern her life had taken for almost a decade suddenly altered. Between the ego-merge, her enforced vacation, meeting Jaq…and this transfer to Epnoce, where the conditions of the planet itself were so drastically different.

But something in his tone of voice and words struck a chord of wrongness within her. The touch of his hands even felt wrong. And there it was again, the sense of otherness, of some miasma creeping into his being. She nearly pulled her hands away, but the sensation passed before she could, and he was normal again, off color from his stress and tension, but normal.

I have to be imagining it. It's my own stress. Just let it go and don't look at his aura any more.

"I practically threw myself at you from the very beginning," he was saying. "Maybe I overdid it. But since you were on leave in Branch."

Rett returned the pressure of his fingers. "I can never in my life hope to equal what you did for me then. Or before. Or ever since. You're very special to me on many levels. My feelings about you haven't changed. They never will. No matter how many other people I choose to spend time with."

He looked down. "I'm having problems accepting that aspect of your people, at least when it applies to you."

She withdrew her hands slowly. "Are you asking me to make a choice, to stop seeing Etron or anyone else? To make a commitment to you? Using the transfer as…as…leverage?"

He was silent for several seconds and started to shake his head, then let out a breath. "The thought crossed my mind a few times. And again when I first asked Ariam. But I've thought it over thoroughly since then, and there are other reasons."

"We talked about this before. You said you'd wait, as long as it took. I told you that I can't promise anything to anyone until I put this uniform I wear away for good." She had to force air into lungs that suddenly felt squeezed. "You seem to forget I'm under oath and commitment already. Until the Coalition is gone from this system and we're stood down, that's the way of it."

"That gives you leave to—"

She was glad he didn't go on, although she could guess the rest of it.

"I love you, Jaq. But even when the war ends, and you might ask me for something exclusive and permanent, I would like to make sure what I feel for you is as deep and strong as what you seem to feel for me. That it isn't out of gratitude for what you've done. I have to be free to choose, and you have to trust me enough to stand back and to let me do that. Can you understand?"

He shook his head, the motion reluctant, but definite. "No. But maybe one day I can."

She searched the blue depths of his eyes. The light that usually made them so fathomless was lacking, a barrier she felt with all the impact of coming up against a wall. "I'm so sorry," she whispered. "I'm sorry I can't give you what you want from me. I really messed you up, didn't I?"

He smiled a little. "No. It's just life, this stupid war, and these tough times. It's hard. Especially for people who've been fighting something or another most of their lives. Like me." His voice was gentle. "And like you."

"Is there any way we can compromise? Or do you feel really want to leave F-troop?"

"I think leaving would be for the best," he said. "I—we both—would be able to think more clearly. There's just too much tension between us now." He corrected himself. "I'm much too tense about it."

He was tense? How did he think she felt—did it even matter? He had it fixed in his head she'd been having sex with Etron, and nothing she would say would change his mind. She had never given him the impression or idea that he was the only lover she would ever have; she had even told him that. *How do you think I feel, Jaq?* she thought. *You can't even compromise, it would have to be your way, or no way.*

Again she was torn between her position as his commander listening to his reasons for transfer, a friend trying to help him resolve a personal problem, and as his lover not yet ready to make a commitment to settle for one partner. She couldn't respond from any of those viewpoints; she had to balance them all. So she said nothing.

"It would only get worse if we were forced together all the time."

He sounded more confident as he justified his decision. But he sounded like a stranger, a distinct note of arrogant altruism in his voice, backed up by his body language. *Look at me,* Rett heard under the words he spoke, *I am doing this for you. I'm going away to wallow in misery alone so you can be stress free and experiment with other lovers. You know I can't find another, and I'll love you until I die, no matter who you choose. I hope you feel guilty about it.*

"—Personal life aside," Jaq was saying when she opened her ears again to the words he spoke and not the interpretation her mind made, "you don't need that sort of distraction."

She couldn't disagree. "No. I don't. Then you'll be transferring on an open contract?" She pulled her commander persona completely in place. The part of her that was simply Rett had just been seriously disabled.

"I don't know anything about how you work military transfers. What's an open contract?"

"In your case, a special operative, you could apply for an open transfer," she said, keeping her voice neutral. "That leaves you the option to return to the original unit, or a different one, after a certain period of time, if you like. Major Yidnar said he wanted to limit the transfer of Easy Force personnel to be within Easy Force. Normally this would mean you can transfer only to any of the other platoons. But there are exceptions to every rule. Did you have any particular unit in mind?"

"I was kind of thinking along the lines of leaving Special Forces and being something other than a tech advisor."

"Like what?"

"Seacorps, Infantry, Spacemarines—"

Rett shook her head. "You can't. It'd never be approved. The only reason you were allowed on a semi-combat status with Special Forces is that we could offer you some degree of protection. But you're still an outlaw from the Coalition, and not yet a full Nyorfian citizen. I'm afraid other combat operations are closed to you, Jaq."

"Then I'll let Major Yidnar decide," Jaq said with a shrug. "He has to approve the transfer, doesn't he?"

Some of her earlier tiff returned, heating the inside of her chest. She reminded herself he meant nothing by it, conditioned by the Coalition—and maybe his Zetinorian upbringing—that the capability of females was a bit limited. "F-troop's chain of command starts with *me*, Jaq Pym. You're a special operative who was made part of my unit. You answer to me first, the 2023rd second. As your commander, I'm not going to hold you back on any options you have." She leaned forward slightly. "But I'm damn well going to make sure you're not a big, fat, target like I am, because I do love you enough to want to be sure you're reasonably safe."

Jaq smiled then, a real smile, and despite the shield of command she'd pulled over her aching heart, Rett felt its impact. She had to force herself not to respond to it. This had stopped being a personal conversation a while ago.

"How about transport and supply? You know how well I can drive a rover. And I'm good with machines."

"You are. Skills like that are needed here on Epnoce, and you'll meet a lot more people that way. You haven't had much opportunity to be around those who aren't as driven as we are." Rett didn't make the pun intentionally, catching it only after it had left her lips. *Almost like something Pam would have said,* she thought. Of course, it went right over Jaq's wild-haired head. "I'll need to know if you'll still be accessible to MainCommand for other information or assistance, the way you have been. It most likely will be a condition for approval, since the fact you're here right now, assigned to us, was also dependent on your cooperation."

"Of course I will. You'll take care of it?"

She took a quick sip of her tea to ease the ache in her throat. "Yes."

He reached for his shoulder harness and withdrew a folded sheaf of forms from the inner fold. As he slid them across the table, Rett noticed his hand trembled slightly. "I started filling them," Jaq said. "The rest is for you."

Rett finally looked up from the reality of the transfer forms in front of her. "Open?"

"I guess. For a year?"

Rett cringed inside. A year? A lot could happen in a year. "Half that," she countered. "The shorter half. Six months."

He laughed, but it sounded forced. "It's open. Six months."

"Very well. If the Major or Lieutenant Evetez have any problems, I'll let you know so we can discuss alternatives."

"Thanks, Rett." Jaq stood up and came to her side of the table. "I have to go. I promised Trebor to go over some plans he's come up with for some new low-light targeters. And Major Yidnar wanted me to meet with a few people from MainTech who are on this problem we're having with the Omni network. I'll see you later."

Rett stood. "I'll give you an update." She gave him a nod of dismissal.

For a moment he stood there, as if undecided. *What, does he expect me to kiss him and pretend everything is fine? Or, does he expect me to beg him to change his mind, tell him I'll do anything to make him stay?* For a moment she was almost tempted. It was hard to stay there and make herself look as if they'd merely completed a businesslike meeting.

Well, so maybe they had, but that wasn't the point.

"Then later it is." With that, he stepped back and was gone.

She sat down and reached for the tea carafe. After filling her mug, she pulled a marker from her pocket, and started to fill in Jaq's application. "That's it then. I really blew it." Her eyes stung and ruthlessly she fought back the tears that threatened to burst free. Damn it, she refused to feel guilty over this. It wasn't her fault. Jaq had avoided her ever since the night Etron had shown up in their mess area. She'd never done anything to deserve his coldness.

She ached at the unfairness of it all. Jaq had made his own judgment and he wasn't about to change his mind.

"Maybe it's for the best." She started filling in the forms. "I couldn't live with someone who couldn't trust me."

Etron wasn't someone she'd imagine having children with, but he was caring, fun, and made her feel good about herself. She wondered how he'd react if she demanded he stop seeing his other friends. She couldn't imagine such a thing, didn't even want to try.

She pinched the bridge of her nose between her thumb and forefinger, feeling a stress headache coming fast. She should go to the gym and work until she dropped, that would help. At least until Med found out.

But no. She had to find Semage and Ariam and get this all out in the... Her head jerked up. "Is there a flaming sign or something over the door outside? Wait your turn to break some devastating news to Rett day?"

211

"I'm sorry, I thought you might have a few minutes so we could talk."

"Have a seat, Semage," she said without looking up. "I was actually just thinking about you. Tell me what's on your mind. Let me get it all now, in one straight shot, right to the bottom line. After the way you were last night, I'm not even trying to guess."

Semage pulled up a chair and sat down. "What did I do last night?" he demanded.

"Evasive action," Rett told the B-troop leader, still looking down at Jaq's application. "It's not like you. You were very diplomatic about it, but you always said what you had to say."

"You don't miss much, do you? Sometimes you're as bad as Major Yidnar."

"Except for lately," Rett said with a self-mocking, bitter laugh. "Obviously I've been missing things so large that if they were holes, entire solar systems would disappear into them."

"Seriously, this doesn't seem to be the best time." His chair scraped back.

"I want to know. We're here, I'm listening. Let me have it."

She heard him take a deep breath and let it out slowly. Responding to the increase of tension in his aura, she kept her head down, and braced herself for more upsetting news.

"Okay. Coming to the point, it's Ariam. I'd like her in B-troop as second."

Rett finally looked up, staring hard at the husky, freckled platoon leader. "You know, it's times like this when I'd rather be cornered, alone, and looking down the hot ends of Coalition SMGs?"

"You can say no. I'm not making a demand. If it's that much of a problem—"

"Hold back, 'Mage. I didn't say it was a problem. It's just I should have expected it. Damn it, no wonder she-" Rett shook her head and forced a dry laugh, amazed at her own lack of foresight. "Of course it's a logical step for her. It's perfect. But deities, the way things are going, the entire platoon's going to be transferring right out from under me next thing!"

"I know it's been rough, but it's not as bad as you think. What makes you think that? Who else wants to leave?" her friend asked carefully.

"Jaq Pym."

"Well, shit, he's a Zetinorian, and you and Captain E—"

Her frustrated thoughts became spoken words. "Professional obligations aside, which I shouldn't have to explain to you," she said, "do you think I'm supposed to change how I make my own personal choices so as not to offend him? Because he can't adapt and accept our ways—which he stated he was willing to do when Major Yidnar sponsored him for citizenship, mind you—I have to? Because he says he's in love with me and there will never be anyone else—I'm supposed to instantly agree without exploring my options? Or not to disappoint others who expected or thought things were a lot different between us?"

"Now, Rett—" He looked as if he thought she should, and she had never heard such a tone in his voice before. Focusing hard on his body energy, she saw that elusive flicker of darkness flit across his normal earthy brown and green like heavy storm clouds over clear sky.

213

What's going on? First it's me. Then Evetez, then Jaq. Even Ariam. Now Semage. Who next?

"You can't expect Jaq—"

"No. Stop." Most of the fraying thread of control to which she'd been clinging so desperately snapped as Semage started to give his opinion. Her hands bunched into fists. She wanted to hit something, see it break.

"Stand down, Rett. I didn't come to fight."

"Don't say another word. Leave the application. I'll take care of it."

Semage didn't move from his place. He met her eyes calmly, although she could see the hot orange tension of combat readiness in his energy aura. "I didn't mean to tiff you. I apologize."

"Leave me alone. I value your friendship but I'm in no mood to be rational right now."

"Rett, Ariam's—"

Rett bared her teeth and cut him short with a gesture. Whatever fragile controls she tried to get back into place were rapidly failing. Before she lost it again, she managed to spit out an explanation, her words fast, low, and hard.

"This has nothing to do with Ariam, her going to B-troop would be good for the both of you, I approve. It's a perfect move for her. It's wonderful you both are getting along that well. I mean that. Now Semage" said Rett, dropping her tone even more, "if you don't know the way out, I'll show you!"

He left the application.

The fire inside banked. Feeling betrayed, cold, and utterly alone, she hugged her arms across her chest and closed her eyes for a minute, fiercely concentrating on pulling herself together.

You are not *going to throw up,* she told herself as her guts twisted and threatened to turn inside out. Regaining control, she stared at the hardcopies in front of her for a good ten minutes before she picked up both sets of forms and left the common lounge.

She needed to think. She needed to talk to someone who really knew her, for an outside opinion. Someone like Pam, who tried to figure out everyone's side and find a middle ground. Someone like Jaq, who always listened…or Semage, who was always steady and levelheaded. Except she'd just run him off.

Pam wasn't here. Jaq definitely wasn't listening any more, and he wanted to leave. Semage, well, he was part of the problem she needed outside opinion on, like Ariam. She wanted opinions outside of F-troop, so that left out anyone else she would think of to ask, especially the older ones like Trebor and Pipano.

Who? She considered. Sergeant Wreagor? She'd confided in him more than a few times. No, he was busy training.

Evetez. He'd always been able to restore her sense of balance. She started to pcom him, but hesitated. All of Easy Force was on free time now. *If Evetez was napping or enjoying some personal time with someone, he wouldn't have his headband on.* She started to reach for her Omni, which would send a message with an audible tone. Then remembered she couldn't reach him that way any more.

You know what I really want to do? I want to—

"Ah, there you are, Rett. I thought I might run into you here."

She wanted to cry. Maybe scream. Instead, she spun smartly on one heel and saluted Major Yidnar.

* * * * *

YIDNAR DIDN'T MISS THE SERGEANT's internal struggle to keep standing still and looking properly emotionless, although why she took such a formal stance with him when he approached her on free time, using her name, he had no idea. He decided it would be best to respond in kind.

"At ease, Sergeant," he said quickly, his attention leaving her face to focus on the forms in her hand. "What's up?"

"Transfers, sir." She almost snarled her reply, her chin going up another notch.

"I see." Deities, she was tiffed and hurting bad, enough to lose her usual control over her face and voice while in a public area. "Why don't we take a walk? Take a few moments and settle down before you tell me anything. Is that all right?"

"Yes, sir."

After a few minutes, Yidnar felt confident enough to give her a supportive pat on the shoulder without risking getting tossed on his head. "All right, my job isn't only to threaten you with suspensions and hand out orders, you know. What's up?"

"I wish it were all as simple as *something*, sir. It's more like an avalanche of things."

"Why don't you let me in on them, sport?" he asked gently.

She didn't answer right away, instead coming to a stop. He angled his body to face her and was startled to see tears in her eyes. He waited silently, knowing how hard it was for her to speak sometimes.

She looked away for a moment, biting her lower lip, then took a breath and met his gaze. "Major, am I supposed to give up any free choice I have as an individual to satisfy popular expectations or opinions of me?"

"Of course not. What's this about?"

"Jaq's applying for transfer, sir, here's his form."

"I think we'd better go to my office." He placed a hand lightly on her back, nudging her, unresisting, in the new direction. "We'll both be better off there."

2.1.21 2023RD CO'S OFFICE, EPNOCE MAINCOMMAND
0535.09.11 (LOCAL RECKONING)

MAJOR YIDNAR PUSHED A TINY GLASS of distilled spirits toward the sergeant, then looked at Jaq Pym's application. He took a burning swallow from his own glass, and studied the uncharacteristically slouching figure across from him as she fiddled with the second set of forms.

The way she sprawled, all sharp angles, arms, and legs, almost reminded him of the girl she had once been. That tall, gangly seventeen-year-old girl whose every graceful motion belied the awkward impression her body made at rest. He'd first met her when he and Mahrhys had been invited to Treetop by her father, Colonel Reve, then a SubColonel, for a few days of leave and some fishing, just about eleven years ago.

He'd never had to work so hard in his life to make someone feel at ease. Although that lanky teenager had guided him and Mahrhys with assurance and skill, she was like a wild creature, hiding shy and wary behind a thicket of long black fringe. She'd long ago shortened the hair to face the world eye-to-eye. Yet even now she retained her feral nature; an impression that she was only here temporarily, and, given the chance, she'd fade back into her mountain forests as quietly as she'd come out of them.

"Jaq didn't list a reason for transfer," he said finally. "And you left it blank."

"There wasn't enough room to list his reasons, sir."

Despite his concern, he had to chuckle at her reply. He picked up his marker and printed PERSONAL on Jaq's form, in the appropriate section. Then he signed his name under Rett's. "Evetez can see this later. Is the other application completed?"

"No, sir. I haven't even started it yet."

"Who is it?"

She looked up briefly. "Sergeant Ariam, applying for the opening of B-troop second." Her gaze shifted to the little glass that waited, and she reached for it, staring ahead while her brown fingers lightly traced the deeply cut geometric designs cut into the outer surface.

"No wonder," muttered Yidnar under his breath. "And? Why the delay?"

She had brought the glass closer and was eyeing it with something that looked like suspicion. "I didn't know until Semage told me about twenty minutes ago. For some reason, Ariam felt she couldn't bring it up to me herself."

Low punch right there, he thought as she shifted uncomfortably in her chair.

"I should have expected it. I saw them getting closer." She sniffed the spirits. Her lips twisted a bit and the slightest of headshakes, almost like a tremor, shivered her features. "It makes sense and I think it would be good for her. I think she'd team up well with Semage on all counts. As she did with Kraym."

"No doubt." Yidnar picked up his stylus and quickly scribed a note on his workstation tablet for his Exec. Rett would need to have a heart to heart with Ariam, and he wanted them to have some uninterrupted time for it.

"You've always approved of putting likely pairs in tandem, Major."

"Yes. But you and Ariam are also a likely pair, who work well together, and the reason I assigned her to you in the first place. What do you have to say?"

"I always thought Ariam would take F-troop if anything happened to me, but that was always with Kraym backing her. They balanced so well. She gets on well enough with Trebor, and they've managed well without me recently, but I know also the two of them have conflicting personalities." She shrugged. "Semage, he's more like Kraym, in personality, I mean. He's also strong enough to stand up to her when she gets into her moods, and she can keep him from getting too…serious. They're a good fit."

"How's your drink?" Yidnar asked. He didn't see the glass anywhere, and the hand she'd been holding it with wasn't in his view.

"Thank you, sir."

He was surprised when the sergeant set the empty glass on his desk. Alcohol was a drug her odd system metabolized without unusual complications, sure, but her limit was very low. As far as he knew, she'd never had anything stronger than ale. He wondered if she'd even tasted it.

"Ever had this before?"

"No, sir. It was very nice. A bit strong. Whatever it was just put me over my one-off limit. I had an ale earlier."

"We're not going to worry about that," Yidnar said. He picked up Jaq's application and slid it precisely into a file slot. "Now, what about you?" He refilled her glass and added a bit more to his.

"Trebor will fit the opening neatly, sir. Those times when he's filled for Ariam or Kraym just went so naturally and smooth for him you'd think he was born to it. We get on well, he's always right in step with me, maybe a half step ahead sometimes."

Either she'd completely missed his meaning or this was one of her very effective attempts to nudge the focus away from herself. *I wonder if she's even aware of it.* Since his goal was to get her talking, about anything he didn't interrupt. So far, it was working.

"He takes a serious responsibility for details," she was saying. She gave the refilled glass a doubtful look. "Worren will move to third-up. He has plenty of combat experience, but needs more hands-on experience with the managerial details. Part of that's my fault. I've never really fostered the idea in him of being so close in a direct chain of command. But after Gerrale, and then Kraym, and now with Ariam leaving..." She took the glass and sipped, making a face. Her expression was one of speculation rather than distaste.

Yidnar was relieved she didn't toss that one down, but had to wonder if she was feeling it yet. She wasn't displaying any physical signs of intoxication. It was a known fact that three ales zoned her, four zoned her stupid. He'd accomplish nothing by rendering her incoherent.

"If Trebor moves up to second, and Worren third-up, who will take Trebor's squad or co-lead with Worren?"

"Corporal Nerrah for Trebor, and Corporal H'tenneck for Worren."

"H'tenneck's very young."

"He's more than capable, sir. And respected. He's been Worren's squad junior ever since the attack on Circle."

He winced when she gulped back the remainder of the spirits, but had to admit that Rett was definitely more relaxed.

"I know Kraym's death hit you hard," he said, "especially coming so soon after your other losses at the Wide River Gap and Circle. You've barely had time to adjust."

"I wasn't the only one who had to adjust, sir."

"You were," he reminded, "the only one who had to adjust initially without having the family of your platoon around you."

Her shoulders hunched and although her face wasn't in his full view, he saw enough of it to detect a glisten of moisture on her cheek. With almost anyone else under his command, he might have offered some physical sympathy, a touch, even a hug. There had been times, more than once, even the toughest of his juniors had broken down and he'd held them while they wept. Rett wasn't someone to whom he could offer a physical shoulder. All he could give her now was a chance to unburden herself and a sympathetic ear.

219

"And now, two more people very close and important to you want to leave that family of their own accord. How will you handle things without either Ariam or Jaq, not as second in command and advisor, but as people you love?"

She swiped her arm over her face, then shifted in her chair and straightened, dark gaze steady. "I might run a bit hotter than normal, sir, but I can handle it. I've handled it before Ariam ever enlisted, and Jaq's only been with us a short time."

"I suppose Med can always keep you throttled back," Yidnar said.

She glanced briefly toward the ceiling. "Deities know he tries, sir. So does everyone else."

"All right, then. We'll run all this past Evetez later, but I don't think he'll have any problems about it, do you?"

One corner of her mouth quirked up in a familiar half grin, but there wasn't any humor in the expression. "If we stand back and look at this objectively, we're not affecting the structure of Easy Force at all. We're simply losing our tech advisor. Except for that, which is going to have an effect on quite a few people, Evetez won't have a problem."

Setting his glass down and steepling his fingers, Yidnar gazed at her for a moment, then said, "What I *meant* was: would he have any problems concerning how these moves will affect his combat team leader and second in command? Who is, last I checked, Senior Sergeant Rett."

"No, sir. Of course he'll be concerned, but Evetez will do whatever he can to support me."

Rett's voice held a warm confidence in her friend that pleased Yidnar right to the bottoms of his feet. At least those two were back on common ground. It gladdened him, because they needed the friendship they had forged during the grueling Special Forces training.

As if reading his thoughts, she added, "I'm very glad to be working with him, sir. And Semage, although I tiffed off on him just before. Both of them have always been able to keep me balanced."

"Good. So we'll go ahead right now and make the changes on file, and tomorrow, start making them official. Ariam goes to B-troop. Trebor moves up to direct second. Worren to third-up."

He glanced toward her for confirmation, then called up the F-troop roster from the workstation on his desk. He made the tentative changes. "Looks good." He idly coded a message to his Exec, asking him to contact Lieutenant Evetez about a few immediate changes in the duty roster. "I'll remind Evetez he may need to allow more time for you to spend with your juniors in regard to the shifting."

"Yes, sir."

"And please, encourage them to take their upgrades. Every one of them turned down upgrade on their last review." He glanced up with a frown. "No one's going to make them leave F-troop or Easy Force. If they want to reconsider taking an advance in rank with this shift you'll be making, we'll go ahead and catch them up instead of waiting until the next review to come around."

"I'll do that, sir." She was still slouching in her seat, but it was a very different sort of slouching now.

He filled their glasses again and nudged hers a little closer until she had to rescue it from the edge of the desk or let it fall. She picked it up.

He hoped she'd forgive him for this. He'd better make sure the ingredients she used for hangover tea were handy. They would both probably need some in the morning.

"It's the moons, you know."

220

She wrinkled one side of her nose, spared him a moment's glance, and stared back into the deep coppery hues of her drink. "Moons, sir?"

"There are three of them up there, all conspiring against us." He smiled at the confusion that knit her eyebrows over her wrinkled nose. "We have no moons on Nyorfias, so we don't think too much about them, other than it looks strange and beautiful to see them in the sky over Epnoce. When the weather is clear, at least.

"And with the war occluding such immediate thoughts regarding the effects of lunar bodies on humanoid ones, and our being indoors most of the time, this aspect of acclimating to Epnoce has gone overlooked. Until someone pointed out that all three of them visible—and full—at the same time was a rare event, something that hasn't happened in the time anyone has lived on this planet. It explains many things since we've arrived: the intensity of the storms, the quakes. The locals have adapted to the lunar cycles, but even some of them were affected by the recent event. As were all of us, to various degrees. You and Evetez were really hammered. It should start getting better now, over time."

Rett shook her head. "I don't get it."

"Gravity, sport. Not only from Epnoce. From her satellites as well. Essentially, we are being pulled in four different directions at once. And it's wreaking havoc with things from the planet's surface to people's brains and bodies. Med said your chemical balances were off, for no reason he could figure. Just like Evetez, and more than a few other people throughout the base who've recently arrived from Nyorfias and were showing some extreme reactions."

"The moons can do that?" She scratched her head.

"Doesn't it make sense that something that can cause earthquakes and tidal waves can also cause personal upheavals?"

She looked so intent for a moment he wondered what it was she thought about. "Yes, now that I think about it. It makes a lot of sense, even though I'm not completely understanding the process. I'm still trying to make sense of the weather patterns on this planet, and haven't even considered the moons as part of the factor." She shook her head. "So we were caught unprepared?"

"Totally." Yidnar nodded, spreading his hands. "Like I said, it was easy to overlook. There's still much about Epnoce we don't know, our people only started living here fifty years ago. But now, Epnoce MainCommand is in the process of completing an information update that will explain it all neatly, and medical personnel are being advised as we speak. Fortunately, it is something that can be prepared for, and compensated for."

"But you said it was a rare event."

"The three moons all visible at once and full, yes. But there are other, more regular events. Those can be prepared for."

Rett puffed a breath out through her teeth. "The moons, who would have guessed?" She rolled the little glass between her fingers and frowned at the ceiling as if she could see the celestial bodies in question.

"Now, what about you?"

She blinked. "Me, sir? You already asked about me."

"Yes, I did, and you started talking about F-troop, so I went with that while it was fresh. I meant you, the individual."

222   "One thing is for sure," she said, "the moons or this planet weren't the origin of my problems in the first place."

"I'm aware of that, Rett," Yidnar said. "However, I'm of the opinion they affected you and everyone else enough, in whatever varying amounts, to help them blow out of proportion like this. I've been concerned enough to ask those gifted among us to be alert for outside influence."

She sat up straight. "And?"

"No one's scoped anything, if that's what you mean," he said, wondering what had put her on alert. "I didn't expect them to, but I wanted to be sure. You're sensitive enough to Talent, by way of your siblings. Have you been probed?"

She hesitated. "I almost felt something like that. To the point I asked Ariam to check me especially."

"She told me. If you makes you feel better, a lot of us have felt the same way."

She slumped back again, frowning into her drink. The deep hurt and confusion that had nearly thrown her into tears earlier was back on her face, along with something else. She looked lost. And lonely. Why?

"What aren't you telling me? Did something else happen I should know about?" he asked.

She started to say something, then shrugged and shook her head.

He backtracked to what she had mentioned earlier, when he met her in the corridor. "Gossip, rumor, and speculation are very normal traits for humanoids," Yidnar said. "Someone says 'What if?' and someone else, 'It would make sense if this happened or that happened'. And the next thing you know..." He flicked his fingers. "It's off and running, by the time it gets to a fourth or fifth party, people tend to take it as fact. None of us are immune to it, or from it.

"And life would be sad indeed if we shut ourselves away to avoid it, at least from others. But as locked up as we can become from the world at large, we still have to deal with the speculations we make about ourselves."

She nodded slightly, not looking up. She closed her eyes for a second. A muscle twitched in her jaw and she swallowed.

At last he was reaching her. "I can guess there's pressure on you from many directions," he continued, "and I don't mean from gravity, this time. Might it help if I mention that this popular opinion that's hurting you so much is limited to a very small handful of individuals completely within this battalion? And not from F-troop." 223

Her look of relief was so strong he had to ask.

"You expected your own people not to back you?"

"I don't force their opinion, sir. They're very fond of Jaq. They're all especially fond of thinking of us as a couple."

"That may be true. But I was assured, firsthand, by your new second in command, that as fond as they are of Jaq Pym, something had to be done about the way he's acted toward you since the first night Captain Etron showed up in the mess area."

"Trebor?"

Yidnar nodded. "They'll do anything for you, you know. He came to me because he wanted to know, exactly, how tiffed Main Command and I would be if my *pet Zetinorian was ass-kicked from here to GTC Central*."

Rett stared at him, openmouthed and wide-eyed, for a full count of three before recovering. "*Trebor* said that?"

"In those very words."

"Trebor." She shook her head.

"Your people might be very fond of Jaq, but they won't tolerate anyone doing you injustice, not even a member of their own unit. As for others, hardly anyone outside of the 2023rd even knows of him, his assignment, or what a Zetinorian is all about."

She swallowed again and looked up, gratitude warming her face. "Thank you for telling me, sir, it does help."

"I'm sorry it came to this."

"Don't apologize, sir. We're all humanoid, last I checked. Our only difference is in how we fight." She sighed gently through her nose. "I know this whole thing got away from me too, and it shouldn't matter what anyone thinks. Deities, F-troop's been speculating on me forever. If only they'd cut me in for two percent of any of that, I'd be set for a couple generations."

"It's just a matter of some really bad cosmic timing for you, sport. On top of a prolonged period of relative inactivity." His voice lowered in compassion. "Now I want to know if there's anything I can do to help you handle it until matters pick up around here."

"Sure," Rett said without hesitation. "Get Med off my back and let me work these things out the way I normally do."

"No, I'm taking Med's side on that," Yidnar told her. "You don't need any more physical work. You need to put those clever brain cells of yours to more creative and challenging tasks instead."

"Well, then, I'm open to suggestion, Major."

"How about a transfer?"

"That'll be a nice diversion, sir." She snorted. "No matter where I would transfer, there's not too much I would qualify for outside of ground combat. Unless you've a need for my skills at foraging or harvesting trees."

She left herself wide open and he swallowed a grin, making his face completely serious. "Not according to this." He reached beneath a notepad in the usual clutter of things on his desk, and withdrew a set of blue forms. "Here."

She reached for them. "What's this?"

He watched as Rett focused her vision on the blue forms. In another moment she was sitting up straight.

"What in two worlds?" And then her eyebrows completely disappeared beneath her headband. "Section Five Combination?" Her breath came out in a shocked whistle. "Captain Etron of 114th AirSpacefighters Squadron applying under Section Five guidelines for permission to sponsor and oversee instruction of Sergeant Rett of the 2023rd Special Forces in combat flight operations…fighter pilot? Instructional and practical to take place in free time—"

Yidnar struggled to contain the grin and the laugh trying to escape. It became especially painful when she reached the bottom on the forms, where his signature was already in place alongside those of Captain Mahrhys, Lieutenant Evetez, several AirSpacefighter officers, and two from MainCommand.

Only the space for her name remained blank.

He couldn't remember her ever so shocked—at least not in a good way. She had to clear her throat twice before getting words out. "W-what's this about, sir? I've never heard of Section Five!"

Major Yidnar gave up any remaining effort to hold back his satisfaction. "I didn't think so. Neither did Etron."

"And you've known? You've known how long?" she exploded.

His grin widened. Oh, he'd known, ever since Colonel Centra had come to him for permission to have Captain Etron start showing up at Easy Force's drill sessions. "Rett, sport, I don't give away all my secrets. But I'm always ready for ways to keep my stars happy—and keep them from running too hot!" He enjoyed the next sip of the deep amber liquid in his glass, congratulating himself for her reaction. "I would have guessed before long that something a lot more stimulating than a man had you tearing across the base a few times a tenday."

She'd gone back to studying the papers again, but at this, her face rose just enough so her guilty dark eyes appeared over the top of the forms. A deeper wash of color glowed beneath her golden brown skin.

"It was the best thing you could ever have done for yourself, in my opinion." He laughed.

225

* * * * *

Rett felt as if she drew the first truly deep breath she'd taken in tendays. Strangely enough, almost everything seemed all right. Almost. Still confusing, but all right. Damn it, if it wasn't so entirely inappropriate, she would jump up right now and hug the breath out of the Major. Instead, she looked expectantly at her commander, waiting for him to explain.

"This has something to do with that cross-training idea you've always had."

He nodded, still looking extraordinarily pleased with himself. "Since the time I helped start Special Forces. It's not a new concept. Our earliest records show that the original settlers routinely doubled, even tripled primary occupations in matters civil and military since there was a need and a shortage of personnel."

"I didn't know that."

He chuckled. "There aren't many who do. In a Section Five combination, qualified and approved personnel not occupied for the time, like you, can occupy their time with a second occupation."

"Cleverly worded, sir." Since he'd looked so smug with his own resourcefulness a moment ago, she didn't resist the temptation to snipe.

"Don't get fresh, Rett, or I'll rescind this. I've spent a lot of time going through centuries of old records in order to dig this up, and I lost count of the hours spent with Etron's CO and several other officers trying to make a proposal MainCommand and the Council would accept. Looking up stuff without using our Omnis was a pain."

"And here I thought you knew everything already without having to look it up," sniggered Rett, then pasted an innocent look on her face when he glared. "Sir."

"Now, what this means is that you," he pointed at her, "will be officially Senior Sergeant Rett, of the 2023rd Special Forces. And when not involved in training or combat maneuvers with us, once you qualify as a pilot, you'll also officially be Senior Sergeant Rett of the 114th AirSpacefighters."

She found it hard to imagine.

"If you want to go through with this, that is," added her commander. "As much as I want all of us to cross-train into as many different skills as possible, I can't say I'm overcome with joy at the potential thought of losing my hardest hitters to some other operation. On the other hand, this is exactly what you need, and will help you during the periods Easy Force might be in between assignments. Apparently, you can't stay out of action very long without problems."

"No kidding," grumbled Rett.

"See to it you take the time off due you when it comes around then, and there won't be such a long interval next time," Yidnar snapped, his pleased expression dissolving into a frown so deep his thick eyebrows formed a single line over his nose.

"Yes, sir."

He continued, voice normal again. "We also considered the advantage of having our own people available for advance aerial surveillance. That factor helped decide MainCommand to conditionally preapprove this upon your agreement. Colonel Centra really pushed it through the Council. She's thrilled at the opportunity to share you with us. She wants more of us, and apparently Etron has already supplied her with a list of interested people from the 2023rd he's scoped out as potential technicians, pilots, crewmembers. We're going to see how this continues to work with you, first."

"Colonel Centra knew all along, too. No wonder she allowed Etron's experiment." Rett said. "I've yet to meet her."

"You'll get along very well with her. An amazing woman; a brilliant officer. She'll be good for you. Don't feel afraid to talk to her about anything; she'll certainly bring it up if you don't."

"I'd heard she has a talent close to Adept level."

"Close? If that's what you were told, you were deliberately misled. She *is* an Adept. A trace of mindspeak ability, as well, but only in proximity." Yidnar leaned across his desk and retrieved the blue forms from her loose grasp. "Think about it."

"What must I do?"

"Of course your first priority must be to this battalion. Nothing with AirSpacefighters can be arranged in advance, it'll be assignments as you report in to the flight officer. For the next tenday, you'll train with them in the afternoons, after you finish in drill, and after you spend time with your juniors and Trebor. Are you sure about letting Ariam go to B-troop?"

"If that's what she truly wants, yes, sir." The matter of Jaq was still a heartache. Not his leaving, which she'd already logically admitted was a sound idea, but his behavior and attitude toward her.

But she'd get through it. Especially now.

"Well, then—"

Rett knew that tone of voice and she stood up, a little bit unsteadily. *Great,* she thought. *I'm zoned. Shit.* She blinked a few times.

"—straighten this up, Sergeant Rett. Take Ariam out for a few drinks, and talk."

"Sir, I'm well over my one-off limit already."

"I'm aware of that, Sergeant."

"I'm going to have to report myself to my commanding officer."

"I've already made a note of it."

"In that case, sir, taking Sergeant Ariam out for a few more drinks, when most likely she's had her one-off already, will be—"

He interrupted. "For someone who is inebriated, you have an extraordinary and annoying attention to detail."

"We were trained that way, sir," she reminded.

"Have tea or something then. Just find Ariam, go somewhere where no one is going to bother either of you. Take these," he thrust Ariam's papers at her. "And meet me back here before curfew. I'll get Evetez in here and we'll finalize things. Okay? Get going."

"Yes, sir! Thank you sir."

"Oh, Rett?"

She paused before she opened the door, and turned. "Sir?"

"Remind me never to give you distilled spirits again."

"I'm supposed to remind you never to give me distilled spirits again, sir."

He glanced to the ceiling and groaned. "Bring Ariam back here with you. I've already changed the duty schedule, you're both off until third shift tomorrow. Mahrhys said Evetez has already informed Trebor. So you're clear."

She let out a small breath of relief. "Thank you, sir."

"One more thing. Inform Captain Etron that I absolutely forbid you flying outside the training area until I feel your unit is sufficiently prepared to deal with a possible absence of their fearless leader. Understood? Now, get lost, before I change my mind about the lot of it."

Rett started to laugh. There wasn't much that went past the Major. "Yes, sir!" Still laughing, she exited the office, entered the corridor, and collided solidly with Sergeant Semage.

"Deities, excuse me, Semage!" gasped Rett, hastily getting to her feet. She tried to give him a hand up, but ended up falling again, taking him with her.

"Damn it, Rett. Let go of me."

He rolled away from her and stood, backing off warily.

Rett got up and stayed that way this time, trying not to giggle. He looked so...*serious*. And defensive. She must have really shaken him up before in the common lounge. "Look, I apologize." She took a step toward him, her hand opened in a peace gesture. "I didn't mean to lose my head when I tiffed off at you before, I totally overreacted."

Semage backed another step. "Don't come any closer. You don't know what you're doing."

"I know perfectly well what I'm doing. And just to reiterate, my temper had nothing whatsoever to do with Ariam, she's all yours. Well, as soon as I talk to her and get these forms filled out. And hey, I'm glad you and she are getting along so well. You know, back when I went home, before going to my first assignment, she wanted to see my friends. So I showed her on my Omni. She said Evetez said looked troublesome, but thought you were pretty cute."

"You're rambling." He sniffed suspiciously. "You've been drinking."

"I have, yes."

"You've been drinking something a lot stronger than ale."

"I know that. It's all right," she said, thinking Semage was unusually slow-witted today. "Now look, 'Mage, I really, really, mean it. I'm sorry. Forgive me?"

"I think you went way over the one-off limit."

"No shit," she said in deep disgust. "So hear me out and then you can haul me into the Major's office, okay? I'm sure he'd love to hear it. Did you know it was the moons?" she asked. "All my problems aggravated by the gravitational influences of three innocent little moons. It's true," she said, seeing her longtime friend's expression change from wary defense to one of pity.

"Rett—"

"Hey, *don't* take that patronizing tone with me," she snapped. "That's exactly what pushed me over the edge before. Now listen to me. You're the sailor, Semage. Even though we've no moons on Nyorfias you should know about tides and that sort of stuff. If you don't, you can ask the Major. Now that I know where it comes from, I can stop it." Her tone changed to one of entreaty. "I feel really bad for slamming you like that before."

"Will you shut up?"

"All that time and effort you and 'Vetez took to get me saying more than four words at a time, and now you want me to shut up?"

Semage shook his head. "This is worse than I thought," he muttered.

"Oh, come on. You're usually the one who's trying to fix things—"

He interrupted. "You've short-circuited, Rett. You're rambling, jumping from one topic to the next, and making no sense whatsoever. I'm not going to take you to see the Major, I'm taking you straight to Medical."

"No you're not." Rett shook her head and took another step, her hand still outstretched. "You're going to hear me out."

She really knew she was zoned then, for in the next instant the B-troop leader grabbed her hand and pulled her off balance. Before she could take a breath, her face was mashed against the wall, her body held in place with his weight. He swiftly locked a disabling hold on her before Rett made a move to counter or retaliate.

"You've flipped out," Semage said. "They pull you out of combat for a more than a month and you flip! And you're over tolerance. We both know I would've been flat on my ass before I even touched you if you were sober. Shit, will you stop that snickering, Rett?"

"It feels good to laugh, okay? Well," she had to admit, "it would feel better if I wasn't being flattened into a pulp and pulled apart at the seams at the same time." She hoped he'd take the hint; instead he increased his pressure. "But I just had a chat with Major Yidnar, things are looking up."

"Deities, the only thing up right now is your alcohol level. You're completely stupid."

"But not at the point where I can sing yet. Shall I demonstrate?" she asked.

"Sing one single note," said Semage grimly, "and you're looking at two dislocated arms and a concussion." He pushed her forehead tighter against the wall in threat.

Oh, that went over well. She tried to shift her weight ever so slightly to ease some of the pressure of Semage's punishing, viselike hold, to no avail. She wasn't moving one fingerwidth until he let her go, and even then it would be doubtful she'd be capable of movement for a few minutes. That was the reason he kept her like this: another minute or so and she'd be numb from the neck down, unable to do much more than verbally protest while he fixed a more secure form of restraint in place.

"Uhm, I told you about the moons already, didn't I?"

"Yes," he said very patiently, as if she were a toddler. "I know they create tidal disturbances on this planet, and aggravate the quake potential, especially in the icefields."

Her recently healed shoulder started to twinge in protest. The thought of injuring it again brought a light sweat to her forehead. She swallowed. "This is really starting to hurt." Then she giggled.

"Good. Don't worry," Semage said with grim intent. "Your medtech will take care of it when we get there."

"I'd prefer you just bash my head into the wall, if it's all the same to you," she suggested politely.

"Shut up, Rett."

"Damn it, c'mon, Semage. Let me go. I'm supposed to meet Ariam. And I really don't think we should be arguing out here, in front of Major Yidnar's office." She chuckled again. "If you're going to put me on report, let's just go there. If you really want to beat me up, that's all right too. But at least let's go somewhere else. Outside, preferably, it's too hot in here."

"Shit, you're right."

When Semage suddenly went still and silent, Rett managed to angle her vision in the direction of Yidnar's office door.

Sure enough, he was right there. He leaned against his doorframe, arms folded across his chest. No telling how long he'd been there. His expression was one of mild astonishment and great interest.

Semage let go of Rett so quickly she almost fell over. She was very glad the wall was right there to hold her up. It helped that her face was still stuck to it. She gathered her wits and willed her circulation to relieve those muscles that had started going numb.

"Looking for me, Sergeant Semage?" inquired Yidnar. The fingers of his right hand drummed a pattern on his left biceps.

"No, uhm…yes, sir. I mean—"

"Why else would you be here on your free time?" suggested the Major.

Semage had apparently lost the ability to speak, so Rett tried to cover for him. Peeling her cheek from the wall, she turned all the way around, scrubbing her hands along her arms as she spoke. "He means he was just on his way to see you, sir, but I just had to get him to show me the new way he goes into that hold." Rett noticed the wall was leaning over and pushed against it so it wouldn't fall. "I delayed him. It's my fault, sir."

"Are you having trouble standing, Sergeant?"

Was he blind? "It's the wall, sir," she explained. "It's falling. I think complex maintenance should get right on this."

"I see." Yidnar's mouth twitched slightly. "I'll call them. Meanwhile, you stay right where you are and wait for Sergeant Ariam. She's on her way to meet you for that talk you're supposed to have with her."

A warm sensation of gratitude filled Rett. It didn't last long, since the Major's expression became stern again and he fixed a cold stare on Semage.

"Sergeant Semage, is what Sergeant Rett said what actually happened?"

Say yes, I don't need any more trouble, Rett begged Semage silently.

Semage only sent her a tight glare and said, "No, sir."

Yidnar didn't wait for him to explain. He stabbed a finger toward Rett. "You—hold the wall until Ariam gets here. Semage, in my office. And from now on, please confine your wrestling to the gym!" He put his fists on his hips. "We have a reputation to keep up. This...this... fooling about in the corridors will not be tolerated. Who knows what it's going to cost to fix that wall."

Rett almost burst into giggles again at the naked shock that appeared on Semage's face.

She saw the shift in his personal energy without even trying. Now he was nervous and maybe a bit scared. What was his problem? It was only a stupid wall. "It's all right, 'Mage," she assured him, "I'll cover it."

"Is something wrong with your feet, Semage?" snapped the Major. "In my office. Now!"

Rett adjusted her stance against the wall and tried to stifle her amusement as Semage, now blank-faced, slipped past Major Yidnar and into the office.

Yidnar turned to follow Semage. Before he closed the door behind himself, Rett heard him say: "Did you know that a lot of these problems were caused by the moons?"

2.2.0 SMALL PACKAGES
2.2.1 TROOPJUMPER, UNSPECIFIED LOCATION
0535.11.38 2647 HRS (LOCAL RECKONING)

*H*ER HANDS ARE NEVER STILL.

From behind the shelter of slitted eyelids and lashes, Rett watched as one of her newest transfers checked through her gear. Again. For the tenth time since they boarded the troopjumper, to be exact.

As tempting as it was to put a stop to such nervous energy, Rett mentally ticked items off the checklist along with the young soldier.

Contents of chemical and demolitions pack, check. Utility and weapons belts, secure. The custom-made TA-5 carbine (the newcomer was small, and the TT-1s were too big for her to use with comfort) was ready, clipped in place on the front of her chute harness. The harness: secure. Every strap and loose adjustment end of harnesses and webbing tucked into stays, nothing left to flap around or snag.

From head to boots, the soldier missed nothing of her peripheral gear or clothing.

With relief, Rett noted Specialist Carakenne showed no signs of wanting to unpack the chute and inspect it now. Three meticulous checks before her own inspection, and once again before Lieutenant Evetez had called final gear-up, was plenty. Not to mention there simply wasn't room for that here.

The soldier's bark-brown fingers next went to her lenses. She checked the safety band that kept them in place, made sure the glare shield was tight. At last, having gone through everything she was capable of checking without getting out of her seat and stripping down to her skin, she sighed gently through her nose.

Rett echoed the sigh inwardly. As much as watching Carakenne helped divert her mind from depressing topics, she had to do something about the younger woman's fidgeting. She needed all the energy her people had to give for this mission. She tilted her wrist enough to catch a glimpse of the time without changing her lazy sprawl.

"You okay?"

Specialist Carakenne's face jerked toward her. Rett kept her face still, a half grin in place as the younger woman met her gaze. As always, the initial glimpse of sky-colored eyes and pale golden hair against such night-dark skin brought a moment of surprise. Nor could she help thinking it seemed impossible for that innocent countenance to ever harden into a combative expression. Yet, since Carakenne had come into the unit, Rett had seen several degrees of transformation there, from cold, deadly calm to the fiercest of snarls, depending on the situation.

"Umm-hmm." The younger woman nodded. "Just checking, Sarge. And thinking."

Thinking. What else? Rett let her grin widen. *She's always thinking.*

Carakenne had a frightening intellect. It was that intelligence, along with an affinity for chemicals, tech-mindedness, and a reputation of being clever in adapting Coalition devices—or creating new ones to counter them—that had made her a top level pick when Rett was choosing replacements to fill the empty spots in her platoon a few months back.

"Thinking about anything interesting?" she asked. Quickly, she added with a light laugh, "that I might understand, that is."

"Hmm," was all Carakenne replied, giving every indication she would follow up soon with an answer.

But moments passed, and nothing had changed. Rett was still waiting, and the small brown face that looked so pensively off into nowhere remained still and thoughtful.

There had been those who warned her about taking on a soldier who didn't fit the average physical profile of most in a frontline combat unit. Even Major Yidnar had expressed some concern. Rett pointed out that Carakenne obviously passed any tests and completed her Special Forces training in an acceptable manner, or she wouldn't be wearing a headband in the first place. So the kid had to have more than enough brains to compensate for her lack of brawn. Why should she let such a valuable asset get transferred to another unit?

Rett knew for a fact that Yidnar was *also* trying to pick up Carakenne during the 2023rd's transfer and exchange lottery as someone for his personal team. He wasn't above trying to talk people out of something they wanted to get what *he* wanted. He was good at that. After all, before the war, he had been a successful and ruthless LawRep who negotiated offworld trade agreements.

He didn't succeed this time, thought Rett with an inward smirk. She didn't often win a battle of wills against the 2023rd's commander, on her own merits or otherwise. This time, it had been the luck of the draw—since it was a computer program, not a humanoid, that compiled the selections and made the assignments.

But once the assignments were official, the real trouble had started— between F-troop's squadleaders. And not because they had reservations about bringing in a lightweight comrade whose head only came up to the chin of even the shortest of them. No, it was because each of them felt Carakenne should be assigned to his or her squad. H'tenneck insisted someone so clever with tech should be with him. Nitraym wanted her for her talent for chemicals and demolition. They had gone from trying to persuade Rett to arguing and insults, so Rett had stepped in and ended it by assigning Carakenne to Nerrah's squad. She told them in no uncertain terms that the newcomer would help H'tenneck as needed, as well as serve on Nitraym's demolition team when the mission called for it—*if* Nerrah, and Rett, decided she could be spared.

As far as Rett was concerned, Specialist Carakenne's major weakness didn't have anything to do with her intelligence or physical assets—or lack thereof. No. Carakenne, growing up in an isolated community of scientists who lived in their own little bubbles of research, was over- whelmingly shy, even more so than Rett herself had been in the past. Not even Special Forces training had taken that out of her. Her records stated that on duty, she was fine. But on free time, she usually isolated herself, hiding behind her Omni, busy with a book or some kind of research. Rett had managed to change that slightly since Carakenne's

237

arrival: the younger woman still tended to bury herself behind an Omni, but at least she did so while sitting near, if not with, a few of her new comrades in a common area.

Of course it helped to have other tech-minded people for her to interact with, too. People who actually understood what she was talking about. More and more Rett would walk through the common area and actually witness Carakenne in a fully animated conversation with H'tenneck, Steffi, Mikel and Jessek.

And no doubt, had Jaq stuck around, he'd be part of those in Carakenne's new circle of friends, too.

Rett sighed inwardly. *Damn it, stop thinking about him already. I'm supposed to be thinking about Carakenne so I won't think about Jaq being gone. And Pam being gone. And Ariam being gone, at least from F-troop.*

And Jaq.

238   *Jaq is gone.*

Thinking the words brought a sharp ache to her heart. Almost three months ago and it hurt as much as it had the first time. *I'd better let it bother me while I still have time for it, and then put it away,* thought Rett, even as she waited for Carakenne to speak.

When he had taken his leave of them, Jaq had promised he'd always love her and they would always be friends. His goodbye had been cool and distant, unlike her own. It had been all she could do to restrict her outward reaction to a clogged nose and eyes that were so filled with tears she was afraid to blink. Several escaped anyway, and she hadn't really cared who saw them. Trebor, thank all deities, had automatically taken custody of Jaq's headband as if it had been his job to do so all along instead of hers.

That had been it. Jaq went off to his short-term assignment with a busy Transport and Supply unit. A few letters had come her way, but they were unvaryingly generic and never said anything personal. Sure, the TRANS units were often incommunicado and personal communications weren't allowed to go into detail. But he was sending letters to her that read as if he were writing them for her to share with F-troop, instead of to her personally.

And she missed Pam, her friend from Earth, the mental companion somehow merged with her body and consciousness in an event Nyorfians called an ego-merge. Missed her more than ever now that Jaq was gone. She might not have missed Pam so deeply if she could talk to Ariam about missing Jaq. But Ariam was gone now, too. Transferred to B-troop. It wasn't as if Ariam had transferred to the other side of the planet. But their opportunities for personal interaction were few; their off-shifts rarely coincided.

Sergeant Trebor was Rett's second in command now, and, as she told Major Yidnar, he filled the position as if born to it. Although he'd been with her the longest of anyone else in F-troop, Trebor wasn't her sister, much less someone Rett ever had discussed her personal life with.

And that's enough of that, she told herself as Carakenne finally indicated she was ready to speak. With relief, Rett pushed her problems firmly into the vault where they belonged while she was working.

239

"Well." Carakenne paused to bite her lip for a half-second. "Well, actually, Sergeant, I have been wondering about something. But it's… it's a personal question."

Rett waited patiently for her to continue, keeping her expression light and eye-contact casual. Carakenne was flushed—impossible for most anyone else to tell since she was as dark as H'tenneck. But Rett's sensitivity to energy auras, as well as her proximity to the younger woman, didn't allow such things to hide.

"There's not too much a lot of people don't know, haven't guessed, or made up about me already," Rett prompted after a few more seconds of delay."So ask."

Carakenne's pale eyebrows rose, making half-circles of golden light against her forehead. "What are you going to do after the war?"

Always full of surprises, this one. "I don't know." Rett leaned her head back against the bulkhead. The ache she had thought she'd pushed away returned. Damn it. She should have never allowed herself to start thinking that way in the first place, Jaq or no Jaq. "I wonder about it. I suppose I'll wait and see if I survive that long first."

"Didn't you intern or train for anything? What sort of work did you do before you enlisted?"

"I was born and raised a logger. I certified in forestry management before I enlisted and was almost a year into my internship, and was this close," said Rett, illustrating her point with her thumb and forefinger, "to finishing my quals as an eco-biologist, too." She'd passed by a hair, but she'd passed. She'd never done well on tests, in a classroom or orally in front of a panel. It was a good thing her chosen career field wasn't heavy on the hard science and tech, and she had been lucky to demonstrate practical know how and experience on the final section of her quals.

Would I be a better student now, after how I've changed? Rett had to wonder. She didn't think she'd become any more a scholar, but she had eliminated or learned to compensate for many of the hangups she'd had before enlisting. As for getting through flight training, that was different. She still got a headache when doing flight-related figures and calculations and didn't fully understand how a few things worked, but she managed to pass by a respectable—if yet far from perfect—margin.

"The eco-biologist qual would enhance the forestry management rating," Carakenne replied with a grave nod, popping Rett's momentary bubble of speculation.

"Yes. It did. It helped learning hands-on as I grew up, too. Back then, I never thought I'd leave home for longer than an internship year. But plans changed when the war started." Rett leaned her head back and stared at the ceiling of the jumper for a moment. "Like they did for a lot of people."

"You have the pilot ratings now, too, for jumpers and fightercraft. Like some of the others are getting now, too."

"Yes." She lifted her head up again. "So I've a couple options I can go back to."

Rett's success with cross-training into AirSpacefighters had opened the prospect for more personnel. For her, flying was a most excellent diversion from her troubles. It lifted her mood as much as it lifted her body from the planet's surface.

"Umm-hmm! Have you been home at all since you enlisted?" Carakenne sounded a bit wistful.

"No." Rett didn't want to talk about that. There were many reasons. Time. Distance. That period Treetop had been under enemy occupation. Not wanting to see what the big fires that happened during the occupation, or the battles that reclaimed the area, had done to the landscape she loved. Fear. Her gut twisted with it every time she thought that once she did go home, she'd find everything so changed it would be unrecognizable; no one she knew living there. That it would be as alien to her as her first experience of the Barrens in the extreme southeast of Nyorfias.

She shook off the unsettled sensation. "What about you, Carakenne? Back to the lab and your study?"

"Probably." The younger woman nodded, a small smile curving hers lips and a faraway look softening the bright focus of her eyes.

She's gone off again, where to this time? wondered Rett.

The smaller soldier's tense sitting position began sliding a bit more toward a relaxed curve than absolute perpendicular. "Ever fall out?"

"What's that?"

"Of a tree," clarified Carakenne.

The younger woman's display of bemused astonishment and Rett's personal surprise at the question brought a laugh. Had Carakenne expected her to follow her exact thoughts? The memory of the first and only time—so far—Rett had ever made an involuntary descent from one of the big trees of Nyorfias' northern mountains rose in her mind, and she laughed again.

"Yes. Once," Rett admitted. "With a bit of help from a Coalition trooper's ML-12."

Carakenne's eyes widened.

Sergeant Trebor leaned across the aisle. "It's a good story. I'm surprised you haven't heard it yet, Cara. Then again, it was Ariam who always brought it up."

Rett glared at her second. There were some aspects of Ariam's constant presence that she didn't miss. Why did Trebor feel it was necessary to fill them in? She had to give up the glare for a chuckle, though. Ariam liked bringing up such stories because they broke the ice, made people relax, and reminded them Rett was as humanoid and capable of making mistakes as anyone else. She'd given her newest team members the speech already, but a good story helped send the message home.

"Which, unfortunately, we don't really have time for right now," said Rett.

"But it really is too good to miss," said Trebor, settling back.

"Yeah," muttered Rett. "And you should see the report she filed on it." She rolled her eyes. "I had to spend more time explaining Ariam's report to Major Yidnar, in person, than she must have taken to write it."

"So remind me or Sergeant Nerrah," said Trebor, "and we'll get Ariam over during some free time to tell that story. No one can tell it like she can."

Carakenne's expression was caught between astonishment and disappointment. "Yes, Sergeant Trebor." The younger woman nodded again, and before Rett had time to take a deep breath, Carakenne's attention already had gone elsewhere.

With a small headshake and a half-grin on his fierce face, Trebor tipped his head back and closed his eyes.

Now what? Rett glanced in the same direction, forward, where Lieutenant Evetez was talking to the jumpmaster. Flirting, no doubt. He never passed up an opportunity.

Another sigh came from the small figure to her left.

Rett's interest perked. *Evetez?* She followed Carakenne's line of sight again to be sure, then focused her energy sense on the younger woman long enough to confirm her suspicions.

She'd had words with Evetez about his sudden interest in Carakenne, but she'd assumed it was more from the young woman's social reticence and reclusive nature—so much like hers had been. Outgoing and sociable, and keenly aware that teamwork took a certain degree of social interaction off duty, Evetez naturally sighted in on those he thought needed extra attention.

He had tried the same thing with her when they had been in Special Forces training together. Since she had found Evetez's attention annoying to the point of wanting to cause him physical harm, she decided to intervene. She wanted to use a different approach on Carakenne, so she'd told him to back off and let her handle it.

She'd never dreamed there was anything but professional interest involved, from either one of them. But from that sigh and the unconsciously longing glance Carakenne was giving Evetez right now, maybe she was the one who should back off.

Was Evetez mutually interested? She had to think about that for a moment. He had been finding excuses to come around more than necessary while Rett was processing in her new platoon members, or sitting with them at mess, that was for sure. Maybe the bubblehead didn't realize he was interested in more than bringing Carakenne out of her social shell.

"You like him." Rett kept her voice low and non-carrying, but Carakenne reacted as if Rett had shouted into her ear. All at once the younger woman was sitting up straight and on the edge of her seat again, her small hands tightly clasped over the assorted straps for packs, weapons, and harness.

"Take it easy, sport. It's all right, you know."

The smallest of headshakes answered. Carakenne's face remained downward, refusing to turn in Rett's direction.

"He's not bad for a bubbleheaded idiot." Rett leaned over confidentially. "He's been watching you, too."

"Really?" Cara's voice squeaked. The younger woman cleared her throat and stared toward her knees again. "But of course he does. It's part of his job, to watch us. Like yours, Sergeant."

"I'm not talking about when we're in drill or combat alert. Maybe you'd better stop hiding behind your reading during free time."

For once the always busy brown fingers were still. Carakenne's shoulders sagged and she slouched, crossing her small booted feet in front of her. Thoughtful. Relaxed. All right, maybe astonished. But for now, thought Rett with a satisfied, inward grin, her mission was accomplished.

Chew on that for a while, kiddo. She let her head tip back again, intending to relax. Instead, she was surprised by a sudden wash of loneliness and that cold, empty feeling that had been with her since the ego-merge with Pam ended. Since Jaq had transferred out, that void had grown, a great wide gulf that made the Rift Canyon look like an insignificant crack. Didn't matter how much she tried to fill it with her new dual status as a pilot with AirSpacefighters and the pleasant attentions of Captain Etron.

Too many changes. She still expected to see certain faces when she glanced down the line at her platoon; the faces she'd grown used to seeing every day for almost three years. The new faces that took their place still startled her.

The troopjumper's engine sounds muted as the pilot switched into the less efficient but near-silent combat mode. Grateful for the timing that checked her darkening thoughts, Rett checked her chrono, slapped the quick release catches of her safety harness, and stood.

"Ten minutes, Fang team, run finals. Specialist Carakenne and Sergeant Trebor will be coming 'round to inspect." She glanced toward Trebor, sending a silent message to which he responded with approval. Rett patted Cara's shoulder. "Come on, check me, then off you go. You're set, I watched your last gear check. The last four or five of them, to be exact."

Silently Carakenne rose, her small face settling into an expression devoid of emotion, all business. Her inspection of Rett's harness, gear, and weapons was as quick and thorough as anyone could want. She added extra streaks of camo paint to Rett's cheekbones, chin, and nose, the parts most likely to reflect light. All shyness aside, the younger woman had no problem pointing out an unfastened corner seal on the utility belt pocket containing Rett's VARs. Or that loose half-finger-length loop of boot binding that might very easily snag on something on the ground, possibly resulting in either a minor stumble or major disaster.

See what I get for trying to divert myself, Rett grumbled inwardly, but made the necessary corrections. Only proved distractions made one careless. *And careless gets you killed. Or worse.* She vowed not to give her personal issues another thought. *At least until we get back.*

Leaving Carakenne to finish inspecting the others, she went to join Evetez and the other platoon leaders up front for a final update. The red ready lights flashing from the panel on the forward bulkhead switched to blue as the combat teams signaled their readiness.

Rett made her way down the file waiting for the signal. A final check, a few quick personal words she liked to have with each of her people, time permitting, before a mission. She saw that Bhayorn, last in the file, was bristling more than usual under his load of weapons and extra gear. Then she saw small fingers busily tucking up a few loose ends of harness and rigging the burly man couldn't quite reach.

Bhayorn dropped a wink at Rett as she grinned at him, his bright green eyes twinkling from beneath a thicket of shaggy eyebrows and surprisingly long, curly eyelashes. "Next time, Sarge, Cara gets to load me up," he said. "She says she can make me more aerodynamic."

Rett nodded. "We'll make sure of it then. You're good to go?"

"All go," he agreed, a grin flashing from beneath his heavy black whiskers. He had to turn his entire upper body to make eye contact with his smaller comrade. "Thanks, Cara."

Rett's gaze went to the figure who shifted now from one foot to the other, only the end of her nose peeking from a tightly drawn hood.

You're hoping I can't guess how much you hate this, Rett thought with sympathy.

Carakenne had a professed fear of heights and was night-blind. She wore corrective lenses to compensate for that disability, but Rett knew the younger woman had something far better than that—guts, combat sense, and an incredible ability to hear beyond the normal range for most Nyorfians. It was time Carakenne was reminded to use those gifts.

Rett gripped the small woman's shoulder. "Carakenne, nothing to it, sport."

"Umm-hmm, yes, Sergeant!"

"Remember to control your position; try not to land atop anyone. Use your ears, your combat sense. You'll hear and feel stuff before you see it. Trust me, none of us are going to see too much going down. Fog's that thick. No trees where we're headed. Listen for your partner's whistle. Jayord?"

245

The commando ahead of Bhayorn, also a recent addition, turned at the sound of his name. "Sarge?"

"Nitraym paired you with Carakenne for this?"

"We're a great team, Sarge," Jayord said with enough confidence for any ten individuals.

Which was, reflected Rett, one of the reasons he teamed well with Carakenne. Somehow the extremes between their personalities balanced out perfectly on the job.

"You're good to go then, Carakenne?" Rett felt the acknowledgment through her fingers more than she saw an outward, physical motion. "Don't disappoint me."

This time, a big, beaming smile angled up from the small dark face, a bright, gold-washed light replaced the gray, subdued colors of the younger woman's energy aura. The change warmed Rett inside and out, especially the strong, heartfelt "Never, Sarge," that came with it.

"Good." Rett released her grip, gave Carakenne two light taps with her fist. "See you below, then."

She went back up the file, stopping briefly with each F-troop member for a personal word or two. Any dark thoughts had been banished. Before rejoining Evetez, she turned toward her platoon, soaking in more of their strength, their confidence, their trust. She hoped, as always, she wouldn't disappoint them, either.

The regular lighting inside the ship faded into the red nightlights. Foggy or not, the switch would give most of them the chance to adjust their vision for the darkness.

Up front, the jumpmaster waited as Lieutenant Evetez gave everyone a met update: winds aloft, winds at thirty lengths, winds at ground level, temperature, and current precipitation.

"Who first this time, me or you?" Rett asked Trebor as he sidled up to stand alongside her.

"You," Trebor said promptly.

"I went first last time." Rett tightened her hood closer around her head and face and adjusted protective goggles over her eyes.

He shrugged. "You've seniority."

"You're older."

"Smarter, too."

Rett made a face.

"Besides, you're the pilot, not to mention you come from the province where everyone climbs trees and mountains and icebergs and things. You like heights."

It had been Trebor's personal aversion to jumping out of perfectly good aircraft that had started up the running argument of who went first. Observing how the exchange lightened the tension for a lot of people, Evetez had become involved in it, too. Now it was part of the jump routine that not only F-troop, but all of Easy Force, came to expect.

"Sure, that's why I'd rather stay up here, thank you. You go first, that way I'll have something nice and soft to land on. Like your head."

"Deities, not this again." The jumpmaster groaned, but it was obvious she was trying to swallow a grin. "Better decide quickly. Half a minute more."

Rett kept part of her attention on the jumpmaster's fist as it hovered over the status alert controls. She wondered what Lenna was seeing on the backs of those specialized lenses that served dual duty as wind protection and data display. Then she saw the shift in the woman's energy, the curve that had been threatening the jumpmaster's lips flatten.

Now what?

"Whoops—looks like a little seismic action down there."

Rett gritted her teeth and swallowed a groan. *All we need is one hard shake once we get down. On that marshy footing, we'll be bogged under before we could take a deep breath.* Watching the jumpmaster closely, Rett felt her own tense concern reflecting from Evetez and Trebor. *Lenna's an expert. Trust her. She's Epnoce-born and has jumped us safely for twelve missions already.* In spite of that, Rett still wished she could see the data for herself.

"Ah, it's over. Telemetry says ground conditions are stable. We're still all-go."

"If we get any more, they'll be minor." Lieutenant Evetez sounded confident.

"Let's hope so." Rett gave a tug to one of her pack straps. As good as their seismo and met people were, Epnoce always managed to surprise them.

"You go first, Fang Lead," Evetez said. The twinkle was back in his eyes as he moved to stand opposite the jumpmaster near the big sliding door. "If there's any Coalition troopers waiting for us, tell them who you are. Then start running. That way they'll follow you and leave us alone."

"Good gods and deities! That's what you said last time, too. All I'm good for is a moving target, is that it? Why can't Trebor be the target this time?"

"Because you're bigger than I am." Trebor crossed his arms, a stubborn set to the already harsh planes of his hawklike face.

"Better looking, too," added Evetez.

She glared at the lieutenant. "Can you at least *try* for a little more originality?"

"He meant Trebor," snickered the jumpmaster, then called "Time, Easy Force!" Her hand hit the ready light and the blue signal went to yellow. "GO!"

Evetez leaned over, giving Rett a smoking hot glance at point blank range. It was enough to startle her, since she thought both of them were well beyond anything but a friendly physical affection.

"Bye."

Then he shoved her out the door.

His motion was more action than applied force, since she'd already been on her way out. As Easy Force second in command and the combat team leader, it was her place to be on the ground first, or heading the advance line into a target area. Trebor would be last off the jumper for F-troop.

Lieutenant Evetez would make sure everyone made it out of both troopjumpers before taking his own turn. Normally, he'd hang back with S- and D-troops, who were coming in thirty minutes behind them as the second line. This time around, he was going in with the first.

Rett laughed as she hurtled into the open, still feeling some lingering effects from Evetez's hot eyes. Deities! Good thing she was in mid-leap when he'd pushed. For a moment there her knees had gone numb.

The night was thick, the frigid air so saturated with moisture she was sure it slowed her descent. She entertained a thought that it was almost better to jump in straight rain or sleet, both of which they'd had on previous missions, than this. After all, rain and sleet, if the winds were reasonable, went down. This fog went everywhere: a writhing, cold moisture that grabbed and clung to her body with heavy, wet fingers.

On the count, she deployed her chute and hoped the oversaturated air wasn't going to cause problems.

The stop-short jolt of the canopy snapping open didn't normally bother her, but this time she nearly blacked out and completely lost her sense of direction and balance. Before a confused rush of panic could even begin to gather momentum, she tentatively identified the source and gasped aloud, "Pam? *Pam!*"

~Where the hell are you?~

Good gods and deities! This time, Rett kept her jubilant shout inside.

~No gods and deities here, just a dimwitted alien mindforce.~

Is it really you?

~I'm baaacck!~

The bright, warm flare of Pam's aura left no doubt.

Gladness filled Rett, warming the place deep inside that had felt cold and empty since Pam's departure. Her throat went sore and tight and she was grateful she didn't have to speak to express her feelings at that moment.

Likewise, Pam's joy felt strong enough to overcome the force of Epnocian gravity, which even the thick mist couldn't fight.

Gravity?

Mist.

Shit. The shock of Pam's reentry vanished completely as Rett tried to calculate how much airspace she had left between her feet and the ground.

249

Damn it Pam, I've lost the count. Rett raised her head a bit, snarling softly to the sky and the mysterious beings they referred to as gods and deities. "You people have incredibly bad timing!"

She strained every sense to the utmost in the effort to gauge her position. It was the nearby warble and whoop of a low-flying Epnocian nightwing that warned her contact with the ground was imminent. The fat nocturnal avians, probably the closest thing in the Nyorfian system to one of Pam's Earth "chickens", never flew more than six lengths above the ground. She scrambled to make the necessary adjustments. A breath later, something crunched under her boots: the ground-hugging, weedy growth they'd been told to expect.

Damn it. That loss of focus might very well have left her on the ground where she landed, either dead or injured too badly to go on with the rest of Easy Force.

~I'll just move on back into my space and clear out the cobwebs, shall I?~

Please. Deities, I have so much to tell you.

~Later.~ Pam already was settling into her place. The imaginary door—that seemed more solid than it used to be—stopped short of clicking shut.

Missed you, thought Rett and felt her sentiment returned even as she refocused focused her mind and body on the mission.

She gathered the chute, releasing the harness with quiet, speedy efficiency. No human sounds reached her ears. Only the wind, the eerie calls of nightwings, and the soft rustling of small animals moving in the brush. Common enough night noises for this part of Epnoce.

Rett whistled, a single, high piping note that trilled away to nothing and then suddenly resurfaced into the nightwing's characteristic whoop. Other whistles answered, the only thing distinguishing those made by the commandos from the avians were the subtle variations in pitch and pattern. She named and counted off each individual in her head as they came to ground and responded. *H'tenneck, Pip, Nerrah, Jayord, Med, Steffi, Worren...*

...that's thirty-two, Mikel, Kuitan, Ewayn, Bhayorn, Carakenne...

And finally: *there's Trebor.*

Forty-one, counting herself. Relief. She felt a bright spot of surprise and alarm start rising from Pam, but pushed it back with a sharp warning. Whatever it was, this wasn't the time or place.

Those brighter areas up ahead had to be the lights from the huge building. Soon, the thick fog took on visible structure. Spooky swirls and currents of vapor curled and eddied around her. Rett pulled a hard focus on her ability to identify energy sources from living or inanimate objects. A swirl of mist might easily be mistaken for the movement of a body, weapon, or vehicle.

Dampness and potential tremors aside, Rett was grateful for the conditions. It was cold, yes, but still unseasonably mild for the time of year. At the same time, she couldn't deny the return of deep cold would be far more of an advantage to the Free Army's ground efforts. She took a moment to recall when an eighteen-year-old version of herself paid close attention to her first platoon leader, Sergeant Utahe, as he told her *"Most Coalition troopers hate the damp. And most of their officers—not all—have a hard time dealing with the cold. The Yixolryn and those Voi, their best friends, the scaly looking ones? Especially them. They would have left Epnoce alone and came straight here if we hadn't had habitats set up there already."* 251

She halted her troop with a hand signal for those who could see her and a soft, animal sound for those who couldn't. Amplified by the damp, the soft "hmm-click!" of the VARs seemed to make a crash of sound loud enough to startle even the nightwings into silence.

2.2.2 OUTSIDE COMPLEX 412, EPNOCE
0535.11.38 (LOCAL RECKONING)

RETT DIDN'T HAVE TO HEAR MUCH to know her unit was splitting up. The demolition teams would execute the first phase of the plan: putting the underground railtubes that connected most Epnocian complexes out of commission. Despite the frequency and potential severity of earthquakes, the weather on Epnoce's surface was even more of a hazard, so traveling underground was popular. The tubes were constructed to withstand the most severe quakes. Phase one was to disable critical sections of the tubes, without making much noise or attracting attention. If successful, the damaged tubes would prevent the current Coalition garrison from escaping as well as prevent the arrival of reinforcements.

So she waited with the rest of her group, still and watchful in the freezing fog.

About one hundred running strides from the outermost entrances of Complex 412, Rett's group was one of two dozen small Easy Force units awaiting the last signal before the attack. She kept one eye on the time display of her VARs as she continued to scan for enemy movement, for anything that might present an unexpected hazard or require some last minute plan changes.

If she had been allowed the choice of carrying only one extra item into a mission like this one, besides herself and her TT-1, she'd take the VARs. The device performed far more complicated tasks than distance viewing or rangefinding under any kind of lighting conditions or weather. VARs also detected metal and heat sources, recorded images and plotted map data when uplinked to an Omni or larger computer, and gave environmental information: basic air quality, movement, humidity, and temperature.

~These were Kraym's?~ Pam asked.

Yeah. Surprise came at Pam's intrusion when the time was so close. Rett allowed herself a half second to remember how Kraym always seemed to have these VARs in her hand before she reached for her own. The thumb she'd been digging into her temple rubbed lightly over several deep scratches in the outer casing of the device.

~You're not stressing, Rett. Where'd this headache come from?~

Weather, maybe. Atmospheric pressure. Shit, I don't know. This planet, the moons, and the flaming gravity are still playing all sorts of games with me. I can't explain that now. But once we get moving, it'll be fine. Pam, I know it's been a while, but if you don't mind?

~What happened to Ariam? And Jaq? Why aren't they here?~

Oh, so that was it. No wonder that alarmed sensation had rose so strongly before. Rett was quick to send reassurance to her friend. *Ariam's gone to B-troop. Jaq is elsewhere. I can't explain it all now.*

Pam was satisfied for the moment, her relief strong. ~All right. And I'm backing, I'm backing. Sorry.~

Deities, but the air was thick. Rett rubbed her forehead, wishing the cool moisture there would seep through skin and skull to her brain. Scowling, she studied the readouts in her VARs again. Air temperature constant, no wind to speak of. She didn't even hear the trill and whoop of nightwings any longer and wondered if something about the huge building kept them from coming close. The ground beneath them shivered. *Not now. We don't need another tremor or quake right now, of any intensity. Not on this mushy ground.*

The tremor subsided. Nothing moved but the mist, swirling thickly around them. It didn't take much to imagine it as a living thing, some alien predator, seeking to appease its chilling, wet hunger, clawing into their clothing in a mindless quest for warm living flesh. Still eyeing the target area with the VARs, she blinked hard a few times and curled her lip in annoyance as the throb of pain in her temple increased in intensity.

The time display in the lower right hand corner of the viewfinder started to flash. *Five seconds…wait for it…three, two, one—*

Rett signaled her people forward.

A shrill whistle shattered the eerie silence and froze her advance.

As she reached for the utility belt pocket containing the breather unit, her head turned sharply in the direction the whistle had come

253

from—behind them. From F-, B-, and R-troop's chemical and demolition teams. Despite her familiarity with the various vocal ranges of her
unit, she wasn't sure who had given the signal. But it was one she hadn't
heard for a long time, and never in an outdoor situation.

Airborne chemical! What sort of chemical? Where was it coming
from, going? Didn't matter. It was a problem. Shit.

What went wrong? It can't be anything we brought with us.

After adjusting her mask, she lifted the VARs and spoke a terse, soft
voice command to enhance the environmental readings. Nothing was
popping any alerts she could see. Coalition had never used chemicals
before, not in the open. Only in enclosed areas.

*But no wonder I'm starting to feel hung over! We've been sitting in
more than weather-produced mist for deities know how long! Why didn't
this set off a hazard alarm before now?*

Taking a breath before pulling her mask aside, Rett put her fingers
to her lips and signaled for all units to pull back. She only hoped there
was time to get clear of this and into cleaner air. And to get clear before
anyone came out of the complex ahead and decided three platoons of
half-zoned Nyorfians would be perfect for some target practice.

Or something worse.

-Weather conditions couldn't be more perfect for a gas attack, too,-
observed Pam. -The stuff won't dissipate in this soup—it'll cling with
the mist.-

Oh, yes, perfect, returned Rett as her signal relayed and echoed in the
dense night.

"Runner," said the muffled, hollow-sounding voice of Ewayn behind
her.

In Rett's mental vision, the runner's combat ready orange aura was
outlined in the hard brassy edges of anxiety. *It's Carakenne.* When the
speeding figure showed no sign of slowing down, Rett growled a sound
that was both a proximity warning to the runner and a *keep going* to the
others with her. The filters weren't exactly suited to the type of breathing
required by fast travel. As a matter of fact, strenuous activity was something to avoid in these situations. *Nitraym wouldn't have sent her on the
run without good reason.*

Catching the breathless commando by the shoulders, Rett steadied Carakenne as she almost fell.

"What's up?"

"Traps," gasped Carakenne. "Gas traps. Have 'em rigged in the vents from…the railtubes 'n underground loading areas an' storage, from back there…maybe farther," she gestured vaguely from the direction she'd come, "right to the complex wall."

Recalling the schematics everyone had studied before the mission, Rett cursed again. The various underground railtubes, passages, storage rooms, conduits and other portions of the complex extended in all directions, like twisting shallow roots from a tree on rocky ground, for almost a mile in a complete circle around the building itself.

"Jayord kicked up a motion detector when we got a length or so from our access hatch." Carakenne gulped in another breath. "We've been triggering traps off for lengths already. Without knowing."

"Motion detectors!" Rett didn't want to believe it. Why hadn't her energy sense caught that? And was there something wrong with her VARs? No, anyone using VARs should have seen an alert. No one had.

The lightweight body in her grip wobbled for control. How much of the gas had Carakenne absorbed or inhaled already? Even as she guided the younger woman back, retracing their steps, Rett lifted her voice enough to call Med to her.

As usual, Med had already been vectoring in on the individual in distress. Rett's voice simply fine-tuned his trajectory through the fog. "Stop for a minute," demanded the medtech.

"I really don't think stopping for anything is a good idea, Med, you'll have to hit her as we go."

The hiss of the injector was followed by a shudder from Carakenne. Med's remedy took effect immediately. As the soldier straightened and steadied, Med traded the breather unit for an oxygen mask. He held the unit to her face and told her to breathe deep and slow.

"Go on if you can, Carakenne," urged Rett.

"Mnf 'ew ube—"

"Wait." Med adjusted his hand and the device. "Okay."

"We fixed the transit tubes, went perfectly, everyone was synched and Sergeant Nitraym sent the activation signal—"

"Yes." Rett curbed her impatience, trying to blink away the blurriness clouding her vision even more than the fog surrounding them.

"Didn't figure it out until Jayord fell over. We helped him up and found a section of clear cable that had been underground; maybe a hard tremor earlier forced it up. Cable for the motion detectors. Looks like darklight technology. Invisible unless you know what to monitor for, even then easy to miss."

From the mental image Cara's words produced in Rett, Pam was able to deduce the clear cable was a fiber optic bundle about the thickness of one of Rett's fingers. But what did Carakenne mean by darklight technology?

It's not my field, so don't expect me to explain.

~I wasn't trying to let that come up,~ apologized Pam.

Don't forget you're as affected by this gas as I am, so don't worry about it. Aloud, Rett said, "You mean those azurium-based lasers? The ones that need those really rare crystalline forms?"

Only the nodding motions of Carakenne's head answered her.

No wonder we didn't pick them up, they're supposed to use so little energy they're practically undetectable. At least in theory. And unless I came in range of one, I'm not sure if I'd be able to scope one, either. "I didn't think that got off the design board yet. Damn. What about the gas? Med? Any ideas?" Rett missed a step, her boot catching in the low-slung branches of the weedy plants. This time, it was Carakenne who reached a steadying hand.

"I can only guess it's a soporific at this point," muttered Med, suddenly having trouble keeping his hold on the breather unit. "Keep this on," he ordered Cara. "What sort it might be, I haven't a clue."

"Neetramsys'inkststm'edcal 'nstheticnsynt 'tect." Cara mumbled from behind the mask and the hand that held it tightly in place.

Rett ground her teeth in frustration. "Carakenne… I didn't understand a single word."

The smaller woman pulled the mask away enough to speak clearly. "Nitraym says it's some medical anesthetic the scanners aren't coded to detect. I think so, too."

"Oh," said Med. "I think, then, we were far too late to do much about it. Probably inhaled enough that the effects have to run their course. Sarge, head hurts, does it? Bad?" As he dug in his pack, Med lost his footing and fell to one knee.

The only good news Cara's announcement and Med's comment brought to Rett was that the agent had to be inhaled in a certain quantity and wasn't absorbed through the skin. "I think most of us have inhaled too much already."

Letting go of Cara, Rett reached behind her for Med's arm and yanked him upright. "Keep moving, Med. No, Cara, keep the mask on."

"But Sarge, you—"

"*Keep it on.* Med, if whatever you gave Cara can induce enough motivation in anyone else to clear this, start with yourself and hit as many as you can. Move it." She gave him a light push away and he reeled off, still mumbling to himself, into the fog.

~Can you call for retrieval or get the second line units up here?~

No, answered Rett shortly. *It's too complicated to explain fully, but right now we can't use certain frequencies until daylight because at night the Coalition can pick them up.* The effects of the three moons and the planet's practically unpredictable weather weren't the only baffling peculiarities of Epnoce.

Her own voice started sounding blurry and strange in her ears. Damn it! The coldness that puckered her skin from top to bottom with chillbumps had nothing to do with the weather.

"Sergeant—" Carakenne began again.

Rett placed her hand over the one the small soldier used to remove her oxygen mask, preventing Carakenne from continuing. She recognized her reaction to the anesthetic as soon as Med voiced her symptoms. It wouldn't have as adverse an effect as other drugs did on her, but instead of going off to sleep without a fuss as quickly as almost anyone else would, she'd have something like a SMG stun hangover before becoming unconscious and after recovering.

"No, I would need too much of it to shake it off what's already started. I don't think any of us are going to clear this before going down. But you can—if you keep that on."

After feeling Carakenne's head move in reluctant acquiescence, she let go and reached for the catches on her utility belt. "Take this—" A jolt of nausea coincided with a sharp escalation of her headache. Vaguely Rett realized she was on her knees. "Take this, Carakenne, I'm having some problems here."

2.2.3 UNDETERMINED AREA, COMPLEX 412, EPNOCE
0525.11.38 (LOCAL RECKONING)

CONSCIOUSNESS RETURNED. A THICK BLUE fog swirled and pulsated inside Rett's mind like some otherworldly afterimage of the weather. Nausea and headache escalated with every waking second, almost as strongly as if she'd caught a full stun. Other than that, her body felt… weird.

Remembering what happened, she thought, *Damn it, not again*, and forced herself fully aware. She concentrated, rerouting any pain or discomfort for the energy she needed to check out her current predicament. Fog first.

What in two worlds?

Almost gasping aloud in her surprise, Rett realized the swirling clouds surrounding her had nothing to do with the weather.

259

Some bizarre energy field. Must be inside it.

It had to be powerful. The blue miasma permeated her mind, making her feel as if the pulsating swirls extended along every nerve ending of her body, filled every space inside her skin. The field all but blinded her ability to decipher any other energy output. But since it didn't seem to be affecting her physical or thought processes other than making such a mentally visible statement, she ignored it for the moment.

Pam?

-Right here.-

Acknowledging that, Rett went on with her usual checklist.

Where am I and is anyone close? Can I push past this? She sent a silent thanks to all good deities as she discovered that was possible. A little extra concentration sent her awareness beyond the lurid blue envelope, and she let it flow away from her, sounding the area.

She was indoors. No windows. One door. No furniture. Physically alone, for the moment. Shadowy energy traces marked movement and activity from outside her immediate area. No one was near the entryway right now, or else she would have a clearer impression.

Then she pulled in for a more detailed physical and local assessment. Definite air movement in the room, probably from the ventilation systems. She wasn't at all surprised to be missing uniform. In a habitual order, she discreetly tensed and flexed various muscles. No injuries. Not even a fresh scrape, cut, or bruise—which did surprise her. The average uniform removal process was anything but careful.

Not restricted as far as I can tell, no restraints, she thought to Pam, puzzled, *but am I standing up, lying down, sitting, what? I can't feel any surfaces in contact with me at all. All I feel is cold air on my skin.*

-Like there's no gravity at all, yet you're not weightless,- agreed Pam. -This is weird. And then there's that prickly tingly thing going on. Like your hair is standing on end.-

I think it is. I'm freezing.

-You're naked.-

Pam. This isn't the place for your cultural hangups.

Rett opened her eyes abruptly and wished she hadn't. The floor was about a length below her face; her body parallel to it. Nothing but air, and a coherent form of the same blue light that was in her mind, filled the open space. The glimpse of her own shadow combined with the leftover effects from the gas brought on a sensation of falling and a sick rush of vertigo that almost got the better of her.

She stifled her exclamation of surprise, but the reaction from the rest of her body she couldn't contain. It was then Rett discovered that her motion *was* restricted, after all. Her muscles had gone all out in the effort to twist her body around and break the fall that wasn't happening.

She'd moved perhaps half a fingerlength to the right, no more. Her altitude remained the same. She swallowed. *This is...certainly different.*

-You were talking about cultural hangups?-

Rett couldn't help a laugh, but she kept it on the inside. *Deities, I'm so glad you're back. I've missed you.*

-Same here. Well, as long as you're... hung up, at least if you pass out again there's no chance of hitting the floor and breaking anything. Unless someone comes along and pulls the plug on whatever it is keeping you suspended.-

I'm glad we can have a conversation without speaking. Damn it, I don't like not being able to move!

-I guess we can call it 'suspended animation', because of the non-movement factor.-

This time Rett rolled her eyes—at least she had control over them, and her facial features, internal bodily functions, especially important ones, like breathing.

She gathered herself for a concentrated effort, throwing her body to the left this time. From the sudden sharp increase of her headache, she felt a muzzy hope that she'd broken loose from whatever this was and had fallen on her head. Every muscle, tendon, and joint in her body ached. No, her eyes and nose weren't bleeding, but they felt like they were. Blinking hard, trying not to gasp, Rett finally focused her vision.

She'd moved, all right: right back to her original position, exactly half a fingerlength to the left. "Shit!"

~Easy does it.~ Pam's mental voice was low and calm.

Moistening lips gone dry, Rett pulled herself together. A small flare of living energy spiked through her headache. Someone was nearby. *Listen, I don't know what's going on with me. But I have to find out if the others are still alive. And if they are, we have to try and give Carakenne some time to get back with backups.* 261

~They might not give you a chance,~ Pam said. ~If she even made it.~ *She's F-troop, Pam. Of course she made it.*

~I hope so. I don't know her. But we don't know if she was affected by the gas, too. Even with that shot Med gave her, and the oxygen.~

No, Rett allowed, *I don't know that. But I'm hoping she managed, and until I see evidence otherwise, I'm going to believe she's on her way for help. If not already on the way back. I don't know how long I've been unconscious. In any case, don't assume the worst. We need to operate like it's going to be a matter of when, not if. And please, if something happens that's really going to freak you out, give me a warning so we can try to do something about it before you make me react.*

~I'll try, Rett, but I just got back. While I remember how to do things, I'm out of practice. It's been a long time for me.~

How long? Rett asked. *It was almost four Standard months for me.* She grimaced, inside and out. It had seemed like a lifetime, with everything that had happened.

~Just over a year for me,~ Pam answered. ~I was giving up on ever having anything left but the stories I wrote, and sketches I made. And yes, I know, now's not a good time.~

The ambient lighting brightened, washing out the weird blue glare a bit. A hand—at least Rett had the impression it was a hand—closed on her left arm, the heat of it shocking against her cold skin. Quite easily, this hand turned her to face its owner.

"Greetings, Sergeant. Glad you're awake."

She identified the alien as a Coalition officer only by the rank sigils and uniform. Whatever else it was, she had no idea, although after a few seconds she felt certain it was male. A large, bulbous head, which contained an outthrust, chinless jaw, tilted to one side. Small, oval eyes, the irises striped with dark and light bands, regarded her from deep sockets shadowed by sloped, overhanging brow ridges.

Despite his thin frame, the visible portions of his torso and limbs were stumpy, rounded, and liberally adorned with fleshy rolls and bumps. A few of the larger bumps bristled with hair. Or were those spines? Some kind of feelers, or sensory organs? She didn't bother trying to guess the exact shades of the alien's eyes or skin; since the cerulean corona of light surrounding her cast its own coat wherever she looked.

As far as topographical features of the being standing before her went, Rett felt very safe in stating she had never before seen anything like him. And she'd seen a lot of different varieties of people since the war began.

~He looks like some sort of thin, lumpy, bulldog-jawed walrus man, without the tusks.~ Pam's thought-picture made the point.

Doesn't matter what he looks like, thought Rett grimly in return. *What matters is that uniform he wears and what he has planned.* A sharp spike in the intensity of her headache blocked her ability to define his aura.

"Comfortable like this, or would you prefer a vertical position?" His voice was low and guttural, yet the words were clear and easy to understand.

Rett raised an eyebrow, allowing the slightest shadow of sarcastic expression to show on her face. She didn't trust herself to speak at the moment. The rotten smell coming from the alien, which Pam described as "five day old roadkill", didn't help her already queasy stomach.

"Of course, you would prefer to be upright. I would prefer you that way as well." Again, a single-handed manipulation rearranged her position without effort, as if she was mounted on some magnificently balanced gyroscopic frame instead of suspended somehow in…air.

"Better?" asked the commander.

She didn't answer. Instead she studied him as openly as he did her. Now she could feel the heat from his body and mentally noted it was much higher than any humanoid or alien temperature range she was familiar with. Little curls of vapor swirled from the alien into the colder air of the room. Almost as if his odor, rather than his body heat, had a visible presence.

~Sort of reminds me of the fog outside.~ Pam's uneasy observation was right in tune with Rett's thoughts.

The being spoke again. "Please do not expect me to comport myself in the manner of my colleagues. I find torture and other personal violence abhorrent, I leave interrogation to my subordinates, and I am not into games. The only reason I took the lot of you alive was that, in addition to the bounty on large groups, I would have an opportunity to test a few of my devices."

Alive. Large groups. The others are still alive. But how many of them?

As much as the news filled her with fierce hope, she had to wonder if their enemy would ever learn that leaving them alive was a very bad idea.

"I was all set to test my restraining field on the senior officer we took, Sergeant Rett, but when my troopers identified you, well. A nice bonus. Better yet, choosing you would all but guarantee I would find no unusual chemical residue other than that left by the gas, which will dissipate completely in a short time."

He actually used my name. Now I know both worlds are coming to an end soon. Concluding her initial assessment of him and how she should respond for now, Rett said, "I thought you people had orders to shoot me on sight."

"The reward is for the delivery of IDs, with an added bonus for any identifiable remains. Shooting on sight is the Leader's preference, not a rule."

Taking the idea surfacing from Pam, she went with it. "I must say this is different. No one's ever tried to nauseate me to death before. How long do you figure I'll have to look at you until it's all over?"

The alien laughed, a bubbling chuckle that sent more putrid gusts of breath in Rett's direction. "Would that you applied such a quick wit to science instead of sarcasm."

She fiercely concentrated on the physical characteristics of the creature and every movement he made, hoping to get her mind off her rebelling stomach. Either she was going to lose all control over it or pass out, and right now she had no desire for either option. She had to find out what this alien was up to, try to find out what happened to the others.

His short arms raised a Coalition version of an Omni to his sight. For such an ungainly creature, his hands were surprisingly human-like and dexterous; the slender fingers nimble as they skated over the touchpad.

"Two, perhaps two and a half hours total for the chemicals to dissipate, almost one and a half gone," he mumbled to himself, eyes nearly disappearing beneath his brow ridges as he squinted at the display. Taking a smaller device from his belt, he made several close passes up one side of her and down the other. "Interesting." A hideous parody of disapproval increased the forward thrust of his chinless jaw and twisted his wide, thin-lipped mouth.

~A medical scanner?~ wondered Pam.

Something like that, I guess. Not like any I've seen before.

Replacing the device on his belt, the officer went back to his Omni and conversation as if the interchange between them remained constant. "Add to your reward the group bounty, the bonuses for the two empaths, the other platoon leaders, and the officer. You can easily deduce this has been a most excellent night for me."

"I've no idea of the current figures. Your Leader hasn't sent me a cost analysis update lately," Rett said.

Her sarcasm didn't go unnoticed by the alien, since once again, a soft bubbling sound emerged from the creature's throat. "No matter."

The officer glanced up from his device. "Never fear, you will be delivered, quite dead, although minus a few parts. Before we proceed, a delay is necessary until I am sure the anesthetic is out of your system."

He's not the average Coalition officer, not even close. He actually has a mind and knows how to use it. We'll have to watch this one double-sharp.

~What, for the next half hour or so until he—or the smell—kills you? Sure.~ Had Pam been a physical presence, Rett would have been worried that her friend's eyes might get stuck permanently backward in their sockets.

"Commander!"

"What is it?" The officer asked it mildly, but the subordinate who had slipped in reacted as if slapped.

"It's the Nyorfian officer, sir. You wanted to see if we could find out more about tonight's attack, since we didn't expect it here. I'm afraid the troopers became a bit frustrated with him—"

~They didn't expect it?~ repeated Pam.

The Major had sent decoy jumpers in the direction of another nearby complex ahead of us, and obviously the sector commander took the bait.

However, this commander and his experimental devices made up for their lack of preparation, and then some. Rett's roiling stomach froze.

The Nyorfian officer.

He means Evetez!

"—he's rather seriously damaged, sir."

"Recognizable?"

"Not very, sir."

The way the subordinate answered made Rett wince. The Yixolryns were always careful not to damage a prisoner's head or face too much. Evetez must have really provoked them.

The alien officer's voice didn't change, but he became very still. "Is he still alive?"

She swallowed her anxiety and waited for the answer. The subordinate was acting so nervous she prepared herself for the worst. At the same time, she realized that when the commander had said "the lot of you" earlier, he'd meant more than F-troop. It wasn't hard then to conclude that B- and R-troops had been taken as well. But—

~That's right,~ Pam put in, picking up on the track of Rett's thoughts. ~And you haven't added another empath to your unit, besides Med, now Ariam's gone, have you? You'll have to explain that later, you know.~ Pam sounded miffed.

Remind me. The way Pam picked up stuff from between her surface thoughts never failed to amaze Rett.

~Anyway, he said he'd taken *two* empaths.~

He only mentioned two empaths, and I know Tris has two in R troop and that Semage's fourth-up can mindspeak with a physical contact.

~Remember, Rett—those command level records that Mott and Shamos stole only dealt with F-troop. They'd only know about Med and Ariam. Even with Ariam in B-troop now, they'd still have marked her name.~

Chagrined for that oversight, Rett twitched in frustration. It was all she could manage. The muscles in her hands ached with the need to make fists.

"Why am I plagued with substandard, mentally deficient parasites such as you? I made the orders perfectly clear. Can't I trust you to take care of these things on your own?" The alien's voice conveyed long-suffering patience and gentle rebuke.

The subordinate turned a pasty shade Rett saw even through the blue haze. His gulp was loud. He was gone in the next instant.

Still in a mild and conversational manner, the officer spoke to Rett. "I noted your lactic acid levels are elevated. It must have been quite a physical effort you made right before I came in. While I am gone, Sergeant—and it will only be for a short time—please do not exert yourself any farther attempting to escape the field. Escape is not impossible," he admitted. "However, the chance of making the escape in an acceptable timeframe without sustaining crippling injuries, or being discovered and stopped, is close to nil. Besides, physical exertion will only exacerbate the amount of chemical residue we are waiting for your system to filter."

Then the commander turned and followed the path the junior officer had taken, leaving Rett mystified and alone in the eerie glow and choking reek of death and decay.

2.2.4 UNDETERMINED SECTION, COMPLEX 412, EPNOCE
0535.11.39 (LOCAL RECKONING)

STRONG ARMS KEPT HIM FROM hitting the floor face first, which would have wreaked more havoc with his mashed face and broken nose.

"Lieutenant!"

Incapable of making any sort of reply at the moment, Evetez muzzily identified the speaker as Semage.

The harsh compression around his chest and arms lifted, allowing him to expand his lungs in the first truly deep breath since becoming conscious. Big mistake, but his body demanded it. So did his mind.

Coughing violently, he wondered how it was possible someone could survive with lungs turned inside out. Because that's what it felt like his were doing now. Didn't help to feel his inside-out lungs were scraping against sharp edges of rib bones, either.

Well, I'm not dead yet. You only have to worry about that when it stops hurting.

Thankfully the coughing fit ended before he passed out from it.

"Easy does it, 'Vetez." Semage's support, strong and unwavering, was more than physical, giving Evetez the strength he lacked.

Finally, he lifted his head. "Thanks, 'Mage," he rasped. The comfortable nicknames from the earliest days of their friendship helped ground him. Gingerly swiping the back of one hand across his abused mouth, he blinked, hard. "Am I blind or is it pitch dark in here?"

"Soon as they shoved you through the lights went out. No, don't try to sit up yet."

"Damn it, I'm *fine*." Evetez growled as his friend's hands checked quickly for more disabling injuries.

"That's not what my hands are telling me," Semage countered. "Ears, either. They're saying you were pretty well pounded."

"Then tell them to shut up." He pushed Semage's hands aside and sat up, swallowing down the groan and gasp that wanted to escape as something grated in his side. "Who else is in here? Anyone?"

"Almost everyone," said another voice. Sergeant Tris, from R-troop.

He probed at his face, grimacing at the lumps, dents, and raw patches he encountered. He was quite sure that, even after the swelling went down, he'd not need any camo paint for a Standard month. At least. Then he checked his teeth with his tongue. Two missing, three loose back there.

Coalition troopers did not take insults well at all, and Evetez had incited the junior officer questioning him, as well as the guard detail, so much that they forgot all about their strict rule to avoid damaging the head and face of a prisoner. The Yixolryns had a point—one didn't get much information from a prisoner unable to hear or speak, no matter how many drugs or devices they used. And they had various reasons for wanting Nyorfian authorities to identify faces and features, mostly to undermine morale. The biggest reason for this peculiarity, however, was to keep captives conscious longer, their full range of senses on the abuses taking place elsewhere.

Provoking them had been deliberate. The Yixolryns had been about to start on some drugs, and no matter how much training he'd had to resist or work past the effects, there was always the chance of failure. So he'd taken the chance to turn things in his favor. If getting beaten to a pulp counted as such. He gave a small, philosophic shrug—which hurt. At least his efforts resulted in one of the answers he'd sought.

Easy Force was still alive.

He'd never expected to see—rather, be with, since he wasn't seeing much of anything at the moment—anyone else from the unit. Officers, unit leaders, and any other people of Coalition interest were usually separated.

"Everyone?" Forgetting his personal aches and pains instantly, Evetez stared in the direction of Semage's voice.

"We're missing Rett, Ariam, Carakenne, and Med Rhozev," said Semage. "Other than those, everyone's here."

"Everyone," Evetez repeated. The sensation in his guts had nothing to do with his beating. "All in one place?" No matter his first impulse to feel good his people were alive. Most of them all being together, in one place, was definitely not a good thing.

"Yeah. We assume they identified Ariam and Med Rhozev and pulled them aside for some special care."

"They would have those two flagged, complete with visual IDs," Evetez said, "since the Leader has F-troop's command level records. Shit."

"And you know how they want psi talent," agreed Semage grimly. "That's about all we had time to figure. We woke up maybe ten minutes before you were tossed in."

"Hmm. They must have given you another whiff of gas or something. I've been up for about thirty minutes."

"I thought I remembered waking up once." Sergeant Tris' voice came from his left.

"As for Rhozev and Ariam," Evetez said, "it's likely they'll keep them alive and in reasonably good shape for the moment. They're more valuable that way. What about Rett? And Carakenne?"

He'd developed a peculiar interest in the spunky little commando who treated any senior to her rank—outside of F-troop at least—with such precise formality, even on free time. It was odd to see such stiffness within the Battalion, especially from someone who'd worn her headband for well over two years. After going over her records, Evetez realized it was a cover for her shyness, a problem that had manifested early on in childhood. She'd been raised in a community of researchers, one in which she'd been the only child. Evetez only guessed that while she had her parents and an entire staff of well-meaning people looking out for her, she'd been lacking in certain types of attention and social interaction.

Ever since, he'd become determined to fill in the gaps. There was something about the wistful manner in which he'd catch Cara watching others that demanded it. So, Evetez had started to go a little farther in his attempt to draw her out. He didn't get far. Rett had come down on him so hard his head still spun to think about it.

So he'd backed off and let Rett do things her own way. No one could deny the time spent with F-troop had made noticeable differences in the young woman's social skills. That was, at least between F-troop and most non-officers in Easy Force. Carakenne still had trouble looking him or Major Yidnar in the eye without breaking into a sweat.

"We don't know about the Sarge, but it's no surprise she's not in here with us." Trebor's calm baritone managed to convey a bleak message. "As for Carakenne—"

269

Evetez's intense worry for the yet-to-be-determined fate of Easy Force or Rett's current condition vanished at Trebor's pause. The thought of Carakenne dead or wounded slammed him right in the guts with more force than any Coalition trooper's boot.

Get a grip, Evetez. You care about everyone in your command. "What happened?" Was that hollow voice his? Deities!

"Sorry," Trebor said from his place in the darkness. "I thought I heard something. Last I saw him, Med mumbled something about the Sarge sending her for help."

"She wasn't affected?"

"She was behind me," someone else said, "and when I got dizzy and tripped over one of the motion detectors setting off the traps, she alerted us."

"Who is that?" Evetez demanded, wishing, like Rett, he was good at remembering everyone by voice.

"Specialist Jayord, sir, F-troop."

"Jayord and Carakenne were one of the railtube demolition teams," Sergeant Nitraym said. "They had some trouble underground with a Coalition patrol on the way out and had to wait for them to move on, so they were bringing up our rear. She didn't seem as affected as the rest of us, makes me think the gas was released from above. I didn't have much time to think about it. I told her to mask up and get to the Sarge to explain, and then whistled the alert."

"And Rett sent her to warn our backups?"

"Yes, sir. I was nearby." That was Junior Corporal Heime, another of the newer transfers to F-troop. "Med hit her with a stimulant and some oxygen. The Sarge sent Med to try and hit a few more of us—I was one of the first of those—but it was too late. In any case, I remember hearing the Sarge telling Cara to take her Omni and VARs and go."

Relief. Evetez felt dizzy, different. He tried to tell himself that the relief was that one of his team had managed to get out and could get help. Wasn't that why he felt such strong emotions? He shook those thoughts aside. They had no place here. His fingers dug into his own limbs with more force than necessary as he kneaded out his confusion along with the muscle stiffness.

Tris spoke up again. "I don't like the fact they dumped us all together."

"And without any restraint," agreed Trebor. "I'm glad of it, mind you, but that's strange. They left us uniform after we were ambushed at the Wide River Gap, but they had restraints on us quick enough."

"Well," said Semage cheerfully, "at least we're not freezing."

Not wanting to dwell on possibilities in those directions, Evetez spoke aloud his other huge worry. "I wonder if S- or D-troop with the infantry ran into this stuff, because as near as I can figure, they should be outside this place right now."

"Carakenne would have notified them first thing," said Sergeant Nerrah, Carakenne's squadleader, from the darkness. "The Sarge would have made that the first order before Cara went on to bring any other backup."

"You're right. While we're waiting for that backup, we still must find a way out. I don't like our options otherwise. Either we get zapped again and wake up as new toys for various Coalition officers, or find ourselves packed on a starship getting sent to deities know where for various purposes, or else the garrison here hits the panic switch when they come under attack, and we end up as corpses."

"That would seem to be the usual pattern," admitted Tris.

Evetez flexed his fingers and thought hard, bringing the building schematics to the front of his mind. There had to be a maintenance access, an air vent, something—he wished he knew what level they were on. While the vertical accessways were generally in the same locations on every level, the lateral ducts and crawlspaces were not. On this storm scoured, earthquake-prone continent, the structural asset was a blessing; but to Evetez, right now, it was a problem.

We'll have to start with all the usual spots, then. We really need to find someone else with the same kind of energy sense Rett has. Then we'd have no issues spotting topographic anomalies in the dark. Before he could name several likely pairs to team up and check the ceiling, a prickle of premonition shivered his nape.

"What's that sound?" asked someone.

A dim light came from high on a wall, then a series of glows sparked across the ceiling of the room, starting close by the exit. The glows slowly brightened, accompanied by a threatening buzz.

"Back!" The command came as one from Evetez and a score of others, but already those closest to the front were in motion. The buzz deepened and grew into a hum. The glowing spots of light on the ceiling fired into painful brilliance and sent deadly bars of energy crackling to the floor. The scent of ozone and smoking hot pourstone filled the room.

At the same time Evetez spotted his hatchway—on the other side of the beams, of course—his nose identified another unpleasantly familiar scent, charred flesh.

"Who got hit?" The beams of light cast a lurid glow in the room, but Evetez couldn't see much through the group.

"I'm over here. It'll be all right," B-troop's medtech answered.

"Who is it, Shenyver?"

"Dinnold." The medtech named one of R-troop's squadleaders. "Nasty deep graze down the backside, but not life threatening."

"I won't be sitting too comfortably for a while," came the tight response from the squadleader, followed by a remorseful chuckle. "Not that any of us will."

"Before anyone else makes a comment," Med Shenyver said swiftly in a tone both droll and serious, "we've a more serious set of issues here."

"Yes, we do. The beams are moving in, the smoke isn't venting any-where, the heat's increasing, and the floor is already starting to melt." Lieutenant Evetez swore. "Damn it! All right, who forgot to bring the spiced meat patties and knotroot again?"

"Maybe F-troop's Cara is bringing them back with her," someone from R-troop called over the resultant laughs and snickers. "Our Sergeant Dinnold has very kindly provided us the toasted buns." More laughs.

There. All I wanted to hear. Satisfied, his spirit buoyed by the high morale of those he was responsible for, Evetez turned serious again.

"Well, two things. We don't have to wonder what they intend to do with us any more. And there's our escape route." He waved his hand in the direction of the ceiling panel in the front right corner. "Can we hope to be on a lower level? With nothing reflecting these beams, I hate to think of them burning out the floor and us falling on anyone below."

"We can hope we fall on Coalition instead of civilians, that's about it." Tris growled. "We should have noticed—"

"Listen, none of us were exactly in any condition, much less had time, to think clearly or see too much before the lights went out," Med Shenyver's soft voice interrupted diplomatically. "And had we been able to see, we'd likely not made much sense of it."

R-troop's medtech added his support. "All of us have been either under anesthetic, stunned by energy beams at various levels, or hung over. Keep in mind how alert you were—or weren't—when you came out of those situations."

"The medtechs are right," Evetez said. "No blame. We deal with what we have. Keep changing positions so no one stands too close to the hotspots for any length of time. Use uniform for smoke filtration. Anyone in distress, we want to hear about it. And any good ideas, don't keep 'em to yourself."

"Anyone who wears lenses still have them?"

Evetez identified the speaker as Junior Sergeant H'tenneck from F-troop. "Rimms? Torleyne?" Besides Cara, those two were the only others among Easy Force who wore corrective lenses.

"Mine are gone," said Senior Corporal Rimms from B-troop. R-troop's Specialist Torleyne echoed the same.

H'tenneck sighed. "Okay, I'll think of something else."

"Hey," said Sergeant Trebor. "While H'tenneck and the rest of our geniuses are thinking, I'm speculating on what time Cara's going to show up. It'll cost you a tenday's paycredit and the total take will be divided among the three closest times, sixty, thirty and ten percent. Anyone?"

273

2.2.5 UNDETERMINED SECTION, COMPLEX 412
0535.11.40 (LOCAL RECKONING)

PAM'S UNEASE WITH THE ENTIRE situation was escalating to a point that threatened to eclipse her curiosity. Hanging naked in an energy field, unable to move, might be fine with Rett, but it wasn't something she was prepared to deal with at all. ~Aren't you even going to try to get out of this?~

Pam. You know as well as I do that if I try any harder than I did before, I'm going to rip, sprain, or dislocate something. I think I already pulled something in my back. If possible, I'd rather save more damage like that for a last resort, since if I break free and can't move at all, I'll be in the same fix. Rett took a few slow, deep breaths and concentrated again on her body. If she could breathe, move the muscles in her face, swallow, there had to be something else involved. Surely an energy field on its own wouldn't be so exclusive. She tried a tiny movement with her fingers. *Feel that, Pam? I can* move—

~Oh sure, yes. A fingertip at a time.~ Pam's inner voice dripped sarcasm. ~So, say by the end of the week—I mean tenday—you should have your hand, maybe a foot, in the open.~

There must be something else on me, even though I can't feel it. If I can angle my head enough to see what it might be…

There was a sudden shift in the quality of the auras outside the room. The officer had returned, his mood as dark and foul as the reek from his body.

"Damn." Rett tried to keep focused on tracking him through his aura at the same time she concentrated on the incremental motions she was capable of making.

~What do you think this field is?~ Pam asked.

A pain in the neck, Rett thought back, as twisting agony spread from shoulders to ears. *Either I really hurt myself before, or he increased the power on this field.*

~Or it's having secondary effects,~ guessed Pam.

Or all three, Rett concluded, and stopped trying to move her head. It was one thing fighting with an arm or leg out of commission. If she got out of this field and couldn't lift her head or turn her neck, she'd really be in trouble.

"I tell you, Sergeant," the Coalition officer was saying, "I am looking forward to being rid of the burden of command and the imbeciles that come with it." He pushed a floating tool tray into the room ahead of him. "I am not a soldier, nor an enforcer, and yet here I am, expected to fulfill those roles. That was not part of the initial agreement I made for military service."

~For someone who seems so intelligent, he completely overlooked the keywords there—military service. Hel-LO!~ Pam gave a mental roll of her eyes.

"All I want is peace, quiet, chemical-free food, my own research facility, a reliable source of material, unlimited funding, and recognition for my work. Is that asking too much?"

"Not at all," Rett said. "I'm not so sure about unlimited funding, but we might be able to cover the rest."

He made a guttural snorting noise. "The query was rhetorical, and your reply was not humorous."

"I wasn't being humorous."

After eying her for a moment, he shook his head. "It is impossible the Nyorfians will win this conflict, much less accommodate someone of my…needs. I shall stay with what I know."

She wasn't going to push the matter. His fate was sealed, if it came to that, of his own free choice. If he were truly interested, nothing would have kept him from asking for more information; from seeking some sort of compromise.

~He's not interested in any sort of data from you, is he?~

Rett manifested Pam's mental swallow. *Doesn't seem that way. Nothing verbal anyway.*

She decided to try once more to move her head. She managed just enough to see the tray without feeling as if her eyeballs were going to end up stuck to the side forever. She examined the contents with an

275

escalating sense of unease. It contained two large, lidded containers, several shallow bowls in various sizes, some normal looking medical supplies, and both her knives, large and small.

"Let's have a look at you."

There's not much he could have missed.

~Oh, that drizzle of sarcasm trumps my drips of it.~ Pam sounded pleased.

Seriously, Pam.

~Seriously, you're right. There's not much he could have missed—on the *outside*,~ agreed Pam. She reminded Rett of the contents of the tray. ~But what if he's not interested in what's on the outside?~

Again, the scanner came out, as if confirming Pam's thought. Neither of them felt the least bit sarcastic now, especially when the alien pressed the side of the device into Rett's neck. She tried to pull back but the field held her fast. For a long second or two, she fought back a rush of panic that nearly blinded her.

Breathe, breathe, breathe, easy, easy, easy...

She wasn't sure if the thoughts came from her or if they came from Pam, but she managed to contain most of her reaction—except for a small shiver as the device beeped and several small, sharp points pricked into her skin.

"I'm getting a more detailed report," intoned the being, his striped eyes fixed on the readouts. "Please don't struggle. I prefer not to render you unconscious at this point, as this will work so much better with you awake."

The scanner clicked into place on his computing device. "Good." A cheerful note entered the commander's guttural voice. "Excellent! A most advantageous metabolism. I wish there were time to study it at leisure, but we cannot always have everything we want." A reeking gust of breath whooshed from him. "Nevertheless, I can get you started. First let me decide what I want to keep of you."

Rett didn't like the sound of that.

Detaching the scanner from the Omni, he again passed it along her body, very close but not making contact. In a precise, orderly fashion, he went down one section and up another, not missing a fingerlength. All the while, his tiny eyes never left the display on the larger device.

"There is not much of the larger muscle groups that is not completely ruined by scar tissue," he complained in the next foul breath.

Pam's flare of indignation on this statement reinforced Rett's reply. "Hey, I'm the first to admit I'm not flawless, in any aspect. But at least everything works. Turn off this light thing. I'll give you a demonstration."

Again he chose not to respond, or else was so intent on his scanning he didn't hear her comment. At length he replied, "Your muscles are indeed operational. But for my purposes, they are ruined. Your internal organs, however, are mostly unblemished. The heart, most notably, and there are no lesions on the brain. A remarkable pair of lungs, no significant scarring past the outer layers. Which is just as well, since internal organs as unblemished and clean as yours are exactly what I have needed lately. And any thickening on bone doesn't affect the marrow within. That, too, I have been wanting."

Do I want to know what for? Rett thought with another hard swallow.

277

-I don't think you want to know.- Had Pam spoken aloud, her voice would have been a tremulous, squeaking whisper.

On the contrary. If you have any of your far out Earth ideas, now's the time to let me in on them.

The scanner went down and the commander reached to the tray. He picked up her big knife, extending the blade for his inspection.

"Beautiful weapon," the officer commented. "Perfectly balanced. Miraculous substance, azurium. So versatile, no matter what form or state it is in, alloyed in metal, as a crystal, as a gas. I have been doing much of my work using it."

He began stripping the camo tape from the blade. The blue glow surrounding Rett reflected dully off the brushed finish of the flat metal surfaces.

"May I ask a question?"

"Certainly, Sergeant."

"Is that why this light—"

Pam's mental tones came as near to a shriek as Rett ever interpreted them.- I can*not* believe you are asking him about the freaking light!-

A new voice at the door interrupted. "Commander."

The officer spun, for the first time raising his voice to a furious bellow. "*Get out!* I don't care what it is this time. Get out and handle it or it will be *your* heart for my dinner!"

You were saying, Pam?

~Never mind.~

Is that what you were thinking before?

~Yes.~

Good deities! This sort of thing common on your planet?

~Only with a side of fava beans. But you don't want to know that right now, do you?~

But Rett couldn't let that go. This time it was her turn to lift something from between Pam's surface thoughts. *Oh. It's one of those entertainment things.* What passed for entertainment on Pam's world was mind-boggling, and not in a good way. *I don't even want to know the details later.* She dismissed the notion and returned her attention to her current situation.

The alien turned back, utterly calm again. "Your question, Sergeant?"

Rett swallowed. "Is that why the light is blue? Is an azurium crystal the focus, or are you using azurium gas as a medium for particle acceleration? Or both?"

"You're familiar with light physics, Sergeant?"

"Only the basics."

"Then I won't burden you with the details, since it would take much more time than I have made room for in my schedule to explain in terms simple enough for you to grasp," said the alien in a patronizing tone.

She didn't expect that to sting so hard. Maybe it was due to Pam, who instantly became defensive. ~What a pompous ass!~

Rett didn't rebuke Pam's strong reaction. Instead she took it to put an equally condescending tone into her reply. "I'm the first to admit I'm not a scholar, but all my question required was a simple *yes, no,* or *I won't answer that.*"

The Coalition officer paused, the incredibly ugly countenance regarding her thoughtfully. "I meant no insult to your intelligence. I do believe you posed the question with genuine curiosity, not as a mere ploy to delay my procedure. My apologies." He actually sounded as if he intended to soothe her somehow. "The answer is yes, to all three counts. However, I truly do not have the intention, or the time, to explain how it works."

I don't give a pile of flaming—

~Ooooh. Now, now, now. Let's not get upset over this. Releases nasty tasting chemicals in the body, you know.~

All the more reason for me to get tiffed.

~Maybe you can get steamed. He might not like his Nyorfian hot, either.~

"This won't hurt a bit—"

"Easy for you to say," snarled Rett.

"—and once I get this cleaned and sterilized, I'll make a nice diagonal cut here, and another here, like so." He touched the back of the blade to the inside of each of her thighs, not quite halfway up."

~Let's not hit a major artery or anything,~ thought Pam.

Why can't I be the one dreaming for once, and you be the one hanging up here? Rett complained.

~Even if we were reversed, we'd both be feeling the same thing,~ returned Pam.

"As you lose blood, you'll go quietly off to sleep—"

Rett interrupted with a growl. "Yes, yes, I know that, been there, done that. And for the record, it's not as simple as people think. Besides that, it's *boring*. I'd die of boredom before losing enough blood to go 'quietly off to sleep'!"

The officer actually took two steps back and stared up at her in quiet astonishment, the lighter stripes in his eyes widening.

"Look, I'm *stuck* here. Stationary target. You're never going to have a better chance. Why not kill me and get it over with? Or cut me open and take what you want right away? Does this have to always be a big, drawn-out production with a running commentary?"

"My reasons for this procedure are quite different from any previous attempts. Come now, Sergeant, most of you Nyorfians hunt for your meat. You should know better."

Rett didn't have to fake the weary note of resignation into her voice. "Of course I know what *I* would do with an animal. But," she pointed out, "the animal would, first of all, be completely dead before I started cutting it anywhere, and if I wanted to bleed someone or something out, I wouldn't do it like this. But I have no idea how you go about things. After all, this is the first opportunity I've ever had to compare notes with someone about to have me for lunch."

She forced herself to keep her eyes on him while her mental focus extended. *Something's happening out there.* "Tell me, is it Nyorfians you've developed cravings for, or anything that's meat? Or only meat that talks back?"

"One of your race's most endearing qualities, this insatiable curiosity. What's more, most of you have the sense to satisfy your need to know with solid, well-documented research. The libraries your people maintain are remarkably excellent and up to date despite the location of this system."

"Really. I had no idea. Thanks for sharing."

The commander was swiping some medicinal-smelling stuff on her knife now. The sharp chemical odor hit her nose like a breath of fresh air. "You will be my first Nyorfian," he said then.

"I'm honored."

~Yep, folks, we have it here. Grade A certified organic Nyorfian. A bit battered and bruised, tough and gristly, but no artificial flavors, colors, or preservatives.~

I suppose my hormone implants aren't a problem.

~If it keeps people who eat you from reproducing, I'd say it was an asset. But don't mention it now. Bad for advertising.~

"Keeping a measure of discipline among my humanoid officers and troopers has fulfilled my needs adequately, although each requires at least several days to detoxify," the commander said. "Yet, after that, there are still portions I cannot use. Fortunately, I have a small appetite."

"Are you going to cook me with vegetables and things?" This from Pam. Rett wanted to keep the alien talking as long as possible, so she relaxed some of the barrier she kept against Pam inadvertently taking over her external functions, like motion and speech. Motions didn't matter much at this point. And since the alien wasn't interested in information, she didn't worry Pam was going to blurt out something classified.

The officer made an approximation of a humanoid smile. It was something Rett would have preferred not to see at all, for not only was the cavernous maw of a mouth—and the foul breath it emitted—repulsive to her, it was filled with narrow, sharp-pointed, brownish-red teeth.

"I'd guess you'd leave out the vegetables," observed Rett.

"You will not be cooked."

"That's such a relief. I feel much better about this now."

"The reports of those I work with are often highly exaggerated. I see, in your case, they are not. In fact, your coolness under stress is underrated. I assure you I'll take the time to savor the results."

"Great. I like to know I'll be appreciated for my good taste."

"Not to mention there is a certain satisfying and amusing aspect in the prospect of disposing of one of the Coalition's most wanted enemies in this manner."

"I wish I can be around when you tell Iheolon and the Leader about it." Rett let out an exaggerated wistful sigh. "Especially Iheolon. Will you save a special piece out for him so he can pretend to kill it himself? A sort of consolation prize, my right leg, perhaps. You probably noticed it's a lot more messed up inside and out than the other. He never finished dissecting—"

~You were worried about me going too far with the wisecracks?~ Pam's warning came strong and bright through the surfacing darkness of memories Rett had to leave firmly buried. ~You'd better stop right there.~

Rett let out a soft breath, reminded herself not to overdo it, and sent silent thanks to Pam.

The officer spared her another glance, this one almost sparkling with amusement. "All the Leader wants is proof you're dead. As far as Iheolon—" He swabbed off the smaller of her knives and made a sound of contempt. "I no longer answer to him."

Rett's mental ears pricked up at this. *No longer answered to Iheolon?* She opened certain memories just enough to know she'd never come in contact with this being before, not even remotely. Even if for some odd reason she didn't recognize his voice, she'd certainly remember the smell.

Then again Iheolon had possessed a number of highly unusual devices.

Is it possible this is the person who created those devices? Rett restrained her shudder.

~Do you have any idea where he is right now? Iheolon?~

Intelligence is fairly certain he's on Aurora continent, returned Rett. *Then again, if there's one thing the Coalition's learned over the years, it's how to say and record that certain officers are posted in one location, but have them in actuality somewhere else altogether. Even the complex residents who manage to get information out to MainCommand aren't all that sure of the names of their garrison commanders.*

"His feelings on the matter are no concern of mine. He's on Aurora continent, and he has his cousins with him now. I understand Sclamuse is a skilled technician. His specialty is with drugs and biological weapons, but he's come up with some very interesting devices as well. Of course he's stolen some of my ideas, twisted them, and turned them into toys for Commander Iheolon's use. No doubt he will be put to work until he and Motuk Iheolon can be taken offworld."

"Iheolon has relatives?" Rett couldn't keep the surprise from her face or voice.

"But surely you knew this. You were partially responsible for their exposure as Coalition agents on Nyorfias."

Rett's heart nearly stopped without benefit of blood loss. *Deities! He means Mott and Shamos!* "I wasn't aware of the relationship."

The alien shrugged and placed the smaller knife precisely alongside of the big one. Then he selected a narrow strap from the tray. "All the same, I hope Iheolon suffers an aneurysm when he finds out that I deprived him of you."

I can almost get to like this guy, thought Rett wryly. *Almost.* And as much as she wanted to ponder the news and its possible implications, she filed it away and concentrated on her current predicament.

He tightened the band around her thigh like a tourniquet. "There. Don't try to move."

"Wait a minute," Rett said. "There's something I need to tell you before you start."

The officer glanced up briefly, his hand pausing over the smaller knife on the tray. "Yes?"

"There's a Nyorfian commando standing behind you," Rett explained in a conversational manner. "I don't advise picking up the knife. If you step aside and allow yourself to be disarmed, you'll be treated fairly. You have information we need, skills we can use. We might even be able to find an acceptable solution—for everyone—regarding your particular needs. Or, you can go ahead as you planned, in which case you'll most likely die first. This is my second offer, the final one. Now it's up to you."

The commander stared at her for a solid count of fifteen, then sent an unhurried glance over one lumpy, rounded shoulder, then the other.

"I thought better of you, Sergeant. I suppose I cannot blame you for trying." His fingers closed over the knife handle. Blue light gleamed off the freshly cleaned blade as he lifted it.

283

There was a wet, crunching sound. The hand holding the weapon stiffened, went lax. The alien's misshapen head jerked up, his large mouth gaping in a soundless gasp of surprise.

Wrinkling her nose from the fetid stench that gusted into her face, Rett earnestly hoped the now-bulging eyeballs, the lighter stripes almost disappearing into the black, wouldn't pop from their sockets and hit her anywhere. If she had to factor that in with the smell, the suppressed remains of her hangover, and the prospect of having her heart and whatever else cut out and eaten for dinner, she definitely might have to throw up.

Staggering to one side, then back, the Coalition officer gave another long gasp and fell twitching to the floor. Behind him stood Specialist Carakenne, both of her knives smeared past the hilt with dark, reddish-orange fluid. More blood covered her small, strong hands and stained the uniform material up to her elbows, occluding its light and color reflective properties.

The ferocious snarl on her dark face changed to a shy smile of greeting. "Hi, Sarge." She gave the body a careful nudge, then bent to make sure the alien was dead. "Phfew! Stinks."

Rett didn't even try to contain her relief. "What in two worlds took you so long to get in here? Did you find something to read out there and get distracted, or what?"

Using the material of the officer's uniform, Carakenne swiped some of the gore off her blades. "Dramatic effect?" She sheathed her long knife, and slanted a sideways glance up to Rett, a mischievous glitter belying the tone of uncertainty in her voice.

"Dramatic effect, my frozen ass!" Rett shot back after experiencing a sensation of surprise. She'd seen Carakenne warm up and get animated in a conversation before, but had never witnessed spontaneous, playful humor. "Commander Nauseating there was about to prepare his lunch, and I was the main course."

Carakenne made a gagging sound. "I guessed as much from what I saw on the way in here." She shook her head, a motion that continued all the way down to her feet, as if she were shaking off the memory.

Rett didn't want to think about it either. "I hope you can get me out of…this."

"Electromagnetic plasma field." As the alien had done, Cara simply reached into the field, unbothered and unhampered by it. A delicate motion from the tip of her short knife released the tight band from Rett's leg.

"How come it doesn't bother you?"

"It tingles slightly. Then again, I'm not reflecting the wavelengths between the echo generator and reflection coils."

"In GTC Standard?"

"Hmm."

"You'd better make it *really* simple. And while you're thinking, can we do something about the temperature?" The tense energy Rett had generated, which had held back the full extent of her reaction to the cold, had reached bottom with the death of the alien. "I'm freezing. I think it's colder in here than it was outdoors."

"The positively charged poles of magnets repulse each other. You're a negatively charged pole in the middle getting pulled both ways."

"I see." Any second now Rett's teeth were going to chatter like her TT-1 on semi-auto.

"That's a simple, generic analogy, Sarge, the science behind this setup, until now, has been entirely untested. As far as the temperature, I'm sorry, but I think it's better if I get you out of the field instead. Trust me, you don't want it to get warm in here."

"I suppose you're right," Rett had to admit. Until now, the thought of how the air temperature would affect the aroma of the area hadn't entered her mind.

The younger woman took a step back. Rett swallowed her impatience, recalling Carakenne's need to study something unusual for an extra second or few while her mind worked through deities knew how many possible solutions at light-speed. When she chose to move, it would be on a decisive and swift course that brought results.

Sure enough, when Carakenne's glance settled on the floating tray, the small soldier no longer hesitated. With a sweep of her arm, she cleared the surface and hopped up. The table dipped slightly, then steadied at its former height, putting the younger woman's head at a level with Rett's. Soon small fingers plucked at Rett's skin here and there, each pluck accompanied by a twinging pinch.

For a moment, Rett didn't understand what Carakenne was about with this plucking and pinching. "What's that you're doing?"

Carakenne held something up to Rett's view. Something tiny, shiny, and pronged.

~It looks like something off my computer's motherboard.~ Pam had to make a sharp visual to illustrate her point.

"These things are stuck in you."

Trust me, that's nothing from the inside of a computer. At least not one of ours. Rett shuddered from more than the cold air. She'd seen devices like that before—had them inserted into her body before. Her hands clenched into fists so tight she felt her nails slice into her palms. *That's what he meant. About his ideas, stolen and twisted. He was right about that.*

"These things are what's really keeping you in the field. I'm sure they're using some combination of magnetic and light reflection. I also think they're emitting some other frequency that is interfering with your large motor responses. I didn't see any obvious way to turn off the field from out there. No time to search for one."

Rett swallowed and jerked her eyes and thoughts back to the present. *When Iheolon used these things on me, it certainly wasn't to float me in some electromagnetic energy field.*

Pam gave Rett a firm mental shove farther away from thoughts of the past. ~Well, you can thank all your good gods and deities that he won't be making any more of them, for anyone.~

But he mentioned Shamos—I mean Sclamuse—

~I refuse to let you think about that right now,~ Pam stated firmly, and in the face of the silent threat behind her words, Rett agreed.

"Who'd you come back here with?"

"Major Yidnar, Captain Onelya, and Lightning Force."

"Lightning—I didn't know they were back in from their last mission."

"Right before I got in. They were geared up and Captain Onelya said they were good to go, so they rearmed while the jumpers were getting refueled. It took forever," grumbled Carakenne. "Twenty minutes to refuel those jumpers. But it was good for me because it gave me time to get back up there. I thought they weren't going to let me come back. Are you getting movement back where I pulled these things so far?"

Rett flinched. The leftover frustration evident in the younger woman's voice was manifested by an extra-sharp twinge. "I noticed I have feeling back in my hands. That's good. Why did you start at the top instead of the bottom?"

"I hope that by starting at the top," Carakenne was saying as the pinching and plucking resumed, "that you'll have more balance and feeling back so you can hang on to something, if you must, once your feet get onto the floor. You notice you're coming down, right?"

"Definitely. Good thinking." Rett's body was starting to feel normal again and had without doubt come down a handspan or so. She gingerly tested the range of motion she'd regained, glad to note she hadn't injured herself after all. Must have been part of the secondary effects of the field and the devices.

"You're not bleeding very much, either, but you do look a little prickly. I'm almost done. Arc they—were they hurting you?" Carakenne jumped off the table to finish.

More pinching. "No. It only hurt when I tried to force my movement." Rett hoped she wasn't going to throw up, because she was closer now than before. "Why were they going to keep you at the base?"

"Oh, something about catching SMG. There. You shouldn't have any permanent damage."

"Maybe not physically," muttered Rett, all the same reveling in feeling her icy feet firmly planted on the surface and a completely free range of motion returning with gratifying speed.

"You should be able to step out of it. Can you walk?" Cara's small dark face wore a mask of anxiety. "You don't look too good, Sarge, and I don't think it's the lighting or the cold. Here." She reached out to lend support.

Rett took a long step forward, out of the pulsating blue light. The immediate *quiet* in her head and along every nerve ending in her body was jarring.

Pam?

~Still here.~

"Sarge?" Carakenne sounded a little stressed.

"I'm okay. Thanks." Rett found her balance and straightened.

"Found these as I came through the other room."

Rett snatched the bundle Carakenne produced next, not even caring that the untidy arrangement had allowed some lingering dampness from the mist outside to spread to her inner clothing. "Deities, Carakenne, this is great." She was grateful to find the garments relatively undamaged, not that it mattered. What mattered was putting those layers around the body heat she had left, before she turned into the block of ice some people believed her to be.

~Beats the alternative of stripping down some dead trooper for clothes,~ Pam said with appreciation.

"Didn't spend time looking for your boots and liners," Cara apologized as Rett all but dove into her clothes.

"Trust me, I'm glad you found this much." Rett scrubbed her hands up and down her arms to speed some circulation and warmth. "Let's get out of here. Tell me what happened. First, where's Lightning, the infantry, and the rest of Easy?"

"Scattered. The Major and Lightning are on the upper levels, Easy and the infantry are on the other side. They found where they were keeping the civilians fairly quick, before I split off from them. So, the people who live here are mostly all right, I think. I didn't hear they weren't. Last I heard on com is that they're cleaning up, but there are still a few sections putting up a fight. Uhm…this section's still occupied, not this level, though. Shouldn't be many. The Coalition's understrength here."

"Sure," mumbled Rett under her breath, "given their commander's appetite, I shouldn't wonder."

"A trooper I ran into along the way told me they thought we were going to hit Complex 44 instead, since that was the direction the decoy jumpers went earlier."

"I heard they weren't expecting us." Rett blew out a breath of exasperation and rolled her eyes, indicating the situation most of Easy had fallen into despite that fact.

"Yeah. Well, shit happens, no matter how many angles are covered."

Rett took a second look at this talkative Nyorfian in Carakenne's uniform.

"The sector commander ordered half the garrison here to leave and bolster the defense for Complex 44," Carakenne continued. "Stupid move. This place is hotter than Complex 44 as far as strategic locations go."

"Did you run into this trooper you chatted with—or run him over?"

"I guess I scared him a little, Sarge. He never saw me until he was flat on his back and from that angle, I looked bigger than he was." The younger woman turned and led the way to the outer room, sending Rett a fierce grin over her shoulder. "I asked him then if the barrel of my carbine looked clean. He asked me very politely if I would like to take his weapons and name now. Stunned him in case he changed his mind and left him for the infantry to pick up later."

Rett nodded. "What section of the complex are we in?"

"We're in the storage wing, close to general maintenance materials and the reservoirs. The same side as we were going to enter when we hit."

~Why this side?~ Pam wanted to know.

Quickest way we could get a foothold—generic material storage isn't as closely monitored or guarded as other sections.

288

Once over the threshold, Carakenne stopped long enough to reach into a utility belt pocket. Turning, she offered a black headband. "Forgot this." She pulled another headband from the same pocket, unfolding it slowly. Her voice lowered a bit. "This one's the Lieutenant's, but I didn't see him. Or any of the others."

"He was mentioned," Rett said, hoping that was enough to reassure the both of them. "I think there's more than a good chance he and the others are still alive. They love catching us in groups, you know.

"We must find them, then. Soon."

"Agreed. I was worried before, but now…" Now that Rett was out of the vicinity of the energy field, the deep psychic link she shared with Ariam burst into a sense of urgency like a fire given oxygen. "Something's really wrong."

She took two more steps and stopped short, looking around the outer room in astonishment and distaste.

It wasn't due to the double handful of dead Coalition troopers who had fallen so silently to a Special Forces operative's lethal skill. It was in response to the condition of the room itself. A few large monitors and computing units occupied one of the long counters, all of which were covered, like the floor, in a wide variety of…stuff. Junk. Dirt. Things better suited to various forms of recycling or in bad need of cleaning. Still other things Rett preferred not to identify.

Her bare toes curled. "I see what held you up. It's amazing you found a path, much less those guards, in this mess. Good gods and deities! It's filthy."

"It's not typical," agreed Carakenne. "Especially since the Yixolryns seem to have a fairly high standard in regards to hygiene among their troops."

That much was true—the Yixolryns were surprisingly fastidious. Their aversion to cold and dampness wasn't nearly as great as their collective dislike of filth and strong odors. This place would be enough to horrify Iheolon. No wonder they shipped the alien officer here and left him to do as he pleased with his experiments.

"They probably staffed his garrison with the undesirables among their regular soldiers, too," Rett said aloud. "Hoping to make them improve themselves for a better assignment—or to get rid of them."

289

"I didn't think of it that way," Carakenne said. "From the smell and the apparatus I've seen strewn about, I'd say that commander spent a lot of time down here on this level. This was probably his main lab."

"Yuck." Something Rett preferred remain anonymous clung to her foot and she shook it off. "And I'd say he was about as untypical as any Coalition officer I've personally dealt with. In spite of his—peculiarities—and dietary habits, I actually had some hope for a minute…" Rett shook her head. "I never expected this. No offense, Carakenne, but on a few levels, I really think you and he would have understood each other perfectly."

"None taken. Although I doubt the 'perfect' aspect. We could have learned a lot from him, if he chose to cooperate. He was a genius, Sarge," said Carakenne with soft regret.

Rett shook another clinging something off her foot and turned her head enough to catch the other soldier's eyes. "Have news for you, sport. In case you were unaware of the fact, so are you."

For a moment Carakenne ducked her head, her more familiar aura of pale reticence returning to sap the bolder primary shades of outgoing confidence Rett had been interpreting to that point.

Then the younger woman's head came back up and she squared her stance. "Sarge, I noticed some of the data and schematics displayed on the screens as I came through. I think he may have invented those azurium lasers. And that electromagnetic field you were in. What little I saw—" Cara blew out a forceful breath and picked her way through the mess. "The applications it might have been put to. Good ones. Who knows what else."

"He mentioned experiments." As she gingerly continued toward the exit, Rett glanced over her shoulder, to the blank, dark display screens and back to Cara. "Wait. *Was* displayed on the screens, you said?"

The younger woman nodded, pausing to crouch near the dead trooper closest to the exit. "He may have had a biomonitor attached to them. When he died, it crashed the system, wiped the data. Doubt we'll recover anything useful."

"We don't need technology like that. I don't even care if the applications were good ones. I don't care if we recover any of it."

"Not even these?" Carakenne displayed her prizes. "I didn't take a lot of time to notice what this guard was doing on the way in. Now, I know."

Her boots. "If you ever need me to push to get you anything, anything at all, for your gadgets or study when we get back, you just tell me."

"Really? I've been working on a few new incendiary devices and had trouble finding some—"

"When we get back," Rett answered, a little worried to have made such an offer so spontaneously.

"And I want to hear that story."

"I'll tell it to you personally." Rett grinned and motioned Cara to keep going. "I'll put them on out there." She took the ML-12 and powerpack the trooper had put aside before shedding his own footgear in favor of Rett's.

I don't blame him. The trooper wasn't a humanoid type Rett recognized, but the shape of the foot was similar. The Coalition didn't spend much time designing personal gear to fit every variation of the people in their military ranks, expecting one generic design to accommodate everyone. Jaq had gone into raptures for a solid tenday after he received footgear actually shaped to his measurements.

~Maybe it's not that armor and weaponry that slows them down, after all. They simply can't move because their feet are killing them.~

Either way, Rett agreed, *we take tactical advantage wherever we get it.*

The air in the corridor was colder and a thousand times fresher by comparison, and most of the churning in Rett's stomach subsided after a few breaths. Taking an extra few seconds to use a cleansing wipe Carakenne handed over, she made sure nothing disgusting was clinging to her soles or squashed between her toes before burying her cold feet into the insulated interiors of her boots.

She let out a sigh of relief. "Much better." As she settled her headband in place, her eyes inspected the younger woman closely. "I grabbed you on that shoulder to keep my balance before, didn't I? Sorry. How badly were you hit?"

"Nothing much, Sarge."

"But they wanted to keep you in Medical."

Carakenne's little chin came up. "I'm good to go," she said firmly, a hard light in her eyes.

Rett wasn't going to argue with her. "Right, then. Let's move." The smile she gave Carakenne didn't last long as her unease edged toward dread. *I hope he had nothing else rigged to activate when he went down.* "You came back a lot faster than I expected, thank all deities. Give me the short version for now, but later I want to hear everything." She adjusted the ML-12 powerpack and checked the settings on the weapon, then started off, following her instinctive pull toward Ariam.

"Well, it was mostly luck. I had a little trouble along the way, but then I reached the thicker brush and they gave up on me. Then I heard something and used your VARs to scan ahead, through the thicket. I saw one of our jumpers had to come down. The same one we were on. I don't think they were hit by weapons fire, but something had gone wrong and they had to land for repairs. So I rushed over and hitched a ride with them and didn't have to wait to break com silence—instead, we dropped in on the rest of Easy and the infantry and warned them before continuing on to MainCommand for backups."

"Good job." Rett put solid feeling behind the words, yet it didn't seem like enough. It would have to do for now. "Do you have com? I'm on, but not getting any outside signals."

"Ever since I came down to this level there's been some sort of interference. I'm not even getting through to Battalion, and I know they're on com. Must be one powerful generator somewhere."

"Look sharp, then."

"Umm-hmm!"

Good deities, Pam, she's talked more in the past ten minutes—I mean a lot more, voluntarily, and in complete sentences—than she has since coming to F-troop. And before, I think that was the first time I heard her say something in fun.

Rett sped through the corridor, Carakenne behind her, silent as a shadow. Echoes of battle reached her ears from other areas of the big complex, but nothing sounded close by. Trying one door after another, they searched for the rest of Easy Force.

Crouching on her heels, Rett studied one mark among the many on the scuffed and dirty corridor floor. Her gaze traveled ahead. There was something there, a corner of it white and shining in some congealed blood. A tooth. Molar. Whose?

She tucked it into a pocket and examined another mark. Finally, she rose and moved on, more confident in her direction—if not the condition in which she'd find anyone. Her only certainty, at that moment, was that Ariam still lived.

In a storage room at the end of the corridor, she found a cache of Easy's gear. From the way things looked, each unconscious commando had been relieved of peripherals right outside. Headbands, utility and weapons belts with the gear still attached; rifles, kitbags, and equipment packs lay in a haphazard jumble. She nearly stepped on someone's corrective lenses. Those, too? Rett picked them up to check the ident strip. They belonged to B-troop's third-up, Corporal Rimms. She put them aside carefully.

~No uniforms here,~ said Pam.

I noticed. Maybe they're somewhere else.

~Maybe they didn't take them. It doesn't always have to mean they killed them—maybe all it means is that they were in a big hurry and planned to take them later.~

I'll go with that thought.

Spotting her personal weapon and belt in the pile, Rett dropped the ML-12. For a second she was tempted to take some of F-troop's gear with her.

No. I don't need anything slowing us down. Better here for now.

"Come on," she said grimly to Carakenne, nodding toward the trail she followed. It stopped at the lifts. "Good bet they went down. Think so?"

"Uhm-hmm."

They went for the stairs. The lower level appeared a lot cleaner. The air, too, was fresh, without the putrid taint of carrion. Rett sucked in several deep breaths and exhaled forcefully to clean her lungs from the upper level. She let out another breath in relief when she was able to pick up her trail in front of the lift doors down here.

It continued for about ten paces. Then the dribbles and smears of blood she'd been following disappeared, wiped clean. The cleaning equipment left against a nearby wall explained that. Well, she knew she was on the right trail. They'd have to check every door and access now, that was all.

293

Rett's anxiety and frustration ramped up from one disappointing failure to the next. Then she came upon a door that was secured. The control pad didn't respond to any command she tried; even the master override was locked out. Carakenne suggested she dismantle the mechanism. Rett had other ideas.

"We don't have time." The urgency from the emotional link she shared with Ariam nearly choked her. "Back up."

She checked to make sure Carakenne was safely to one side before leveling her weapon at the control panel. It exploded, sizzled, and smoked. The door slid aside…for perhaps the width of a hair.

"I can—"

"No. It's time for one of my personal laws of physics this time, Carakenne." She put all her frustration, anxiety, and weight behind her right foot, slamming it into the wall right below the control panel.

The pourstone wall cracked. More sparks burped from the smoking panel. With an electronic gasp, the door opened the rest of the way.

Cara instantly flattened to the left side, Rett to the right.

"F-troop?"

Answered by silence, they looked into the space over the barrels of their weapons. The storage room, like most of the others, held stacked pallets of supplies in packing crates. Unlike most of the other rooms, this one was filled to capacity. Only a pathway wide enough for a cargo floater extended to the far wall, and it was open and empty.

She has to be in here!

The emptiness mocked Rett. Not even a tinge of Ariam's physical aura tickled her awareness. She still knew her sister was very close, and whatever was worrying her, they didn't have much time to find.

"I—" started Rett.

"I hear something," breathed Carakenne, and slid closer to the opening, head tilted and face intent.

Rett nodded; Carakenne's senses of sound, smell, and touch were definitely more acute than hers. "Go in. I'll watch the door."

She waited, impatience and anxiety making her attention flick from corridor to storage room. Carakenne's small form was soon lost in the forest of palletted supplies. Each row looked exactly alike: an orderly stack of crates secured to the pallet with a tight net of cargo webbing. Carakenne finally reappeared, moving slowly, her face scrunched up in concentration.

No luck? Rett felt like screaming. At that moment, though, Carakenne brushed against a crate, whipping aside as loose cargo netting fell, nearly entangling her.

Then she froze. Rett's breath froze, too. Was it a trap? Or had the netting been arranged to only look as if the pile was untouched?

She saw Carakenne go up on her toes, reach up just as high as she was able, hand flat against the side of one of the crates. "Sarge!"

Rett rushed to Carakenne's side, eyeing the crate. "In there?"

"I heard something. When I touched it, I felt movement. I think it's Sergeant Ariam."

"Deities! Watch the door." Shouldering her weapon, Rett closed her hands over the handles of the crate Carakenne indicated. She brought it to the floor and went after the one below it, hoping it held Med. "Packed up all nice and neat and ready to ship no doubt," Rett snarled under her breath as she heaved the second crate from the stack and lowered it to the floor. She reached for the lock but a strong current slammed up her arm the instant she tried to manipulate it. "Damn it, Carakenne, back here now!"

Carakenne quickly came alongside.

"Can you do anything about these locks? Careful," she warned as the small woman leaned close to the first crate. "My arm's numb just from touching it."

"It seems to be similar to the newer mag restraints," said Carakenne after a moment. She reached to her utility belt. "I assembled an opener of my own after the one Sergeant H'tenneck made. Mine can be adjusted to almost any frequency they use. It should work."

Rett bit her lower lip as Carakenne brought her device close to the lock. But the result wasn't at all dramatic. The locks on both crates popped open and she was quick to yank the lid open on the first container.

"Ariam!" Sliding to her knees, she leaned close to hear what Ariam was mumbling.

295

"Find the others fast, Rett. Now." The B-troop second's voice was weak and hoarse, as if she'd been straining to speak as loudly as possible even before they opened the crate. She'd probably been screaming for Carakenne to have heard from the doorway.

Ariam lay on her right side, thick foam padding wedging her slender form tight from top to bottom. There had been a mask of some sort affixed to her face, probably to feed both air and sleeping gas to her while cocooned. Somehow, she'd managed to work it loose. And somehow, she must have found a balance between giving in to the gas and the air she had left to keep conscious.

A few more minutes and she would have suffocated, thought Rett. "Take it easy, Ari, just try to breathe."

Ariam hadn't been stripped, but a hasty cut had been made in her left sleeve, and the material pulled away enough for a biomonitor to be fastened to the upper part of her arm. Small sensors clung to her forehead and neck. From the position of that same arm, it looked as if her wrists were secured behind her; no doubt her ankles were restrained as well. The padding hid most of the details.

"Get the other one open and those things off Med," snapped Rett as she reached for the monitor with one hand and the mask still emitting the mixture of sleeping gas with the other. Carakenne jumped to obey.

"I'm fine," Ariam insisted hoarsely. "They're somewhere close. They don't have much time left. Pull the stuff off Med, leave these crates open. We'll be fine with clear air, go!"

Rett pushed back, turning to the second crate to check on Med. She almost gasped aloud as she stared at the figure Carakenne was attending to. Did they put someone else in Med's uniform as a decoy? This man was the same size, had the same sandy hair, but he looked at least ten years younger than the Med she knew.

But this *was* Med.

"He looks so different." Carakenne said as she slid a finger beneath the arm monitor. A slight pressure released it instantly. Then she plucked the sensors away before pulling the mask from his face.

As Carakenne turned Med's face toward the open air, Rett knew why.

"He's not scowling, that's why. He's been anesthetized enough that all his muscles are smooth. He'll be all right. We have to go."

"I'd rather see him grumpy than see him like this," muttered Carakenne as she stood up to follow Rett.

"I know. Me too." Rett reached for Carakenne's uninjured shoulder, wishing she were an empath so she could express the deep gratitude that was almost choking her. She cleared her throat. "Let's move."

The next corridor was totally dark. Rett paused before entering it, pushing out her energy sense. She didn't register any auras, but if there were any troopers hiding down here with active targeters, the two of them would be easily spotted.

"Jammers on?" she asked Carakenne softly.

At the affirmative, Rett directed with a jerk of her head, sending the younger woman to the left. She stayed on the right.

"Something smells hot," Rett said after a few minutes.

"Pourstone," said Carakenne. "Can't be a regular fire, Sarge, this section would've been cut off with blast doors and fire controls activated."

"Unless fire controls were overridden or destroyed," countered Rett, the ball of cold dread, augmented by Ariam's empathic link, moving from her throat to her stomach. *I know you had a very bad day, but behave!* she ordered her belly.

The acrid smell and smokiness thickened as they moved on. A tiny crack of light above a doorway revealed the source. Rett moved to Carakenne's side of the corridor, and again they stood, one to each side of the portal.

"You're fully kitted? Put your mask on, then." Rett tried the control board, which refused to light. But the tone response on contact—and her energy sense—told her it was active. It wouldn't open to a voice command. "It's locked, but it should open to the complex override. I'll try that in a minute."

She felt the door, first with her hands, then leaning close. The door was warm, but not hot. Someone was going on behind it. Pushing her energy sense, she visualized the hard yellow outlines from power supply lines running through the wall overhead—normal enough—but when she tried to go beyond the wall...

~What about fire?~ Pam asked.

Fire isn't steady. This is fairly steady. It's more than a light. "Carakenne, there's something strange going on in this room. I agree, I don't think it's a fire, but the door is warm and I'm scoping a lot of loose power on the other side. So move aside and stay low, we could get caught in a backdraft."

Leaning flat against the wall, she made double-sure Carakenne was ready before entering the code.

The door opened easily. A huge gust of hot air, followed by a choking swirl of smoke, escaped into the corridor. There was a lot of coughing.

"Easy Force?" queried Rett from behind the pulled-up collar of her uniform. The puzzling energy aura she'd scoped outside sharpened into distinct vertical yellow bars in her mental vision, but her physical vision was assaulted by smoke backlit with lurid orange.

"You're clear, Sarge." Trebor's deep voice sounded rough. "Wait for the smoke to clear, parts of the floor aren't safe. Watch where you step— hold on, is Cara with you?"

Rett threw her companion a puzzled glance. "Yes."

More coughing. "Wait a second."

From the change in his voice, he'd turned his head away. "All right, who had twenty-five minutes and forty seconds?"

"What in two worlds? *Shit,* Trebor!" exploded Rett. "Let's go, Carakenne." Narrowing her eyes to help protect them from the smoke, she moved into the doorway and then stopped so suddenly that Carakenne bumped into her.

Through the heat and thinning haze glowed a deadly barricade of narrowly spaced energy beams. Behind that was Easy Force.

"No wonder the door was easy to open," Rett noted sourly.

"Did you bring the spiced meat patties and ale?" someone asked hoarsely.

She cleared her throat and swallowed. "Please don't mention food right now, all right? Is everyone okay?"

"More or less, for right now, Rett. Not for much longer," replied Lieutenant Evetez.

In the coherent light from the beams, his sweat- and smoke-streaked face looked blotchy and strange. His hair, which had come loose from the tight tuck and braid he usually confined it in, made a tangled halo around it. A torn, bloodstained piece of uniform covered the lower half of his face.

"Deities, we're glad to see you two," he said. "It's been twenty-five minutes since these things came on, and the smoke was starting to become a problem." He pulled down his makeshift smoke filter. "Now the door is open, though, it's already improving"

"You'd better keep that on until we can get more air going, or turn these things off."

A motion at her side caught Rett's attention. Carakenne started to take off her breather unit, and it wasn't hard to conclude she thought someone in the group might need it more than she did. Rett's "No, Carakenne, leave it" was echoed quickly, simultaneously, from four different voices. "They need us operational, and I need you fully operational," Rett clarified. "So keep it on."

"Yes, Sergeant."

299

"Lieutenant?" Rett turned back to Evetez for a report.

~He looks awful,~ Pam said. ~That subordinate officer before wasn't kidding.~

"The heat's getting stronger but we're rotating positions as much as we can," Evetez said. "Have a few people out from heat and smoke. The real hazards right now are these beams. You noticed the condition of the floor?"

She had, but her first concern had been for the people in the room. Since entering, though, her feet were getting warmer by the minute and it wasn't going to do anyone any good if she and Carakenne weren't careful.

"I don't know how much longer it'll last. The beams don't quite stay in place long enough to burn completely through, but I'm sure it's destabilizing. They're squeezing in on us, too."

"How fast?"

Evetez shook his head. "At random intervals, but the motion increment's been the same, fingerlength at a time." The lieutenant glanced over his shoulder to Trebor. "And talking about time, I won, damn it. I had the closest time, so—"

Sergeant Rett growled. "Shit, Lieutenant, if you're more concerned over your bet on what time we'd get here, I suppose we can go help Lightning and come back later."

"Sarge," squeaked Carakenne in protest, "we...Oh."

Rett signaled she had no intention of leaving.

"Oh." Carakenne's response was more sigh than spoken word.

Rett turned to study the situation, wincing at the smoking, blackened furrows that already marked the track and movement of the beams. The path started a length inside the doorway and stretched two lengths to the current position. The pourstone material was definitely soft and melting around the edges of that path.

"It doesn't look as if the beams stay in any one place long enough to melt clear through, which is good," said Carakenne, already intent on the problem. "We might have opened the door into a hole that went three levels straight down. Maybe farther."

"Three levels?" someone from the group repeated.

"What's beneath us?" another wanted to know.

"Complex water reservoirs—three levels deep," Rett said.

"Well then, at least any of us that were scorched or flaming would be drenched," said Evetez, then coughed so hard he nearly lost his balance and fell into the beams.

Rett clenched her teeth. Easy Force didn't have much room left. Even if they were to stand atop one another, the beams were going to angle in as they closed. The bottom layer of support would give way as their legs burned out from beneath them, the pile would collapse, and everyone would be toasted. The narrow spacing of the beams made the prospect of anyone escaping alive impossible. "Ideas, people, let's have them!" *You too, Pam,* Rett urged.

"Must get closer," muttered Carakenne, removing her handlamp and brushing a trickle of sweat from her forehead. She started moving toward the beams, but Rett grabbed her arm.

"Hold it," Rett said. "Before we do anything, I'm going to cover that doorway. Just because we didn't see anything on the way down is no reason to get careless now." She left Carakenne frowning at the ceiling and mumbling to herself. The corridor was still clear, and although she saw the fire controls had indeed been disabled, the environmental controls on the outer panel were still active. She dialed the ventilators to maximum, and the *whoosh* sound, followed by a brush of cooler air moving past her cheek, took some of the edge off her anxiety. The powerful system that made air quality in these big complexes so fresh wasted no time making a difference. Now all they had to do was get Easy from behind that deadly curtain.

~It's a good thing that room isn't any smaller,~ Pam thought. ~I don't think you'd have found any of them alive, whether or not the beams reached them.~

I know. Rett sent her awareness up and down the corridor again, as far as she was capable. Still clear, but she couldn't count on it. Then she stepped back inside the room. Carakenne was standing near the bars, shifting from one foot to the other. Squinting past the brightness of the barrier, Rett recognized H'tenneck and Jayord on the other side.

They're my two best techs right now—Carakenne and H'tenneck. If they can't think of anything, I don't who can.

~What's she doing?~

Rett watched the younger woman unclip something from her weapons belt, hold it tight in her fist a moment, and then cautiously, using only her fingers, pass it through the beams to H'tenneck.

It's an explosive. In case we fail. They won't have to wait for the beams to kill them.

Rett felt a negative reaction from Pam start to build, but at the same time, the gratitude and relief on the faces of those she could see of the group began to register with her ego-merge friend.

~I have to admit, it's better than waiting. And they're all for it, looks like. But what about you and Carakenne?~

I'll worry about that when the time comes.

And then Carakenne turned around, standing as tall as she was able and so determined her aura flared into Rett's consciousness brighter than the energy beams.

"Sarge, I need to get up *there.*" She pointed at a powerunit cluster on the outer wall, about three lengths above the floor.

"Can't we blow it off the wall? Or get those reflectors?"

"No," Carakenne said firmly.

301

~I don't think she approved of your scientific application of brute force earlier, even though it worked,~ snickered Pam.

"Has to be too much power running this thing and no telling what might happen. It might be trapped. The reflectors appear to be synched—if we hit one, the rest might go wild. With normal fire there's no way only two of us can hit all of them at once, or even fast enough, to stop any that from happening. If you went full auto on your TT-1 it would work, but it would also bring the roof down. I don't think we're looking to do that. I have to take a closer look. I might have to disconnect it."

Examining the spot at which the younger woman still pointed, Rett nodded. She'd need both hands free; so would Carakenne. "We'll make certain someone can cover the doorway first. I'm not closing it, it's still too hot in here, and if those ventilation fans cut out, we won't have to wait for those beams to kill anyone." As she spoke she began to disable the bio-safety of her weapon.

Enabling her TT-1 so someone other than herself might use it was something Rett hadn't done too often in her military life. All Special Forces personnel carried firearms coded to their own body chemistry. Rett, like the others, had become inured since earliest training to any discomfort from the momentary prick of the tiny device that identified her every time her finger touched the trigger. Rather than an annoyance, the bio-lock was a blessing.

Only unit leaders and seconds knew the codes to override the mechanisms. Since the weapon's owner had to remain in constant contact for the weapon to fire, the bio-safeties ensured an enemy couldn't operate the weapon against its owner, or anyone else.

She then took two steps closer to the barricade and gestured for Trebor and Jessek. Without a doubt they were the best sharpshooters in this group. *Semage had to finally admit that, although he has Ariam now*, she gloated to Pam for a second as she started to hand her weapon through the beams. *But as fast and accurate as Ariam is, Trebor's better.*

A sharp inhalation from Carakenne nearly startled Rett into a fatal extra movement as her arm reached its fullest extension through the narrow gap in the beams to hand off her TT-1 and extra rounds to Jessek. She'd only a half-fingerlength of clearance to either side. Rett withdrew her arm once Jessek had a solid hold on the weapon.

Closing her eyes for a moment, she let out her own soft breath with a softer warning. "Don't do that again, Carakenne."

An apologetic gulp sounded in reply.

"Let me have your carbine."

The weapon was presented as if for formal inspection. Taking it, Rett repeated her operation, disabling the safety. No gasps this time as she gave the TA-5 and two extra ammo clips to Trebor.

Pulling her boots from the hot mineral mud that part of the floor had become, Rett stepped back and turned. *I am really, really glad she came up with my boots. I'd hate to be barefoot right now.*

~You wouldn't have any feet about now,~ came dryly from Pam.

My point exactly. "Ready?"

"Ready." Carakenne rose from the crouch she had dropped into and shoved a handful of tools into a pocket on her shoulder harness.

"Let's do this." Rett positioned herself on one side of the powerunits, about a handspan from the wall, facing into the room. Then she extended her hand and arm at a slight angle, palm flat and upturned.

Without hesitation Carakenne took a running step into Rett's hand and timed her jump with the extra upward boost. When the smaller woman's boots landed on Rett's shoulders, she shifted her balance and stance to compensate.

"Perfect," said Carakenne from overhead. "A bit smoky up here, though, like my head is in a cloud."

The light from the younger soldier's handlamp reflected from the wall to Rett's uniform and into her corners of her vision. "Good thing you kept your breather on, huh? Careful up there."

"Don't worry, Sarge." Already, Carakenne's voice had taken on the distant, concentrating quality more familiar to Rett. "If I do something wrong, we'll never feel a thing."

Rett grinned and patted Carakenne's left leg above the boot top. "All I was worried about was you kicking me in the ear. Be a little hard to stay up there hanging on by your teeth."

303

The room became silent. Rett heard only the hum of the generators, the hissing, bubbling sound from the floor where the beams made contact, and occasional coughs. And then Carakenne mumbling to herself from above.

A sharp pain against her scalp made Rett let go her grip of the uniform material of Carakenne's right leg. Her fingers snapped tight around whatever it was—one of Carakenne's tools. It was damp with sweat—no wonder it had slipped.

"Sorry, Sarge."

Rett wiped the tool against her chest and stretched her arm up, keeping hold until she was sure Carakenne had gripped it. Even as she made the transfer, there was a click, a soft whir, a flicker of the beams—which sent Easy scrambling back and closer together. They couldn't pack any tighter; already those who were unconscious were being held up by virtue of the fact there wasn't a fingerwidth of space between anyone behind the barricade.

"No guess who built this," Rett heard from above. "Stinks."

Then the body standing on her shoulders jerked. A sharp gasp made Rett clench her teeth even tighter than they already were.

"What is it?"

"It's trapped. I nearly set it off. Sarge—in the lab, he had it set so that if something happened to him, his research wouldn't be compromised. Or so no one else would profit from it. I think that's what started this unit up—when we killed him."

"You killed him," reminded Rett.

"I hope there wasn't anything in the room with Sergeant Ariam or Med."

"If you think this laser thing started when the commander died, we likely would have already encountered something in the room with Ariam and Med."

"Oh."

Rett was grateful for that. Being helpless and unable to solve a problem so technical was frustrating. So was being unable to help in any way except as a ladder. Being able to offer a logical explanation that made sense even to someone far more intelligent than she—well, that was as reassuring to her as it was to anyone who heard.

But the beams shifted again. This time, there was a sharp hiss from someone in the bunch, followed by a whiff of scorched uniform and burnt flesh.

Something peculiar was happening with the floor, too. As she focused on them, a few of the furrows widened. The floor, already half-mud in places, shivered beneath her feet. And then a hole large enough for a body to fall through opened up. The hot slush of melted pourstone around it immediately started to ooze toward the hole.

"*Hurry*, Carakenne, there's not much time. The floor is destabilizing. Another shift and people are going to die."

"Sarge?"

"Yeah?"

"This thing is a mess. I almost set off two traps already. And there's no way to shut it off without setting them both off for sure this time. The only thing to do is cause an overload big enough to take power down in this entire section."

"How are you going to do that?"

"I can do it from here. This thing's sucking so much power and running so hot already it's a wonder it didn't burn itself out...ah, I see why not, these heat sinks and housing are azurium-alloy..."

"Carakenne!" Rett growled the name out this time.

"One more gadget drawing power on this line should be enough to overload the section generators and either trip off breakers or burn out the entire grid. All I need is something that can draw power from a live feed. I'll wire it in through the main power line right up here, not the unit itself. My lamp would do it, but I can't make the connection in the dark. An ML-12 powerpack would really be nice—"

"Carakenne."

"Sarge?"

"We don't happen to have anything like that. And I don't think there's time to run back to that storage room where we found everyone's gear."

"Oh."

"Any other way?"

"Yes. But not if we want a sure chance of recovering anyone alive."

"Wait a sec, you still have my VARs and Omni? The Omni can run off an external power source, and if you uplink the VARs and run something, it'll draw even more. Use them!"

"Yes, but didn't those VARs belong to someone—"

Another chunk of floor disappeared. Rett tightened her fingers forcefully into the slim legs they steadied. "*Now,* Carakenne!"

This time, Rett ignored the sharp boinks and thumps on her head and chest as Carakenne dropped any tool she held. *Just don't drop the VARs. Don't drop the Omni. I don't think we'd have time to pick them up.*

She heard Evetez ask who had the explosive, if it was ready. Inside her, Pam was frozen into stillness, as if any thought from her now would jeopardize what Carakenne needed to do.

"Brace yourself, Sarge, there may be some backlash from this," warned Carakenne.

"Ready when you are," Rett replied. The small body she supported shifted its weight to the left. So Carakenne would go left, she'd go right.

"Don't try to hang on to me, Sarge, let me roll! Calculate and display!" shouted Carakenne.

Pam—Before Rett's next thoughts surfaced she felt every hair on her body stand at attention. The buzz in her ears deafened her. Every muscle and tendon contracted and froze into place.

For a second she thought an energy field like the one she'd been held in upstairs had been activated. There was a deep, jolting shock. A gigantic shove. There was a bright actinic flash followed by utter blackness.

Stunned, breathless, prickling all over, Rett managed by force of will to pull her face away from its hot contact with the floor.

Am I blind or is it dark? she wondered first.

Then from Pam:~ How many sections are we in?~

If we're in sections, it's a good thing it doesn't hurt as badly as I thought. Yet. Couple more seconds, though, and I'm going to start melting.

~There's no satisfying you. Thirty or so minutes ago you were freezing.~

The numbing paralysis locking Rett's muscles ebbed. Turning her head, she noticed a crack of light to her left: Carakenne's handlamp, still clipped in place on her shoulder harness and now beneath her still form. And dangerously close to one of the holes in the floor.

"Shit. Carakenne?" Rett struggled to get up, but her body wasn't listening to her brain.

Then there were hands on her, lifting her away from the soft, half-melted pourstone. Hands. More than one set. Whose? More shadowy forms blocked her view of the crack of light. Only for a moment.

"Careful, watch that hole!" That was Jayord's voice. Then light flared out brightly as Carakenne's body was lifted, illuminating the faces Rett wanted to see.

Those of the formerly trapped members of Easy Force.

"How is she?" Rett managed to actually make sound come from her mouth this time.

"She's all right. Singed. Stunned. Out of breath. She'll be fine, Sarge."

Elation and relief rose strong. It had worked. The light still clipped to Carakenne's shoulder showed at least a double handful of sweated, smoke-blackened, grinning faces surrounding them, with brighter gleams marking the locations of those outside the reach of the ambiance.

"Way to go, Carakenne!" Unable to come up with anything more original on her own, Rett heard her voice speak with Pam's thoughts.

This time the younger woman moved on her own, lifting her head to give Rett a puzzled stare. "Way to go where, Sarge?"

"I meant well done."

"I think I am," the small soldier said ruefully, shaking any clinging pourstone from her hands.

Laughter followed. "Aren't we all," said Sergeant Tris.

"Steamed, smoked, and toasted, but we're alive. Thanks to you." Trebor added, and thumped Cara lightly on top of her head as he and Jessek slipped past them to cover the doorway and the hall outside.

Feeling was coming back to her feet, her legs. Rett straightened, balancing on her own. Corporal Rimms from B-troop kept a hand on her anyway.

~And I thought I was a smartass,~ snickered Pam. ~You have an entire assault group filled with them.~

Rett sent a glance toward the ceiling. *Just wait until you've been here a little longer. Some of them can give you lessons.* Aloud, she said, "What I really want to know, Carakenne, is if you're all right."

"I think so." Carakenne sounded strained, but she straightened.

The light wavered and shifted as someone—Nerrah from the shape—unclipped the light from the small soldier's harness and adjusted it to illuminate more of the room. What Rett saw wasn't encouraging, especially factoring in the intermittent trembling that she determined wasn't the backlash of nerves from a close escape.

The holes that had started opening in the floor were getting bigger.

"Secure the corridor, Trebor, we have to move out of here quickly before the floor caves. I think there's more than a quake shaking us right now. Everyone else, get the wounded up front now—and once Trebor calls clear don't stop moving until you're well away from this room!"

Once Trebor's whistle sounded, people moved. A sharp crack and jolt sped the last of them into the hallway. Rett started to follow when the entire building pitched up, then down. The level surface beneath her tilted sharply. And she was falling, sliding backward toward what her energy sense sounded as a huge gaping expanse of nothing.

Fingers clamped around her forearms, dug in to her flesh. Finding strength in her still partially numbed body, she dug her knees into the pourstone that was still hot and soft from the sustained assault of energy beams. She hurled her weight forward, toward those who had grabbed her. All three of them landed against the wall across the corridor, less than a length of solid floor between them and what had been a storage room.

"Thanks, Rimms, Jayord." Rett puffed out a breath. *Pam?*

~I'm still here. That was a little too close,~ Pam answered.

"If we stay close to this wall we should be all right. You good to go, Sergeant Rett?" Corporal Rimms asked.

She nodded, again waving them ahead of her. What was left of the corridor might be safe enough, but she was heavier than either one of them. Soon they rejoined the rest of the unit, safe for the moment at the far end of the corridor.

"Everyone here?"

"All accounted for," Sergeant Tris confirmed.

"Fabulous job, Carakenne. Very well done." Lieutenant Evetez appeared in the lighted area. Med Shenyver from B-troop was close by, ready with a supporting hand. "And just in time."

Any new-found display of confidence Rett had been seeing from the small soldier vanished. Maybe not on the outside—no, Carakenne, as any of them would, appeared composed, alert, and ready for orders as the Easy Force commander addressed her. Rett's energy sense told her a different story as the younger woman's internal and surface temperatures shifted; causing telltale ripples, streaks, and fluctuations in her energy output. It had little to do with any attraction she might have felt for Evetez, either.

Knowing exactly how it felt to be the unwilling center of attention, Rett took pity on her and moved a step closer to Evetez, breaking the line-of-sight between him and the younger woman. Carakenne's sigh of relief was audible.

"Heard you gave them some trouble, Lieutenant." Rett ran an assessing eye over her friend's battered countenance. The left side of his face and both his eyes were swelling nicely. His nose looked broken. "It must have been your blood I followed down here. Thanks for the trail."

Evetez shrugged. "Don't mention it. Where were you?"

Rett pressed a hand to her belly. "Me? Hanging out with the local Coalition commander. He wanted a Nyorfian for dinner."

One of Evetez's sandy eyebrows rose at that, but thankfully, he didn't ask her for details. "Have any idea where Ariam and Med Rhozev are?"

"Ariam and Med were packed up and ready to be shipped out to deities know where. They're safe for the moment. We'll need to pick them up. How about you? Going to be okay?"

He grimaced. "Eventually. But not right now. If you're operational, you're going to have to take over. I'm mobile but I'm not going to be able to see at all in a few more minutes, much less keep thinking straight."

Rett nodded, and swung away from Evetez to give orders, impatient to put distance between her butt and this part of the building. "Tris, our weapons and gear are cached in a storage bay a level up." She gave him directions. "The way was clear when we came, but take Jessek to cover you."

Sergeant Tris gestured to R-troop and disappeared into the gloom. Rett noticed most of them managed to pass close to Cara on the way, a word, a touch, or a glance expressing appreciation. Poor Carakenne still looked as if she'd much rather disappear.

Rett spoke to her pcom, opening the general frequency they used. Then she pulled off her headband and handed it to her third-up. "Worren, get with Trebor and start clearing us as far as you can to the main level. We have to get past this com blockage, so as soon as you start hearing anything relay it back vocally. As soon as Tris brings up the gear, we'll get that handed out and go the rest of the way."

"Right, Sarge."

She swung back to the B-troop medtech. "Casualties here besides Evetez?"

"Six from smoke and heat, three beam grazes, but all mobile. Sergeant Dinnold will need some help if fast movement is needed."

"Anyone need you in attendance?"

Med Shenyver shook her head.

"Nerrah, take your squad to retrieve Sergeant Ariam and Med. If it's all right with you, Semage, I'd like Med Shenyver to go with them."

Sergeant Semage nodded to both Rett and his medtech.

"Thanks. Go, Nerrah. Carakenne will show you where."

"May I have a few moments of Specialist Carakenne's time first?" asked Lieutenant Evetez.

Rett took him from Bhayorn and moved aside, modulating her tone so it didn't go past him. "Can it wait?"

"I think it waited too long already. Are you going to be difficult about it? Going to toss me down to the floor and twist my arm again, like you did the first time I tried to be nice?" A belligerent note crept into his low voice.

She eyed him in the dim light, having trouble swallowing her grin. "Make it quick." She turned him over to Bhayorn and moved aside. "Specialist Carakenne. The lieutenant needs to talk to you."

* * * * *

He tried to set her at ease first thing. "This isn't anything official, Carakenne."

"Yes, sir." She nodded but didn't relax her formal stance. Evetez regretted the change that had come over her ever since the moment of crisis had passed. Genuine concern leaked through the set expression on her face, though. The passing of several B-troop members, each one giving her some sort of touch—a tap on the back or shoulder, a brief mussing of her hair—gave her an excuse to break the eye contact he wanted to hold.

Evetez grimaced inwardly. He couldn't blame anyone for not wanting to keep eye contact with him at this point. He was sure his eyes had all but disappeared into his face.

For a long moment he didn't say anything, just looked at her. She shifted, glanced down, back up, took a breath.

"Uhm, I-I…I have your headband, sir." Pulling it from a belt pocket, she unfolded it and held it out to him.

"Deities, thanks, Cara. Another pcom will come in handy." His fingers closed over her hand and the headband. He squeezed her slender fingers gently and kept his hand on hers until he saw a reaction.

Her eyes went wide. "Yes, sir," she said weakly.

He took his time letting go of her fingers. "Are you good to go? You were injured." He nodded at her left shoulder.

"Uhm-hmm. Yes, sir. Good to go."

His voice lowered so no one else would hear him. "I know this isn't exactly the right time or place, and it might seem like…uh…the line you may have heard that I usually use, but it isn't."

His angled his mashed nose toward the corridor floor, mustering up one of his best pitiful expressions. He didn't have to fake it very much. A moment of vertigo made him stagger back a step, into the wall. He leaned against it, unsure for a moment if his knees were going to hold him.

She stepped in closer, reaching to steady him. "Sir, you need—"

His lightheadedness passed. He straightened. "I'm all right. I need to finish talking to you."

"What is it, sir?"

"If you've no objections, I'd like a chance to know you on a bit more of a personal level. I didn't ask you sooner because…" He glanced toward the spot Rett occupied for a moment. "Well, because I seem to make you uneasy. Is it because I scare you, or you don't like me?"

Slowly, she shook her head. "Neither, sir," she whispered.

"Then is it okay if we meet in the common area when we're both on free time?"

Her mouth opened, then closed with nothing more than a short exhalation. Her lovely sky-colored eyes were huge. "Yes, sir."

He managed a smile. "Great. Give my headband to Sergeant Rett. Oh, and Cara," he added, in a normal tone and volume, "when your squad gets caught up with everyone else, make sure Trebor's covered. He owes me and I intend to collect."

"Let's go, Cara," called Sergeant Nerrah.

"Told you he was a bubbleheaded idiot," muttered Sergeant Rett loud enough for him to hear as Carakenne went past her.

As soon as he felt better, he was going to get her for that.

2.2.6 SECTION C, EPNOCE MAINCOMMAND
0535.12.01 (LOCAL RECKONING)

~H'TENNECK AND NITRAYM FOUGHT OVER her assignment?~ Pam asked incredulously.

Almost came to blows. Rett flashed Pam a glimpse of the incident, as always surprised how easily Pam managed to enhance the details.

~Actually, they did come to blows.~

I meant to each other, not to me. I'm glad I stopped it.

~With your ribs?~

Rett shrugged. *Nitraym might have caused some real damage if he hit H'tenneck.*

~But is that sort of thing allowed?~

Pam, we're like a family. You know as well as I do, we argue and squabble off duty just as much as we have good times. And sometimes arguments get out of hand. It usually works out just fine, but after getting suspended, I didn't need any internal platoon dynamics drawing attention from anyone. So I settled this argument for them.

~By putting Carakenne in Nerrah's squad.~

I did. Rett grinned inwardly. *So we all benefit. Besides, Nerrah is quiet by nature, too. Not the same quietness as Carakenne, but similar enough so she doesn't feel overwhelmed by the more talkative personalities, like H'tenneck's.*

"Aren't you ready yet?"

Rett had, at that moment, finished cleaning her teeth. She glanced at Trebor as he leaned against the lavatory/bathing alcove's entrance, trying not to look too impatient.

She smiled at his turnout. "I've never seen any of us in dress uniform."

"We usually don't have time for it," said Trebor. "I suppose we might have gone formal at the official functions after the battle for Circle, but we weren't exactly in the mood."

That was an understatement. She frowned as she dried her hands. "I'm done."

He stepped aside for her. "Shall we, then?"

313

"I'm not sure about springing this out of nowhere this way."

"That what took you so long? Don't forget this." He handed over her headband after giving a little adjustment to the brushed metal finish of the Freedom Star gleaming against the black material.

"Me? *Me?* I was ready in less than five minutes." She slid the headband in place, pausing long enough to check the lay of her hair around it in the mirrored panel near the door. "*You* were the one taking up space in the lavatory. If it wasn't so blasted small I would have been in and out before you finished counting how many new gray hairs grew in since yesterday."

He laughed and followed her into the corridor from the quarters they shared as platoon leader and second. "I don't think we need to worry about Carakenne, Sarge. She'll hit the ground, but she'll hit it on her feet."

314

"Yes. After all, she's F-troop." Rett gave a final adjust to her utility belt and lengthened her stride. She wondered if it was right to feel so much love and pride for her entire platoon, enough that she couldn't express it sometimes.

~You express it, all right,~ Pam assured her. ~Trust me. And they know it.~

Sergeants Nerrah and Worren waited for them outside the quiet annex designated as a library and study area. Carakenne, not surprisingly, had been spending a great deal of her waking hours here since Med grounded her.

Rett complimented them both on their turnout. Witnessing Trebor almost falling over his own feet at his first glimpse of Nerrah was priceless. She pretended she didn't notice her second in command giving Cara's squadleader a more personal sign of approval as she asked Worren, "She's occupied?"

"She's so deep in whatever she's reading I can probably blow the door down and she wouldn't notice," said the F-troop third-up.

"Time she comes up for air, then." Trebor, his color a little higher than normal, made a pretense of adjusting his shoulder harness.

"Go in and get her," Rett said to Nerrah and Worren.

＊ ＊ ＊ ＊ ＊

As they entered a conference room filled with serious faces above formal black uniform, Rett didn't have to strain any ability on her part to imagine Carakenne's reaction. The maelstrom of emotions causing the small soldier's energy to resemble a strong auroral display was erratic and turbulent. So much, in fact, Rett was surprised that the younger woman remained so still—for once—and composed. On the outside.

~You might have given her a chance to change her clothes. I think her shirt is bigger than she is.~

Hush, Pam. She's not supposed to twist or bend too much. She's burned all across the front.

~So were you. Taking a belly flop into a floor of melted concrete tends to do that.~

Yeah, but she caught SMG before that.

It hadn't taken long for a recovered Med to declare the small soldier on disability for a tenday. By the time they had returned to the base, Carakenne had been having trouble moving without pain, and couldn't lift her left arm at all. Since Rett was also being treated for surface burns gained by "romping in melted pourstone", as Med put it, she'd seen the full extent of scrapes, painful looking bruises, and energy weapon scores Carakenne had sustained on the way to get help for Easy Force. Now, six days later, Carakenne's surface burns, like Rett's, were no more annoying than a fading sunburn. But her injured shoulder and arm was still in a sling, and she had been forbidden, on pain of being incarcerated in Medical, from wearing closely fitted clothing or making any motions that would cause stress to the healing burns across her midsection.

"At ease, Specialist Carakenne," Major Yidnar said.

~I'll bet she's anything but at ease. I think this whole surprise-hush-hush thing is sort of mean,~ Pam commented. ~She probably thinks she's in trouble.~

"Thank you, sir," Carakenne's voice was strong, if a bit breathless.

She's scared and confused, yes, but she knows she not in trouble. Major Yidnar or anyone else wouldn't have put her at ease if she were.

~Even so, if that was me, I'd probably be peeing my pants.~

Rett, outwardly as still, formal, and devoid of any expression except for detached calm, swallowed the laugh that nearly escaped, almost choking herself in the process. It was a good thing attention was on Carakenne right now.

Major Yidnar continued. "As you know, we have our traditions in Special Forces. One of them is that the Battalion commander has the privilege to present an individual with commendations for distinguished service. After some tough deliberation over this instance, we're changing that tradition."

~You *were* tough on him,~ chided Pam. ~I must admit, though, you managed to thrash him into agreement without showing one single sign of disrespect. I thought you people were more into non-physical forms of argument.~

I can't help it the discussion arose while we were both in the gym. Hoping she showed no outward sign of movement, Rett shifted her weight to her other hip. The right was still rather tender. *You know damn well it was Major Yidnar's own idea to settle the matter with a three-minute takedown.*

~All the same, I thought you both held back a little there.~

Yes, we did. Killing force. That was about it. I was lucky because the Major was one second short of landing me on a tenday vacation with Med when I got my opening. I might be stronger, but he thinks faster and has more tricks than all of us put together.

Rett directed her inner attention back to the wildly shifting colors of Cara's emotional energy. The small woman's apprehensive curiosity and uncertain panic was ready to give way to complete chaos. Since it was a good sort of chaos, not the dark, oppressive kind that Rett had felt threatening her sensibilities over the past few months, she didn't worry.

Few more minutes, sport.

"Sergeant Rett?" Yidnar said then.

Taking the opportunity to clear her throat, which still ached from holding back amusement, Sergeant Rett came around smartly and took a smooth step to the left to face Carakenne head-on instead of at a right angle. In an automatic response, the younger woman again came to attention.

"On behalf of every single one of us in F-troop and Easy Force, I would like to present you with this Freedom Star in appreciation of a job well done under tremendous odds."

~Pacing, pacing,~ prompted Pam. ~Slow down.~

"You were nominated for commendation by a unanimous vote upon the completion of the mission at Complex 412."

Sergeant Rett paused again, the interval for her as agonizing as it was for the woman she faced. Although the emotionless façade never changed, a visibly pale cast cooled the rich, deep color of Carakenne's skin.

"May I have your headband, Specialist Carakenne?"

There was the tiniest of trembles in the younger woman's lips as she pulled off her headband. It was then that Carakenne's hair—which had been loose before their arrival and given a hasty braid and tuck by Sergeant Worren—erupted, spilling down her back and tumbling over her face.

Rett continued the motion of taking the headband, trying to send silent encouragement with the brief contact of their fingers. Carakenne never moved. Rett was quite sure she'd stopped breathing a while ago. She didn't waste any time attaching the Freedom Star to the headband, although she did brush her thumb over it once with a heartfelt thought of gratitude that she—and everyone else—was still alive to have this chance.

She had to close the younger woman's icy cold fingers around the headband. *It's almost over, sport. I know—stuff like this makes getting shot at during missions seem a lot simpler.*

Then Rett stepped back a pace and saluted. A breath later, so did everyone else.

Carakenne stood frozen one heartbeat, two. Then her eyes moved, making fleeting contact with Rett's. A spark of comprehension rose. Belatedly, a return salute followed. Since her headband was still in the saluting hand, it went flying.

Rett managed to catch the headband before it got too far, a bubble of laughter nearly choking her.

"Thank you. And congratulations, Corporal."

Cara's stare went from Rett's face to the gleaming platinum-and-gold medal on her black headband.

"Did I look that bad when I got mine?" Rett asked her second in command.

Sergeant Trebor's fierce face and the hard, serious line of his lips softened in a grin. "Worse. Cara's quite a bit cleaner and doesn't smell as bad as you did."

She smacked his arm. "That's not what I meant."

"Corporal ?" Carakenne repeated faintly. She looked up, uncertain.

"No one in the Battalion protested against it so we bumped your review up a few months. Do you accept the upgrade?" Rett asked, trying not to laugh.

"Yes, Sergeant, I accept," Carakenne managed.

"But, yes, Sarge, I'd say the level of panic and confusion were about equal." Trebor's golden eyes twinkled. "Thank you, Corporal Carakenne." He handed her a new set of rank patches and all the forms that went with them.

318   Major Yidnar inserted his rangy body between Rett and Trebor. "When I mentioned a change in tradition, I didn't mean for you two to make it a comic occasion," he snarled at them. Punctuating his remark with a very loud sigh, he shook his head in a resigned manner. "I suppose I should be grateful you're both serious when you have to be. Corporal!"

"Sir."

Rett watched as the Major took the headband and new rank insignia from Carakenne's fingers. "Sergeants Rett and Trebor might have ended anything formal about this presentation, but I still get to do this part." He removed the single open circle of the specialist rank from her over-large sleeve and replaced it with the double interlocked rings of a junior corporal. And after making tiny adjustment to the Freedom Star on the headband, he went to fix it in place on her head.

"Never forget to wear this with pride, Carakenne. No matter how you feel about it personally. As others in your platoon, and in the 2023rd, you've earned that right, as well as been given the responsibility."

~He said something like that to you, didn't he?~

Rett nodded before she remembered that no one else would have heard Pam. It didn't matter, for once, since no one was paying any attention to her, anyway. The Major's fingers seemed to be tangled in Carakenne's hair, and she wasn't sure if it was for real, or a move by him to get the younger woman to relax. If it was the latter, he failed. With her hair all over the place and her commanding officer apparently entangled in it, Carakenne's expression said plain as daylight that she wanted the floor to open up and swallow her. The moment was fleeting. The headband was in place, the loose mass of sunny hair arranged over and around it, and the Major was smiling.

"You're in good company, Corporal Carakenne." Major Yidnar said. "Look around. You probably won't see as many Freedom Stars in the same place again."

Rett also cast her glance around the room. The formal, metallic versions—not the near-invisible field variation—of Freedom Stars and other awards and commendations on Special Forces headbands winked and flashed like stars against the blackness of space.

"I'm very pleased with you, Corporal."

"Thank you, sir."

"And here are your orders. You are to come to the Common lounge immediately following this meeting—which should be just about now. What did you say the youngsters were calling the lounge, Trebor, the Drop Zone?" Yidnar asked over his shoulder. "I'm buying. Except for Sergeant Rett. She'll be on a duty shift for AirSpacefighters in another hour anyway. And," added the Major, raising his voice so everyone heard him, "to complete a very nontraditional occasion, in deference to Corporal Carakenne, those of us with long hair can, and will, let it down while in uniform."

Rett chuckled along with everyone else and watched as every man and woman in that room with braided, tucked, or pinned locks promptly reached up and loosened the constraints on their hair.

The Major's attention returned to Cara. "Let's go. The rest of your comrades are there now, waiting for you."

"Yes, sir! Thank you, sir." Carakenne's voice almost cracked. Then she looked up at Rett. "Thank you, Sergeant."

"You have it mixed up, Carakenne. We're thanking *you*."

"And may I have the honor of escorting you to the Drop Zone, Corporal Carakenne?" asked Lieutenant Evetez.

His face still showed some bruising, and the dark circles under his eyes from his broken nose looked like streaks of camo paint. Rett didn't realize that he had so much hair. It sure was a lot longer than it had been all those years ago back in training. The long dark gold waves went past his shoulders.

For a moment she thought Carakenne was either going to pass out or reach up with both hands, grab those long waving locks, and—

Pam! Stop it!

She shook those thoughts clear and watched as Evetez offered his arm and the young woman took it like someone in a dream.

Rett felt rude for eavesdropping as she overheard Evetez's voice, low and soft, as he addressed Cara. "I like your hair loose."

"Same here," the young woman answered.

And then, as the small face dawned with a smile as brilliant and dazzling as sunlight on dark water, Rett let out a satisfied breath. Maybe the assignment at Complex 412 hadn't gone off completely according to plan. But this more than made up for it.

320

"Good job there, Rett," Ariam said, sliding her arm around her sister's waist for a quick hug.

"Me? I had nothing to with it. Things happened on their own."

"Don't tell me there wasn't a nudge here and a push there. I've been around you too long. Besides," reminded Ariam, gray eyes sparkling, "Tovadan and I used to push and nudge at you like that when we were kids. Until a year or so before you left for the military, you were the shyest thing on two legs in Treetop."

"Evetez and I had our hands full with her in training, too." Semage came from behind and urged them forward. "Every time we had a minute or two for socializing, Rett would disappear. We'd find her hiding in a brushpile or up in a tree somewhere, taking a nap."

"Only way I got any sleep with the snoring I had to put up with." Rett rolled her eyes. "Semage, I need some alone time with Ariam. Give us a few minutes, okay?"

He nodded and moved to the door to wait for them.

Rett pulled her sister close. Ariam hugged her hard, shivering a little. "Are you really okay?"

"I don't think I'll look at a cargo crate in quite the same manner again. Med was lucky he never woke up until the others came and took him completely out of his." She shivered. "I can appreciate your phobia about being in tight places and unable to move a little better now. And not being able to breathe."

Rett tightened her hug briefly, then stepped back to look into Ariam's face. "Are you still having problems going to sleep?"

"Some. I miss sharing a room with you."

Rett nodded. "Me, too. But we'd better get used to it. Again."

Ariam smiled. "And we'd better get going."

Semage came back to see what held them up, worming his way between them. Sliding an arm around each of their waists, he urged them toward the door. "Come on, you two, we're going to be the last ones there. I'll admit I'm relieved you won't be drinking anything stronger than tea, Rett."

"That's not what you said before," Ariam pointed out with a wicked laugh. "You suggested maybe you could get her zoned enough that she'd swap Cara—"

"Ariam!" He bumped her with his hip.

"I only negotiate in the gym," Rett said.

"Never mind then, I've heard your terms."

"And saw them. Everyone could see the Major was having a bit of trouble with his left arm," Ariam said.

"Yes. Don't worry. I'll save the sweet-talking for your sister. And if I want any of your personnel, I'll be sure to ask them first, not you. Since you've never refused them any reasonable request."

"Ow! Direct hit." Laughing, Rett didn't resist as Semage swept her and Ariam toward the common area.

321

2.3.0 CHILD'S PLAY
2.3.1 UNDETERMINED AREA, COMPLEX 63, EPNOCE
0535.13.24 (LOCAL RECKONING)

RETT SWIPED HER FOREARM ACROSS her chin, smearing her face with blood. "Fang Med, I need an ETA."

The medtech's reply was lost in a blaze of static from energy weapons.

Jessek stiffened and ground his teeth together as she used her knee to apply pressure over the blood-soaked bandages at the top of his thigh. She'd applied them in haste, with no thought other than to keep his leg attached long enough to move him into a safer area. Well, they weren't going to get much safer than this, and now that they had the time, she had to think about him bleeding to death.

I have to do better than this. She put her weapon aside and rummaged in her utility belt for more medical supplies, laying them out in easy reach.

"Stay with me, Jess. I'm letting up. Deep breath."

The partial release of pressure on his groin pushed Jessek beyond all temptation of movement. What smidgen of color remained in his cheeks washed out with the clammy sweat that slicked his skin. The young sharpshooter's nostrils flared with each breath with his struggle to keep his pain in control; to regulate his breathing and heart rate as he had been taught.

Stripping the old dressings away with careful speed, Rett poured the antiseptic coagulating powder liberally into the wound before pushing the mess of torn and crushed tissue together as best she could. She opted against the adhesive. Strong as it was, the adhesive wasn't meant for something as massive and deep as this, unless she started applying it from the inside out. Instead, she reached for the specially pretreated bandages they carried as part of their personal medical kits.

To her eyes, his leg was all but severed; the heavy thighbone crushed and fragmented. Deities knew what had kept the big femoral artery from rupturing. As far as she could see, that artery and the long muscle on the inside of the thigh were all that kept the limb attached.

In her former life as a logger, crushing accidents happened occasionally, no matter how careful they were. She recalled with graphic clarity the first time she'd seen the victim of a similar accident. That one had died as they performed emergency treatment—much the same as Rett now was performing for Jessek.

-All right, now I am going to interrupt.- Pam's thought came with the bright cold slap of an icy wind.

Not now, Pam. Can't you see I'm busy here?

-I understand that. But you can't think about whatever happened to those people in the past. Or just a few minutes ago.-

Rett bit the inside of her cheek. Jessek wasn't the only casualty, but the other two with her didn't make it. She'd left them back there, one of her newest personnel and one of R-troop's longer-term people, who'd come along to relay information back to Sergeant Tris.

-It's awful they died, Rett, but right now, what matters is that it didn't happen to Jess. If he was going to die of shock, he'd be dead already, especially considering it took you a couple minutes to get him out from under that door. Immediately after which you dragged him a hundred or so lengths and around a corner or two before ever slapping on the tourniquet, much less the first bandage.-

That's just it, I should have—

-What, stopped and given first aid right then? You're both still lucky to be breathing! I don't think that a mosquito could have made it through the SMG at the time, and the way the shots were bouncing everywhere. Now, focus!-

Rett winced. Pam was right. But who knew what she added to Jessek's trauma by that rough handling—

-Hel-LO! That's not the point! Jess knew how bad it was before you ever got him out. If he was worried about permanent damage, he wouldn't be here with you now.-

A sharp twinge twisted in the muscle of her left upper arm. Ow! Damn, how did Pam do that? *All right. You're right.*

Jessek was determined to live, no matter what. He would have asked her for mercy otherwise. Rett sent gratitude for Pam's heading her back on track.

She compressed her lips in the same manner her bandaging compressed Jessek's mangled flesh. Of course there was a chance to save the leg, but only with the timely arrival of a medtech and a quick dispatch of Jessek to a hospital facility.

And we were just about set to pull back. Come ooonnnn, Tris, com me! she growled inwardly.

Then she realized her thoughts showed on her face, and Jessek was watching her.

"Back with me then, Jess?"

"Ass is smoking," he informed her in a raspy grunt. "Come'ere." He lifted his right hand.

She swung her hips a bit closer to his reach, since her hands were occupied. Strange how she only noticed the spot of heat after Jessek flicked away whatever it was that had been slowly charring its way deeper through her uniform and into her flesh.

"Check for anything else, Jess, would you? I'm a bit busy here."

His contact was firm, although as his fingers felt along her length for any hotspots, a steady tremor betrayed the weakness and pain. "That was it." Jessek let his hand fall to his chest. "Guess I bled on you enough to put out anything else. Shit. It's bad, isn't it? How's it look?" He tried to lift his upper body enough to see.

"Lie still. It's bad enough. A few fingerlengths higher and to the right, you'd have to learn a new way to piss."

Jessek's answer was a short laugh that sounded more like a groan.

"Easy." Making sure the bandage lay snug and smooth, she finished it off at the top of Jessek's thigh, watching as it puffed up and tightened to keep its own pressure on the wound. She slid a finger beneath to check—good, not too tight, just enough. She hoped. "Easy. Don't move any more. Just breathe."

He had a good grip on himself now; it would just take a minute or so more to coordinate everything and lock it down…if he stayed conscious for that long.

"Stay with me." Rett smoothed the furrowed lines in his forehead with her filthy hand.

"Minute," he murmured. "Just a minute."

"One minute," she allowed. "You're on the chrono."

If he can't lock it down, I'll have to get him to go into deepsleep. It was a last resort, and while it had its advantages, it had just as many drawbacks. If it came to that, she'd have to guide him down, and do it while he was still coherent. For someone not in total control of the process, there was the risk of the sleeper going so deep he or she would die instead of merely slowing metabolism.

Rett sat back on her heels, easing some of the pressure on tired muscles that had once again forgotten what it felt like not to feel pain of some kind. Then, using the plotters on her VARs, her senses—natural and trained—and factoring in the terse communications over her pcom, she updated herself to within several fingerlengths as to the current location of her people and what each of them were doing.

Two days earlier, the infiltration of Complex 63 had started right on plan, but all sorts of minor complications had cropped up. Since they left plenty of room for alternate plans and quick changes, the overall progress was still on the chrono. Although Easy Force's units were still fighting on this level, Rett was ready to receive the order to start replacing her people with the advance infantry units.

As second in command and Combat Team Leader for Easy Force, she'd been directing the replacement of teams from the four other platoons besides F-troop that made up the special assault group. Since then, however, F- and B-troops had encountered a stiffer opposition, requiring Rett's direct attention and participation. So she'd turned over the matter of redeployment to R-troop's Sergeant Tris, who acted as Rett's backup.

F- and B-troops were engaged, yes, but nothing they couldn't hand off to the infantry now. And by her estimation, Tris should have finished routing the new teams in place for her so they could start the transition. Rett took a breath, ready to com him herself.

As if cued by her thought, Tris's voice sounded in her ear. "Fang Lead, we're all go for—"

Sergeant Trebor interrupted on the priority frequency. "Fang Lead, there's a group of kids between us and the rest of the complex. Just spotted them moving into a side corridor. If they keep going that way, they'll be heading into a live sector."

You just had to tempt more bad luck, didn't you? Thanks a flaming lot, Pam, groused Rett.

~I didn't do anything!~ Pam protested.

You were thinking we were almost finished up here.

~Well, sure…but so were you. Don't blame me. It wasn't like I was bored enough to yank kids out of my ass and throw them into the live fire zone.~

The static from Trebor's end was answer enough why he hadn't sent anyone after the kids himself. His group was hot.

"You saw what, Fang Two?" The Easy Force commander, Lieutenant Evetez, jumped in on the conversation. "Kids in…Sector 17?"

To hear a report of a civilian in that location was something unexpected. Sector 17 housed the main power units, generators, and machinery that ran the basic environmental controls for the west side of the complex. Even under normal circumstances, it was a low-maintenance area, always monitored and routinely inspected, yet never assigned permanent staff. As such, the sector was far from any areas normally frequented by the civilian inhabitants. Occasionally a maintenance worker, but they'd stay away if the area was hot.

Unstaffed or unpopulated as those areas might be, Coalition troops were aggressive in safeguarding them. Not all of the various humanoid and alien races filling the ranks were able to adapt to sharp changes in heat, cold, or air quality, so a drastic, sudden change in environment might cause unexpected and intense problems for them.

"Fang Two has never made a sighting report in error," Rett reminded the other unit commanders, her tone very dry. For once she wished he had.

"Damn." This from Tris, and he sounded tiffed. "No time to wonder how and why. Better have someone from your group get them, Fang, you're closest. Can you spare a team? What about Razor Fourteen and one of yours?"

Rett kept the sigh in her thoughts. "Razor Fourteen and Fang Thirty-two didn't make it. But we're on it, Razor Lead." Already she was checking the gear she carried.

"Good," said Tris after an extra second of hesitation. "We've already started deploying infantry into this level, so we'll keep them there since they're needed, and advise extra confirmation before they shoot at anything."

"We can't finish our pullback now in any case, until we make sure no civilians are going to get caught in the line of fire," Evetez said.

Rett signed off her direct links with Tris and Evetez and spoke to her second in command. "Fang Two, I need details."

"I saw three, but caught only enough to identify two. Boy, red-brown hair, about a length and a quarter in height. A teenager, girl or boy, hard to tell. Thin, length and a half, can't miss her, her hair is as silver-white as Razor Lead's." He followed with coordinates of the place they were spotted; the direction the children were headed.

Trebor must have only seen them for half an eyeblink not to have more detail to report than that. She was glad he'd had that much time. She briefly consulted her Omni, calling for the map of their level to match the picture she'd formed in her head with Trebor's coordinates.

"That means if I cut through the service corridor at 45 West B345 I should intercept."

"Yes. But you'll have to move fast. Must go, things have just heated a bit more here. Luck, Fang Lead."

Rett glanced down at Jessek. His eyes were closed, but he was listening, to her and whatever was coming over his pcom on the general bandwidths. She touched gentle fingers to his throat, noting his pulse was steadier now. "Good, that's it, sport. Lock it down. Com connect Fang Med—how long?"

This time Med's answer was clear. "Two minutes. I heard. I guess there's no protesting your going this time." He sounded resigned. "I have help with me. So go ahead, be careful. Did you give him anything?"

"No. He has a grip, and I thought it was best he stay alert until you or someone else had matters in hand."

Med spoke Jessek's com number to include the wounded man in the conversation. "Once Fang Lead gets you situated, don't move. You move and I'm going to kick your ass. Dead or not."

"Yeah, Med," mumbled Jessek, rolling his eyes.

Rett tousled Jessek's straight hair as she signed off with Med and opened a direct link to Trebor. After getting the accessway location where his sighting had occurred, she gave him a quick update and switched back to Tris. "I'm on it. Fang Two has the team until I'm back." Rett cut her com with a voice command and looked down again.

Jessek was alert and in solid control. He pushed something damp into her hand—a wipe. "Better use this, Sarge. You don't want to scare those kids off, and your face is all over blood. At least get it out of your eyes."

"Suppose you're right." She scrubbed the treated material over her face and hoped she exposed some skin instead of smearing the mess even more. It would take a lot more than one wipe for a thorough clean, but there wasn't time for that.

~You're going to be more visible out there too, with blood mucking up your uniform,~ said Pam.

Rett acknowledged the reminder, grateful for it.

"You'd better get going," Jessek said. He lifted his head and shoulders, his forearms and fisted hands pressing hard to the floor.

Guessing his intention, Rett quickly intervened. "Damn it, Jess. I said don't move, so did Med."

"Med said after I was situated, and I want to sit up," said Jessek with a determined frown.

"Then I'll help you," Rett said. "I've time enough for that." She settled him in a sitting position, his back braced against the wall. "Better?"

"Little easier to shoot this way than flat on my back." The senior corporal's skin was as pale as the snow outside the complex, his dark brown hair and eyebrows making the contrast even sharper. Tense lines tightened and aged his face, but his lake-blue eyes were bright, perhaps too much so. He bared his teeth at her in a grin of sorts. "Good to go," he told her as she handed him his weapon.

She nodded, made sure anything else he would need was in easy reach. So many words rose into her throat, but she swallowed them, unable to find the right ones.

Instead, it was Jessek who spoke. "Sarge, I—"

She completed Jessek's sentence for him. "—am going to hold this section of corridor until relieved. And you're going to damn well watch my smoking hot ass until you can't see it any more."

329

The apologetic expression that had started creeping into Jessek's too-bright eyes transformed into purpose, and as he nodded, Rett tightened her utility belt a notch.

"Depending on where those kids are by the time I catch up, either I'll be back with them or we'll sit in a safe spot until the shooting stops." She slapped the outside of her right boot to make sure her locator was active. "I'll check in when I can."

"Jammers," reminded Jessek.

"On," Rett said after taking a moment to feel the subtle vibration from her wrist bracers, which indicated the targeting jammers were active. "Don't disappoint me, Jess."

He gave her a smile. "Never, Sarge. Get those kids safe."

Keeping to the shadows, Rett raced through the narrow accessway to where she hoped she'd intercept the group of youngsters Trebor reported. Sounds of battle echoed into the access from the main corridors and open spaces in the local area. She kept every sense she had wide open, and found time to wonder just why in three moons, and how, these kids had become separated from their parents at a time the citizens of the complex were told to hold tight.

The Yixolryn Coalition troops had learned to contain complex inhabitants in their residential areas at the first sign of trouble. They'd found out the hard way that the majority of Nyorfians on Epnoce, for so long a time sulky and compliant under Coalition occupation, made an instant transition to fierce guerrilla fighters once Free Army forces backed them up.

Except for here, Rett thought. *We haven't had any contact with civilians here at all.*

While the greater part of her was on alert as she moved, a small inner part of her fretted over Jessek. The responsibility to protect civilians at all costs came first, but it didn't mean she had to like leaving one of her own alone in such a condition, and in such an unsecured area.

The Coalition troops pinned inside, especially those guarding the complex commander and any escape route they had, would hang tough no matter what. The enemy needed this place. Complex 63, devoted to agriculture and food production, was an important, renewable source of food and the only one the enemy had access to. Food—prepared food—was something the surface troops of the Yixolryn Coalition were hurting for. They slaughtered large numbers of animals on Epnoce, like they had on Nyorfias, but much went to waste, since many of them hadn't the slightest clue how to prepare or eat something that wasn't packaged or ready-made.

The lack of culinary skill was a good thing for the families that lived here. Since the Coalition desperately needed bodies to make the food they couldn't make for themselves, the people of Complex 63 received a better level of treatment than civilians elsewhere.

-Not to mention the kids would be the first ones threatened if the adults failed to produce said food,- Pam put in. -That could be why you didn't get any civilian help on this job like the others.-

Rett had to wonder if Pam wasn't absolutely right.

Jaq had told some unbelievable tales of troopers going hungry amidst some of the lushest supplies of naturally growing food plants on Nyorfias. Rett wondered what sort of impact that dependence made on this agricultural community. Would the average Coalition trooper starve if nobody existed to prepare what was harvested here?

Maybe the GTC reinforcements produced the most visible results in the Nyorfians' twelve-year struggle for freedom. But the matter of food and fuel, especially food, and the Coalition's complete dependency on technology to get both, was rapidly becoming the Nyorfians' greatest asset.

-Wise Earth generals, even in ancient times, said that an army marches on its stomach-, Pam thought. -I guess they had a point.-

And for once, Rett had to instantly agree.

As more distance and time opened up behind her, temptation to pcom Med about Jessek was strong. She told herself there wasn't a damned thing she could have done. At the same time she was sure two extra seconds and her own body length would have made the difference between the young sharpshooter's coming along with her on this retrieval, or his sitting back there wondering if he was going home with one leg or two. That was, if he didn't bleed to death first. The pressure properties of the bandages she used only lasted so long.

As she emerged into a slightly wider corridor, she focused on her mission. If she'd timed it right, she should—

Yes. There. She caught sight of a small figure with red-brown hair. If there were others, they must be ahead; already around the corner this one was fast approaching. In that same moment, the child's face turned toward her. Trebor had nailed the gender correctly—a boy. She saw his mouth open in an expression of astonishment. With a yip, the boy broke into a run and turned the corner.

Rett launched herself after him, wishing she had been closer before allowing herself to get spotted, but then again, she wasn't expecting Nyorfian kids to run *away* from her.

The russet head peered around the corner. Rett gestured, a sign that any school-age child would recognize and respond to from an adult, especially during an emergency.

Stop. Wait for me.

But the child quickly pulled back.

Anywhere between seven to ten years old from her guess. But why the avoidance? Surely the kids knew the difference between the Nyorfian and Coalition troops. *Must be he's seeing something else I'm not scoping yet.*

Before she focused her awareness ahead, a niggle of warning from a different direction had her flattening to a wall. A stray SMG shot from a side corridor on her left zinged past, well spent by the sound of it, but still hot enough to cause serious burns. The bolt hit the opposite wall, the glossy smooth surface bouncing it up toward the ceiling, where it ricocheted at least five times from wall to wall before vanishing with nothing more than the scent of ozone and a wisp of smoke.

When a startled yelp reached her ears from the direction the boy had gone, concern overshadowed her caution. She took the same corner a second later.

2.3.2 UNDETERMINED AREA, COMPLEX 63, EPNOCE
0535.13.24 (LOCAL RECKONING)

WHEN CONSCIOUSNESS RETURNED, RETT HAD no idea what had happened or where she was. She didn't have the usual hangover feeling that resulted from SMG stun, just a little headache, and figured she must have been hit with a smaller handheld stunner of some sort.

Shit. Stupid. Very, very stupid. What's it going to be this time? She couldn't help but wonder.

She soon discovered the position of her body was awkward. It felt as if she were bent at a backward right angle, with the small of her back at the highest point. To add to her discomfort, she was twisted to the right at the hips. Beneath her was an uneven mound composed of hard lumps.

Maybe it was a mountain range. By the size and feel of some of the lumps grinding into her, probably the Skyrakers of northern Branch.

Routine wakeup procedure continued. She briefly acknowledged Pam was still with her and in the same split-second opening sent an extra caution to sit tight. Deities, she was bruised just about everywhere, although none of them were crippling from what she could tell at this point. The mountain peaks grinding into her from below didn't help. The next obvious fact that registered was that someone performed a really bad job of tying her up.

~Or good job,~ Pam put in quickly. ~For you. Maybe.~

There was a lot of narrow webbing, or maybe a cargo net, wound around her body, from chin to heels. No matter the material, it was in no way tight, or even snug. Not by anyone's standards. There had to be three or four layers of the stuff, but slipping free would be easy, and the task made even simpler since her big knife was still in its sheath on the weapons belt. Its solid presence made itself apparent between her right hip and the mountain range. Since her left arm lay across her waist, she also felt the cold, hard edge of the hilt right below the skin on her littlest finger.

333

Damn it. The weapon was so convenient, her fingers started twitching toward it. She could have it in action before most humanoids could even react to her movement. *Not yet. Not yet. Keep still,* Rett ordered herself.

As her self-inspection continued, the weight and feel of the familiar accessories of ten years allowed her to discover what remained and what was missing. No VARs—she hoped they wouldn't get broken; they were brand new. Weapons belt, still there, still carrying ammo for her TT-1 and chargers for her sidearm. The smaller weapon was missing, since it lived right behind her knife sheath and that pocket was definitely empty.

Her right arm was angled across her chest, fingers near her neck. Beneath her forearm were the flat pockets of her shoulder harness, where the smaller throwing knife was missing, along with most of the sundry gear those pockets usually carried. As she stopped a frown from wrinkling her forehead, she made the next puzzling discovery. *I have my headband.* Which meant she had com. And the entire mystery deepened.

She went on with the checklist. Bracers and chrono were missing; her wrists only felt uniform and the brush of netting. The left wrist and arm, of course, felt the hardness of her knife and weapons belt. The locator was so light and small she wasn't sure if that was still under the top edge of her right boot or not.

Don't get careless this time, she told herself with an inward sneer of exasperation. *Look where it got you. You're the only one to blame for it. And I'm sure you'll never let me forget it,* she added swiftly to Pam. Rett kept the sigh in her thoughts. *Well, I don't think I've ever claimed to be faultless.*

~If I'd been in your boots just before, I wouldn't have thought twice about going around that corner either.~

Rett didn't dare let herself think about what might have happened to the children she'd been following at this point. Options. Sure, freeing herself might be easy, but it would slow her down enough for another stun charge to slam her right back in the same, or worse, situation.

With no more than a breath she could activate her pcom and dare a direct connect to someone in her platoon, but what if—?

334

I thought that situation a couple months ago at Complex 412 was bizarre. Another event that went on her mental "Experiences I Never Want To Repeat" list. *I mean, I've been tied up badly before. But all those times my headband and gear—or everything on me—had also been taken. Now here I am, like a steelhead in half a net. With almost everything.*

~Never a dull moment,~ Pam thought.

How Rett wished for dull moments in times like this. Summing up her physical evaluation, she decided she was fit enough; nothing a change in position wouldn't cure. Her back and right side would be stiff unless she shifted position soon. But not yet.

Of course, things would be different had her restriction been up to the usual Coalition standards, which she thanked all good deities was not the case. She could free herself in a matter of seconds. Then again, there were those among the enemy who enjoyed peculiar games. If this was a setup for one of them, she wasn't about to indulge them by playing along.

I have to com someone else to look for those kids. Then I can figure out what to do about me.

Sensing living energy somewhere nearby, she flowed more awareness away from herself, feeling along a floor bare of furnishing or covering. Except for whatever was beneath her, the immediate area was cold, flat, open. There. Five auras. Wow, were they a mix-up of emotions, all of them negative, the sick gray green of fear predominant.

The beings were whispering. Hissing sibilants of consonants gave them away although she couldn't distinguish any words. Whoever they were, they were not physically close enough to worry her at the moment.

Puzzled, uncertain, Rett pulled back her awareness. She left enough around herself so any movement past that mental perimeter would alert her if she started thinking too hard about this with Pam. If there was a need for an expert imagination, it was now.

Ideas where we can be, Pam?

~Colder in here than where we were. Air feels a bit humidified, too. And it's circulating. Smells a bit musty, earthy…like a big bag of potatoes. A climate-controlled storage unit?~

335

Pam's interpretation matched hers, well, except for the potatoes, and from the quick mental image they seemed to be some kind of big, smooth, oblong tubers. Yes, the cool, circulating air would be ideal for root vegetable storage.

Rett agreed.

~Do you think someone's hungry again? You're forming a distressing habit of finding yourself as food lately.~ Pam rolled mental eyes.

That's life, you're either eaten or eating something else, in one way or another. Stay around, but easy does it, advised Rett, turning her attention back to the speakers. Her impulse to make a communication would have to wait for a moment. Since the whispers were gradually increasing in volume, she stopped thinking about her surroundings and concentrated on the voices.

They escalated to murmurs, to mumbles, to tense, high-pitched mutters just below normal tones. When one voice rose to a near shout, she opened her eyes wide in surprise.

If that's a Coalition trooper, I'll eat my Omni.

First, she strained her peripheral vision as far as it would go. Then, she began to tip her head in fractional increments until she caught a good glimpse of the speakers.

Rett's first thought took off but never got altitude. It lost any forward speed and lift it had, and stalled, crashed, and burned.

Her second thought had a bit more luck—she shut her mouth and nipped back the whistle of disbelief that would have given her away.

The third thought formed coherently.

I don't get it.

~Kids!~ thought Pam at the same time, sounding just as astounded. ~Are they the same—~

Looks like one familiar head of hair. Unless Rett missed her guess, the youngster that she'd been following was beneath that russet mop.

~Well, this answers your question about where the children are.~

Rett's only response to this was a soundless groan of exasperation. Time for a reassessment of any ideas she'd started to get.

"We have to!" The girl's voice was rough with anger. She stood in the center of a circle of children, gesticulating in irritated, nervous, and wide movements, a small weapon clenched in her right fist. "You know what She said!"

There's the second one Trebor saw. Pale hair, thin. And no problem guessing who zapped me.

Closing her eyes again, keeping her breathing shallow, Rett remained motionless as the circle of arguing children swirled in her direction. A solid something, that weapon most likely, poked Rett's ribs—and hard. Hard enough to indicate she'd been poked in the same spot enough times to have a deep bruise well started.

"She's still out," said a boy's voice.

"But she's going to be waking up soon." The angry girl nudged Rett in the bruise again, this time probably with her foot. It was just slightly softer than the weapon.

"We're never going to find out anything if you keep stunning her," said the boy.

"She said—"

"I know what She said," snapped the girl. "But we don't know how to tie someone the way they wanted. And I couldn't find an Omni to read her IDs, or know if anything she has on her is going to blow up if I touch it."

"But she has senior sergeant's circles and the group leader's diamond. How many of them would wear that?"

"There's more than one platoon of Special Forces here, from what I heard one of them say."

"She doesn't look like the picture they showed us," said another boy. "That one looked mean."

I look mean?

Aside from some teenaged anxiety about a few blotches, Rett had never concerned herself over her facial features, which she felt were plain and serviceable. Others had different opinions, which Rett appreciated while firmly keeping her own view. A face was a face, and as long as all the parts of hers were arranged—or rearranged—in a more or less normal pattern, she was okay with that. She had a handful or so of facial scars, but they were small; the most noticeable one bisected her left eyebrow. She had one thing to thank the Coalition for: their rule about not damaging the head and face of a prisoner. If her face was as scarred as the rest of her, she wouldn't blame the kids for being scared. But it wasn't, and she'd never thought of herself as mean-looking. That she would appear that way to a child really bothered her.

Do I look mean, Pam?

~You can look pretty scary sometimes,~ Pam admitted, her mental voice apologetic. ~You take that completely expressionless look you guys wear sometimes—that puts people off and makes them uneasy, because they don't know what you're thinking. Then out comes your war face, and people run. Then again, most of the time I can only make a judgment call from what I feel on your face or see from people you look at, since it's hard to see the outside of it from in here. On the other hand—~

Please. I didn't ask for the complete history of the universe. Stop. You've said enough.

~But I didn't get to the good p—~

No more, Pam. Forget I asked.

"And She said Killer hates kids. If she's Killer, I don't want her to wake up, Shannai." That was a different girl. The hesitant, soft voice dropped to a whisper of dread. "Her face and hands have blood on them. Even her hair. There's blood all over her and you said it wasn't hers."

Shit. That doesn't help, does it? Rett groaned inside, having forgotten she was all but covered in Jessek's blood, most of it dry now. Even under the best of conditions, one didn't perform emergency treatment on a partially severed limb without wearing some of the results. She was sorry it frightened them, but there wasn't any help for it. What really bothered her was the first sentence.

Hate kids? I hate kids? Me? Since when? Good gods and deities! Rett loved children. Of all ages. She clung fast to her dream of the day when she would have a handful of her own children.

"She doesn't look mean. She's nice," said a third boy's voice, this one very young. "Even with blood."

Mollified somewhat, Rett throttled back her growing impatience and confusion, and kept still.

"We don't know that, Olvero."

"I know it. And she looks cold. I'm going to get my blanket and cover her." That was the little boy again.

"No, Olvero, stay away from her," said the first girl, she of the angry voice and waving weapon. "I said no, Olvero." Her angry tones gentled for a moment. "That's very nice of you, but you need your blanket, and if you cover her, it's going to get blood on it."

"The blood isn't wet. I'll show you."

"I need to see her hands. I don't want you to get any closer than this, okay?"

"But she won't hurt us."

"Olvero, please. I don't want you to get any closer." As if someone flipped a switch, her voice turned harsh again. "Thalom, Labonne said—"

How do I get myself into these situations? Rett wondered as the row erupted again, five or six voices all speaking at once.

~At last. Something you're not blaming me for!~

Rett gave Pam a mental shove and a firm thought that unless she had something constructive to contribute to keep still. *Time I said something.* She took a breath. "Excuse me." Her voice, low, strong, heavy with command, brought instant silence.

While her insides tensed for a stun shot, Rett fixed a calm, level gaze on the pale, angry face of a girl no more than fifteen Standard. Her glance had already assessed the four other children, who seemed to cover a range of age between four and fifteen. Yes, the middle boy was he of the red-brown hair.

"What's going on?" Rett kept her tone low and quiet. *No wonder I don't have a hangover.* Just as she suspected, a low wattage stunner. She was getting a good close look at it, especially since the teenager planted the business end of it right between Rett's eyes.

"If the object is to kill me, just do it. Please. But use the weapon. Arguing someone to death takes too long."

"That's not funny. And it's just a stunner," the girl snarled.

Rett wiped any lightness from her expression. "Stun someone from this close up in the head, they're dead." Despite her deadly seriousness, she kept her tone conversational. The bright insignia on the shoulder of the girl's overall denoted her school section and her status as a junior safety coordinator. "The backlash'll burn your hand as well. Also, a body shot with any stun weapon—even one as low power as yours—on a kid smaller than you can kill them. No matter the distance."

"I'll do the talking."

"I'm sorry, Citizen, but your safety training apparently didn't cover handling of weapons intended to disable or kill. You were waving that thing about without any regard whatsoever."

"Shut up!" Nevertheless, the teenager's weapon withdrew by half an arm's length. Rett's words had definitely shaken her. "Who are you?"

Rett shrugged. "Depends who's asking."

"The one who didn't get caught and tied up by a handful of kids," snarled the pale-haired girl.

Rett had to scramble to temper her reply to that one. She let frost creep over her face and into her eyes, replacing the friendly attitude with indifference. "You have a point."

Total surprise flickered through the girl's eyes, cooling the molten silver of them. "Give me your name," demanded the teen.

After holding the contact for several more seconds, Rett deliberately let her head drop to the lumpy stuff that had pillowed it before. She closed her eyes and counted.

"What are you doing? I asked you a question."

I'm impressed. Barely made it to three. Rett lifted her head and cracked one eye open. "I'm going back to sleep." She resumed her position.

"Shannai, we don't have to—"

"Be quiet," she warned the boy Rett had followed.

"We need to catch Sergeant Killer for the—" This voice, huskier than Shannai's but not much deeper, had to belong to the oldest of the boys.

"I'll handle this, Thalom!" the girl hissed.

"Shannai, we have to tell her," Thalom shot back. "We can't treat her like...like *they* would. That why she's not going to talk to you. Deities, it makes us just as bad as She is."

"You know just as well as I do what She said we had to do."

"So we try to explain it!"

There's definitely something wrong here, thought Rett in growing bewilderment. *All these kids are so scared they can't think reasonably. And who is "She"?*

"Thalom's right," said the youngest girl. "You're acting different and scary. I don't like it."

One of the other children started to cry. It sounded like the boy who'd wanted to give her his blanket. Lifting her head and turning it toward the sound, Rett had a clear view of the smallest of the group. Crouched on the floor, arms wrapped around his knees, he sobbed as if his heart would break.

Hers very nearly did. It lurched inside her chest so painfully she had to bite the inside of her cheek to remain still and silent.

"What do you expect?" This time, although Shannai's voice was angry, it held the same notes of desperate, uncertain fear the others did. "Do you expect us to tell her we need Sergeant Killer, then what? Is she going to turn around and call Sergeant Killer and say, 'oh, come here, the Coalition commander wants you?' Especially after what we just did?"

*Explains who *She* is.* A vague sense of unease grew. Not many Coalition officers were female. Those who made it into the upper ranks were mainly pureblooded Yixolryns. Maybe a double handful of officers fit that description at the last reckoning of intelligence reports. Less than three of those served in combat positions, which included commanding a complex garrison.

Great. Pushing the track of her thoughts aside for the moment, Rett focused on the situation at hand.

"Shannai." Rett used the same strong, low commanding voice as before. The beginning argument cut short before it ever got started. Gentling her tone, Rett continued. "You can try asking me."

She's naturally that pale, thought Rett as the teenager turned toward her again. *I was worried she might be sick. Ariam looked that way those years when she was sick, and for so long afterward...*

Rett ached anew as she looked deeper, beyond the fair skin and hair. Shannai was much too young to have such a hard, bitter expression.

"I asked," said Shannai. "You all but said you weren't going to cooperate."

"That wasn't asking. That was sticking a weapon in my face and making demands. If you expect me to respond to that, to cooperate as long as you treat me like an enemy, you're going to be at it for a long time."

"Told you," muttered the older boy, earning a withering glare from the girl so obviously in charge.

"Someone as desperate for help as you," Rett added, absorbing every nuance of aura she could from Shannai, "shouldn't alienate someone who might be your only chance."

"What makes you think we're desperate?" The girl forced a cooler expression to her narrow face.

"Look me in the eyes and tell me you're not," Rett replied softly. The girl's glance, and gun arm, dropped toward the floor. "Did you and your friends give up your Nyorfian citizenship to join the Coalition?"

342   The proud flashes of defiance and the indignant huffs from Shannai and the children with her, even the one sobbing, answered that question.

"That's good to know. But last I checked, the insignia on my uniform is Nyorfian, too. You all should be old enough to know what else it means. From what your parents told you, and what your hearts tell you—not what the Coalition tells you."

"Mom said any Nyorfian soldier's supposed to protect us," said the other girl. "No matter what. Even them, Special Forces."

The way the girl mumbled it, added to some of what she'd heard earlier, made Rett wonder just what Coalition propaganda had sunk in and taken root over the long twelve years behind them. Complex 63 had always attracted and supported a large number of families with children. This made it an ideal environment for a relentless Yixolryn campaign aimed at subverting the young.

Complex 63 was very different from most others. It only had two aboveground levels and three below, and sprawled across five times as much space as the largest installations on the planet. The agricultural station boasted over two hundred square miles of controlled environment; most of it open space. Acres of it dedicated to the growing of plants, the raising of meat and dairy animals. But since Easy Force's

operations were mainly to secure points of entry and exit from the complex and undermine the mobility of the enemy garrison, Rett had yet to
see any of the true interior with her own eyes.

She'd seen fascinating vids in briefings of huge indoor fields, gar-
dens, groves of fruit trees, a herd of small dairy animals especially bred
for this place. Even domesticated flocks of breekies—a tall, lean, flight-
less bird so named for the sound it made. Rett wasn't familiar at all with
the species, found in the wild only in the extreme southwest of Main
on Nyorfias. From several enthusiastic ex-farmers in Easy Force, among
them her own third-up, Sergeant Worren, Rett learned more about
them then she ever might have otherwise. The bottom line was that
the birds adapted well to domestication. Domestic breekies carelessly
dropped prodigious amounts of eggs as long as they had enough food,
light, and room to wander, just as they did in the wild. The eggs were a
superior source of protein.

Rett didn't let Worren or anyone else go on into the other uses and
breeding and whatever else, although under other circumstances, she
would have listened, since she was unfamiliar with domesticated animals in any aspect and was curious. There hadn't been time.

And one wing of the huge complex even boasted a lake stocked with
fish. Sergeant Semage had commented that if the complex ventilators
could get up enough wind, the lake was big enough to sail with a small
boat. Rett didn't remember when any other target area had generated
so much intense personal interest from just about everyone, even Pam.

~It's a paradise in the middle of a hostile wasteland~, Pam said.
~Come on, if you heard they had mountains and big trees in this
building, you'd be just as extra curious.~

*I never claimed not to be. But we never get a chance to stick around
and explore, why waste more time than I did already wishing I could
satisfy my curiosity? Especially now? All I can do is thank all the gods and
deities, good or evil, that the Yixolryn Coalition's still hoping to take all
this, and the civilian population, in as intact a condition as possible. I'm
grateful for it every day, especially every day we come closer to getting the
enemy out of this system.*

Pam had to concede the point. She, too, thanked the forces responsible for the inflexible Yixolryn mindset—one so convinced of the

343

eventual Nyorfian capitulation, so sure they would have the people and resources under their complete dominance, that they waged their war carefully. What was the sense of destroying their slaves and resources? That rabid fanaticism, the same that kept Rett and any other military person as the primary focus of Coalition violence, was another of the many factors that were giving Rett's people an ever-growing hope of ending this war. Ending it soon, giving children just like these a chance for a good future.

"Your mother's right," Rett said to the little girl. "Anyone in the Nyorfian military makes a commitment to protecting others, whatever it takes." She nipped back the *Then again, we don't expect our own people to attack us* comment that longed to follow without any encouragement from Pam, and might have, had she been dealing with adults. "I'm going to help you."

Shannai's gaze came back up. "You would com Sergeant Killer to come here—just like that?"

"You never know," Rett said dryly. "Even so, I know for certain she'll want more details. So if you want me to help, it'll cost you some information."

Shannai hesitated, but the younger girl spoke up. "She took our families and said we would never see them again unless we catch Sergeant Killer."

"Does She have a name?"

"Commander Avok," spat Thalom as if the very words tasted bad.

The younger girl shuddered. "She said They would kill them if we didn't!" Her voice broke.

Rett closed her eyes and let out a breath. *Avok.*

How do I get myself into these jams? she wondered again. *It's not enough the Coalition's been after me for years. And then there was—is— the ego-merge. And everything that happened from it and after it started.*

~Are you blaming me again?~

No, the deities with the warped senses of humor that keep pushing me into these situations. Obviously, I'm not providing them enough entertainment on my own, so they had to dredge up Avok.

~I assume you've met Avok~. This time, Pam's mental voice was flat.

Oh yes, Rett acknowledged, hating the sudden cramping pain that rocked her guts. *We've had several memorable encounters. My second most devoted fan after Iheolon.*

~I thought the Leader had that distinction.~

Rett nearly snorted aloud. *You have to remember that the Leader's only reason for wanting me dead is so that certain of his officers don't spend valuable time obsessing on what they're going to do with me once I'm caught. I'd heard Iheolon's original command staff had been broken up, and that alien officer at Complex 412 hinted at it as well. This just confirms it.*

~And this female was one of Iheolon's command staff?~ Pam sounded amazed. She now knew enough about the Yixolryn Coalition to realize what sort of being—especially female being—would be allowed such a high position under an officer like Iheolon.

Used to be his fourth in command, confirmed Rett.

~Now I remember you hinting about her, back in Branch, when Jaq saw your scars— ~ Pam stopped short, her tone turning defiant. As if, should Avok show up, Pam might suddenly jump right out of Rett's head, assume physical form, and attack the Yixolryn female with her bare hands.

~Well, she's not here yet. ~

Taking heart from Pam's staunch support and sending her friend a warm inward smile, Rett firmly pushed back her apprehension. *You're right, Pam. And I'm glad you're with me. We have more important things to worry about right now. Like the kids. If I start going off, will you head me back so I can focus on them?*

~Yes, ~ said Pam. ~I understand. ~

Rett returned her full attention to the conversation taking place, grateful as usual that her internal conversations with Pam took moments instead of minutes. .

"She gave us a stunner and told us to get one of the Special Forces people, and Killer would come to rescue or look for whoever it was— you, I guess," said Thalom. "Then we would stun Killer, and She would come and get her from us. The other one, too. Only then would we get our families back. She's coming at new day and if we don't have Sergeant Killer by then …"

By that point, Rett had an excellent idea of what she had to do. But on top of everything else, hearing the name Killer eight times more than she wanted to triggered an extra rush of impatience that nearly blinded her. Adding unadulterated outrage to the mix was Avok's audacious, deliberate callousness that had sent five children and a stunner into a combat zone to catch a Nyorfian commando. Luckily, it worked. But it might have backfired with fatal results. That bolt that had prompted her around that unlucky corner with such careless haste might have very well hit the middle boy. She had yet to hear his name.

Avok. Rett fought to keep everything she felt beneath her skin. *Still a solid azurium bitch. Not that I expected any improvement. There has to be another way,* she thought.

~We'll find a way. Don't worry about what isn't happening right now. Worry about what is. ~ Pam's thoughts were firm.

346 "Has Avok…" Rett paused slightly as all the children cringed, "been commander here long?" None of the reports or rumors she'd heard about Avok mentioned the Yixolryn female getting her own command.

"Almost a half-year too long," snarled Shannai. "The first one was bad enough, and he was here as long as I remember, but She—"

"She's a very mean, very bad person," said Olvero, creeping closer to Shannai. "And her guard Wik is mean, too. And scary."

"Wik ripped one of my friend's uncles right in half," whispered the middle boy. "Just for looking at Her right in the face." He shivered and swallowed hard. "Right in front of everyone in our section."

Rett's headache zoomed up a few more degrees. Seeing stuff like that as a result of an accident was bad enough and couldn't be helped. But no one, adult or child, enemy or friend, should have to see such senseless, barbaric acts of cruelty. Unfortunately, the Yixolryns thrived on having as many Nyorfians as possible witness such brutality to selected victims. And although—by orders from their own High Command—they were supposed to lay off the civilians, a lot of occupying troops and their officers ignored those orders. They thought it undermined morale; weakened the Nyorfian resistance.

Rett knew better. The terror and horror of those acts instead increased the Nyorfian hope to drive the enemy from their system. And failing that, their resolve was to go out fighting, right down to the last old person; the newest baby.

"Anyone who She catches looking gets killed," Thalom added.

"So?" asked Shannai. She placed a sympathetic and supportive arm around the middle boy's shoulder, her eyes never leaving Rett. Her voice was less hostile, less demanding, yet still challenging. "We told you. What will you do about it?"

Despite Pam's obvious efforts to help dampen Rett's personal feelings on this situation, they leaked through enough to keep that trace of nausea going in her belly. Rett let out a breath and took a moment to formulate her reply.

"I knew you wouldn't help," Shannai said with deep bitterness. "You just wanted to know, and now you won't do anything."

"Shannai," Rett said with gentle patience, "on my utility belt—the one that didn't have the handgun—is an Omni. It's a bit different from the ones you probably use in school or at home. Smaller. Lots more dents and scratches. Probably why you didn't recognize it, besides the fact it's in the flat pocket right in front on the left. See it? It's not going to explode, I promise." 347

The girl glanced to the smallest child, but Rett didn't take her eyes off the teen's tense pale face to see what passed between them. After a sullen nod, Shannai hunkered alongside Rett's body to retrieve the device. "All right, so it won't explode. But how do I know it is going to work? Isn't this coded to your voice only?"

"For most things, yes. But to find out the owner's name and obtain public level information on the internal storage, or to read the primary levels of an ID disc, no, anyone can do that."

"Owner and primary function. Verbal response." Shannai spoke to the Omni in the normal, businesslike tone one usually took with such devices.

"*Rett, 90674SF. Rank senior sergeant, primary function, platoon leader, F-troop, 2023rd Special Forces.*"

Shannai and Thalom gasped and exchanged glances.

"It *is* her," said Thalom, almost whispering.

"We're supposed to get Killer," said the youngest girl. She finally emerged from Shannai's shadow, a thin, leggy child with tangled wavy hair the color of spicebush stems. Rett guessed she was probably about nine years old.

"Rett is Killer's real name, Safkas," said Thalom.

"Is 'Killer' her family name?" The middle boy looked appalled.

"No, Kallet. It's a special nickname. You know, like your mother telling us that they used to call your big sister 'Blaze' because of her hair being so red?"

~Blaze? Seems to me that name's familiar.~

Rett thought it at the exact moment. Taking a longer look at Kallet, she compared him to the memory of the friendly Spacemarine she'd met on the troopshuttle journey from Nyorfias. And Blaze had said home—of which she had been out of communication with for while—was here at Complex 63!

Maybe you should mention it?

I'm not sure this is the right time—as a matter of fact I'm sure this isn't the right time. Look at him.

At the mention of his big sister, Kallet's face twisted. The battle for control there was cruelly plain. "I think Mom and my sisters just made those stories up. I don't have another big sister. My brothers don't even remember if it's true or not."

Oh, deities. That's right, they've never even seen each other. Rett bit the inside of her lower lip as just another aspect of the tragedies of the long war played out in front of her. *I can't bring it up, it would hurt him too much, whether or not he chose to believe me. And even if I could, as stressed as she is, Shannai's sharp and on her toes. If I just come out with 'Oh, hey, I met Blaze on the shuttle', it might seem convenient enough for Shannai to let me find out just how much charge she has left in that stunner.*

"I'm sorry for making you sad, Kallet." With an adult gesture of tenderness, the older boy smoothed the younger one's russet hair. "But it was the only example I could think of. Am I right?" Thalom appealed to Rett. "About your name?"

She nodded at Thalom. "Yes." She again met Shannai's gaze. "My name is Rett. If you need to verify that, just slide my ID through."

Since her fingers were right there, near her neck, Rett carefully slipped them beneath her collar and hooked the slim lanyard that held her military ID and public information. With a slow motion of her forefinger, making sure Shannai clearly saw what she was doing, Rett drew it to the outside of her uniform. "There'll be an image as soon as you've inserted it. Use your own Omnis if you prefer—if you have them."

"It'll work on them?"

"It'll work on any GTC compliant device," replied Rett. "Even Coalition ones. That's what it's for."

Shannai reached for the slender thread, and Rett lifted her head a little more so the girl could remove it.

"I might not be smiling in the picture, but I don't think I look mean." Still vexed over that, Rett allowed her head to go back with a thump to the lumpy stuff under her. *Ow! What is this shit anyway... rocks?*

~I can't imagine why they would want to keep a pile of rocks in humidified cold storage on an agricultural station. Maybe they're breekie eggs. Or, maybe you're truly a princess after all, lying on thirty mattresses of finest swansdown—er, breekie down, or maybe the down of nightwings I mean, if they even have any—under which was placed a single pea to test the sensitivity of your fair royal body. ~

Pam, Rett thought wearily, *please, if I want bedtime stories from your planet, I'll let you know.* Despite her mental tone, she had to smile inwardly, and she couldn't resist asking, *Are these the same princesses who throw fits of tiff at their friends when they're frustrated, or when their lover accuses them of something that never happened?*

~Oh, yes, the very same. You see, royal princesses can't show too many emotions, or people might think they're ordinary and take advantage of them. So the princesses either lose their tempers at the ones they love, or hold everything inside so much that they bruise as easily as ripe peaches. ~

Rett's amused, inward smile grew at Pam's double-edged comments, for the intentions behind them were loving and well-meant.

~Maybe you can leak some of that smile onto your face where the kids can see it. As we say on Earth, you catch more flies with honey than you do with vinegar. ~

It was just as well Rett obeyed, for both she and her image were under minute inspection.

"Well," admitted Kallet, sounding reluctant, "it's hard to tell with all the blood, but the eyes look the same. And we know they can change how people look." He dropped his voice to a whisper. "You know they make Her images look nice. And Yixolryns aren't nice looking at all."

The other children crowded around Shannai and the Omni as she read the information displayed there. A nearby little hiccup brought Rett's head back up and her gaze straight into the sorrowful, round dark eyes of the youngest child. He appeared more interested in watching Rett's face than the Omni.

Any deep fears or misgivings she had went forgotten. The closer sight of the child's trembling lips and tear-streaked cheeks hit Rett harder than any weapon ever had. Her hands clenched into fists but she remained motionless, biting back a groan of deep pain. All she wanted to do was grab her big knife and clear enough webbing so she could hug that child to her and tell him everything would be all right.

When one of the older children blocked him from view, she let her head drop back again. Despite the cool air of the room, a trickle of sweat slid off her forehead. She felt as if she'd just run the distance between here and the Base under water.

If I move now, while they're still scared, no telling what will happen. I doubt Shannai will give me a second chance.

Trust couldn't be forced. The confidence of these children had to come of itself.

~It's the same thing with horses, ~ agreed Pam. ~Except horses will try to get away before turning around and hitting you with a stun beam~.

Remember that and don't do anything spontaneous. All it would take is for me to sneeze at the wrong moment, and Shannai might shoot that thing off by reflex…no matter what direction it's pointing.

She managed to keep the shiver that thought produced inside. Damn it, and that Coalition commander probably knew the likelihood of a child under sixteen on this complex—occupied for twelve years—would have never had any firearms instruction. Not even for the sort used in hunting. No one did much hunting here on the semi-frozen steppes of the main continent. Nightwings didn't taste good at all, from what she'd been told. Besides, in this complex, there should be no need to hunt or gather outside the sheltering walls.

Avok.

That bitch is probably enjoying the thought of an accident, even hoping for one. Something to use to undermine the confidence any citizens in her control have in the homesystem military and government. Oh, she'd make it look and sound so very convincing! Damn it. Getting her breathing under control, Rett clenched her teeth and sternly told herself to pay attention. She couldn't blame Pam or any mysterious outside agency for the distracting thoughts that came now. Each and every one of them was hers.

"It is really her," whispered Shannai.

Rett stared at the ceiling. "Yes, it's really me, and if you let me, I'm going to help you all I can. But if anyone calls me Killer again, I'm going to get really tiffed."

351

2.3.3 UNDETERMINED AREA, COMPLEX 63, EPNOCE
0535.13.24 (LOCAL RECKONING)

"Fang two to all fang coms," Trebor said, opening pcom channels to all the F-troop members. "Anyone heard from Fang Lead yet?"

The replies came back all negative, and Trebor cursed. No one had com from the Sarge, no one at all. It was going to be another one of those times. As usual, he felt gray hairs multiplying even as he had such thoughts. He'd be lucky if he managed to make it to the end of the war with any hair at all, much less gray ones, at this rate. He'd have to use camo paint on his head, like Pipano did.

"Fang seventeen." Jessek's voice was much softer than normal, but clear. "Forgot to relay Fang Lead said she might be sitting tight until we give an all clear."

Trebor grinned, even though the other man couldn't see it. "No one's going to blame you for that. Even so, it's been hours. Not like her to check even once. How's it going with you, then?"

"Med's not being very nice to me," responded Jessek with good humor, "so I guess I'm not dying any time soon."

Trebor told the wounded man he'd check on him in a bit and switched channels to the unit's third-up, Sergeant Worren. "Try to get a fix on her locator. Maybe her pcom's gone bad."

After Worren replied with an affirmative, Trebor opened the platoon bandwidth. *Damn it, Sarge, com me.* "Fang Two to all Fang team, hold your positions until we get instruction. Clear com. Fang Two connect Bronze Two."

"We're hot, Fang Two," Sergeant Ariam's voice answered, the static of energy weapons discharge distorting the sound. B-troop was in a different section; from the sounds of it they were still busy. "I know it's important but make it fast, what's up?"

His question wasn't urgent enough to distract her and get her hit. They didn't need more casualties. "Com me back when you get a clear minute," replied Trebor. At least he knew now his platoon leader's situation was nothing immediately dire, because Ariam would have known already. "Com connect Razor Lead."

"Infantry will take your position in ten minutes, Fang Two," Sergeant Tris said after the update.

Lieutenant Evetez spoke up on the command frequency. "Fang Two, once infantry units relieve you, go ahead and try to get a track on Fang Lead. Keep us posted."

Trebor relayed the information to F-troop's personnel, giving them coordinates for a meeting point. No sooner had he cleared F-troop's frequency, he was commed back by Sergeant Ariam.

"What's up?"

"Fang Lead is missing and off com," Trebor returned. "Wondered if you scoped anything."

He waited, knowing Ariam would need a moment or so to focus her attention on her sister. The pause reconfirmed his assumption that while Rett was definitely late in communicating, she wasn't seriously hurt or killed. Nor was she about to become that way any time soon. No matter Ariam was in B-troop, or busy. Her link to her sister Rett— to all of F-troop, actually—was strong. She'd know if any of them were in serious trouble. 353

"I did get something before, but it wasn't ominous." Ariam went silent for another moment. "All I get now is she's not anywhere close. And she's not alone. Strongly concerned about something, but not injured. I have to clear. Keep me posted, I'll get back to you if I can go any farther or feel anything stronger."

Thanking her, Trebor cleared com and followed it with a very deep and heavy sigh. *I wish I remembered Jessek was down. The Sarge mentioned it, but it completely went out of my head. I could have spared two as backup. She would have been able to leave one with him and take the other with her.*

Yet more gray hairs sprouted on his head with every breath he took. *It's not like she goes looking for these situations. But whenever she gets into one, it's always something bigger than it looked at first.*

Trebor cocked an eye ceilingward. He addressed his thought to the alien entities that, for lack of better terms, all Nyorfians referred to as gods and deities. *If you beings have anything to do with what's been happening to the Sarge, back off. I need a break.*

2.3.4 UNDETERMINED AREA, COMPLEX 63
0535.13.24 (LOCAL RECKONING)

RETT GRIMACED. THE KIDS HAD withdrawn to a corner of the room. Making a tight huddle, they spoke softly, no doubt discussing their next course of action. Or what sort of wrapping they should deck her in for presentation to Commander Avok.

After the children had pulled away, Pam had distracted Rett from darker thoughts by explaining a custom in her culture of wrapping up gifts in fancy trimmings, sometimes more costly than the gift itself. Trimmings one couldn't reuse or recycle. They were usually ripped to shreds and thrown away upon the giving of the gift.

That sounds about dead on target, Rett observed, giving in to pessimism. *Hmm, Ariam always said I looked good in black. Maybe I should suggest it.*

~You're stunning in black. I got a good look at you while you were getting ready for Carakenne's award presentation. We need some slick black Mylar with a nice, shiny, metallic purple ribbon.~ Pam created a thought picture of the materials. ~When wrapping something as expensive as you are, you have to do it with a bit of style. This icky-yellow webbing you Nyorfians use for almost everything just doesn't do anything for you. It's like wrapping a bottle of Dom Perignon in old dirty newspapers. Hmm. I'm having a bit of trouble putting you into the basic slinky black mini dress and stiletto heels. Barbie, you are not. With your figure, you definitely need something classic. ~

Of course, Pam had plenty more visual images and explanations to get the points across.

Good gods and deities, do people really wear stuff like that on your planet? Why?

~Because it's fashionable~ answered Pam. ~Some people on Earth are conditioned to feel good, even superior to others, when they are fashionable, especially if they've spent a lot of money in the process.~

Money? Oh, credits. Rett wrinkled her nose. *That's really important to you, isn't it. To your culture.*

Pam's mental frown almost reached Rett's face. -Yeah, well, it is, yes. I'm not going to get back into it. The point is that, yeah, to some people in my culture, having clothing that is fashionable and trendy is important, even if it's uncomfortable. Don't people dress up here? I mean, do men and women wear different styles, put on fancy clothes and makeup other than the camo paint and uniforms I've seen? Even most civilians I've seen wear kind of the same thing…these kids, for example. -

Rett was at a loss, even for thought. She hadn't been exposed to many people outside her own district before joining the military. She never paid much attention to what anyone was wearing, unless it wasn't right for the job or the weather. *I guess the only time I ever thought about it,* she told Pam, *was when I asked Jaq what how people dressed on Zetinor Prime. Because of the hair. I have some memories of the time we went to Circle Spaceport as kids…I suppose there was a lot of different styles being worn. But whether they were worn by Nyorfians or visitors from outsystem—I can't recall. I have to think on this some more later, when it's the right time and place to let you help me bring out more details. That imagery you gave me though… was that for real? Or something you made up? Do you dress like that?*

-No. Well, I might put on something nicer if I get invited to a wedding or something like that. But for the most part, I wear what I think is comfortable instead of popular. And reasonably clean, if I'm going out in public.-

But you're still hung up over how you look on the outside. As soon as Rett let that thought loose, she felt the shift in Pam's defenses. She expected that, just as she expected her ego-merge friend to sidetrack right off the topic. *Pam, we're both too good at sidetracking when we don't want to talk about something, so don't bother. I love you the way you are, no matter what. As for the fancy packaging, for people or their gifts…* Rett held back an amused snort. *You can keep that shit on Earth where it belongs. I prefer the old Nyorfian custom of giving a gift wrapped only in the intention in which you want it received. In Avok's case, it would be my knife wrapped in my fist.*

For now, enough of this. High time she took advantage of the resources her inexpert captors had left to her. She spoke to her pcom with the barest exhalation of breath. "Com connect Fang Two."

355

"Damn it. Where under the flaming sun are you?" Trebor's voice was prompt in her ear and so tight with frustration it made Rett cringe.

"Don't know," she said. She kept an alert watch on the group of children, who paid no attention to her at the moment. They were eating something. Whatever it was she couldn't identify, but it smelled interesting.

-Eggs,- Pam informed her, interpreting the odor that was so unusual to Rett. Certain food items were regional for most Nyorfians, including those living on Epnoce. Rett had told Pam she'd never tasted any dairy products until her second year in the military. Pam was surprised. She thought eggs would be common enough as a food even to the hunter-gatherer types from Rett's province. Maybe when it came to eggs, they bypassed gathering them in the nest to hunt them later when they were meat.

"You don't know!" Trebor shot back. "What do you mean, you don't know?" The phrases that followed those words contained a long string of highly descriptive metaphors not normally heard on military com channels. At least not all in the same sentence.

Pam was so stunned her aura went pink, and Rett marveled at Trebor's creativity. Even after six years, he managed to surprise her.

"—and we haven't heard from you in *four* hours." Trebor finally paused to fill his lungs. "We're not even getting a reading from your locator."

One of the children chose that moment to glance over, so Rett took a slow, deep, breath and let it out through her nose in reply.

"Can't talk much right now?" Trebor's query reflected more of his usual control. "You're in trouble. Coalition?"

"Wouldn't be on com if that," she said without moving her lips.

"I suppose not. What's up?"

"The children have me."

"Have you? The kids?" His end went dead for a count of ten. When it came back, Trebor's deep voice was nearly soprano in disbelief. "The kids we spotted—the ones you went after? *Captured* you?"

"Uh-huh."

"But…why?"

"Not now," Rett said as Shannai stood up and turned to look at her. Damn it, and she was going to ask after Jessek. She hoped she'd have a chance later.

"Leave the com open. Something's bouncing your signal and I can't get a direction just yet, but at least I can listen in to what you say and try to figure what's going on."

Again Rett didn't answer, since Shannai's eyes didn't leave her as she walked over, a shallow bowl in her hands. "Are you hungry?" Shannai crouched on her heels, set the bowl beside her. A wisp of steam curled from it.

"No," answered Rett.

"Need a drink?"

"Are you going to let me loose later to handle the results?" She wasn't about to let on that she was good for the next day or so in that department. One of the first body functions they'd learned to control back in training was elimination.

357

"I can't." Shannai shook her head, a flash of discomfort and regret darkening the natural pale hue of her skin.

"It's all right. I don't need anything. Thank you for asking."

Shannai indicated the bowl. "I'm going to clean the blood off your face. It's…really bothering the little kids. Us. It was hard to compare you to the picture. I mean—is it all right if I do that?"

Rett shrugged. Frustration prompted an entire array of sarcastic answers; patience substituted a single alternate. "I don't mind."

"You're going to let us give you over—just like that?" Shannai dipped a rag into the bowl. The faint chemical smell of the soap brought Rett a wistful, tantalizing vision of a deep tank filled to the brim with hot, hot water.

"You told me they're going to kill your families unless they get me, Shannai," said Rett. The touch of the warm cloth against the skin of her cheek was hesitant, tentative. She remained perfectly still, as if nothing at all was unusual about being tied up on a mound of sharp objects; having her face washed by a teenager who would just as soon shoot her. "Did I misunderstand you when you said that?"

"That's what She told us."

Shannai applied a bit more pressure to her scrubbing, taking a firm hold on Rett's chin with one hand. There was nothing tentative about the procedure now; this was a competent young woman who had obvious experience at restoring dirty faces to some semblance of neatness. She wondered if the girl had younger siblings.

"She told us," Shannai said, "that if we didn't get you, have you here, tied up a certain way, by new day, then she would have the guards watching our families kill them and all we would see would be…what was left."

~Would Avok do that?~ Pam wanted to know. ~I thought—~

It's possible Avok was making an empty threat, answered Rett, *but she'll do anything she thinks would give her leverage. And find a way to get away with it, turn what happens to her favor and credit.* Aloud, Rett said to Shannai, "Then we'll see Avok gets what she wants." *And I'll make sure she gets what she deserves.*

Shannai's cloth paused near her headband. The girl's fingers slid beneath the top edge of the material. A soft rush of coolness against her forehead stopped Rett's breath in her throat.

Deities, if Shannai takes my headband there might not be a chance for Trebor to get here and get these kids before Avok will. Because if I know Avok, nothing these kids do will make one bit of difference for the plans she made for them originally.

"It didn't go underneath," said Shannai, as if to herself, and when the cleaning continued, the motions went carefully around the headband without touching it again.

Rett was glad to be lying down at that point. She squeezed her eyes closed as liquid dripped close. "I wish you would let me try to come up with another way. My platoon is out there, wondering where I am. They could be looking for your families instead of me right now. They could even be establishing a safe route to get us from here to wherever they are."

"No." A deft swipe of a finger diverted liquid from getting into Rett's mouth. "She said if a bunch of Nyorfian soldiers showed up, especially Special Forces, that she would know it, and kill our families that very same minute."

"They're probably tracking me now." Rett carefully cracked one eye open to see a frowning Shannai shake her head. Whether it was about what she said or any remaining stains on her face, she had no idea. When the girl applied upward pressure beneath her chin, Rett tilted her head back. More scrubbing followed.

"They won't find you," Shannai sounded confident. "Besides, I took your locator and those wrist things and your VARs and dumped them down a recycle chute with your big gun and the smaller one. The chutes are shielded, so they won't even be able to track a signal into one."

Trebor cursed softly, and his connection went silent for several seconds.

Those were brand new VARs, Rett thought with an inward wince.

"We're going to have to start taking collections to get your gear replaced," Trebor came back on, sounding more like the competent, organized second in command she knew him to be. "I don't think you can afford to lose any more. Put two of our own on the problem." 359

Carakenne and H'tenneck, most likely, thought Rett, in no doubt that pair of clever minds would find clues. "Why didn't you take everything I carried and dump it?"

"I couldn't figure the catches on your belts and they were too snug to pull off you. And if something didn't come off easily I was afraid to try to fool with it," Shannai admitted. "They said sometimes you guys make stuff explode when people touch it." Apparently finished with her task, she sat back on her heels and made a ritual of folding the rag she had used into the smallest possible square.

"If we walked around with stuff ready to explode with just a touch, there'd none of us be left. Can we discuss alternative—"

Shannai dropped the small square of cloth into the bowl. "She said you would try to talk us out of doing this. I don't want to do it. But She said she'd be watching, and if anything happens that isn't supposed to, She'll kill everyone. Including the little kids. Whether we had you or not. I can't let that happen!"

"How under the flaming sun do you get yourself into these situations?" wondered Trebor, voicing her earlier thoughts.

"No." Rett let out some of the tension in her shoulders. "We can't let that happen."

The rest of the kids joined Shannai around Rett's body on the mysterious pile of sharp lumps.

"I told you she looks nice," said Olvero, pointing to Rett's clean face as evidence.

Kallet and Safkas looked a great deal less apprehensive, daring to edge closer than they had before. Safkas stayed close to Shannai but didn't try to hide behind her. Thalom, without a word, bent and whisked away the bowl of dirty water and the rag. He was back again before Rett took a deep breath.

While she was being re-examined and again compared to the image on her ID, Rett took a good close look at them. "Is anyone hurt? Sick? Have enough food and water?" Although she saw what she wanted to know, she asked the questions for Trebor, who would need details for a variety of reasons—not the least of which were the parents of these children. Once the parents were located, they would want to know everything. It would help if Trebor could reassure them he had heard the children speaking for themselves.

Other than being tired and scared, they seemed fine. They had food; plenty of water; and seemed clean—there weren't any telltale odors that indicated they didn't have access to lavatory and washbasin. No one appeared to be ill or in physical pain. Seeing they were all dressed for the colder temperatures of wherever they were brought Rett personal relief.

"What is this stuff under me, anyway?"

"Knotroot," said Shannai.

"Knotroot? The size of mountains? Is it some kind of giant mutant knotroot?"

The kids giggled and the faintest glimmer of a smile softened the Shannai's lips. She lifted her chin with pride. "Complex 63 grows the biggest and best knotroot on Epnoce."

"Get me the location of every single storage area with knotroot," she heard Trebor tell someone. "Yes, *now*."

Must have not asked anyone in F-troop, thought Rett with an inward roll of her eyes. An internal groan followed, heard only by Pam. *There are no crop storage areas close to the last position I remember being in.*

For all I can guess, we could be sixty miles and three levels away with Coalition troops between us. We might as well be on one of the moons. No wonder my signal's bouncing.

"Uhm, do you mind if I move a little that way? There's a lump of the biggest and best of this lot mashing directly into my butt, if you know what I mean." Rett's explanatory grimace brought more giggles from Kallet and Olvero.

Shannai's little smile disappeared. Her stunner came close. "Shift over, but move anything else and I'll stun you."

"Understood." Rett eased her most pressing problem of the moment with a sigh of relief mental and physical. "Thanks." Who would ever guess the ubiquitous, everyday Nyorfian knotroot was hard and sharp as rocks when massed together?

~Who would have ever guessed that a small, peace-loving, pioneering society on the ass-end of nowhere would hold their own against, much less kick butt on a huge, technologically superior invasion for over twelve years?~ countered Pam.

Hmm, I see your analogy. But I still would like to shift around more. The lump in my ass was one thing. I don't want my right side to go numb, either. I still have my knife and if I get two seconds to get out of this, I don't want half of me to be asleep.

"How much time is there until new day when they come to pick me up?" Rett asked aloud.

"It's just after 2600 now," Thalom said.

Rett felt that peculiar mental shift when something from her world clashed with Pam's interpretation. ~Sorry,~ said Pam, ~I have to keep reminding myself your Standard day is thirty hours... Standard hours, not Earth hours. These kids are up awfully late, even on your time.~

These kids aren't exactly in a normal situation, either, reminded Rett. *They're scared to death.*

"Labonne should be coming soon, right?" asked Safkas hopefully.

"He said he would," answered Shannai. "Labonne always keeps his word to us."

Four hours until new day. Rett calculated the time. *I was on com with Tris and Evetez around 2145. Trebor was right. I've been gone almost four hours, out a little less than that. Must have been zapped every fifteen to keep me out that long!*

Trebor's voice spoke in Rett's ear. "You sure know how to find trouble. I have people checking on knotroot, civilians who are missing children, and recycle units. We've secured two habitat areas of the four, and there's one school central to the complex that's off the first habitat—so we should find someone who at least knows one of the children, if not the families."

Good work as usual, Trebor.

"No surprise that the Coalition's hanging in here," he continued. "It'll be a slow go to clean them all out. Plans changed and Easy's staying on to help the infantry. Not that we'd leave without you anyway. I've heard three names from you—try to mention the rest in conversation. Fang Three's come up with a few teachers from the school, he's bringing them over. I'll stop talking now, but I'll be right here listening."

"That decoy was a neat trick," Rett admitted.

"She said once any of the Special Forces caught a glimpse of us that someone would be sure to come after us." Shannai's narrow shoulders lifted in a shrug.

"We're supposed to," reminded Rett, deciding not to mention anything about the terrible risk they had taken. That was an issue she would love to take up with Avok, in person. To these children, the only risk they understood was the one of never seeing their families, alive, again. "You run fast, Kallet."

"He's the fastest in the eight to tens for the whole complex," said Safkas with pride.

Kallet's face reddened. "Shannai and Thalom are faster."

"How did you move me once I was stunned? I'm pretty heavy, especially with all my gear."

"Cargo floater," said Thalom.

Explained that. Most cargo floaters had forklifts and netting capabilities to keep cargo from shifting, or to wrap pallets and crates for shipment or storage. Some of them were capable of moving quite fast as well. *Stunned, scooped, wrapped, floated, and rolled off onto Knotroot Ridge, slick as anything.*

"Thalom can drive good," said Kallet. He hesitated when Shannai sent him a significant glance of warning.

"But had a bit of trouble with the cargo lift and pallet wrapper?" Rett supplied with a lift of her eyebrows. "You didn't have to stop him from saying anything, Shannai. I can feel that I was dropped a few times in the process."

The deeper color that flooded the cheeks of the oldest children confirmed the source of the majority of Rett's newest bruises.

"Not surprising, considering those attachments aren't meant to handle people. It's okay. I'm hard to break."

The smallest child moved closer to Rett, his round eyes studying her. "I like you."

She smiled at him. "Thanks, Olvero. I like you, too."

363

"Are you cold?"

She shrugged. "Don't worry about me. You look tired. All of you do." Shannai worried her the most. "You don't have to worry that I'll try to leave."

"You kids get to sleep," Shannai ordered the others. "I'll watch her."

Olvero didn't move away, he moved closer. "I'm not worried," he said. "Can I call you Rett?"

"Of course you can."

His head cocked to one side. "You look like my mommy. 'Cept she's darker than you, like me. See?" He held a dimpled brown hand close. "And you're bigger than she is, even lying down. You're even bigger than my dad. You know what? That mean commander says you hate kids and chew them up and spit them out just for fun. And then the others eat them for lunch."

"And you throw babies out windows," said Kallet in a mumble.

Rett and Pam together struggled hard to moderate Rett's reaction to a disbelieving "Good gods and deities!" instead of the more descriptive sentiment concerning Avok, her personal habits, and her ancestors, which Trebor so vehemently expressed at the same time over the pcom.

"I didn't b'leve Her," Olvero said with a reproachful glance at the middle boy. "But Kallet and Safkas did. They think the blood on you is from some kids you—"

"Olvero," Shannai said sharply, "go with the others and lie down."

"Don't you start acting like Her again, Shannai," he yelled. "Rett is nice, she's not lying to you. She's not!" He stamped his foot. "She will help. And she's cold. We're the ones being mean. Mean like *them*!"

A stricken expression crossed the teenager's narrow face. "We're the ones who are going to get our families killed, too," she reminded Olvero.

"Rett's mommy and brother were killed by the bad people. She won't let it happen to us," Olvero returned with a flat-voiced gravity better suited to someone six times his age.

Shannai fell silent, hunching into herself, her eyes and weapon not leaving Rett's body again.

Rett forgot to breathe and just stared at Olvero. Only his voice, reverting back to that of the small, frightened boy he was, broke her out of the absolute shock that had locked her body and thought functions. *Deities, he's Talented! When I made the association, he lifted it right out of me slick as you please. He must be close to Adept level.*

~Holy shit. Do you think he can sense me?~ Pam shrank behind her door. Rett didn't dare think back an answer.

Olvero pointed to the streaks remaining on her hands and staining her uniform. "Whose blood?"

"Someone in my platoon."

"Did he die?" whispered Olvero.

"I hope not. He was—I mean, he is hurt badly."

"It wasn't your fault the 'splosion made him fall and the door closed too fast."

Rett kept her face from changing expression. *Damn it.* She swiftly pulled up what little mental protection she had learned to use while living in constant contact with two empathic younger siblings. On top of that she imagined the shield stronger, just as Pam was always trying to get her to do in practice.

"I know that," she said. "I still feel bad it happened."

"I hope he gets better."

"Me, too."

Olvero bit his full lower lip for a second. "You'll make Her give back our mommies and dads, won't you?" Hopeful trust shone all over his small brown face.

"I'll do whatever it takes to make that happen." Rett's voice roughened. She cleared her throat, finished pulling up any small mental defenses she had, and redirected her surface thoughts. In complete accord, Pam had practically disappeared, only the tiniest pulse of energy marking her in Rett's mental vision.

Then Rett dismissed any current urges to dwell on Olvero's all-too-accurate statements. When Ariam and Tovadan were younger, if she puzzled over something concerning them for very long, they picked up on it right away. No amount of surface diversion kept them from discerning the nature of her thoughts.

Powerful psi talent in the making or not, Olvero was a small, scared, lost little boy and she wanted very badly to hug him and the rest of his frightened companions and tell them she would make everything right. She wished she could be sure. She was familiar with the empty promises made by the Yixolryn Coalition. And she knew exactly how someone like Avok used such promises to devastate guileless children and adults.

"Do you know why I b'leve you?" asked Olvero. "Because you have nice eyes. Just like Mommy."

His concern, his trust, and his comment touched her deeply and made this entire bizarre situation easier to swallow. "Thanks. Now you'd better do what Shannai asked, sweetheart."

She heard Trebor's connection go silent, and guessed he was keeping busy for the moment. Letting her head drop to its rocky cushion of knotroot, Rett closed her eyes again, hoping everything was going well with the battle; casualties were being kept at minimums for both sides.

There was any number of times, including now, she could have freed herself, relieved Shannai of her stunner, and taken charge of the situation. It would take less than thirty seconds. In three more, she'd find out exactly where they were. F-troop would come and get the kids. Then she would go after Avok, and make the Yixolryn female understand firsthand what chewing up and spitting out involved.

But what she wanted personally had no place here. She had made that choice the day she enlisted. She, as military, was expendable.

Civilians were not. Her main objective was to minimize risk for the children and their families, and that meant not to take chances with their lives. Especially when she had no idea of her location, or what manner or number of enemy defenses and troops were beyond the reach of her energy sense.

~So this means you'll let them deliver you to Avok on a silver platter?~ Pam asked very quietly from her corner.

Until another acceptable alternative presents itself.

~Yes, but will she take you—and leave them unharmed?~

She will if the timing is right. Rett opened her eyes. *Shit. I hope he didn't scope too much of that.*

Olvero hadn't moved, having watched her the entire time. "You think a lot."

"It's part of my job."

"Are you afraid?"

Rett studied him for a moment, then looked past him, toward the others, who'd crept in close once more.

This lot was already on the sharp edge induced by fear, already suspicious. Analyzing her every breath. And the soft, round eyes holding her in such hopeful, serious regard already saw much too deeply beneath her surface.

"Afraid? Yes," she said honestly. "I am."

Kallet edged nearer and squatted alongside Olvero. "I didn't think you'd ever be afraid of anything."

Rett chuckled. "You know, my younger brother once said the same thing to me. But I'm the same as anyone else. I'm afraid of a lot of things."

"Like what?" whispered Safkas.

She made the comparison as simple as possible. "Well, right now, this minute, it's about as easy for me to stay here and know the Coalition is going to take me prisoner as it is for you to be away from your families and not know if they're going to be all right or not."

"That's pretty scary." Kallet nodded.

"I guess that's why no one has slept very much in...how long has it been?" Rett asked. "A few days?"

"We haven't seen our families in over a tenday," the youngest girl said.

"Have they made you stay in here all that time, Safkas?" Rett tempered her outrage at the thought, keeping her voice calm.

"No, just when the attack started. Three days? I forget." Safkas rubbed at eyes already reddened from strain and exhaustion. "But being here is better than being with them. With them, we were afraid to go to sleep even for a minute." She shivered, and Thalom dropped a protective arm around her shoulders.

"Did they hurt any of you? Do anything more than push you around?" One sign that any of them had been abused would change her plans entirely. Trebor's soft growl on the pcom said that he was thinking on the same track.

"They said they would," Thalom answered, his hand rising to cover Safkas' spice-brown curls as she ducked her head against his chest. "Those that She had guarding us said they would do some terrible things. Maybe they didn't say them to us directly, but they made sure we could hear them. Shannai told us not to show them we were scared because that was what they wanted and it would make it worse."

367

"She's right. Some of them are encouraged by fear as much as by a fight." Rett flashed quick approval in Shannai's direction.

"And Labonne told all of us that She told the guards if they did anything to any of us without her permission she'd give them to Wik." Kallet's voice shook.

~Wik sounds like a problem,~ Pam thought uneasily.

I guess I'll be finding out how much of one sooner or later, Rett agreed. *Though why Avok would need anyone as an enforcer when she's quite able to kill or threaten someone herself is beyond me.*

"I know they've injured adults," Rett said, glad to see Thalom so protective of the younger children. He was hugging Kallet with his other arm. "But has the garrison here been injuring children, as well?"

"Not that we know of," said Thalom in a very adult manner that reminded her of Trebor. "But like I said, there's been talk. And they always try to get us to take their drugs, to join them, saying it would be better if we volunteered rather than were forced." Thalom glanced at Shannai, the frown of concern on his face also that of an adult. "They grabbed me a few times, but mostly to push me around. Shannai was—"

"Don't, Thalom," hissed Shannai in warning.

Alarmed at a sudden flux in Shannai's energy, Rett focused on her.

"—pushed around, too, but other than staring or talking, they didn't do anything to the littler kids."

Shannai glared at Thalom but said nothing.

Rett's flattened her lips for a second. Thalom didn't have to say anything more. It was apparent enough from Shannai's reaction that something more had been done to her.

~You think she was raped?~

I don't know. I... Rett closed her eyes for a moment. *I've been with young people who were sexually abused and tortured, by Avok and her people as well as random others. I'm not scoping the same kind of energy from her. Something happened to frighten her deeply—Thalom, too. He must have seen everything. I wish she would trust me.* Her heart twisting in her chest, Rett swallowed back sympathy and frustration to focus on the moment.

~Just be yourself, Rett. With horses—~

It always comes back to horses with you.

~All I'm saying is that you can't always *do* something. Sometimes doing nothing at all, and just being there, quiet and patient, turns things around.

I guess. There's nothing I can do, anyway.

And since it didn't look as if anyone was getting much sleep, it was time to change track. "Are you sure all of you've had enough to eat? I've have rations in those pockets you never emptied. Good stuff. Not that junk the Coalition eats. Fruit bars, too. You should take them. If you don't, the Coalition will. I'd rather you did."

"Fruit bars?" Kallet cast a pleading look in Shannai's direction. "We haven't had fruit in a long time. Just breekie eggs. Lots and lots of breekie eggs, knotroot, and greens."

"They take all the good stuff." Thalom reddened, as if he wasn't supposed to complain.

368

"Labonne said he would try to bring us some grain rolls," said Safkas, but her eyes went to Rett's utility belt. "We haven't had those in ever so long, either."

No wonder they looked so thin and tired. A prolonged diet of nothing but protein and fiber was better than nothing, but it wasn't the best choice for growing kids, especially those under stress.

~You give them free access to a combination of protein, fat, and carbs like you have in those bars, and it'll go straight to their heads like alcohol. Or straight into a major tummy ache.~

I don't think so, Pam. I was thinking the regular fruit bars, not those super concentrated meal replacement ones—although Shannai could use a couple of those. And the energy they get from a fruit bar or two is exactly what they need. It's not as if they're going to swallow them all at once. I think Shannai's too smart to let that happen.

Shannai was trying very hard not to look interested or even affected by the mention of fruit bars and the assault of hopeful glances from her companions.

"What kind of good stuff?" asked Olvero, sidling closer.

"Oh, you know, the usual stuff Special Forces eats," Rett answered. "Booger berries and metal slivers in blood. Mashed beetles, stingflies, and slimefruit—that one has little crunchy bits in it. Baby fingers in spicebush syrup. Stuff like that."

The kids giggled, even Shannai cracked a smile.

Then Olvero's eyes narrowed. "I *don't* b'leve it."

"You're right. I was trying to be funny. It didn't work?"

"No." Olvero crossed his arms and frowned. Then he ruined it by giggling. "Yes."

"Make up your mind. For those of you who thought it was funny, there might be some mixed berry, stonefruit, and blackhip bars. Maybe even some packets of spicebush shoots and nuts. You'll have to check the third and fourth pockets on the left. Those who didn't think I was funny are just going to have to starve."

"It was funny, Olvero," said Shannai, and without further hesitation, she retrieved the coveted goodies from Rett's pockets. A fruit bar and spicebush stem to each, a pack of good, rich, longcone nuts to share. "Don't swallow them down," was all the warning Shannai gave,

369

but combined with her stare, it was enough for Kallet to turn the big bite he was ready to take into a small one; for Safkas to close her eyes and chew as if she intended to make her first nibble last until tenday's end. Shannai and Thalom carefully stashed the rest for later, out of sight and reach of the smaller children. Shannai didn't take any for herself.

"Didn't Shannai tell all of you to get some rest?" Rett saw another general protest starting. Suddenly they expected Rett, as the adult, to take charge of the situation, tied up or not. "Who has taken care of you all this time you've been away from your families?"

"Shannai," said Thalom.

"Labonne was allowed to check on us once in a while, but Shannai," admitted Kallet.

"For over a tenday she's been your leader," Rett pointed out. "Don't back out on her now."

Thalom put his fruit bar in a belt pocket and took Olvero's hand with his right, Safkas' with his left. "Come on," the older boy said. "You too, Kallet. You can finish eating your treats while I tell you a story."

From Shannai came a hint of surprise and grateful warmth. Knowing that would disappear with a direct glance, Rett pretended not to notice. She stared at the ceiling again until she heard the rest of the group settle back into their corner.

The stress and glassy-eyed fatigue she saw in the girl concerned her. That was something Rett had only seen, until now, in the eyes of other soldiers; something she had experienced for herself. Shannai, as oldest of this group, paid a hard price for the responsibility of leadership. And despite her exhaustion, stress, and fear, the gutsy teenager was still determined to save her family and the families of those with her. No matter what it took.

-Just like someone else I know,- came from Pam.

"You should rest. I said I wasn't going anywhere, Shannai," Rett said.

"You can't. They told us if we tied you up you couldn't go anywhere, and you had to be tied up when they came. She even said it had to be a certain way, and if it wasn't she would be tiffed. None of us knew what she meant or how to do it."

~In contrast, since such things are part of entertainment, there are plenty of kids in my society who would know exactly where to begin.~ Pam's thought was bitter.

"I know you can get loose any time you want. So I have to make sure you won't try to get your knife and escape. I'll use the stunner again, just like before."

"The charge must be pretty low by now if you've kept me out for four hours," said Rett. "Probably why I woke up before you expected me to this time."

"It's not long until new day," said the girl ominously.

Rett felt another stress headache coming on. "I'm glad, that after all you've been through, that you still have faith enough to trust the promises of the enemy."

"Labonne never broke his promises to us."

We need to know who Labonne is, thought Rett at the same time Pam did. Both of them had the uneasy feeling that Labonne wasn't a Nyorfian. "Is he the one who made the threat against your families and put you down here?"

"No, of course not. He'd never do that. And I know there are some things he can't do, but he always kept his promises, and I've known him a lot longer than I know you. All my life, I guess."

"I can't contest that," Rett said. "But, Shannai, I'm not your enemy."

"I know. But I can't let you loose. I can't let you go."

"I'm not asking for that. I suggested those fruit bars and snacks for more of a reason than a treat. We carry them to help keep up our energy when we're under stress. As you've been. There's more stress to come. Has Avok spoken directly to you?"

Shannai gulped. "Well…not directly."

"What happens if you collapse before this trade is made?"

Shannai's thin shoulders fell slightly.

"There's a few, in the second pocket, that are a bit more concentrated that the regular ones. 'More bang to the bite', a friend of mine likes to say." She gave Pam a friendly mental nudge.

Reaching over, the girl slid one of the bars from the indicated pocket. "Those belt pockets of yours hold a lot more than they seem to from outside."

"When they're full of gear, they probably weigh as much as I'd guess Safkas to be. Not counting the extra water or TT-1."

"Is that why you were so heavy?" Incredulity cleared the guarded veil from Shannai's face and another half-smile made pleasing transformation of her face. "Sure, you're big, but we couldn't figure out why the floater scale said you weighed so much more than any of us would guess."

The moment of normalcy didn't last long. Shannai realized she'd overstepped her self-imposed limits, and fell silent as she bit into the ration bar.

At least she's eating it. Rett resigned herself to waiting again, a sense of misgiving growing with each beat of her heart. Before Shannai took the last bite, Rett's combat sense was on full alert and she put everything she had into pushing her ability to sense energy auras through the walls and door,

Someone's out there. A faint orange trace, moving…stopping. Right outside the door. She couldn't focus enough to assess the threat level beyond the orange tones she associated with alert, combat-ready tension, which were very different from the colors she assigned to those intent on killing or malicious harm.

It might be that the new arrival didn't guess anyone was in here with the children. The wariness, then, was for other reasons.

"Your friend Labonne…he isn't Nyorfian, is he."

"No. But he's our friend. He should be here any minute. He promised to check on us before She came."

"Then you'd better open the door for him," Rett said.

Shannai crumpled her wrapper and shot her a distrustful glare, which faded at a sound from the door. The teenager's animated response to what was obviously a prearranged signal prompted an echo reaction from Rett.

As Shannai leapt to her feet and sped to the door, Rett finally went for her knife. The long blade sliced through the cargo netting as easily as her hand through water. Before the outer door was open more than a crack, Rett was in a ready crouch, prepared to launch the long azurium alloy blade.

"Labonne!" The joyful tone of greeting was quite different from the tone of voice Rett had heard until now.

Again Rett pulled hard on her ability to interpret the energy aura of the newcomer. She found some reassurance there, more in the instantly brightening auras from all the children. Releasing the tension that would have sent her blade to the hilt right through his armor, she let out a breath, retracted the extra length of blade, and returned her knife to its sheath.

I must be insane.

~You know firsthand not all who wear that uniform are bad. These kids seem like good judges of character,~ came softly from Pam.

It's not an easy call for me to make.

~No. But you have to trust your instinct—and theirs.~

Rett released her misgivings with the catches on her utility and weapons belts.

"I brought you some—" started a man's deep voice, his accent strong and stressing vowels in a disturbingly familiar manner.

Shannai didn't let the man finish. "We caught her, but we didn't know how to do anything right. She said it had to be right. Can you help?" Shannai's words tumbled out so fast and in a tone so breathless Rett barely understood her.

"Caught who?" the man asked in some perplexity. "Take a breath, Shannai. Slow down and start over."

"Sergeant Killer," said Shannai. "We caught her—"

"You did?" The man sounded shocked. "You went out, all the way to where the fighting is? And came back? Are any of you hurt?"

"No—"

"Thank the One. You might have been killed. Move inside, quickly. I can't be seen out there."

The words, the accent, and the raw emotion from the newcomer told Rett than more than a tenday of conversation ever would. Before Shannai closed the door behind Labonne, Rett's belts, and their contents, landed at the trooper's feet. He swung around to look her straight in the eyes. At least she guessed he did, since, as usual, it was impossible to tell with the targeting goggles that hid the top portion of his face.

"She's loose," gasped Shannai.

373

"I'm unarmed." Rett's hands, open-fingered, were stretched forward, away from her body. Her gaze never left the targeting goggles of the Coalition trooper Shannai had greeted like an old friend.

The others, alerted by Shannai's outcry, swarmed toward them and stopped uncertainly a length away. Glances went from Labonne, who had brought the ML-12 across his back into a firing position, to Rett, who remained crouched and motionless on her lumpy mound of knotroot.

Before anyone did or said anything, Olvero pushed his way to stand between Rett and the rest. "No, Labonne! Don't shoot her!" he said in a trembling voice. "She just wanted to make sure it was you and not someone bad."

"Olvero, get out of the way!" ordered Shannai.

"No!" he hollered. "I won't! She has eyes like my mommy, and I want my mommy. I don't want her tied up. I don't want Shannai to make her to go to sleep again. I want..." Olvero gulped in a breath. "I want to go home," he wailed, and burst into tears as he spun and flung himself between the arms Rett had outstretched for quite another reason.

Olvero hugged her around the neck with a grip so fierce it nearly choked her. Sternly, Rett ordered herself to hold her position. Her body ignored her, knowing the proper humanoid response for situations like this.

So her arms folded protectively around Olvero.

And Labonne's energy flattened into the murderous blood-red shade of definite threat.

Letting out a harsh exhalation, she pulled Olvero tightly into her body and twisted so her back was to the ML-12. "Don't shoot—don't shoot—give me a second to get him clear!" Her back tensed. *I hope it's on a stun level, at least I can absorb most of it before it affects Olvero—*

The moment of immediate danger passed. Closing her eyes in relief, Rett let her butt drop to the bumpy mound. But for those she used to hold Olvero, the muscles from the nape of her neck right to her heels unknotted.

"Olvero," she whispered to the sobbing child. "You'd better move away from me."

Again, her physical response belied her words. Even as she said them she knew she wasn't letting go. Instead, she curled her body around the child and changed her grip, hugging him just the way she had wanted to from the beginning. His choking hold loosened but remained strong, and he nestled his small body snugly against hers in need and trust.

"Olvero!" gasped Shannai. "You let him go right now! Or I'll—"

"*Kelani*, if you shoot, you might surely harm Olvero." Labonne's voice, though calm, carried a sharp, deadly edge. "She won't hurt him."

~He's Zetinorian.~ Pam sounded stunned.

Took you long enough. I suspected it from his energy signature—confirmed it the moment he started to talk.

~Jaq's accent is no way that broad, and I haven't had as much time to hear him speak as you did.~

Back down again, I have Olvero, Rett reminded Pam. Now that the immediate threat of weapons fire had passed, she addressed the overwhelming need of the frightened child in her arms. "Shh, it's okay. It's okay." Cuddling Olvero, rocking him just a bit, smoothing his hair, she dismissed all her other concerns for the moment and gave her entire being into offering comfort to the boy.

His sobs diminished to jerky gulps, but his grip stayed strong, his face and nose stayed plastered damply to her neck. His heartbeat hammered right through his chest into hers.

Rett lifted her head and turned it partway toward the others. She didn't have to exert any effort to feel the lingering tension from them: the atmosphere was painted with it. Nor did she have to see to know that Labonne's ML-12 was still aimed at her, now at her head instead of her back.

"Sergeant, I suggest you let the boy go."

"I'm not keeping him here by force. He's clinging on to me, and he's not ready to let go yet. Please hold your fire. Even if you hit me in the head with a stun, he can get some shock from it, or more likely I'll be thrown forward on top of him. I'm going to turn around now. That way if you feel a need to shoot, at least I go back, away from him. I'll move slowly. If the knotroot pile shifts and I lose balance, any movements I make will be only to keep Olvero from getting hurt. Is that agreeable?"

"Do so," responded Labonne.

"No!" Olvero gasped when her body shifted in preparation to move. He started to cry again. "No! I want you."

"Everything will be all right, Olvero, and I won't let you go yet—but you need to breathe. And I need to show the others that I didn't hurt you."

Without letting him go or looking up, she shifted her seat on the mound of knotroot, angling her body so the others had a clear view of Olvero. Or as much of one as his clinging form allowed. "Come on, sport." Rett teased his face away from her neck. When he turned it to open air, she kissed his forehead and brushed his tears dry with careful, gentle fingers. "Just breathe. Nice and slow and even. Your breath won't stick that way."

Olvero took a deep breath and promptly hiccupped.

"Oops, too late."

He was far too tired and overwrought to give her much more than a token little grin, only for the space of an eyeblink, but it was there.

Reluctantly she lifted her head from the private little world into which she had slipped for those precious seconds. The first faces she saw belonged to the younger children. Kallet's face was pink and screwed up, his fingers knotted and twisted together. Safkas was biting her lips and blinking tearfully. For a rare moment in Rett's adult life, she had no idea what her own face displayed. All she wanted was for them to understand she cared. That she'd never hurt them. That she only wanted to help.

She opened her mouth, not knowing what to say, hoping something sensible would come from it. Faster than even Pam could supply her with an ever-ready comment, she found herself with two more sobbing, terrified kids who needed a hug, needed reassurance. Somehow Safkas joined Olvero on her lap. Kallet leaned close to her left side, and Rett didn't remember getting that arm around his waist, but it was there.

She blinked, once, twice. Even Thalom crouched close by, eyes hooded, arms wrapped around his knees. Trying, perhaps, to absorb some of the comfort the younger children started to feel.

Deities, now I'm going to start crying. I think I need someone to give me a hug, thought Rett whimsically to Pam, and was promptly rewarded by the fleeting sensation of her ego-merge friend's strong, warm embrace around all of them. With emotions running this high and a powerful little Talent coming out of his own misery enough to start picking things up from Rett and the others again, Pam didn't dare more than that at the moment.

"Good gods and deities, Fang Lead," Trebor's perplexed voice said in her ear. "I'm off for less than two minutes and what in two worlds is going on there?" A puff of exasperation came over the speaker. "Hold on, I'll get back to you." Again his com cut off.

2.3.5 SECURED AREA, COMPLEX 63, EPNOCE
0535.13.24 (LOCAL RECKONING)

"WHAT NOW?" IF IT WERE not for the seriousness of the situation, Sergeant Worren would have laughed outright at the bewildered expression that left Sergeant Trebor's craggy visage looking so unfamiliar.

Trebor raked a hand through his hair in what Worren figured was an unconscious imitation of their platoon leader, scratched the back of his head, and stared blankly into some infinity only he could see.

"Let's go over here." Worren nudged the F-troop second aside with his right shoulder; plucked lightly at Med's sleeve with his left hand. There were some very upset citizens waiting for some word or action from Trebor, and right now the man simply wasn't in control of his face. "Med?"

Med, waiting to give his report, glanced up from the Omni in his hand. He moved aside with them, and after giving Worren a questioning look, studied Trebor. "Trebor?"

"You know," Trebor said to the space he stared toward, "now I know what the Sarge means when she says that she'd give everything she owns right this minute for one solid hour of boredom."

"What's happening?" prompted Worren.

"There's a bunch of kids crying, must be right on top of her."

"Are they hurt?" Med asked sharply.

"No, it wasn't that sort of crying."

Worren listened as Trebor updated them on the latest from the platoon leader. "The trio over there is missing a child named Shannai." said Worren with a quick glance toward two men and a woman who stood in an anxious knot. The paler-skinned of the two men joggled a baby on his shoulder, and the woman clutched a toddler into her body as if the Coalition was going to appear suddenly to snatch that child from them as well. "They said Shannai and four others have been missing about twelve days. The commander of the garrison here took the children hostage."

Trebor rubbed his eyes. "Shannai. Yes, that's one of them. The oldest, the one in charge. Deities. I'd better let the parents know, as soon as I've updated the Sarge and get the latest. Worren, give Lieutenant Evetez an update, will you? Med, why don't you move that family and any others missing kids over there."

"Right. Don't forget to mention Jessek this time."

Trebor nodded. "I will. The Sarge's probably a little crazy about it by now. She's not sure if he's still alive as it is. Wait a sec—what's with this Labonne I keep hearing about? Have you found out then, Worren?"

"Yes. School warden," said Sergeant Worren. "He's—"

"What a mess," sighed Trebor. Not waiting for Worren to continue, he moved aside to make his communications in relative peace.

"He's a Coalition trooper," finished Worren to the empty space where Trebor had been.

"Oh, goody," said Med at his most sour, which Worren thanked all deities was nowhere near any dairy animals like those he used to care for back on Nyorfias.

379

* * * * *

When Sergeant Trebor finally turned to the group awaiting him, he was very nearly mobbed by overwrought, anxious parents. Three other parental groups had joined the original trio, all eleven people speaking at the same time. Trebor tried to be polite, but no one heard him. With his current level of frustration he felt strongly tempted to yell them down, but doing so would only add to the confusion. It would also be damned unprofessional. He cleared his throat.

"Hold up!" The chilling note of command and threatening rumble in the quiet, deeper tone cut through the higher-pitched voices of nervous, stressed parents and produced instant silence.

He'd never had to use what most military personnel referred to as "That Voice" before. It was usually reserved for discipline, and he'd only heard it, fortunately directed elsewhere, back in training. The Sarge used variations of it from time to time, but not the real thing—not in Trebor's hearing. She tended to yell at someone without letting her voice go past the unfortunate who earned her displeasure. Most of the time, though, one significant glance from her was enough to produce the same effect. Most certainly the Sarge had heard That Voice from

Major Yidnar a time or two. Just thinking about being nailed between Yidnar's gunmetal blue eyes and That Voice gave Trebor the shivers. But whichever way one heard it, it never failed to get results.

Like the absolute attention he had now from the F-troop members within range, despite the fact they knew he wasn't speaking to them. And the taken-aback expressions—even steps—from a few of the now wary civilians. That Voice had that kind of power.

Trebor's face matched the tone until he was certain he had the complete and undivided attention of the parental group. One quick glance and a flicker of his eyebrow sent F-troop back to their duties.

"Now hear me out first, then you can each speak in turn. We won't get anything accomplished otherwise. I know you're all upset, I got that—no, Citizen, I asked you to hear me out." Trebor held up a hand to forestall a question as the shorter of the two males in the trio started to speak again.

380 "Our primary concern is your children, and so far they're physically unharmed, no one is injured or sick. They're frightened and tired, but otherwise all right. They think *you're* the ones being held hostage. The Coalition commander here apparently gave them some kind of story and deal that all of you would be killed unless they cooperated and came up with Sergeant Rett for trade."

He allowed a semi-humorous grimace to come and go on his face. "As things turned out…they succeeded. I'm in contact with Sergeant Rett, for the moment. And no, we can't trace back the signal."

Trebor wasn't about to explain the secure pcom frequencies had a limited range within the huge Epnocian complexes. Had he never heard the storage room and its contents mentioned, the com signal problem was enough to prove Rett and the children were too far away for comfort.

"I have people trying to target definite locations, but if you have any clues to lock down a storage area with knotroot and close to free access of breekie eggs and greens—now is the time to tell me. That's all I know. I'll need to know if any of the children might need some sort of special attention, medical or otherwise. All right, you can go first." He nodded toward the trio. "*One* at a time," Trebor added as all three mouths opened at once.

He glanced to his left, where Worren had again silently made an appearance. Before the spokesperson for the trio had a chance to get started, however, Trebor lifted a silencing hand and addressed the F-troop third-up. "What's up? Did Lieutenant Evetez have anything?"

"Not yet. But you left before I could mention Labonne, the school warden, is a Coalition trooper," said Worren in a voice that didn't go past Trebor's ears.

Trebor very politely, yet in no uncertain terms, informed the parents he needed another minute and excused himself. Taking a long step aside with Worren, he prompted with a tense: "And?"

"The person who told me wasn't really concerned about that fact. Apparently Labonne's been here since the complex was first taken twelve years ago, and most of the residents think of him more as protection than threat. Most of these kids have known him since they were babies." Worren poked at a crust of dried blood on his forehead, just above the headband. "The first response I received from adults was a very concerned: 'Deities, is he all right?'"

Trebor grunted. "Can't discount twelve years of approval from the locals. Well, we know there are some decent people among the enemy, humanoid and alien. But we also know what happens when we take things for granted." He swatted the third-up's hand away from his face. "Stop that—you'll start it bleeding again. Dripping blood isn't good for public relations."

Worren made a face but lowered his hand.

"No telling what this Labonne will do if he's forced into a choice?" Trebor asked.

"No. Not yet," said Worren. "That's what concerns me. No matter how much they say they like him, there still seems to be some sort of line between them. But I can't figure if it's because the residents are trying to protect him from us—or protect him from the Coalition."

"Protect him from us?"

"I received the impression that a few are already upset that we mean death to anything in a Coalition uniform, and others are afraid they'll never see him again once we reestablish Nyorfian claim to the complex."

"Well then, sounds as if the locals need an update on Nyorfian military policy. It's been a long twelve years for these people. Make it clear to them that if this Labonne wants to cooperate he won't be harmed—and he might not have to leave." Trebor paused. "That is, if he survives long enough. If he's that well-liked by the locals, Commander Avok is more of a threat to him than we are."

"Does the Sarge know it's Avok yet?"

"I'm not sure, but I'm going to tell her."

"Shit."

"Would you prefer it remain a surprise?"

"No!" Worren bared his teeth for a moment. "But damn it, I would have preferred a rematch between the Sarge and any of those Coalition nasties would find her a bit less disadvantaged than usual."

Trebor had to agree. He didn't want to admit that the situation was actually ideal for improving their chances of getting five live children returned, and that was all that should matter. But that wasn't all that mattered. "Are you thinking what I'm thinking?"

Worren met his gaze. "Probably. I'll try to find out more about Labonne. You might want to ask these people as well."

Trebor nodded. "Let's hope we manage to get a plan together before the Coalition commander does, then."

2.3.6 UNDETERMINED AREA, COMPLEX 63, EPNOCE
0535.13.24 (LOCAL RECKONING)

RETT KEPT ONE EYE ON LABONNE, who hadn't moved much more than to lower his weapon. The other she kept on Shannai. The girl stared up at the trooper, a pleading expression on her face. He shifted his weapon to his back and then lifted his targeting goggles.

He reached to touch Shannai's cheek, a similar gesture to the one Rett had given Thalom. "We don't have much time to plan, *kelani*."

As he spoke again, Rett studied the Zetinorian intently. Labonne was an older man, tall and broad like Jaq, but far more streamlined. His features were lean, well-worn, etched with experience, and cast with the rusty overtones that marked his race. The other telling characteristic— his hair—was hidden beneath his helmet, although a few long silver strands escaped from beneath it. His outward expression was neutral, without one trace of the emotion she had heard in his voice when he first entered.

Their gazes met, held. His eyes were a paler blue than Jaq's, with maybe the slightest hint of green, but possessed of the same startling clarity and brilliance. Like unshuttered windows to his soul, they mirrored the greater part of his aura. By the time she had drawn two breaths, she felt they could be allies, even friends.

First, she had to convince him of her intentions. He wouldn't hesitate to disable her if he felt she threatened the children...*his* children. All he needed was one clear track and a good excuse, and she'd be a scorch mark on the nearest wall. Of that she hadn't the slightest doubt.

~And what of the children's safety from him?~ Pam wanted to know.

A Zetinorian would never intentionally harm children, not even in self-defense, answered Rett. *No matter how much conditioning they'd had from the Coalition. Not that they were susceptible to Coalition conditioning in any case, which, according to Jaq, is one of the reason there are so few Zetinorians left.*

~Would you—in self-defense?~ asked Pam.

383

Rett couldn't help a shiver. Disarming and neutralizing Shannai had been the closest thought she'd ever had to it. If she'd realized the children had been converted to the Coalition side and were intent on harming her—or worse: harming a lot of other people—then what?

I can't guess at that answer, Pam. It would have to be a decision I make on the spot. All I can say is that hope I never have to find out. But the issue here is Labonne. Whatever he does for the Coalition, all that matters is he cares—dare I say he loves these kids? And the kids care for him. For that, she made the allowance of dismissing the origin of the uniform he wore for the origin of the man inside it.

Aloud, she said to Labonne, "I think in this matter we want the same thing—for these kids to go home safely. I'm open to suggestion."

His eyes flickered, maybe in surprise, maybe in amusement, but told her nothing. The lack of expression on the Zetinorian's deeply lined face made him appear dour and forbidding, although the reaction of the children to his presence implied the opposite. Right now he was as inscrutable as anyone she'd ever seen, trained or otherwise. Had it not been for her ability to read him on a deeper level Rett would not have been so quick to withdraw her defenses, Zetinorian or not.

"Everyone listen. Shh." The Zetinorian's soft bass voice had an undeniable soothing quality. The weepy group around Rett quieted, although no one showed signs of moving. "The sergeant and I need to talk."

"Don't hurt her," sniffled Olvero with a hiccup.

"I can't promise anything, Olvero, but I'll try not to."

"Are you going to tie her up again?" Safkas wanted to know.

"I think I should. That was something the Commander said must be done, wasn't it?" Labonne eyed the twisted pile of netting that had been wound around Rett so uselessly. "Did you use all that, and she still got loose?"

"We tried to use the wrapping tool on the cargo floater we took, and did a really bad job," admitted Shannai, "and we were afraid to take all her things away and she still had a knife. I couldn't get it off her belt. That's why I was waiting for you, and keeping her stunned until a little while ago. But my stunner is running out of power. And we had to find out who she was, so I didn't stun her again. She didn't try to move or anything until you came in."

He put a reassuring hand on Shannai's upper arm. "You did well." That was exactly what the girl needed to hear, and her tense shoulders relaxed. Her soft sigh of relief was followed by a tired smile for the older man. Rett's estimation of the newcomer went up.

"Why do we have tie her up now?" Like Olvero and Safkas, Kallet still clung to Rett and showed no indication he wanted to move any time soon.

"Because the Commander isn't going to wait until new day." Labonne rubbed a hand over his face for a moment, a gesture that expressed the frustration and weariness he didn't otherwise reveal. "You're all lucky I managed to come at all, and managed to come first. Had it been the Commander or anyone else…things would've been very bad for all of you. No matter what we decide to do, there isn't much time. Please, move over there. Go with Thalom. Here, take these. They may still be warm." He handed a small shoulder pack to Kallet. "Shannai, you stay here."

"You've more trouble by the sound of it, Fang Lead," Trebor said over the pcom.

Rett exhaled softly through her teeth.

"It wasn't easy for me to get away," Labonne said gravely to Shannai. "I'm glad I managed. *Kelani*, I can't lie to you, the situation is not good. The Free Army is taking over this complex."

"But that's good, right?" Shannai was confused.

"In one way, it is. For us—for you children, it isn't. The Commander is going use you children to get herself out. That was her plan all along."

"Us! But what about our parents and families?"

"She doesn't have them. She never did." He glanced at Rett. "I don't know how you did it, capturing this one. Now that you have her, though, the sergeant is a bonus. The Commander never expected you to succeed. Don't expect her to thank you for it—but now I think you might have a better chance."

The emotions flying across Shannai's narrow face deepened the fresh aches in Rett's heart.

"You mean we might have escaped instead of catching her?" Shannai whispered. "I took them into sections where the fighting was, and we could have gone with her—with any of them we saw—and been safe?"

He nodded. "Yes."

The girl looked ill. She buried her face in her hands for a moment, a low moan escaping from behind them. Then she lifted her head. "Why didn't you tell me before now?"

"I didn't know her true reasons until a short time ago." He sounded upset, tiffed, but it was obviously self-directed. "I should have guessed, of course."

For a moment Labonne appeared as if he would continue, as if he would offer more explanations and reasons. Rett was sure he had them; it was easy to guess that as a Zetinorian under a Yixolryn commander like Avok, Labonne would be thwarted on many angles. Instead, he kept it simple. "I'm sorry."

"Well," Shannai allowed, "we're not the only kids you take care of here. Does She suspect you? Is that why you weren't allowed to be alone with any of us once we'd been taken?"

A corner of Labonne's mouth twitched. "Commander Avok's been watching me since she took command here. Yixolryns do not like Zetinorians, you know, no matter how useful we are to them. But she has watched me all the more closely since your group was taken, yes."

"Will you get in trouble?" Shannai's hands clasped together so tightly Rett feared those slender fingers would break. Her naturally pale complexion took on an alarming gray hue. "Labonne, will they... if they..."

Rett readied herself to catch Shannai should she suddenly collapse.

"You must not concern yourself with that," Labonne said, voice sharpening enough to bring color back to her cheeks. "But I'm not supposed to be here now. I barely slipped away just before, and I have to get back before I'm missed." He let out a breath. "I wish I was able to get away earlier. I would have told the sergeant to go, and take all of you with her, and made sure no one followed. But now it's too late. The Commander's troops are concentrating in this area, since it is near the outer perimeter and is her only way out right now."

Shannai, silent, the silver of her eyes tarnished, sank to her heels and wrapped her arms around her knees. "What are we going to do?" she whispered.

"Is this a good time for some late breaking news from my end?" Trebor sounded extremely tired.

Keep your headband on, Trebor. "How much time do we have?" Rett asked Labonne.

"I'll delay her a bit if I can, but maybe an hour, hour and a half at most," said Labonne. "It won't really matter. There isn't—" His gaze rested on her black headband, probably taking real notice of it for the first time.

Second test, Labonne, thought Rett. She didn't move.

A muscle twitched in his cheek. The briefest hint of expressions slipped through his otherwise still face: approval, relief, nothing negative. "You're on com." It wasn't quite a question.

"Shit," muttered Trebor.

"I looked for a comlink," Shannai said, raising her head. She frowned. "I didn't find one."

"You wouldn't have known where to find it, *kelani*," said Labonne. "Sergeant?"

"Yes, I am on com. I have been," Rett admitted even as she hoped the brightening in his eyes meant he was pleased.

"Good, are you in contact with your unit?"

She nodded once, reassured he wasn't going to be negative about it. "They don't know where I am, although they've been attempting to find out. They've also been looking for the children's families."

"That can't be true." Shannai rose from her crouch. "I didn't hear her talking to anyone but us. I think you're all lying to me," the frustrated teenager snarled.

"Twelve days, it's a wonder the poor kid's held together."

Rett wasn't sure if Trebor meant her to hear that, but he was right. Shannai was at her limits; Rett wasn't about to blame her for losing control. But neither was she going to allow it to happen. She caught Shannai's gaze and held it fast, challenging the teenager to look away.

"FangLead," Trebor went on quickly, "we have the families here, moms, dads, brothers and sisters, everyone. Just verify these names— Shannai, Kallet, Thalom, Olvero, Safkas?"

"Yes," she confirmed, keeping her voice conversational. *This will either steady Shannai or send her over the edge,* she thought, then told Trebor, "Make it fast."

"First off—Fang seventeen is alive, going to stay that way, FangMed's not committing to details, but either way it goes, it'll be a long recovery, so he'll be going home. I'm sorry you weren't told before. Here's the story from this end. The oldest girl, Shannai, was responsible for walking that group back to their homes before and after school. Twelve days ago, they didn't come home.

"The Coalition commander told *all* the parents in the complex that the kids would be hostages against the Free Army's taking back the complex and getting any civilian assistance. This probably explains better than anything why insider assists on this assignment were nonexistent. Not that we count on getting civilian assistance, but it does expedite things when we can."

"Yes, keep going," prompted Rett when he paused.

"And, if we did succeed in taking the complex, the kids would be their barter for whoever was left to escape free and clear. With you as part of the trade, if F-troop was involved, and we were."

"That's what I heard, too," said Rett. "Except on my end, the tradeoff was to be the kids' families."

Trebor's grunt of assent came across as more of a groan. "So now, it's not long until new day."

"I was just told they weren't waiting for new day," said Rett. "We don't have much more than an hour or so."

"Whatever the length of time we have left, if we don't get to you and the kids before that…that…"

Surprised that Trebor failed to find suitably descriptive words when he had so many to say before, Rett filled in the gap. "Commander Avok?" She kept her voice even and didn't let it carry past Shannai or Labonne. Shannai cringed, but didn't drop the staring contest she was having with Rett. Labonne grunted.

"So you know." The undertone in Trebor's voice said everything. "That's why our plans changed and we didn't pull out. When we found out who the commander here was and passed the information back, Force One said he doesn't want Avok to escape. Whatever it takes."

"Understood. And I agree. Whatever it takes." A disease like Avok had to be stopped. Rett wasn't the only Nyorfian that had experienced the Yixolryn's sick cruelty.

"You have to get me a location. This building has three wings that have complete levels dedicated to storage rooms meeting the description of yours."

"I need details, Fang Two, and now," she said pointedly. She softened her air of challenge toward Shannai, trading it for encouragement and entreaty. "Shannai, I wouldn't lie about something so important, even if I was capable of getting away with it. My people found your parents."

"Why are you doing this?" Released from Rett's compelling stare, angry tears started filling Shannai's eyes. "I thought you were going to help. You're just making it worse."

Rett went on. "Their names are Shemet, Zairynthe, and Gulanai. Shemet is your birth father." Details she'd asked for, and details Trebor fed her from a ready supply. "You have a little brother, Irenet, and sister, Gulimethe, ten months and three years old. You call your little sister Guli."

"How do you know this? You don't have a com. Are you gifted?" Shannai stiffened.

Maybe not in the way Shannai meant, she wasn't. But on one hand, Rett counted herself gifted with the most extraordinary personnel in the GTC. And on the other, for now, she had the most doubtful, suspicious teenager she'd ever in her life met.

"Fang Two, get Shannai's parents on our frequency, all of them, the kids as well if they're right there. I don't care how. Do it." She leaned toward Shannai, who had closed her hand around her stunner and looked very ready to use it. "Listen to me. You never asked me if I had a com device—for that matter, any other device besides my Omni. I never claimed not to have a com. I've been in contact with my second in command almost this entire time. Since I've been awake. He's been listening in, and has heard everything all of us have since then. He's been working hard to try and find your parents, and to find a safe way to get you all back together. I told you that I would help you, and that's what I've been doing. I said I wasn't going anywhere. I haven't."

Shannai's chin rose in defiant tiff. "You should have told me. I can't trust anyone. *Anyone*." She glanced to Labonne and back to Rett, shaking her head, her breaths coming sharp. Her fingers tightened over the stunner's handgrip.

389

Rett didn't have time to argue the fine details. "Please, all I ask is one more minute. Your parents are on com right now. They want to talk to you. If I lie, then you can shoot." Slowly, Rett started reaching for her headband.

Shannai leveled the stunner at her head. It was only a fingerlength away.

This is not the time to find out if that thing has any charge left. Rett's motion froze. "All right, I won't move. But give me that minute before you shoot, Shannai. My pcom is open and on my headband."

At the girl's extra-hard stare of disbelief, Rett sent a quick glance to Labonne. "We don't make an issue of it, but the location of our pcom isn't secret. And since it's so sensitive it can be used without making a sound loud enough for someone else to hear unless they're right on top of us, it's usually one of the first things taken when we're caught."

Although she had included him in her suspicions, Shannai turned to Labonne for confirmation. At his affirmative nod, she clenched her teeth so hard Rett heard them grind together.

"*Kelani*, the sergeant's communications may have made the difference between death and safety for you and the others. Put your weapon down. If she lies, I promise you I'll deal with her, permanently." Labonne casually shifted his ML-12 so it covered Rett, but the sergeant noted his eyes didn't stray from Shannai until she lowered her aim. "Good. Now take the headband. Talk to your parents and find out the truth."

His calm, deep voice settled Shannai. She reached over and carefully slid her fingers beneath Rett's headband, slipped it off. The girl fingered the dark layers of material, locating the tiny hardnesses of the pcom's components on the left side, where the band narrowed and angled down to go behind the ears.

Her silver eyes were hard and bright when she raised her head. "This is going in the recycle chute with the rest of your stuff. You're lying! Both of you. Both of you are lying!"

"Com open speaker full!" Rett ordered the voice-activated controls on her pcom. "Shannai's family—*talk* to her!"

"Shannai?" When the female voice practically shouted from Shannai's hands, the girl was so startled she dropped stunner and headband.

With a smooth reflexive action that left Rett wide-eyed in admiration, Labonne fielded the stunner before it hit the floor.

"Nice," she said in a low voice, thanking all deities for Zetinorian reflexes. Shannai's weapon, low on power as it might be, could have discharged on impact with the floor. Unlike most Nyorfian weapons, Coalition issue firearms didn't have a sensor, of either the body heat or biological ID type, which would render them inert once they left the hand of an operator.

"Thanks." Labonne checked the stunner and slid it into his weapons harness.

The other kids were alerted now, and Thalom quickly came to Shannai's side. "I heard your mom, Shannai!"

The oldest of the group stood perfectly still, staring down at Rett's headband as if it was alive.

"I heard her, too. Where is she?" From Thalom's side, Safkas looked around the room.

"Shannai, Shannai love, where are you? Answer me—it's Mom! Please answer!" The woman's voice was thick with tears and high-pitched with tension.

Shannai reached for the headband, her movements slow and trance-like. The astonishment on her face was in no way amusing. "Mom?" Her lips formed the word, but no sound came from them.

"Shannai-baby," said a male voice as the woman's choked. "Are you there? We have to know where you are, sweetheart."

An infant started to fuss. The baby brother, guessed Rett.

"Shannai, can you hear me? Can anyone hear me?" asked the man.

"Shannai's listening," Rett said. "Don't stop talking. Let her hear all of you."

Then a small voice wailed: "Shan? Wan' Shan! Wan' Shan home?"

"Shh, Guli." A second male voice spoke in turn. "The Commander lied to you, and we're safe, Shannai. All of us are safe. It's you and the other kids who are in danger, not us. Some of the Special Forces people are coming to get you and the other kids. I'm coming with them, Shannai. Tell us where you are."

It was the combination of the toddler's plaintive wail and the second man's voice that broke Shannai's trance and with it, and an onrush of tears, the rest of the hard, suspicious shell crumbled. "We're on the storage level in section Y south, room 57," Shannai sobbed back. "Oh, Daddy, hurry. It's almost new day and Labonne said She might come early."

Nearly twenty-five miles as the jumper can fly, but we've three levels of complex and who knows how many Coalition troops between us. Great. "Fang Two, how long?"

"Hold tight, we're already moving," Trebor's voice replied. "We've some armored complex rovers and Shemet and Kalebetha are coming with us to show the shortcuts once we leave the rovers behind, but we'll be cutting it pretty close."

"Hey, Kalebetha's *my* mom. *My* mom's coming." Kallet squirmed into the front of the group. "Hey! You just tell her to be careful!"

"Must be Kallet. I'll make sure of it, sport," Trebor assured him. "She'll see you soon. And you can talk to the rest of your family in just a minute. Fang Lead, if Avok and company get there before us, you're going to have to get them to leave with you and not the kids, or delay the entire group from leaving best you can."

"I had something like that in mind. And, knowing Avok, a delay won't be a problem," Rett said grimly. "Once she sees me, she'll forget all about being on a schedule."

Trebor paused before speaking again. "I haven't heard anything negative about Labonne on this end, and what I heard him say over the com is encouraging. But you're there with him. Is he going to be a problem?"

Rett met Labonne's eyes. "I'll let Labonne answer that."

"I'll do what I have to for the children," replied the Zetinorian evenly, his eyes steady on Rett as his voice was to Trebor. "That's the only guarantee I can make."

"Understood, fair enough," Trebor said. "Connect to Fang Three when we're finished. I guess we've left him with a riot—now everyone needs to hear his or her child's voice. We're going to silence now. Luck and good deities go with you all." With that Trebor signed off.

Rett switched her pcom channels to her third-up's with a voice command, amused inside at the subtle note of panic underneath Sergeant Worren's tone when he answered.

~Poor guy. More deadly than the entire Coalition, enough to strike terror into the heart of Special Forces—a group of anxious parents.~ Pam inserted her own take on the matter.

No doubt, responded Rett with an inward laugh. *If Trebor left on the run, those parents are probably eating Worren alive.* On the outside, she nodded at Shannai to go ahead and take charge of letting the other children have a few words with their parents. "Take it over there."

After the children withdrew to their favored corner, her eyes returned to Labonne. "Is there any way you can take me out of here directly to Avok?"

"I considered that possibility. It would only raise her suspicion, since I am supposed to be elsewhere entirely. Even if I hand you over—probably especially since I did so—she might send someone after them." He glanced toward the children. "If your unit was only minutes away I would take that chance. But not now." 393

"Then I suppose we're back to the original plan."

"The one the children were told to follow? I think it would be safest for them, and best we do it quickly. I can't be certain someone else won't come in here at any time—and if they find me in here at all, it would not be a good thing. Especially since I am supposed to be with Commander Avok's group when she does arrive."

"You took a big chance to come, then."

He shrugged a little. "I promised. And I had to warn them."

"You're a good man, Labonne." Then a shiver skittered up her spine, leaving Rett suddenly feeling very alone. It didn't take long to realize Pam's spot was vacant.

Damn. She nearly knocks me on my butt every time she comes in, but I never know when she's getting pulled out until after the fact. No more help from that direction, although if Pam had come up with another one of her wild ideas and strange, but accurate, insights, nothing would have stopped her from telling Rett earlier.

I can't worry about Pam right now. All things considered, the bottom line remains the same. Avok gets me on a silver platter, as Pam says. What happens after that can go in several directions.

"All right," Rett said aloud. "Once Avok comes, I'm going to do all I can to get and keep her attention. The kids might have several avenues, depending on what happens once she gets focused on me."

Labonne nodded. "There's the lavatory. It opens into the service corridor." His deeply cleft chin indicated the direction. "The outer door is locked. I'm sure you know the access…Shannai or Thalom can memorize it."

"No guards or monitors?"

"No monitors, for some mysterious reason they keep breaking down, and any new ones shipped in are generally faulty. So the practice was abandoned. But it's patrolled, like this level. Right now there are guards only at intersecting halls, lifts, or stairwells."

"If you're not supposed to be here, how did you get past them?"

"One doesn't spend twelve years in a place like this without learning the exact pattern a patrol takes, as well as alternate routes and how to disable any motion sensors placed within them."

Rett nodded. *I wonder how many citizens of this complex he managed to get out of tight situations—like Jaq did.* "Now then." She made sure the children were occupied, glad hope and anticipation had replaced the darkness of uncertain fear in their auras. "Uhm, this will be a lot easier for us both if I wasn't awake for it. Better for all of you if someone should walk in, too."

"Agreed." Labonne reached for his sidearm and made an adjustment to the weapon's power settings. "I won't use the ML-12, too loud. This instead. Lower levels might not put you out completely, or long enough. Midrange acceptable?"

He sounds as if he's asking if I like my mushrooms broiled or steamed. "Midrange is fine, but please, don't get me in the head. I'm going to want to be able to think clearly right away when I wake up."

He nodded. "I'll quickly go over several plans and alternate scenarios with the children. If you have time when you regain consciousness, I hope you might also give them a few ideas."

"Right."

"While they're distracted, shall we?"

"Might as well." Having no desire to see it coming, Rett squeezed her eyes closed. *I've volunteered for a lot of things, but I can't believe I'm doing this.* "Wait." She opened her eyes and held up a hand to forestall the Zetinorian's fire. She almost wasn't fast enough. "Make sure Shannai gets a new charge for her stunner. She might need it if something goes wrong. Labonne—"

She locked her gaze with his, suddenly getting an insight into his reluctance to display his inner feelings to her. Rett extended the hand she'd raised, palm upturned. "My name is Rett, from Nyorfias. If circumstances allow, and it's what you want, you might not have to leave Complex 63. I doubt we'll find too many are unwilling to sponsor you." She motioned with her head toward the children. "And in our government, their opinions and votes count just as much as those of adults."

His eyes stayed with hers, unchanging for a moment, and then an incredible warmth melted the frost there. "Branwud Labonne, Zetinor Prime." A big, bony hand closed over hers.

"What name do you prefer to be called by?"

A small smile deepened the lines around his mouth and eyes. "Labonne has been my only name for a long time."

"Good luck, then, Labonne."

"Thank you. We'll all need it."

2.3.7 STORAGE ROOM 57, SECTION Y-5, COMPLEX 63
0535.13.24 (LOCAL RECKONING)

"Rett?"

Soft sobs came from somewhere close. A little sniffle sounded from even closer, followed by a gust of warm breath smelling faintly of spice-bush. Moving instinctively toward the child and meeting resistance, she remembered what had happened.

Small hands smoothed her forehead, patted her cheeks. "Rett? Are you dead?"

Her bleary eyes also met resistance, a blindfold. While it caused no physical discomfort, she had to put real effort into quelling the deep shudders threatening to come up right from her toes. Taking a deep breath, she instead forced her mind on the task of making a clinical comparison between the wakeup effects from a close-range, medium-power shot from Labonne's sidearm and one from Shannai's little stunner.

"She's not dead, Olvero," said Thalom's voice, patiently. "You should know that. She's breathing. She's moving. She's waking up, I think."

"But I didn't feel—"

"Shh! Just wait."

More feeling came back. Rett lay on her left side, still on the lumpy hill of stored roots, although she noticed right away the ridges had been leveled into more of a gentle slope. Her wrists were snugly lashed behind her back and finished in a large, awkward feeling knot—the sort a child might tie with the "bigger is better" thought in mind. A small, tentative motion of her legs was enough to know her ankles, likewise, were secured. Labonne paid attention to the details, she had to give him that. She could even work free fairly quickly if she put her mind and effort into it.

An ache of frustration and terror added to the post-stun headache and nausea. Just as it had in all of her nightmares since childhood, she feared the blackness would suck her down screaming one of these times. She scrambled to pull herself together now, desperately shoving down the near-panic.

"Rett, you're awake now. Oh! You're scared. Don't be scared. I'm right here." Olvero's sympathetic whisper and the touch of his small hands sent a shock of bright reason into her.

Stay focused, Rett, it's the kids that matter. She dragged her uneven breathing under control and cleared her throat. "Olvero. What's wrong?"

"You're tied up," he informed her.

His light touches were undeniably soothing. Four years old, untrained. What would he be like when he was older? "I know that," Rett said patiently.

"And your eyes are covered. Is that why you're scared?"

She sidestepped the question. "Who's crying? Was someone hurt?"

"Rett's not dead, Shannai," he called, the sound of his voice changing as he turned his head. "You don't have to cry any more." Each gentle pat of Olvero's soft hands sent warm brown and clear green impressions straight to Rett's mind, dispelling the last of the choking miasma of panic. "No one was hurt but you. Shannai is crying. She thought Labonne made you killed."

"Shannai needs a hug, Olvero. Go to her. You give good ones."

"And a big kiss?"

"Yes. A really, really big one. Maybe two."

"Maybe she needs three. Don't worry," the little boy assured her, "I'll make Shannai feel better."

I know you will. His absence left a cool spot next to her side, but Rett let the sounds of the enthusiastic Olvero comforting Shannai soothe her as well. She imagined the older girl cuddled him close just because it felt good.

"Here, blow," Olvero said. Shannai followed his instructions rather loudly and let out a watery, hiccupping sort of giggle.

Clearing her throat again, Rett asked, "Did Labonne say something else to get you upset?"

"No. I was looking over. It looked as if you both had made friends, but then he picked up his gun and fired, just like that. It knocked you right off the knotroot."

Compressing her lips a bit, Rett wondered if she should get into the differences between the weapons involved. Good thing he hadn't used the ML-12. Not only would it have knocked Rett off the knotroot: a close range stun would have sent her right into the far wall like a wind-driven drop of rain hitting a window.

"Yeah, it has a little more kick than your stunner."

"I thought…I thought he would just tie you up." Shannai hesitated again. "I don't understand what happened."

"I'm really sorry that it upset you so much, Shannai. If we knew you were watching, we would've explained. It must have been awful to see us giving names one minute and the next…something so violent."

"Why did he do that?"

"I asked him."

"Why?" Thalom's shocked voice was so closely twined with Shannai's, they sounded as one.

Now this Rett had to explain, to herself as much as the children. She took a breath. "A number of reasons. The main one? At that point, I couldn't trust myself to let him tie me up without fighting, even though my heart and mind said not to. I have limits. When I'm close to going over them, the reactions of my body can completely ignore the orders my mind gives it."

"The bad people hurt her before, very, very badly," Olvero whispered to Shannai. "*She* was one of them."

He's beyond an empath. His parents must know of his Talent. These children—do they take him for granted, comfortable with or unaware of his ability? Or do they consciously know of it? Deities! How many other people in the complex know? Does Avok know, too?

The thought made Rett's blood run cold. Was that one of the reasons Avok singled out this particular group of children? Olvero's value would be beyond estimate to the Coalition. If Avok was aware of Olvero's gift…it would really complicate matters.

"Shannai, I hope you can forgive Labonne."

"I hope so, too. I thought at first you were dead. I told him I hated him. I thought he was turning on us." The girl's voice was thin and tight. "I pretended I wasn't listening to anything he said after that. I didn't even say goodbye to him when he left." She sniffed. "I didn't even look at him."

"Then I hope you can forgive me as well. But listen, sport, I think he understood that you were scared and upset. Zetinorians can be very wise."

"Are there more?" asked Thalom. "There used to be three here, a woman and another man. Labonne said there were a few others, somewhere. But the Yixolryns can't stand them to be nearby. They end up killing them. We're always afraid Labonne will get killed when She finds someone else to do his job. You know a Zetinorian besides Labonne?"

"Yes, I do. He escaped to our side over on Nyorfias. He—"

Olvero crowed in delight. "You love him, just like Mommy loves Daddy! Oh! Is he just like Labonne? Do you know what? He must be very nice. Where is he? Will we get to see him?"

Rett groaned. *Damn.*

"You're in love with a Zetinorian?" This time there was a smile in Shannai's voice.

"Deities help me." Rett pulled her mental defenses into place, berating herself for her oversight. "Now all my secrets are in the open."

"We'll never tell," promised Kallet.

"Better not."

"But something happened—"

"Olvero," warned Rett, using That Voice, "if you or anyone else says one more word about it, I will *personally* make each of you eat stuff with bugs and boogers in it. Understood?"

Olvero gulped.

Thalom chuckled. "Yes, sir!"

Rett neatly changed the subject. "How long was I out?"

"About half an hour," replied Shannai.

"Everyone get to talk to their moms and dads?"

"Yes, a few words each," confirmed Shannai, "it was good but…now it's harder to wait."

Rett sighed and clenched her hands into fists, resisting a fresh temptation to free herself. "I understand *that* feeling. Did you get rid of my headband?"

"Labonne took it with him, and we're to tell Her we dumped it with your other stuff."

Then Olvero whispered to Shannai that he had to pee, and she sent him off with Kallet and Safkas as well, reminding them all to wash their hands.

"The lavatory." Rett remembered what Labonne told her. "Good."

"Why good?" Shannai wanted to know. "I hope you don't have to go. I should have let you before. I'd never get you tied up again, not like he did. It looks so uncomfortable. Does it hurt? Are you hungry? Uhm…do you need a drink?"

"Shannai, I'm fine. I don't like it being like this, and my interest in the lavatory has nothing to do with needing to relieve myself, so don't even think about untying me. Now, Labonne said it has a door going out. Tell me about it and where it goes."

"Yes. It's a regular door, it goes outside to a serviceway as well as here. But it's locked on the outside. I don't know the code."

"I know the bypass sequence that'll open any door or access in this building. Can you memorize it quickly?"

Shannai said she could, as did Thalom, so Rett gave it to them. "Keep that in mind as an escape route. If you get a chance, stay as close to that door as you can. Try to keep out of Avok's immediate line of sight. I'm going to be doing everything I can to keep her attention on me."

"Labonne mentioned that."

"It's very important that no matter what happens, no matter what she does or says, that you don't interfere. Don't worry about me. Do nothing to call extra interest toward you and the other kids. Olvero—"

"He talks a lot. We'll keep him quiet." Shannai said instantly.

Focusing past the hangover feelings of headache and mild nausea that weren't fading as fast as they should, Rett moistened dry lips and spoke again. "I have to know if his Talent is common knowledge. Does Commander Avok know about it?"

"What do you mean?"

Rett growled a soft warning. "Shannai, Thalom, the time to play games between us is long over. If you don't trust me by now, tell me."

"We do," mumbled Shannai.

"I grew up with empaths. I work with them. Olvero is extremely Talented, he's beyond anything I've experienced, and I knew it a long time ago. Now please tell me what I need to know."

"Just us and our families know," said Thalom just above a whisper, "since we're all neighbors, and maybe a few others his parents trust. We're not supposed to ever mention it, not even to Labonne—but I think he knows, too."

"If someone ever said something, we'd just say something else," added Shannai in a tight, low voice. "The Coalition would take him away if they knew. Me and Thalom have been worried about it. Olvero knows he's not supposed to talk about it, but he just blurts out whatever he feels from someone without thinking."

"He's just a little kid, and that's what little kids do, Talented or not. Let's hope that Olvero's gift is still safely unknown." Rett changed topic as she heard Olvero and the other children come close again. "Listen, I'm going to make a suggestion, take or leave it. Don't be afraid to say Avok's name. Avoiding it just gives her more power over you, whether she's around or not."

"It does?" asked Safkas.

"Yes," Rett said firmly. "And Avok loves having power over people, knowing they're terrified of her, knowing they hate what she's doing. Not using her name puts her on a more than humanoid level—"

"Like a deity?" asked Kallet.

"Well, we don't know the deities have any names. But if we knew them, I'm sure we'd use them."

"Is it like calling you Sergeant Killer instead of Sergeant Rett?" suggested Thalom.

"Exactly," Rett said, jumping on that better, more tangible example. "Exactly. People hear or speak of Killer as some superhuman entity. Which, as you all have discovered, I'm not. I'm just me. I make mistakes, I screw up, I'm just like anyone else. If I was so super, would any of us be in this predicament right now?"

"I guess not," said Kallet slowly.

"Same thing with Avok. It's a name all of us in this room associate with bad things, but it's just a name. And one of reasons she doesn't want you to look at her goes with that power she wants you to feel. Not to mention she's about as nice looking as a pile of…"

"Throwup?" offered Safkas.

Rett coughed to cover the more earthy metaphor that almost left her lips. "Yes, that'll do. Anyway, Avok is dangerous, evil, and cruel, and it's okay to be afraid of what she can do. But she's not immortal. She's not a deity, or even close to it. Remember that."

"We can try," said Shannai.

"Good. If there's nothing we can do but wait, we all might just try to close eyes and rest. Just remember this, if the Coalition gets here first, you all act like you know absolutely nothing except what they told you in the first place. All right?" Rett winced behind her blindfold as her headache spiked. She'd have to see if some deep breathing cleared it up.

Trebor, she thought, *you'd better get here first.*

The children moved away, but Rett wasn't alone for long. Material rustled overhead. She identified the object as it settled over her cold body. A blanket.

"I *know* you're cold, and your head hurts."

Before Rett could protest, Olvero slid his warm little figure beneath it and snuggled against the front of her, just as close as he could possibly make himself. Another blanket and a body burrowed close to her back. From the size of the body and boniness of the knees, Rett guessed Safkas.

"The bad people make Labonne's head ache and tummy sick, too," said Olvero sleepily, smoothing his small hand over her hair once, then a second time. Her headache started to ease. The third time, his fingers spread and combed through what short length she had, reminding Rett of the way she used to slide her hand through the sleek black waterfall of her mother's hair.

Maybe that was the reason Olvero's next remark made her nearly choke on her own breath.

"You know what? You have hair just like my Mommy, what's so slippery."

When Rett found words, they had nothing to do with her hair. "Olvero, when the bad people come, try hard not to mention what anyone is feeling. Anyone, the other kids, me, Labonne, the Coalition. Try not to say anything at all. Please, it's very, *very* important. Try really hard for me, okay?"

His arms slid around her neck and he kissed her cheek so sweetly Rett wanted to cry. "I will." Snuggling back down, he was asleep almost instantly.

"We're going to have mashed knotroot here in a minute," Rett said as she felt several more bodies settle nearby.

"We like mashed knotroot," murmured Thalom drowsily from somewhere near her left knee. In another second what could only be his head was pillowed on her calf muscle.

"And it's cold. When you're cold you're supposed to huddle together." Kallet gave a huge yawn that spanned at least eight distinct notes. He made himself comfortable on the other side of Olvero.

Now her arms jerked involuntarily and uselessly, wanting to cuddle Olvero and anyone else in reach, wanting more than warmth. She needed to feel she wasn't alone; she wanted to taste the security they felt. She wanted, for just a moment, not to be the adult.

Wild thoughts, get rid of them now. With a sigh she angled her face down so her chin rested against Olvero's tight black curls. The special perfume unique to babies and small children calmed some of her restlessness.

Even so, all her doubts crowded up again, letting the dark thoughts rise through the cracks in her defenses. *Not this again. So help me, I've had enough of that.* Gritting her teeth, she took a lesson from Pam. She built a sturdy mental box, packed her doubts into it, and wrapped it with an imaginary cable strong enough to support a fully loaded troop rover. *You already made your decision and the only way is straight ahead. No looking back. If onlys waste time.*

"I'm sorry, Sergeant Rett," Shannai said softly.

"For what?" She lifted her head, for the sake of showing she was attentive and ready to listen, if anything. She could only see Shannai with her energy sense, and what she saw wasn't reassuring.

"All this is my fault. You're not tiffed at me?"

"Good deities, not for a second. None of this is your fault, so wipe that thought. You're one of the bravest people I've ever met."

"Me?"

"Yes. You are."

"But I'm scared."

"Shannai, it's all right to be scared. You heard me before, I wasn't putting one on when I said I was scared of a lot of things. Right now we have to think past that. I know it's hard and you're tired, but I need you to stay strong for a while longer. So do the others."

"I don't want Her—I mean Avok, to hurt you either. What's she going to do to you? And I'm afraid for Labonne. He's just about part of our families, too. She'll kill him. And—"

Rett hardened her voice without raising the volume. "You see these kids? You, Labonne, and I have the same mission. The same responsibilities. Until they are safely reunited with their families, nothing else matters. *Nothing* else, Shannai. Whatever it takes."

The startled breath Shannai gulped down made Rett nod in satisfaction. *If she needs orders to focus, then I'll give her some.* "Your part in this mission is to take advantage of any openings Labonne and I create for you to get the others out and away from Avok. You gave the kids the right advice—don't show her you're scared. And don't try to fight her. Stand up to her. And wait for the opening. If you have to be scared—keep breathing, keep standing. Even if you have to stand there in tears, or shaking so badly you can't talk, or even if you pass out unconscious—do it without giving in. The very second you show her you have nothing left, nothing at all, she'll kill you."

Shannai swallowed. "I'll do my best." Her voice shook, but it was strong.

"I know you will."

2.3.8 COMPLEX 63, EPNOCE
0535.13.24 2815 HRS (LOCAL RECKONING)

TREBOR HELD UP A HAND as they came to a crossway. Glancing back, he met the level brown eyes of a short, powerfully built redhead wearing the outfit of a complex maintenance technician. At his gesture, she moved up to stand alongside him.

"This is where we split up?" Trebor asked in a soft tone.

Kalebetha nodded.

Trebor gestured for Nerrah and four others to go with the woman. "You know what to do."

The patrol moved off on the run.

Trebor motioned for Shemet. Shannai's birth-father moved up in turn. After a brief consultation, the rest of them moved. With luck, they'd meet from opposite ends of the same corridor. With better luck, they'd beat the Coalition there, but time was running out fast.

Once they had a definite objective, Lieutenant Evetez and Sergeant Tris had rerouted splinter groups from Easy Force and available infantry units to make as tight of a net as possible around the area—just in case the situation got away from Trebor and the part of F-troop with him.

Good thing Shemet and Kallet's mother knew these seldom-used service accessways. Even better that they had their heads on straight and proved they could move fast and quiet!

Soon, Trebor heard voices from ahead and pulled his people up short. "Com connect Fang Four. This is Fang Two, we're live. We'll have visual in a moment."

Nerrah's reply was gratifyingly swift. "Confirm live. We're in cover position and have targets under visual track. Any time you're ready."

405

2.3.9 STORAGE ROOM 57, SECTION Y-5, COMPLEX 63
0535.13.24 (LOCAL RECKONING)

"WELL, ISN'T THIS COZY? ARE we ready to get out of here?"

Trust Avok to make a big entrance, thought Rett.

The new voice roused the drowsing children as effectively as any Basic training drillmaster. Rett's own low command, which didn't go beyond them, sent the children skittering off the knotroot pile, away from her.

"Look here, Commander," said a raspy alien voice. "Looks as if they actually caught something for you." A scaly hand scraped against Rett's face and pulled her blindfold away. The relative brightness of the room, combined with a gust of breath that had the sickly sweetish odor of small, dead animals, made Rett's dry eyes start to water in protest.

It's one of those Voi. Should have expected a few of his kind to be among Avok's personal guard, she thought grimly, identifying the species before her eyes even adjusted.

"Look at this. It's even the right one." A hard nudge sent Rett rolling off the knotroot to land up against a pair of booted feet.

"Yes, we caught Sergeant Killer for you," Shannai said.

"Omni and IDs here confirm it," said another trooper.

Rett blinked her eyes clear. Whatever the reason, it wouldn't do for Avok to see any watering from them. They didn't have time to stand around while the Yixolryn female made a big production of it for her own amusement.

"A present for me." One of the booted feet slid beneath Rett and expertly flipped her over. "And *exactly* what I wanted."

Unlike the residents of Complex 63, Rett wasn't the least bit afraid to fix her flat stare directly into Avok's tiny, deepset eyes and keep it there. *I do believe there's been some improvement.* Rett noted several small scars, almost like the marks of scraping teeth, across the Yixolryn female's broad grayish-yellow forehead.

To call them humanoid was being as generic as saying they had two legs, two arms, and a single head. Rett supposed they were, after all,

406

there were instances of half- and quarter-blood variations. Commander Iheolon, for example—and the agents she had known as Mott and Shamos, whom she'd only recently discovered were related to him.

Avok stood contemplating Rett the same way Rett would eye a plateful of freshly roasted mushrooms. "So, while all of you were getting acquainted, Shannai, did this one tell you bad things about me?"

Shannai's answer was haughty. "I kept her stunned until just a bit ago. And it's cold in here. I don't want the little kids to get sick. She's big and warm and just there doing nothing, so we took advantage of the heat."

Good girl, Shannai.

"I've watched you and your friends for a while, Shannai." Avok had yet to break her stare with Rett.

Don't let her take you off guard, Shannai, she's going to try.

Avok had worked long years training her voice into attaining the qualities more associated with Nyorfian-type humanoids. It was rich, smoky, and capable of conveying a full spectrum of meaning and nuance. Combined with her solid grasp of Standard, even Nyorfian-localized terminology and context, it was effective as both tool and weapon.

That was, as long as Avok kept Nyorfians from looking her in the face. Having experienced Avok's voice firsthand in a variety of situations—especially one in particular—Rett would be the first to admit the Yixolryn female had an amazing talent. But Avok's complexion and physical features shot down any effectiveness the alluring, compelling voice attained with the Nyorfian variety of humanoids.

It's no wonder the kids thought she was some sort of untouchable superbeing, Rett thought.

Now the Yixolryn officer dismissed her to glance toward the others. "Especially you, Shannai. You're a smart girl. Did you think I'd pick just any group of kids to perform such an important task for me? Anyone can see you're a leader. You will have a great career as an officer in the military. I will make sure of it."

Such warmth and praise colored Avok's mellow tones that Rett felt real worry. She didn't often wish for psi ability, but now she wished she had the rarest of Nyorfian psi-talent: the ability to mindspeak. *Don't let her suck you back in to believing her. I wish you could risk seeing what's on her face.* For of course, none of the children would dare looking up past the Yixolryn officer's prominently boned knees. Rett hoped they wouldn't pick this moment to suddenly decide they were brave enough to do so.

"I don't want to be in anyone's military," a sullen Shannai answered. "I don't want to be a leader. I want the war to be over and I want to be a farmer like my mother and my fathers, and I want to go home to them. You promised us we could if we got you Killer."

"Yes, I did, didn't I? Quessl, put the restraints on Killer and then cut that webbing. Otherwise she'll be out of it fifteen seconds after one of us looks the other way." Avok's tone changed in a flash. "Quickly! Then get out and guard the corridor. Wik and the school warden will stay with me. You two, get Killer on her feet."

Vertigo rose, strong as the pull of gravity as Rett was hauled to her feet. She staggered as the magnetic field contracted between the metallic bands on her ankles and wrists, but didn't once remove her eyes from the Coalition commander. Hard hands held her upright.

"It's been a long time, Killer," Commander Avok said softly. "I look forward to having you all to myself… well, I might share you with Wik. I've been promising him a new toy, and we're starting out with you in much better condition than any of our prior meetings." Cold fingers touched Rett's face in a sharp-tipped parody of a caress, traveling downward to pause above her left breast.

For a long space of two endless heartbeats, every fingerlength of Rett's body froze except for that one spot. Starting with the ones directly beneath the press of Avok's clawlike nails into her uniform, a series of old scars burst into searing pain as if opened afresh.

"It's still there, isn't it, Killer? I've heard reports it was." Avok smiled and exerted just enough pressure to break the skin beneath without puncturing holes in the material. "But there's no blood. How can this be? Being repeatedly stunned and immobilized must have impaired your circulation. You look a bit pale, my dear. Here, maybe this will help."

Pain exploded into Rett's right leg, then the left. Caught unexpecting, she barely registered the first blow before the second landed. Already off equilibrium, Rett went to her knees. A sudden pressure around her throat choked back the hiss of surprise she would have made.

"You're bad!" yelled Olvero. "You're mean and yucky and bad! I'm going to kick you, see how you like it!"

Olvero, NO! Rett projected her feeling with so much effort her brain felt as if it turned inside out. With that same desperate surge of energy, she launched her body from its kneeling position. Too late the grips of her guards, which had relaxed somewhat when she went to her knees, tightened. The control loop they had slipped over her head went slack. Rett twisted her shoulders and was in the open before they could get fresh holds.

Unleashing still more energy from her ready muscles, Rett angled herself to intercept Olvero's rush. His leading foot caught against her hip and he tripped, falling on top of her. A shriek of anger erupted from his throat and the little boy kicked hard at what had kept him from his goal. Since she rolled toward him to knock him flat, that little foot connected a lot faster and harder than either of them expected.

I wouldn't put it past her to be going for a weapon right now. Without hesitation, Rett redirected the sharp pain in her hip into extra energy for her legs. The violent thrust and sweep to the right took the Yixolryn officer off her feet. With a surprised outcry, Avok fell back and to the left, crashing into the wall behind her.

Thalom, who had instantly sprung after Olvero, hardly expected Rett to suddenly be in front of him. His stumble landed him atop both Rett and the younger child. She turned her head so Thalom's eye missed a painful meeting with her chin and just as quickly brought it around so her mouth was close to both boys' ears.

"Olvero, stop!" Rett didn't bother to hide her anger, and in an extremely short-range version of That Voice said, "Damn it, *keep quiet!* Don't *do* anything else, don't *say* anything else!"

Olvero stopped kicking and snarling for a moment, his physical actions daunted by her vehemence. But his attitude remained unrepentant; his bottom lip thrust forward; his eyes dark and stony. Matter of fact, Rett had seen a similar stubborn expression from Ariam many times.

Avok's probably filling him so full of bad feelings he can't help himself. But it's going to get him killed, or worse.

"Thalom, keep him quiet! No matter what. Sit on him if you must."

Thalom grabbed Olvero. Already disregarding Rett's warning, the four-year-old started to rage and cry. "You're bad, Avok! You're a mean old liar! Let me *go*—! You're mean and bad! And you're...you're rotten and slimy and ug—*mmfph fnm io!*"

Thalom moved just in time. No sooner had he rolled away with Olvero and dragged him, kicking and screaming, toward the back of the room, a heavy tentacle fell with a *thwack!* over Rett's body and coiled around it faster than she could twist out of the way. The appendage wrapped three times around her, mashing her bound arms into her sides and back, threatening to dislocate her elbows, shoulders, and maybe even her head from her neck as they constricted with a force that squeezed the air right out of her body.

Over the roaring in her ears Rett heard Avok snarl, "Grab that little brat and bring him here!" There was no smooth richness in her voice now. It was as harsh and grating as any Yixolryns. "Bring him here, I said!"

"Please, sir, I have him, he won't do it again," said Thalom, his tone tight with panic, low with tension.

After a few more seconds, Rett realized she was no longer on the floor. Her feet were at least a half-length above it. The constriction had loosened only slightly. She took advantage of it to breathe in shallow gulps. She couldn't lose consciousness for any reason, not now.

Damn it. Why didn't she keep on me after that? Unless she knows about Olvero...or if she caught him looking at her. He used her name— I'm sure that caught her attention. Shit! Come on, Labonne...get her mind off him.

She remained passive in the grip of the tentacled alien, but gathered her energy into a tight, ready coil. If she had to cause another major struggle to regain the attention of Avok and her guards, she'd need every last bit of her strength.

"Commander, the boy is only a baby," Labonne said. "All he knows is that you hurt the first woman of his race he's seen in over a tenday. He doesn't know any better."

"He was going to attack me!"

"I'm not a baby! I'm four and I *mnphh n bhnff mmer!*" Olvero's incensed scream again disappeared into unintelligible mumbles as Thalom's quick hand clamped over his mouth.

"He has a...problem," mumbled Thalom as if Olvero's problem was a contagious disease. "He gets hysterical and...and has fits." He gestured to his head in explanation. "Didn't take his medication. We, uhm, forgot because of Killer."

The lie was shockingly blatant to Rett, but Avok seemed to accept it. The Coalition officer made a sound of exasperation. "Just keep those brats away from me, School Warden," she snarled at Labonne.

"Did Killer injure you, sir?"

The reminder brought a low growl of rage from Avok's stocky body. As she turned her head slowly to stare at Rett, there was an answering increase in the constriction threatening to crush Rett's ribs against her spine. "Bitch." The Yixolryn swung back on Labonne, her voice soft with lethal menace. "Spare me your empty sentiments, School Warden. Just keep your brats under control. They trust you. That's the only reason you're here. The very instant one of them gets out of line again, I'll turn Wik loose on them."

"Yes, sir," said Labonne, his voice toneless. He backed closer to the children.

"Zetinorian filth," spat Avok under her breath, returning her attention to Rett and the tentacled being holding her. "Let's hope he's the last of those. Keep your eyes on him, Wik."

A flapping, fluttering sound answered her.

This doesn't sound good, thought Rett as she finally made a mental connection of the vocal sounds to the tentacle wrapped around her.

411

Wide River Gap…the ambush near the bridge. *Unethi.* There had been a huge tentacled alien officer there, and in the few businesslike minutes it had handled her she had gained a vast respect for its strength.

Rett groaned inwardly. *Shit, so this is Wik. It must have moved in behind when they first came in. I should have guessed sooner… but there are more than one tentacled race with the Yixolryns. No wonder she didn't bring in more than a handful of guards, she doesn't need them. The creature's worth at least thirty normal troopers physically.*

"Wik, we don't want her dead. Not yet. You won't have anything to play with later if you kill her now."

More sounds, flapping, squishing, a not quite trilling whistle.

"I know what the Leader said. But we have to get out of here, first, we'll need her. Keep hold, but let her breathe." Waiting until Rett's feet were back on the floor, Avok moved closer and leaned her body comfortably into Wik's restraining tentacles. Rett noted that they didn't give a fraction either way.

Gently, as if whispering a secret, Avok spoke. "So you might have spared the child by knocking me over, but that move is going to cost you, Killer."

"Commander, we have to get going. The Nyorfians are going to cut off our outer exit route in no time." The voice came over the comunit on Avok's shoulder.

"Quessl? What's wrong with your voice?" Avok demanded.

"It's the dampness, Commander," rasped the guard on the com apologetically.

"Yes. I'd forgotten how these storage levels affect your kind."

"We have to go, sir, quickly," the voice urged.

"Yes, yes. You said that. Are any of those ragtag Nyorfian soldiers anywhere near this section?"

"I'm not reading movement in our area, sir, but we'll let you know."

I wouldn't imagine any of them are moving at the moment. Rett started to smile, keeping most of it inside, but allowing just a trace to show on her face. New energy flowed into her limbs. *It's about time.*

The voice on the com didn't belong to a scaly Voi trooper with bad breath, it belonged to Senior Corporal Pipano, who could imitate almost any accent with wicked accuracy, especially those of Yixolryns and the reptilian aliens who were their most trusted aides.

Wik's muscular tentacles started to tighten as Rett's hope rose. She had to wonder if the Unethi was Talented, or merely sensitive to body signals that would be invisible to others. She hoped it was the latter. *Squeezed to death. That's something no one's tried before*, Rett thought as her lungs flattened. *I wonder just how sympathetic any others might be to the Coalition... it doesn't stink, it isn't slimy, and it'd be great to have a few of these guys on the logging crew in Treetop...*

Her mind was drifting and she bit down hard on the inner flesh of her cheek to stay focused.

"Quessl, even if they get past you and the others they won't get much," Avok was saying. "I'll kill all of these sniveling brats, right in front of them." Avok, sneering, closed her com. She studied Rett's face for a moment longer before turning again to the guards who had failed to keep her under control. "Incompetent, brainless clods! Didn't I tell you to be ready for a move like that? Even under restraint she's dan-gerous. Look what happened to me!"

Rett knew what was coming next. The troopers weren't allowed the chance to make amends. Avok's sidearm made short work of them both, the thin, lethal energy stream seared a hole through the throat of one; the forehead of the other. There was a murmur of reaction from the children, who were probably too scared now to be very loud about it.

The Yixolryn's hand dropped to her side, but the weapon remained in her grasp. When Rett saw the commander's head turn from the dead troopers to the children, she didn't hesitate to give vocal evidence of her current state of distress, respiratory and otherwise. She hoped it sounded serious enough to distract Avok before the Yixolryn gave in to an angry impulse to shoot one or all of the children.

"Wik, you have to wait," Avok said, surprising Rett by the indul-gent tone of her voice. Anyone else would have been reamed—or killed

413

outright—for forgetting themselves once the Yixolryn gave a command. "I said to let her breathe. Let her loose so her blood can circulate. I need her mobile."

Wik obeyed, flapping softly to itself as it adjusted her restraints. The huge form that had been behind her all this time moved to the right, keeping the tip of one tentacle on the center of her back. To help her balance until feeling came into her feet, or for some other purpose? She kept her shrug inward and took it as an assist. As she stabilized and imagined her body re-inflating like some of the strange images—cartoons—Pam had showed her once, she took the opportunity to eye Wik from its huge flat feet to its face. Or whatever that thing sitting atop its midsection and covered with skinny purple sponges was called.

All the stability in two worlds wouldn't increase her chances if she had to fight it. That much was for sure.

At the very least I'd need my hands free, she thought optimistically. Then she gave her effort to breathing, hoping somehow to store extra oxygen before it was squished right out of her again.

"Wait. We caught Killer for you. You promised us our families back," Shannai said angrily. "Where are they?"

"Dead." Avok's contempt oozed thick, as stifling as mud from a bog. "Now shut up."

The children couldn't have timed their response more perfectly. Olvero, who had quieted for a minute or two, started his incoherent screams of rage from behind Thalom's muffling hand. Safkas started to wail. Kallet made angry noises that turned to sobs. Even Thalom started to sniffle, but Rett suspected that might have more to do with the damage he was taking from the compact little body that struggled, thrashed, and kicked against his. Olvero was probably trying to bite him, too. She'd heard several soft sounds of pain from Thalom already.

"Dead! But...you promised—" Shannai's shock nearly choked her. She swallowed. "We caught her. You *promised!*" Her voice broke on the last word.

"Stupid, naïve girl for believing her enemies."

Shannai was getting the whiplash effect from Avok's well-schooled voice: it was as derisive and cutting now as it had been warm and praising before. Rett longed to give the girl a glance of support, but she had her reasons for holding her stare on Avok. Although the Yixolryn was turned away, Rett knew Avok was very aware that Rett was watching her. That meant a great deal of the enemy officer's internal attention was diverted.

"You don't need your parents any more. The Yixolryn Coalition will see to your upbringing now." Avok's enjoyment of the children's anguish was obvious. "Now come along. We're all going for a walk."

The wails and sobs rose in volume. The children made enough noise for three times their number. If this was one of Labonne's suggestions, it was a good call. With the factors of time and room to run dwindling, making a loud emotional scene was the children's own best defense. If Rett hadn't known that an hour ago all the families were well and each child spoken to by his or her parents, she would have been convinced otherwise.

"Be quiet!" Avok's voice rose, sharp and harsh, but it only made the children cry harder.

"You might have let them hope until we reached our destination, sir. If you want to take them with us now, we're going to have to carry them," said Labonne. "They've waited twelve days to see their parents. They would have gone quietly and quickly had you given them hope." His voice was cold and loaded with exasperation, the low rumble of it cutting through the wails.

The sidelong glance of pure hate Avok gave the Zetinorian sent a flare of alarm through Rett.

"Carrying kids will slow us down, Commander," said one of the surviving Voi guards, casting a nervous glance toward Olvero and a visibly bruised Thalom. "And we need our hands free to make sure we can get you to safety. Wik will be occupied restraining Killer."

"You're right, Ionis. The brats'll slow us down. You, School Warden, since you seem to know better than anyone else, have the task of stunning the little monsters. Make it quick, so we can get out of here."

Deities, she's putting him on the spot—if he doesn't do it, for sure one of the others will. After she kills him.

"Don't," Rett said.

This time, Avok's eyes met hers completely. The thick skin on the alien's ridged forehead lifted in surprised query, a slick expression of pleasure slid over broad lips the same shade as her yellowish-gray hide. Rett knew she was taking a chance, but she didn't see any other acceptable options. She'd have to give Avok something the Yixolryn couldn't refuse.

"Don't?" repeated the commander. A knowing look grew. "Oh, that's right, stuns can kill the brats. And you'll do anything to keep them alive, won't you?"

"You don't need them," said Rett.

The Yixolryn female stood a head shorter than Rett, so when Avok stepped in close, almost touching, her breath puffed hot against the base of Rett's throat. "There's more where they came from. More brats than adults left in this system. What difference would five make? What can you give me to leave them alive and unstunned?"

"Your life, and my cooperation."

Some unseen signal from Avok sent the huge alien, Wik, to stand behind Rett once more. The remaining two guards she ordered from the room altogether.

Good, Rett thought. *That means no one is looking at Labonne and the kids right now. I hope he's taking the opening to work the kids toward the lavatory.*

"Your cooperation!" Avok laughed. Placing her hand and fingers in the exact configuration as she had earlier, she shoved hard, the talonlike nails driving deep into the bloody wounds on Rett's chest. The shove sent Rett back into Wik's solid form and all three of its thick tentacles wrapped firmly around her from ankles to sternum.

"Your cooperation." The nails impaled in Rett's flesh twisted and clenched.

Rett was glad of the pain. She put it between her present situation and the ballooning specter of old nightmares that threatened to break from their confinement. Greater than that threat was her fear for the children. Between pain and fear, she kept her focus. It would be just like Avok to suddenly turn and repeat what she was doing to her on someone who wasn't going to stand there and not show a reaction to it. Avok had done so before.

"And I can give you your life," Rett said. *As much as I prefer to take it.* She resisted the impulse to look down as Avok withdrew her hand.

The officer's bloody fingertips traced along Rett's right shoulder, up the side of her neck, along her lips, and down her throat, where her fingers lightly stroked back and forth above the choke loop.

"You're in no position to be offering me my life, Killer. Let's get back to your cooperation." With her idle hand Avok reached for something in a utility pocket. "Do you mean that you'll cooperate without this?"

The delivery end of an injector was laid lightly under Rett's jaw. She barely managed to turn her impulse to shudder into a nonchalant flick of her eyebrows.

417

"That won't get you what you want. You know what happens when people try to give me drugs," Rett said dryly.

"This is different from anything we tried in the past. Commander Iheolon's cousin, Sclamuse, has been very busy. I know they had hoped for the chance to test this on you. He was very certain it was refined enough to use without a device. That it would have only the…desired effects. I stole it, of course. But at least now I can report on its effectiveness. Or lack thereof."

Rett said nothing. The Coalition was aware of her drug intolerance—even though at first, Iheolon had refused to believe it. His disappointment didn't last long since he also kept a huge collection of devices to satisfy his… scientific need to experiment on Nyorfian prisoners. Or anyone else he took a dislike to. And now Iheolon had Shamos. Or Sclamuse, as she'd discovered his real name was, back at Complex 412 when Easy Force had been ambushed with gas traps.

Not only had she learned the real names of Mott and Shamos—but that they were also related to Commander Iheolon and shared his family name. And that Sclamuse Iheolon was as clever with chemical and biological inventions as he was with tech.

That it was possible the Coalition might have succeeded in creating a substance her metabolism wouldn't reject nearly stopped her pulse.

"Cooperation is an attractive offer," purred Avok. "Very attractive. I would prefer you not to be under the influence of any drugs or gadgets. It seems so much like cheating to use them. But your cooperation might not be enough, Killer."

"The choice is yours," Rett said calmly, as the cold material of the injector dug into her left carotid. "But whatever you decide, you're running out of time. Get me on a com. I'll activate our command frequencies and I'll tell them to clear this area right to your exit point."

"And is that all?" Avok's other hand, the one with the bloody fingertips, played with several strands of hair near Rett's left ear. She seemed fascinated with the way the slick strands kept avoiding her grasp.

"Your primary concern is getting out right now, isn't it?"

"Everyone needs incentive, Killer, even me. Staying alive means nothing unless there's something to look forward to. Your offer of command frequencies will leave two children behind and unstunned, one boy and one girl. Your coming along quietly merits the life of one more. A boy, I think. Yes. One more boy."

"Leave all the children unharmed and I'll do whatever you want," Rett said.

The flash of avarice that leapt into the Yixolryn's tiny black eyes was quickly banked, but not before Rett saw it. *She'd be a fool not to run with this. It can all but guarantee her advancement to direct second in command of the entire invasion force.*

The commander's smile grew, exposing teeth. "Oh? Anything I want?"

The cold alien tentacles were shifting around Rett's body, some sections of them growing while others shrank. The length of them was amazing and quickly banished any ideas Rett might have formulated about the alien having a limited reach. The flexible limb that had been around her midsection now easily covered her from hips to shoulders in six closely spaced loops. Slowly, these started to squeeze. The patch of warmth on her chest grew as the pressure forced more blood from the wounds Avok had made.

When the control loop started to tighten around Rett's throat, she guessed what the free tentacle now held—the leash for the device. Fighting back unconsciousness soon became a major effort.

"And how do I know I'll get it?" Avok demanded.

Rett didn't have breath enough for more than a whisper. "I give you my word."

"Yes. And we all have learned you mean what you say." For once Avok spoke without artifice, showed a split-second of honest respect. But the split closed as quickly as it had opened. "Anything I want. Even change your mind about that promise you made to kill me? I heard how you killed Ngaller. He was one of my most loyal servants."

"If that's what you requested."

"You would do that for me?" Avok's tone dropped, a note of speculation entering it.

"Don't delude yourself, Avok," snarled Rett with all the extra force she could muster. Her state of strangulation and breathlessness added harshness to her words without any effort of her part. "I am doing nothing for you. Any cooperation you get from me depends directly on the safety of these children. Nothing else."

"And if I kill them?"

"If the children are dead, or even harmed in the slightest way, you don't stand a chance."

In response to some unseen signal from his commander, Wik's tentacles contracted. The pressure was stronger than anything exerted before, compressing her chest, lower ribcage, and stomach, again sending what air remained in her body out any available outlet with a rush.

"Very well then," Avok said. Her voice sounded far away. "Your word on it."

Rett felt a vague surprise that it was only air that had escaped her body so far. Wondering if her head was going to stay attached, she managed to move it in an affirmative motion and make a grunt that stayed in her chest. The officer's cruel laughter registered like a distance echo and Avok's face was a swimming, yellowish-gray blur. Rett tasted blood, and the bittersweet, salty taste gave her an anchor point.

419

"Just imagine, they will think you're making the call on your own pcom. Never dreaming you, the unshakable Sergeant Killer, would ever spill any information worth a credit. How delicious. And afterward... think of the possibilities. Of course the Leader will want you, but I don't have to let him know right away, do I? Or perhaps I should, and have you make a personal speech to the Nyorfian people advising them to give up their resistance..."

Yeah. Right. If that's what it takes. But it won't make anyone give up. Fuck, my eyeballs are going to pop out.

"Yet I do have to keep you from Iheolon," Avok mused, tapping a forefinger against her lips for a moment. "He'll be sure to ruin my plans."

Rett didn't have to strain her imagination to see the greedy little fans churning in the Yixolryn's mind as Avok pondered the future. Then the pressure on her throat and body released. Conscious enough only to hear, unable to stand, Rett again slid to her knees at the officer's feet.

"I like you there," Avok purred. Cold fingers stroked through Rett's damp hair. "It feels very right. Maybe I'll keep you collared and leashed like a pet. I've already put my name on you. I knew you wouldn't mind if I added a bit of embellishment to it today." Avok's fingers slid under her chin, thumb toying with Rett's lips. "It is your destiny to serve me."

The change in the commander's voice shocked the haze out of Rett's brain. Chills raced up her spine and horror froze her guts. *Don't look up,* she told herself at the same time the sterner part of her demanded, *you have to, and make sure you have the right face on.* As Rett focused her eyes on the being before her, she expected to see something darker and more malevolent than Avok towering over her kneeling body. But no. Rett straightened her back. *Get back on track.*

Now the knife-sharp edge of Avok's thumbnail lightly raked over Rett's lips. "And you have given me your word."

"The agreement is valid only after we leave here and leave the children unharmed, Avok," Rett reminded, keeping her voice soft so it wouldn't rasp from squeezed chest and bruised throat.

The Unethi flapped something, and the Yixolryn officer chuckled. "Wik likes that you're so strong. Most humanoids would have soiled themselves by now."

Rett was rather surprised she hadn't.

"Now the question is: can you be trained?" mused Avok. "I'm sure Wik would like that."

The alien freed one of its other tentacles from Rett's body, letting it ripple loose and drop in a leisurely movement. It started moving up the inside of her thigh.

"Trained." Rett allowed the slightest bit of a sneer to wrinkle her nose. "You mean, like your pet Unethi back there? What did you threaten it with?"

Avok laughed. "I think she's trying to insult you, Wik."

A peculiar vibration thrummed through the alien's body.

"Wik and I have a mutual arrangement. Which, in time, my pet, you will come to understand the nature of."

I'd bite your entire hand off if I knew no one else would suffer for it, she thought as the end of Avok's thumb slipped inside her mouth, daring to slide against her teeth. Daring even more by adding a testing pressure against them.

"I'm sure you'll keep the both of us very well entertained."

Deities, please…I don't care what she does to me, as long as she doesn't do it to the children—or in front of them. They should be out of here already. She couldn't focus to check for their auras and cursed her weakness. *If they're still in here and she hears Trebor and the others are outside instead of her detail…*

Rett allowed her concern for the children to manifest in an outward shiver, knowing Avok would think it was her touch that caused it. *Can it be too much to hope that if they're still in here, they can't see what's going on?* Rett sent her heartfelt plea to those mysterious beings that seemed to take such an interest in complicating her life.

And then she realized that of all the local presences she should instantly account for, it was Olvero's, whether or not the child was in hearing or sight range. For certainly the talented little boy had established a connection with her the instant he'd thrown himself, weeping, into her arms. *Yes, it's there all right,* she thought, *just like Ariam's and Tova's when they were kids. That's probably why I didn't think about it before. Damn it. If Olvero were in extreme distress, she would know. The bad part of that is that if things start getting extreme with me, he's going to know too.* She didn't want to think about that happening to a four-year-old with such a strong, untrained talent.

I won't let it happen. But now that I'm fairly sure they can't see me, or are safely out. In case I'm wrong, I need options. Rett considered them, ignoring anything connected to Avok or Wik for the moment. *All right, the objective is for us to get out of this room—without the kids. And fast.*

The only way to speed that process and avoid even more of a scene here was to give the officer a sample of what she wanted. Not too much. Avok had no sexual attraction to humanoids. What she enjoyed was the reaction, and even when she wasn't getting one of those, she loved knowing whatever she did caused mental, physical, or emotional turmoil or pain. Rett knew for sure that right now, the Yixolryn was loving that Rett hated every second of being in arms' reach of her and helpless to do anything. But the commander also liked a fight. Offering no resistance at all would be just as dangerous as complete submission or, as Rett would be more inclined to show if the children were not a factor, total indifference.

So she pushed back every trained and natural instinct she had to resist, pushed down the bile threatening its way past the strangling pressure that increased again on her throat. Then Rett relaxed her jaw, just a little, but enough to bring another husky laugh from the Coalition officer that burned in her ears like acid.

"Very good." Probably just to prove that she could get away with it unharmed, the pad of Avok's thumb skated along in the slight gap between Rett's upper and lower teeth. "Very good, my pet."

Hearing the pleased smile in the officer's voice, Rett wondered if it would remain intact if she gave in to her impulse to vomit. *No, that wouldn't do any good. I'll just choke on it while she laughs. Come on, Avok, you've had your fun and the window is closing here. Let's get going.*

The thumb withdrew, traced the dampness from Rett's mouth over the outer surfaces of her lips again.

"Up," commanded Avok. At the insistent upward tug of the control loop and the tentacle now wrapped firmly around her left thigh, Rett struggled to her feet. "Now tell me again what you have to say, pet."

"Leave the kids safely behind," Rett said, trying not to sound strangled, "and I'll do whatever you want."

"Listen to this," said the Yixolryn. "Too bad Tyndal Iheolon never figured this out." Cruel delight flashed in every word. "Just throw a kid in front of her and threaten to kill it."

"Don't be hasty, Commander," snarled Rett. "I haven't heard your agreement to *my* terms. All agreements are off otherwise."

Avok was silent for a moment. "Agreed. The brats can stay behind, unharmed. I can't stand the sight or sound of them anyway."

"Commander, we have to get out of here now," urged a strained voice from outside. Pip again. His words and delivery offered Rett no clue to the situation out there.

A flapping sort of grunt from behind Rett was the agreement of the alien called Wik. Very slowly and deliberately, the grasp around her leg slid away.

Sorry, Wik, but getting groped by you or your owner just doesn't do anything for me, as much as you and she might like to think it does. She wondered briefly just what Wik got out of it. It had to have a weak spot. The effort of thinking gave her something else to focus on besides the increasing possibility of spending the near future as an amusing plaything for the commander and her sidekick.

"Come, pet."

A stinging snap of a tentacle across her lower back and butt sent Rett stumbling after the pull of the control loop.

Ten minutes with you, Wik, hand to tentacle, on even terms, that's all I want. It'll take you a flaming millennium for you to get out of the knot I'd leave you in. The corridor felt hot compared to the storage room.

"No, wait, get the littlest one," Avok ordered. "We'll keep him. Mentally deficient or not, from what I've been able to find out, there's psi talent in his genetic background and I want him tested. If he's not psi-able, well, then we have other uses for such adorable little humanoids.

Give that choke to me, Wik, but keep a hold on her." Avok's abrupt tightening of Rett's loop stifled any protest the sergeant might have made. "Call me capricious. Bring the baby, Labonne!"

Rett thought the words she couldn't say aloud. *Bring him out, and you're going to see just how much resistance I'm* not *giving you at the moment!*

"No." The Zetinorian's low voice was strong.

"Excuse me?" Avok stopped in her tracks and stood perfectly still.

"You're not getting your hands on any of the children."

A profound satisfaction lay behind Labonne's words, and Rett dared a glance toward the last spot she'd seen the children. The room was empty. She started to grin. *Yes. Oh yes. Labonne, if we survive this I am going to kiss you senseless.*

Avok whirled around, her ugly face a nightmare, her scream of rage a terrible sound. "Wik—*kill him!*"

The restricting tentacles slid away from her body, and Rett took the advantage to gulp air down her bruised windpipe. But before she could gather her reserves for a major commotion, another deep voice, this one long familiar, spoke six beautiful words.

"Movement is not advisable, Trooper Wik."

Wik was not inclined to take Trebor's advice. The alien whipped a tentacle toward its ML-12, but the sharp bark of a TT-1 brought an immediate recoil of the limb. Wik's flapping sounds came sharp and loud. A forearm-length section of tentacle wriggled on the corridor floor, leaving a trail of brown and yellow goo in its wake.

"Drop that leash and your weapons, Commander Avok, Troopers, and step back," Sergeant Trebor continued calmly.

Instead of letting go, Avok gave a savage tug that pulled Rett straight back into her body. The Yixolryn spat a hot, angry curse into Rett's neck. "Nyorfian bitch, you delayed me for this!"

Rett would have laughed aloud in astonishment had she been able. *Me? Me, was it? I delayed you? You were the one having so much fun in there you didn't pay attention to the time.*

Although short-statured for any Yixolryn, Avok possessed the heft and strength of her race. The Coalition officer didn't have much difficulty maneuvering them both into a nearby shallow recess housing a ladder that led to maintenance crawlspaces between the building levels.

Rett's inward grin was sudden and fierce: Avok had just trapped herself. She wasn't going anywhere. The Yixolryn was strong, but there was no way she was going up or down, much less managing the manual doors, while holding on to Rett.

Not that she'll have the chance, Rett thought. *Me being in front of her won't stop what's coming. Thank all deities. Avok's finished.*

But a sudden commotion and a babble of voices from the storage room turned Rett's relief into a soft groan of dismay. The sound she made went unheard over the flaps and whistles of pain and rage from Wik. The children had been in the lavatory—but instead of waiting there as the plan dictated, they'd come out. Wik, moving with an agility its size denied, fluidly ducked toward the open door. She heard and saw Wik get hit at least five times, but the bullets didn't seem to slow it down.

Body shots with regular ammo isn't going to do it! Use explosive slugs and aim for the tentacles, the face, just like someone did before! Rett wished again for a telepath's ability.

Wik's destination was soon blocked by Labonne's tall, rawboned frame.

"Stop, Wik!" the Zetinorian thundered.

Uncertain now, the huge alien halted. "What do, 'Bon?" it flapped, agitated.

"Damn it, close the door, Shannai, close it now!" ordered Labonne. He was too far from the door controls to reach them, and it was obvious he knew that if he raised his weapon or made a quick movement, a commando rifle would take him down—possibly leaving Wik a clear path to the children.

Labonne made his choice, and Rett's heart went out to him. The exposed portion of his face was grim and set as he prepared to stop Wik's charge with his own body.

"Sweet lords of mercy, Shannai," the Zetinorian said over his shoulder, "close it!"

"I'm trying…it's stuck!"

Wik's tentacles shivered, the spongy feelers on its "face" vibrating so quickly they were a blur. The hesitation from the Unethi surprised Rett. Was the creature hurt more than she thought? Or was it instead possible, somehow, the Zetinorian had made some overture of friendship or favorable impression on the alien trooper?

"Back off, Wik." The Zetinorian's bass voice was flat and deadly.

"Out way or die, 'Bon!" flapped the alien.

"No choices, Wik! Kill him!" screeched Avok on a note of disbelief that her dedicated assistant would even hesitate.

Whatever the reason, Wik's moment of indecision passed. Labonne and Wik charged each other at the same instant. The Zetinorian never had a chance. One whiplike snap of a tentacle, moving with impossible speed, snagged Labonne's ankles and jerked his feet right out from under him. He went down hard on his back, the sound his helmet made against the pourstone floor loud.

In the next second another commando TT-1 fired and Wik shrieked as its attacking tentacle separated—close to its body this time. The severed tentacle, however, completed its mission and sent the Zetinorian's ML-12 flying before falling to the corridor floor. The larger section of limb flopped like a beached steelhead, spraying fluids everywhere. The children screamed afresh as the oozing appendage writhed and looped toward the open door.

Labonne wasn't done, already reaching for his sidearm as he rolled for a better position. But Wik was faster. Already it had its own sidearm in action and fired the energy stream into Labonne's face as the man started to rise. The humanoid slammed to the floor, inert, not even a twitch from his body.

"Labonne!" The concerted scream of fear and dismay from the children sounded with Rett's sharp gasp of regret.

Wik staggered when the next two shots hit, his whistles and flaps louder than before. The last tentacle hung by a thread of flesh from the alien's thick body.

"Wik!" Avok sounded genuinely upset. One of the hard arms holding Rett moved as if to go for a weapon.

Should have thought of that before you tangled up with me, Rett thought grimly, and kept Avok's attention by giving her enough of a struggle to concentrate on keeping control of her rather than getting to a weapon. Fearing the commander had actually reached her weapon, Rett threw her weight hard to the left. As Avok twisted frantically behind her to retain her hold and position, Rett's effort was rewarded by the sound of the officer's sidearm dropping to the corridor floor.

"No! Back! Get back!" Thalom ordered in a harsh grunt, one of extreme physical effort. Rett couldn't see them any more and the part of her not engaged in keeping Avok busy agonized over what was happening there. "Ugh! There…back inside! Kallet, get Olvero! Shoot, Shannai, shoot!"

"Get inside, Thalom!" The quiet hum of Shannai's little stunner was echoed by the sharp, percussive report of another commando rifle. A high-pitched whistle like nothing Rett had heard before preceded a squishing whack. *Wik's down.* The storage room door finally snicked closed a second later, cutting off the sounds of the scared and upset children.

"Quessl! Ionis!" shouted Avok, her nails shredding through the material of Rett's uniform. "Damn them, where are they?"

Rett's energy faded with every labored breath. She'd better stop giving Avok so much trouble and let Trebor or whoever had them targeted get a clean shot. She let herself go, becoming a dead weight. The sudden change nearly threw the Yixolryn off her feet.

The tension of real fear replaced most of the arrogant swagger of the enemy officer who struggled for balance behind her. *Avok finds herself unsupported. Of course Trebor has her completely cut off. Now if I was positive the kids are finally safe…this would be a lot easier,* Rett thought wearily.

"Commander Avok, are you looking for your guard detail? We had a discussion with them already." Trebor spoke in such a completely relaxed and conversational manner that he might have been leaning back in a chair nursing a beaker of ale. "Odd, isn't it, that most of them decided our offer was much better than any they'd had from you."

"My personal guards were loyal to me," snarled Avok, standing firm now. Her nails dug deeper into the bloody furrows she'd already left in Rett's skin.

"A few of them, yes. The Voi. If you look a little farther to your right, you'll see what became of them." Trebor finally moved into plain view, his weapon in a casual position that matched his tone of voice.

The pressure on Rett's throat eased, and for a moment, she actually believed Avok was giving in. No. The moment of slackening was just so a flick of the commander's wrist could send a length of the leash into a loop that settled over Rett's eyes.

"Oh no, my pet. No you don't," Avok hissed. "No eye contact. I know how that works. I warned both Iheolon and the Leader back in Circle. But did they listen to me? No." With the commander's last word, the pressure returned, forcing Rett's head back and to the left. Rett's gasp wasn't from the choke loop cutting off her air this time.

Ow—shit! She barely managed to keep it in her thoughts. The red line of pain threatening to cut right through her eyelids was checked only by the bridge of her nose.

Then Avok's body molded itself against Rett's back, the commander's hard arms weaving into an even firmer locking hold between Rett's bound ones.

Guessing Avok's intention, Rett fought another urge to laugh. *It's not going to happen, Avok. Not today, not any day. Do you think me being in front of you is going to stop Trebor or anyone else from taking you out? You're not getting out of this. If you wanted to try getting away with a hostage, you should have picked a civilian.*

"I don't know why you're taking all this trouble," observed Trebor. "There's nowhere you can go. If you surrender now, you'll be treated impartially."

"The only way you'll take me is to kill your own platoon leader. Which you won't do."

"If she's the only thing between me and a clear shot at you," Trebor said evenly, "I'll shoot right through her. Besides, if I let you go just to keep her alive, she'd kick my ass into the next inhabited star system. Which, last I heard, is too damned far for me to think about."

That's right, Trebor. An appreciative chuckle managed to slip past the darkening pressure on Rett's throat.

"Sarge, the kids are safe in that room now. Carakenne and Med are in there with them. They went in through the back. That lavatory access had a few guards the kids didn't expect, which is what forced them to come back through prematurely. But we took care of it."

Rett was glad Trebor had told her. That was all she needed to know. Letting go that tension was a great relief. Any elevation in energy she'd felt had vanished, and she had barely enough strength to resist the pressure threatening to crush her eyes to jelly and snap the vertebra in her neck. "Thanks," she tried to say, but only a choking sound emerged.

"What was that? Was that what you said earlier? About doing anything I wanted?" Avok's voice lost any smooth richness, not with anger this time, but outright desperation. Another moment of slack on Rett's head and neck made a small spot of brightness in her brain.

In that moment she thought of a lot of things she wanted to say to Avok, in a lot of ways. For practical reasons, she kept it simple. "You're fucked."

The Yixolryn was doing something with one hand back there, but Rett didn't move, she didn't want to mess the shot she knew Trebor was ready to take. She visualized exactly where it would hit her, where it would hit Avok. Avok would be gone, unable to hurt anyone any more. That was all that mattered.

There was a hard jab and burning sting in her ribs. In the time it took for her to comprehend that Avok had managed to inject her, Trebor fired and a line of heat and motion whined between her ear and shoulder. Rett was jerked back as something exploded in a wet burst from behind her. Then she found herself falling heavily forward with Avok's dead weight locked between her bound arms. The death grip on the leash wrapped around her neck and face twisted her head even more to the side.

I wonder if this is going to hurt.

To her surprise came separation. The dead weight pressing her down was suddenly gone. The burning, choking pressure of the control loop was broken. Strong hands caught her upper arms. They didn't keep her from going down. Rather, they managed her descent into a controlled landing instead of a crash.

A Nyorfian adult's voice rang out in an exultant cheer. "That's the way, Labonne!"

Shannai's father. Rett identified the voice even as she settled like wet toweling over the armored body that was attached to the arms supporting her. And Labonne—it must have been a stun shot Wik hit him with. She knew how well Zetinorians could handle stuns. *Thank all deities he's not dead.* The material of Labonne's armor was cool and hard beneath her nose as she gasped for breath. *Again I owe a Zetinorian for my life.*

"Don't make any more sudden moves, Trooper. Drop the knife." Trebor's voice was closer now, just out of kick range by the sound of it.

So that's what the extra hardness in his right hand is, thought Rett as Labonne loosened the grip on her left arm enough to allow his weapon to fall. Trebor's foot swished it aside.

"Hands off her—slowly. Move them where I can see them—straight out to either side of your body."

Rett lifted her face and tried to get wind enough to speak. Her first attempt made her cough, but the next came out. Sort of. "L'bon... thank—"

"It's all right," Labonne said softly. "I'm glad it's over."

His fingers released her arms. She felt the multiple plates of his chest armor shift under her as her weight settled fully over him. Then a faint scraping sound against the floor as he obligingly moved his hands away from her and any weapons he still had on his body.

* * * * *

COVERED NOW BY A FEW of those who had come with him, Trebor shouldered his weapon and crouched beside the two prostrate humanoids. The Coalition trooper had done more than break the sergeant's fall. If the man's reflexes hadn't been fast enough to slice that choke line and kick the dead officer's body aside, Rett would more than likely have her neck broken right now.

He unsheathed his knife as he addressed Labonne. "I have to admit we came close to nailing you a few times, especially after we thought you were already down. I would have sworn that was a stun on the highest level." Trebor eyed the leftover lengths of the choke loop on Sergeant Rett. Two quick touches of his knife blade released the remaining pressure. "Then I realized what you were doing. Thank you. You also have a lot of supporters in this complex. I was actually threatened with bodily harm by Safkas' great-great-grandmother if anything happened to you as much as the children."

Rett started to laugh at the pained sound Labonne made, but her amusement turned into a fit of hard coughing and strange throat sounds instead.

"If we can expect your cooperation, Trooper, you will not be forcibly restrained."

"I'll cooperate."

"Good. I'll ask you to please remain perfectly still until you are disarmed. I'll get the sergeant off you so you can breathe." As he matched his words with action, Trebor frowned over the magnetic bands that bound the sergeant at wrists and ankles. He'd have to find the control, who would have them? Probably on the dead officer or the tentacled trooper. *Damn, I didn't think it was going down at all. Looks like that description the Sarge gave us of that officer she encountered at the Wide River Gap.*

Wonder how many more of them the Coalition has? Trebor returned his attention to her neck and head, with care removing the cut pieces of the Coalition's control loop. He had a little trouble with the part that had dug so tightly into her throat, and was unable to see the damage it caused through the blood there. His eyes went to the bloody circle just above her left breast and the slashed, bloodstained material from shoulders to wrists. Frowning, his attention returned to the platoon leader's face, where a nasty dark red welt was already swelling over her eyes.

Good thing Avok's dead, he thought grimly.

Returning his knife to the sheath, he glanced up as Pipano respectfully ordered one of the civilians who came with them stay back.

"What is it, Shemet?"

"Please, go easy on Labonne." Shemet looked highly disturbed as he glanced around at Trebor's detail.

Trying to understand the source of the civilian's new distress, Trebor's gaze followed the trail Shemet's had taken around his group. No wonder. Their long-time school warden was flat on the floor and targeted by no less than six weapons.

"Maybe he's in their uniform, but he's always done his best for us, especially for the kids."

"We have yet to use force against him," reminded Trebor, "and will not, unless he gives us reason. For now, we'll stick to our operational procedure. Your opinion and that of others will carry a great deal of weight in his assessment and debriefing. His actions of the past few hours, especially the past few minutes, are also very much in his favor."

Rett tried to add her own statement to that, but all that came out was a squeaking hiss.

Trebor translated. "The sergeant's spoken in his favor as well."

Shemet let out a sigh of relief.

"Besides," added Trebor, finally allowing a trace of levity to lighten his formal, serious tone, "I've no desire to go back and face the wrath of Safkas's great-great grandmother."

The civilian rolled his eyes. "No one does."

"This brings up my next question. Why didn't you set that formidable old woman on Avok a long time ago?"

Kallet's mother laughed. "Maybe we should have, instead of spending so much energy and effort keeping her quiet and out of trouble."

"Both go see the kids." This time Rett managed to form words. "Waited long enough."

"What was that?" asked Shemet, peering down at the sergeant in puzzlement and concern. "Will she be all right?"

Trebor nodded. "Nothing our Med can't handle. Sergeant Rett suggests you both join the children. They'll all be glad to see you. I'll com Corporal Carakenne to unlock the door for you. Stay in there with them. As soon as we've confirmed a completely secured route to the main complex and cleared most of this," he nodded at large to the scene of violence, "we'll take you and the children back."

Shemet and Kalebetha wasted no time going to the storage room. Trebor almost couldn't com Carakenne quickly enough and wondered if they would go through the door before she opened it from inside. Fortunately, she was waiting nearby for his signal, and the two parents didn't even have to slow their stride as they passed through the portal.

"Have a few bodies in here," Carakenne said softly, and instantly Pip and Steffi went to bring them out. Then the door closed on Carakenne's smile and some very happy voices.

"Deities, Trebor," his platoon leader wheezed, "sure you don't want my job? You do it so well."

"That's only because I keep getting the easy parts," he answered with a chuckle. "Com connect Razor Lead."

* * * * *

TRYING TO AVOID ANOTHER THROAT-TEARING bout of coughs, Rett fought down her urge to laugh. Deities, but her eyes burned! The lack of compression across them had felt glorious for the first three seconds. She blinked furiously, hoping the damage wasn't permanent. Then she managed to get a blurred glimpse of the Zetinorian, who remained motionless, on her right.

"Med!" She wasn't going to have a voice at all before long.

"Right here." Med touch was firm and reassuring. "And you're asking for me? Well, so you should be, but I'll have to mark that down."

"You wish." Rett coughed again and forced herself to swallow. "Not me—L'bon," she croaked. "He's all over blood."

"It's your blood," said Med. "Well, mostly your blood, some is from that...female, and some of it from his nosebleed."

"Mine?"

Trebor interrupted. "Labonne caught a stun in the face—"

"Saw that," mumbled Rett.

"I suppose most of it hit his goggles and helmet, which must have, in turn, deflected a good deal of the effect. He went down, but he never went completely out. That's the only way I can figure it out."

"Whatever the reason, it was fortunate for you," added Med. "The way Avok had your head twisted around, you would have broken your neck falling with her weight attached. But that's not what concerns me at the moment." His quick hands had already divested Rett of the top half of her uniform and moved over her slashed arms, the wound on her chest. "Those claws of hers made a mess of you for sure."

Now that she had time to think about them, those scores burned as if made with acid instead of sharp alien nails. *If anything would get past my immune system and give me an infection,* she thought, *it would be Avok's nails.*

"I saw him take the shot right below the goggles, though, Trebor," Med said then.

"Maybe it wasn't as hard of a stun as we thought."

Rett wondered if they had forgotten certain Zetinorian peculiarities so quickly. Then again, she still had trouble believing she'd witnessed Jaq take a direct hit between the eyes from an ML-12's full stun—an even stronger level than the weapon Wik had used—and regain consciousness in less than ten minutes. *Oh. That's right, they don't know Labonne is Zetinorian yet,* she reminded herself. *They'll find out shortly.*

"Jessek?" she asked then, needing a little more detail than Trebor had managed to tell her earlier.

Med sprayed something that cooled the fire in her arms. "He's stable and resting now, in the main med section here. We need to get him back to the main base as soon as we can. All I can tell you for sure is he's alive, going to stay that way, but he won't be coming back to us."

"Mikel and Steffi will get to see him...?"

"Yes," said Med patiently. "We'll do the best we can."

"I don't feel good."

"I know."

"Why am I still tied up?"

"Uhm...good question. Bhayorn—can you see to that? Thank you."

"Ow. *Hurts.*" Rett squirmed in irritation, trying to duck her head away from Med's hands.

"Hold still, Sarge. It's only a little piece, but it's bleeding like you severed an artery."

"Little left, or missing?" Rett's voice squeaked. *Deities! I hate those flaming chokes,* she thought with an outward snarl. *I hate sitting here restrained when I don't have to be.* A growl followed, threatening enough to make Med's hands pause.

Impatiently, she shrugged to let him know her thought hadn't been for him, and turned her mind back to what she hadn't seen or might have misinterpreted. Her head felt funny. Her guts felt worse. There were bugs crawling all over her.

"I don't feel good, Med," she said again. "But what happened to—"

"Not now," interrupted Trebor's voice firmly, and Med echoed him. "I know there's a lot to be covered from all our angles, but those kids and their families are anxious to be back together, Sarge. We can talk later."

She bared her teeth. "Someone get these things off!"

Either they didn't hear, didn't understand, or ignored her. She twitched. It was getting very hot.

She heard Trebor tell Nerrah to see to Labonne's disarming and listened as Nerrah made the formal inquiry of his willingness to surrender peaceably, submit to the disarming procedure, and to state his full name and planet of origin.

Seconds later when, as Labonne gave his name "Branwud Labonne, Zetinor Prime," Rett heard various soft exclamations of surprise come from the other F-troop members with them.

She turned her sore neck and strained her fuzzy, aching vision just enough to note Labonne's shaggy locks were varied shades of silver-gray; the central crest nearly pure, blinding white. After that she had to close her eyes. Not only from the extra sting of the light reflecting off that hair, but its reminder to her of Jaq.

"What is it with you, Sarge?" muttered Trebor. "Starting a collection?"

I only want one of them. And he's not around. How can I collect something I can't keep? The extra soreness in her throat and sting in her eyes had nothing to do with the recent abuse those organs had taken.

435

"I suppose I shouldn't be surprised," said Med finally, "considering the way he shook off that stun, but I am. And here I thought we cornered the market on Zetinorians already."

"What?" There was a hopeful note in Labonne's resonant voice. "You know of others?"

"One we know of," said Nerrah. "He's cursed on the Sarge." There was an unusual note of wicked mischief in her soft, cultured voice.

"Nerrah—" Rett's voice caught and stalled on her protest. She tried to glare in that direction instead.

"Really? There were two others here for a time. No longer. I was beginning to think I was the last." The Zetinorian sounded hopeful.

"Our Jaq's on assignment elsewhere for a term, but he'll be back with us before long. I know he'll want to see you, too. When we get things settled with you, maybe we can arrange something."

436   *Nothing like being sure of ourselves, are we, Nerrah?*

"You'll have to help him a bit," Med said to Nerrah. "He'll be off on the left, he took his entire fall on that side. As soon as you can, I want a gelpack on his face to keep the swelling down. And, Zetinorian or not, he's going to be out of balance from the stun for a while yet."

"I'll take care of him," Nerrah said.

Zetinorian charm at work? wondered Rett. Nerrah had gone all goofy over Jaq, too. Good thing Trebor wasn't the jealous type, although he had been known to discourage a few from expressing any interest in his long-time lover.

"Why'm bleeding, Trebor?" Rett asked then. "You miss?"

"I never miss." He sounded offended at the very idea.

"I 'spected it in the throat."

"You almost got it there. But she was having a hard time believing I was serious. She couldn't resist taking a look."

Rett nodded just enough for Trebor to know she made a deliberate motion. She hurt too much for anything else. "Sure she's dead? And Wik?"

"Yes. Enough for now. I want to move you and Labonne out of here and finish cleaning up a bit. As much as kids seem to like gross stuff, I don't think them seeing Labonne with his face such a mess, or you hair to boots blood with that lumpy shit all over you, would go over well. So if you're ready? Can you stand?"

Med protested, "That's not such a good—"

But Rett had to get up, and Trebor must not have heard Med. As soon as she was vertical her knees collapsed and she started falling again. Good thing Trebor was there to hold her up.

"Why do I feel like I'm zoned? What lumpy shit?" She tried to peer down at herself and gave it up as a bad job. "I'm hot." And she was, she felt sweat breaking out all over her body.

"Trebor hit Avok's left eye with an explosive slug, so you're wearing a good bit of the results."

"Aww, yuck." It didn't help her current state of distress. "Why's happen to me all the time?" She then realized her nose was practically plastered against her second in command's collarbone. He needed a shower. She probably did, too. "There's things crawling on me, Trebor. I'm going to throw up."

"Not on me you're not. Just breathe. Med, I haven't seen her this zoned since…well, never, actually. Do you think Avok—"

A sharp pain in her side was Med's hand, probing the burning spot over her ribs. "Ow! *Shit!* Damn it, Med, that hurts!" Trying to shout started her coughing again, which hurt more.

"Something's not right here, just listen to her," Trebor said, his voice vibrating against her. That hurt, too, and she tried to push away. He held her steady. "Sarge, take it easy."

"I want to go home."

"Shit. Avok managed to inject some kind of drug, and damn it, I didn't notice. There were so many other things going on, some hypoxia, aftereffects of multiple stuns, bruised inside and out—" Med sounded upset.

"S'okay Med, you can be wrong once in a while," Rett whispered, trying to reassure him as she struggled to keep her balance. "I'm hot and I need to pee." Her body wasn't listening to her, and neither was her mind. She tried to stop the words that kept coming out of her mouth but she couldn't. "And I was squished. And I'm blinded, and I only have one ear," Rett mumbled plaintively to Trebor's collarbone. *I can't even blame Pam for what I'm saying this time.*

"Sarge," Trebor said, sounding weary and patient, "you have both ears. Everything's attached. Nothing is crawling on you, either."

Anger sparked through her now. She twisted against Trebor, causing him to take a better grip and shift his balance. "There's things on me, and I'm still chained up! Get them off, Trebor."

"There are no restraints on you. Bhayorn took them off a while ago."

"But why—"

"Sarge, shut up." Trebor's hand clamped over her mouth.

Rett couldn't believe it. She was too tired, all she could do was lean into her second with sweat and blood and crap and things crawling all over her—and wait to die.

438   "Can I have the new command codes for our secure network?" Trebor asked, moving his hand.

Rett tried to glare at her second. "I think I will throw up on you, after all."

"Thanks, that's all I wanted to know." He clamped his hand over her lips again before she could say anything else. She groaned and considered biting him.

"That was… interesting," she heard Med say.

"I had to check. She's spouting off out with everything else on her mind."

Am not! She was going to bite him, hard. Since her teeth were the only things not hurting and his fingers were right there, it would be easy.

"She doesn't need any more agitation," Med said. "I need to shut her down before that stuff goes any deeper, but she's so out of control I don't dare. Move your hand, Trebor, you're upsetting her. I want her to stay calm."

"Allow me."

It was Pip. She wanted to tell him he did a good job on the voice thing. But now she was really starting to twitch, and there were strange prickling sensations going up and down her sweaty spine. Trebor still had his hand on her mouth. Didn't Med tell him to leave off? She growled.

It was just as well at that moment he moved his fingers and handed her off to Pip.

"Easy, Sarge." Again Pipano's familiar voice deflated her. "Come here. I have you."

"Watch out for my back," Rett told him, keeping her tone to a whisper. "It's all over muck. That stuff'll infect you, sure as anything. And don't squish me."

"We'll take care of it, Sarge," soothed Pip. "Don't worry."

She peered at him, trying to blink her vision clearer. He looked different. "Deities, Pip, you really need to do something about your hair. It's all over the place." Something was very wrong with what she just said, but she couldn't figure out what it was at the moment. "Didn't know you had any."

439

"I don't, Sarge," confirmed Pip. "Haven't had hair on my head since I was your age. Just eyebrows. Listen, Med's given us a nice oxygen pack for you and there's transport back to a medical station, but I need you to do me a big favor first."

She loved Pip. She'd do anything for him. "Sure, Pip. Name it."

"Pass out."

She blinked. "Now?"

"Now would be good."

"Maybe it better wait, Pip, you'd just have to carry me."

"Oh? And were you going to walk, Sarge? You can't even stand up."

"Oh," mumbled Rett. "I can't feel my legs either, but they're all itchy and jumpy anyway."

"Besides," Pip added, "even if I did have to carry you—you carried me out of a canyon in the Zen's Glacier River country under enemy fire. I can carry you through a few quiet, level stretches of corridor. But we've a floater ready. You won't be squished that way."

It sounded like a good idea. Pip was so smart. Why hadn't Med or Trebor suggested that? "S'long as it's no problem, then, Pip…"

2.3.10 PATIENT ANNEX 2B, COMPLEX 63, EPNOCE
0535.13.25 (LOCAL RECKONING)

MED LEANED FORWARD, HIS ENTIRE body ready to counter a possible offensive—always a chance when waking any of his wounded charges. He'd lost count of how many black eyes, chipped or missing teeth, or temporarily rearranged facial features he'd sustained over the years. He was lucky Rett hadn't ever awakened violently on him, but there was always a first time, so getting careless wasn't an option.

With a delicate touch, he triggered a few key pulse and nerve points. Then he tapped his fingers on her right knee. "Sarge."

She wasn't that deep; passed out wasn't the same as being asleep. It wouldn't be long. He frowned as a shudder went through her body. No, not a convulsion, thank deities. There had been enough of those.

A strange, squeaking sound came from her throat. Her face tightened. "…Pip?" Her voice was raw, nearly inaudible, but Med expected that.

"It's Med, Sarge. But even Pip was impressed you passed out so quickly when he asked you to."

"Didn't." She looked mortified.

Since she couldn't see him very well, he allowed himself a smile. "Oh yes, you did, passed out on demand. There were witnesses. Why don't you do that for me?"

Her dark eyebrows came together; a snarl wrinkled one side of her nose. "Maybe didn't ask," she snapped in a creak, then hissed and spread her right hand over her ribcage. The left lifted toward her face.

Med intercepted. "Touch it and I'll break both your arms. It's just oxygen, and you need it. Is it bothering you?"

She grunted something he took as a "no".

"Then leave it alone." He moved the sergeant's wayward right hand from her ribcage, being careful of the intravenous cuff covering her forearm. "More pressure isn't going to help that, either. And don't touch this, either." He indicated the cuff with an extra touch, making her aware of it. "You're still hooked in to a scrubber because of that drug

Avok shot you with, and getting fluids, and yes, I know you hate that but if you don't want me to tie you down you'll leave it be. You won't be feeling any urges to get up, I've taken care of that, as well."

"Should have left me unconscious."

"No. It's sleep you need. Which we'll get to in a bit. How do you feel?"

Her nose wrinkled again. "You tell me. Save time." Even at a hoarse whisper, the sarcasm was apparent.

This time Med laughed aloud. "Glad to hear that. Earlier, you didn't have a problem telling all of us exactly how you felt. As a matter of fact, you didn't shut up about it until Pip asked you to pass out."

"Didn't."

"Oh, yes, you did. But don't worry, they haven't discovered something you tolerate. It took a little longer to really start in, which was good for us—that fact and you going unconscious gave us enough time to get you in here and start countermeasures. It was still a bit tricky: some serious convulsions, and you stopped breathing for a while, too. None of that helped the injuries Avok and that Unethi left you with. Fortunately, they've good facilities here. Once you were over the worst of the drug reaction, I fixed most of those cuts, realigned your spine, and ran some deep sonics over your upper half to help with the bruising."

Eyeing the chrono on the wall, one ear alert for what he hoped would be stage one of his relief, Med stood up to finish preparing the poultice he was making for her neck. He pushed the floating tray closer to her bed and kept talking to distract her.

"Carakenne told me to let you know she thinks she can get your gear from the recycle chute Shannai dumped it in—before it is recycled." He set the container with the herb and mineral paste aside. "She went off to see to it with Bhayorn and H'tenneck."

"Kids!" As if suddenly remembering, the sergeant sucked in a breath and started to sit up.

He spun around just in time to stop her. "No. Don't worry. The kids are all right, back with their parents where they belong. Easy had no other fatalities, other than Druden, and Ohmara from R-troop."

He felt her pain spike at the reminder and tightened his hand briefly on her arm. "It was rough, Sarge. There were a lot of injuries, but other than Jessek, no one will be out long term. Infantry unfortunately lost fourteen—thank deities that was all. Five in combat and nine when a storage bay full of fuel went off on two platoons of them. Thirty serious burns in that particular group, but according to their respective medtechs, they'll make it. The rest have some minor burns or debris impact injury. Any other infantry casualties were not serious."

"Civilians?"

"The citizens of Complex 63 are all fine, other than some minor injuries, cuts, burns, and broken bones, a few lost and reunited kids—besides yours, I mean—lost in the confusion when Coalition troops made them move from one section to another. All safe and sound now. No serious casualties, at least not from today's fight. Avok's command wasn't easy on them. As for the Coalition, we took over six hundred into custody, about a third of those are wounded, of those, two handfuls seriously but from what I was told, they'll all recover. Infantry's taken charge of them."

"L'bon?"

"No, we kept charge of him. He's with Lieutenant Evetez. Who insisted I tell you that you can see Labonne later—*after* you've slept."

"Thanks, Med." Then she blinked hard. Her hands twitched, made fists in the covering. "My eyes?"

Med didn't have to strain any talent to understand her frustration, or the real fear beneath it. "Easy, there, Sarge. I know they hurt like fury, but as long as you don't try to strain them, they'll be okay in a day or so, thankfully. Yes, they'll even be fit enough for flying. And so will the rest of you. But *rest* is the keyword. And…hands off."

Giving a small nod, she relaxed a little, the deep lines between her eyebrows smoothing.

"I've something I want you to put on your eyes—and around your neck—but I wanted you to wake up first."

"My Omni?"

Now what? She can't be serious. "I have it, but—"

"Important." The sergeant made an impatient gesture and held her hand open in demand.

442

She is serious. Med retrieved the unit and made sure her fingers closed over it. He counted it fortunate that the military issue Omnis had the same sound sensitivity as the pcoms as the platoon leader whispered something to her device. She then held it back out to him.

Med regarded the display. It took him a moment to associate the name and face displayed there. "Kalenthi…Blaze? Yes, I remember her from the troopshuttle. But—"

"Kallet."

"Kallet? Kalebetha's son—oh!" Med glanced at Rett's notations. *Hasn't seen or heard from her family since the war started. I'd better check her status before I get excited.* Relief washed through him when he saw a bold blue Active marker on the record detail. "You're right. This is important. I'll get a dispatch out to Lieutenant Kalenthi's unit on our secure channel just as soon as I'm done here with you. Do we tell her mother and family?"

443

Rett shook her head, but in very tiny movements. "Let her contact."

"Better that way," agreed Med.

"How long have I been out?"

"An hour or so." He hesitated, chewed his lip, and continued. "I'm sorry, Sarge. "I had to send Jessek back to MainCommand. We had a jumper waiting and a storm coming in, so it couldn't wait."

Her face tightened in disappointment. She looked so sad and lost all of a sudden, her face turned away from him toward the door.

"He'll likely be going home. He said to tell you not to worry." Med settled back. He was worried about Jessek; stable now, yes, but far from knowing if they were going to save his leg or not. But Jess was as tough as an old root and always had a bright outlook on things. No matter which way things went, he'd make the best of it.

The sergeant was going to take his absence hard. Jessek was one of those who always managed to lift her out of dark moods, with some daring teasing, outrageous behavior, or funny story. Med sighed as he intercepted her hands with a sigh, not having the heart to give her the usual threats. "Don't touch."

She nodded and looked like she wanted to cry.

All the times I would like for her to just come out and cry—now is not one of them. Not with the beating those eyes took. It would just make things worse.

"I'm putting some stuff on your neck that'll help. It's warm—at first. Feels like mud, and it'll dry like it, too. That's when it comes off." He spread his concoction on a wide length of bandage, then placed it aside to remove the old dressings.

"I'll follow this up with a sonic treatment." Med applied the poultice and made sure it would stay in place. "Factor it in, since I'll do it whether you're asleep or awake. I prefer not to get a fist or elbow in my eye, thank you."

She grunted again. He left his hands in contact with her to make sure that she made the necessary mental adjustments so that his coming and going wouldn't wake her at all, unless he insisted on it.

"Avok did more physical damage to you—in less than fifteen minutes—than that handful of Coalition troopers did dragging you around the DIPA building in Circle for twice that time."

"Shit. Felt like hours."

"You know every second seems like an hour in times like that," he said, and then smacked her hand away from her bandaged left ear. "Try to touch anything again and I'll make sure you can't move more than your eyebrows for a tenday."

The sergeant subsided, her expression one of righteous affront. She sulked rather well when she put her mind to it. Med had seen it before, of course, but today her frustration, sadness, and the leftover effects from the drug added to it, touching him on a deeper level he cared to admit.

"You'll be glad to know we've destroyed a small supply of substances we found, looks like she had more than the one. I never thought I'd hear myself saying this about anyone, but when Trebor nailed her, I felt like cheering. What a..." Med looked over to the door as movement caught his eye, and made a motion for the new arrival to wait. Thank all deities. His relief had arrived. "Anyway, I'm sure you know what I mean."

"Yes."

444

"I'm glad Major Yidnar told us to stay on and make sure she didn't escape. You should hear some of the stories from the people of this complex."

"Heard enough. Avok won't be missed."

"Rett." He gentled his voice. "I won't take no for an answer. Avok's dead. You need to erase the marks she made, then and now."

After a moment and a hard shudder, she made a motion Med took as agreement.

"Good." He again intercepted her hand as it went after the bandage on her ear, holding on to it this time, hoping the contact would calm her. "I want you to sleep yourself out. Two days complete bed rest."

She didn't offer any resistance, just nodded.

"You should be completely back to normal by then."

A small sniff came from her. He pretended he didn't hear it, and hoped his backup plan, waiting to be called into action, was going to help. "I called a three-day Medical leave for all of Easy Force. We've had a busy time of it the past couple months, and taking this place was rough. We need the break, for some mental health therapy, if anything. So, we'll be staying right here at Complex 63. You don't need to worry about anything else, we'll all be right here."

This earned Med the sergeant's best effort at a suspicious glance, considering the swollen welt across her eyes and her impaired vision.

"If no worries, why being so nice?" She winced when her voice vanished completely before the end of the last word.

"I'm not going to tiff off in the presence of junior medical staffers. My relief is here," he explained in answer to Rett's sound of query.

He turned away from her to talk to the recent arrival, satisfied at the new flash of frustration he felt from the sergeant. Her injuries and exhaustion prevented her from being able to see or tag anything with her energy sense. Getting her frustrated wasn't ever a good thing, but at least, this time, it was for a good cause. She needed a nice surprise.

He greeted the newcomer. "I'm glad you came. And exactly on time—that's good. What's that?"

"A s'lute."

"Where?" Med looked around the room, expecting to see some flying creature or insect he hadn't been told about zooming around.

445

"Right here! I was reportin' for duty."

"Oh! A *salute*. I thought you were trying to catch a bug or something. We don't salute like that, and besides, you're a med assistant. Medical doesn't salute anyone."

"Oh. Well, I'm still here. You said you were going to give me special orders."

"That's right, I did. Well, listen up. She needs a nap. Her eyes hurt, so they have to be closed—if you can, make her put this on top of them."

"It's all squishy and cold," complained the new assistant.

"It'll make them feel better."

"Can I put one on my toe, too?"

"I thought I fixed that. Is it hurting?"

"No, but maybe if I have one, she'll put hers on. That's what Mommy and Daddy do sometimes."

"Then I'll get you one. Her throat is sore; so don't make her talk. As a matter of fact she's sore everywhere. And her neck aches; so no grabbing around there. If she starts picking at her bandages, or anything else, you use the comlink and call me. Other than that, you're in charge. I don't want her getting up."

"What if she has to pee?"

"It's all taken care of."

"Oh. Okay, then. I'll make sure she takes a good nap," said the newcomer very seriously. "Mommy said so, too."

"And like with the gelpack, maybe if you pretend to go to sleep, she will for real," Med whispered loud enough for Rett to hear. He had to wonder if she thought she was hallucinating, still under the influence of the drug Avok had slipped her. He knew for sure she'd never heard him talk like this before, to anyone.

"Can I come up, then? She can't see me down here," the newcomer whispered back.

"Sure," said Med. "Room enough for you."

His surprise was having the intended results. The change in his patient was gradual as comprehension dawned. The frustration and anxiety he'd sensed was soon replaced by hope and pleasure. Her sadness and pain faded the instant Olvero's weight joined hers on the bed. Yet her outward facial expression and body remained frozen, still, not quite certain if what was happening was real.

One touch from him should fix that, thought Med.

"Oh! I know what this is. So people can breathe better."

"Right. And don't let her take it off."

"I won't. What smells?"

"Medicine."

"Oh. You know what? Mommy uses stuff like that for people what has in-in-"

"Injuries," supplied Med. "Yes, she gave me some and I put it in the stuff I used."

"No yucky stuff left?"

"No yucky stuff at all. Pip and Bhayorn slicked her right up."

"She was mad just before. Is she mad at me?" Olvero asked then. "I kicked her."

447

"You told me that earlier, when I fixed your toe. But I seriously doubt she can ever be mad at you. Come on."

At last, some physical reaction. Blinking hard, she turned her sore neck and head toward Olvero, who slid close..

"It's me." He touched her cheeks, her eyebrows above the welt. "Same eyes underneath. I'm sorry for kicking you."

Med felt Rett's reaction as strongly as if Olvero had touched his skin instead of hers. He was glad he didn't have to speak, because his throat was closed tight. He went to get the gelpacks.

"Don't worry," Olvero continued, "Mommy and Daddy said it was okay for me to come. They're worried about you, too. They said I could help Med Rhozev." He patted her shoulder in reassurance. "Do you know what? When I kicked you, I broked my toe."

He turned in time to see her frown, lift her head, and reach in concern for the appendage in question. "Broken?"

"It's all right, Sarge," Med said as her concern started pushing back all the good feelings so recently surfaced. "It was minor. The older boy is fine, too." He handed the gelpacks to Olvero.

"I didn't cry, either." Olvero reconsidered and amended his statement. "Well, I did cry, but not about my toe. Later I did. Med just gave me a squishy thing for it. It's not yuck squishy, but nice squishy. Oh! Hey, do you know what? Mine is little and purple and fits right over my toes. And there is a nice green one for your eyes, too—you can see through it, see?"

He held it up to his own eyes to demonstrate. "Everything looks all pretty and green and wavy. And it's nice and cool. You don't have to be scared. Close your eyes."

She obeyed. Med reached down to help Olvero fix it in place. *I can't believe this is working so well* he thought. *Maybe I'm the one hallucinating.*

"There," Olvero said. "It won't fall off. Feels good?"

She nodded.

"Now sleep. I'll be right here." He planted a warm kiss on her cheek, then nested in close, but not touching.

The sergeant wasn't satisfied with that. She lifted her left arm.

"You're sure? Not too sore?" Olvero sounded worried.

"Not sore," she whispered.

Med knew for certain that she wasn't feeling any pain at all. Smiling, he watched Olvero snuggle in happily. He'd barely straightened the cover over them both before stopping mid-movement to stare.

Look at that, asleep in less than a minute with a smile on her face. "I wish they made them a bit more portable," he muttered. "I'd keep one in my kit."

"Kids, or gelpacks?" A low, warm voice from the doorway made him turn.

"It wasn't a gelpack that put her out without a fight in less than a minute. That was your son." He chuckled. Pip put her out too, of course, but she wasn't in any condition to resist that suggestion, much as she tried.

"Olvero thinks you did the most marvelous job on his toe," the boy's mother said. "Like magic. He likes you."

"Don't tell anyone, you'll ruin my reputation." Med rarely blushed, but he did now, and was thankful no one who knew better was around to see the telltale heat his fair complexion didn't hide. "It was just a crack, and the equipment here set it right in a few minutes."

"You don't give yourself enough credit for bedside manner, Doctor Rhozev."

"You haven't seen me with my regular patients," Med told her with a snort. "I'm sure they'd have a different opinion. Just ask that one over there when she's up for it again."

"I've seen enough since you've been here. I'm sure they all love you for it. Including that one over there."

What was—huh? Deities! Not even the tough fighters of F-troop dared ruffle his hair. Matter of fact, no one had ruffled his hair since he was eight years old, give or take a few years. His heat level deepened; he was positive he was flushed scarlet from top to bottom. And when was the last time someone addressed him as Doctor, with his real name behind it?

I'm going to get all squishy in a minute.

He cleared his throat. "Yes, well, I've some reports to file, and these two will be fine."

449

"Thank you for letting Olvero stay here. I know it was an unusual request, but he was so worried about her."

"I'm all for doing what my patients need most, unusual or not. And they both needed this."

"Com me when you want him to go home," she said, giving him a smile that curled his toes.

"Thank you." Completely recovering his aplomb and reminding himself at one time in his life he knew how to be sociable, Med smiled back at Olvero's mother, then placed a hand on her arm to walk them both out. "He takes after his other cousin. But he definitely has a Talent all his own. I'd like to keep in touch, see how it develops?"

"Yes, please do. I hope we keep contact with all of you."

"That shouldn't be much of a problem. And if he shows any interest in medicine a few years from now, look me up."

2.3.11 MEDICAL SECTION, COMPLEX 63
0535.13.26 (LOCAL RECKONING)

ONE OF THE MOST WONDERFUL SOUNDS in two worlds—the delicious, happy giggle of a child—teased Rett into a gradual, relaxed awakening. Olvero was talking somewhere close by. Two other voices she tagged as belonging to Safkas and Kallet. And an adult—Evetez.

The last identification brought her awareness level up sharply. She raised her head, the pain level diminished, her vision clear.

"See? I told you she'd wake up soon. What time is it? Hah! You owe me—"

"Good deities, Lieutenant!" Rett turned her head just enough to glare toward the bed next to hers, upon which sat or sprawled a half-dozen bodies of assorted size and age. She groaned. "Isn't it enough Pip asked me to pass out and I did? Please tell me Trebor didn't take bets on when I was going to wake up."

"Trebor? Of course not. He's too busy collecting on the wagers put against his gray hair count. But *we* did. Let's see…Safkas owes me two kisses, and Olvero owes me a story, a long one, yes you do, longer than four words. And Kallet here has just won himself a—what was that you wanted again? Me to hold Rett down while you tickle her?"

She felt pretty good. Lazy, in need of a wash and something to eat, but good. Rett stretched and snorted. "Get serious." She decided she didn't much mind being here. Her bed was more than averagely comfortable, and the annex Med had moved her into was pleasant.

"Trust me, I am serious." Evetez sounded closer now. "Thalom and Shannai wanted to watch, or help?"

The answering snickers from the two older children were definitely evil in nature. And much too close for comfort.

"Don't—" warned Rett, going from sleepily amused to realizing, with dismay, she was about to be ambushed and at a strategic disadvantage in a tangle of coverings. Evetez happened to be one of the few people who knew she was hyperticklish. "Don't you dare—*oof!* Hey! *Ow!*"

Too late, she was smothered beneath one commando lieutenant and five happy, squealing children.

* * * * *

TREBOR LEANED INTO THE ENTRANCEWAY, watching the melee in what should have been a quiet, peaceful hospital annex. Instead, it resembled a junior version of combat training. "Are we looking at another two days disability here, or what?"

"When was the last time you had the chance to romp with a bunch of kids, Trebor?" Med leaned against the opposite side of the doorframe.

"An hour ago," Trebor said, still feeling a sense of warmth and contentment. "They have children in plenty here. Just popping out everywhere, wanting to know everything."

Med grinned. "Before that?"

"I don't remember. When did I enlist? Six, seven years ago?"

"The extra time I requested we take here works more than one way," said Med. "A good many of these kids have only known one sort of soldier—your average Coalition trooper. With a few exceptions like Labonne."

"Not many like him."

"No," Med agreed. "And who knows everything the Coalition told these youngsters over the past twelve years about the Free Army. Especially lately, and especially about us. Including Sergeant Killer over there, who hates children and throws babies out windows."

Trebor's peaceful feeling vanished and he nodded. "So now the threat of Avok is gone, you want the kids to see firsthand that she and anyone else who told them such things were lying."

"Yes."

Since Med didn't move when his patient went off one edge of the bed with a yelp and three kids on top, neither did Trebor.

"Okay, okay," Rett protested. "I'm outnumbered here! OW!" A pained yelp came from the floor. "Now I think my other ear's missing!"

Med's eyebrows went up, but again he didn't move. Trebor tried to relax, but couldn't quite manage it. Sooner or later, someone was going to get hurt.

"Not to mention we all need to have this sort of connection," said the medtech as if there had never been a pause in their conversation.

"With the floor?" Trebor nodded toward the mayhem occurring there now. "We get enough of that."

451

"My point," Med continued, "is that we don't often get to make contact with the nicer side of what we're trying to protect." The stare from the medtech's sea-gray eyes was flat and challenging. "However, if you'd like to connect with the floor, I can certainly put you there."

Trebor's took a long step out of Med's reach. "I know you can. Seriously, thanks for coming up with the idea. I have to admit this is the best thing we've done in years. I just hope we don't have to wait as long before we do it again. Without it being a Medical order. And for as long as we like."

* * * * *

"HEY, I THOUGHT I WAS supposed to be the one in bed," Rett said, flat on her back halfway under that furnishing.

Kallet stretched out one side of her, Thalom on the other; Safkas sprawled across her chest. Rett had one hand protectively behind Safkas' head so she wouldn't ram it on the bedframe a handspan over it. That it was nice to finger comb the silky, spice-brown curls was a bonus.

Evetez, Shannai, and Olvero were lying across her hopelessly rumpled bed, grinning over the edge at her. All of them were panting hard and a few hiccups chirruped from here and there.

"Rank has its privileges," Evetez informed Rett. "Not many, true, but being up here while you're on the floor is one of them."

"Oh it is, is it? Maybe I'll reconsider taking my upgrades. Better yet, I'll just come up there."

Evetez sent her a smug and saucy grin. "Take your upgrades or come on up," he challenged her. "Either way, you'll never get here in time to catch us."

"You're right." Rett coughed and cleared her throat. "I lose. Just toss me my blanket, okay? I think I'll stay down here for however much longer Med's grounding me. I won't have to fall down so far." An insatiable tickle caught her throat, sending her into another brief coughing fit.

Olvero's eyes instantly rounded with concern. "Does it still hurt?" the child asked. He reached over to touch her neck, leaning so far Evetez had to grab the seat of his coverall to keep him from falling.

Rett smiled up at him. "I guess I laughed too hard. I'm okay."

Evetez lowered Olvero to the floor. He plopped down next to Rett's head in the fluid, careless manner of small children. And then, as it seemed he always had to do, he reached to touch gentle fingers on the spot he sensed she hurt the most.

"She—Avok—was very bad, wasn't she? She hurt you more after you made her fall. And then she said to get me, and you yelled, and Labonne stopped Wik. I thought Wik was going to grab him and rip him in half. But Wik knocked him down and shot him. We thought he was dead. Then Wik tried to grab me and almost did. I screamed. Really loud. I was scared. And then POW! Its arm fell off."

Rett was glad she didn't have to imagine the details from Olvero's disjointed rendition. "Yeah. That was pretty scary."

"We all screamed when we thought Labonne was dead," said Safkas, still on top of Rett. "And I screamed when someone shot off Wik's other tentacle. It kept wiggling and almost came in the door. Thalom kicked it and it grabbed his leg. He almost didn't get it off in time to push it outside."

Kallet picked up the tangled thread. "Then Shannai shot Wik right in the face and got the door closed."

"Then Cara came in through the lavatory door with Med Rhozev right behind her. Shannai nearly zapped Cara, too. She's only as big as I am," Thalom said with awe, "but I never saw anyone jump like that."

Shannai remained unhappily quiet for the exchange, her eyes dark and troubled. Leaning his head against hers for a moment, Evetez offered the girl one of his best smiles.

"Hey. No one's angry with you. Least of all Rett or Carakenne."

"But I used a weapon against them. I might have killed them—"

He laid a gentle finger to her lips, the blue eyes that were usually so mischievous dark with compassion. "It's okay, remember?"

He must have talked with her afterward, thought Rett. *That's good. Shannai needs people to talk with her about that situation—and what happened before then.*

Right now, the nod and expression of hero worship Shannai awarded Evetez made Rett smile. Her friend had definitely slain some monsters for the girl. He really wasn't bad for a bubblehead.

453

"Did Sergeant Trebor really shoot off your ear?" Kallet dared to touch a fingertip to the forbidden bandage.

"I don't know," Rett said in a forlorn voice. "Med said if I take off the bandage he's going to make me sorry."

"Labonne said there was *this* much room." Shannai made an uncomfortably small gap with her thumb and forefinger just a little smaller than the diameter of one of the cartridges used in Rett's TT-1. "Right between her ear and shoulder."

"And Trebor shot Avok right through that little hole," marveled Kallet.

Rett swallowed. At the time she'd been ready, and fully expecting, to go down with Avok. Her glance went around the group. *I'm glad I didn't.*

"And Avok's head blew up and made a big yucky mess the other grown-ups didn't want us to see." Safkas actually sounded cheated.

"I'm glad he shot her dead," said Shannai fiercely.

"Is it all right to be glad he killed her, Rett?" asked Safkas, suddenly troubled. "I want to feel better about her being dead, too. She was very bad. She killed and hurt a lot of people and was always scaring us."

"Evetez said it was okay to be glad someone who is evil can't hurt anyone any more," said Shannai.

Med joined them before Rett could say anything, for which she felt a huge relief.

Pam would have called me a chicken, and she would be entirely right. But there are things I don't feel at all confident in trying to explain to kids. This fine line—between glad someone was dead and glad they couldn't hurt anyone any more—was one of them.

The medtech leaned down to frown at Kallet. "You touched it. I saw that."

Kallet grinned, unrepentant. In that facial expression was another flashing reminder of his older sister Blaze, the Spacemarine. Rett shot a glance to her medtech, eyebrows raised. *Blaze?*

"Fix one toe, and my reputation is already in shreds. I think it's time you got off the floor, Sarge," said the medtech, a darting flicker of his gray-green eyes answering her query. He'd heard back from Blaze or her unit commander, so one way or another, and sometime soon, Kallet was going to finally get to meet his big sister.

"Hey! Where were you when I was getting knocked off my bed and tickled to death?" grumbled Rett.

"Watching. Seen enough. Come here, love." He snagged Safkas neatly and whisked her up into the air, making her squeal. "That's a hard question you asked. I don't think even I can answer it. I can try, if you want. It might be a better idea to wait until tomorrow. There's going to be a group of people arriving then. They'll talk to all of you about that and can explain much better than we can. They'll be here for a few tendays, maybe longer. How does that sound?"

"They'll talk to us, like Evetez talked to Shannai?"

"Close. They'll make it easier for you younger citizens to understand. Not only that, they can answer all different kinds of questions you might have about what happened."

455

"I'll wait then," said Safkas decisively.

Closing her eyes in relief, Rett thought that she never felt more like kissing Med senseless than at that moment. If she wasn't flat out on the floor, she would have.

Footsteps came near, and soon feet responsible for the sounds came close, closer, pausing only for a second before framing Rett's head between them. Since the familiar energy aura accompanying the newcomer belonged to Ariam, Rett didn't bother to move or open her eyes.

"Rett? Good deities! I came to see if you were ready to visit and have something to eat, and find you on the floor. Are you all right?"

"I was ambushed by Lieutenant Tickle and the Giggle Patrol." Rett did her best to look and sound pathetic. She reached up limply with one arm. "They had no mercy. Help me, Ariam."

"Oh, give here, you big baby." Without ceremony, Ariam pulled Rett to her feet and dusted her off.

"Maybe you can cover for me while I clean up a bit." Rett didn't wait for Ariam's agreement. She snatched up the change of clothing some thoughtful med assistant had left out for her and fled into the lavatory. She wished she had time for a real cleanup, but contented herself in the meanwhile with the basics and a change from the thigh length hospital shirt to a soft gray inner shirt and clean old fatigues. She took an extra minute for a look at her arms and shoulders. Med had done a good job. Only faint pink lines remained from the shredding Avok had given her. A furrow the length of her littlest finger was new. She puzzled over it for a moment, then realized it was from the shot Trebor had made.

The area between left collarbone and breast was still bandaged, so she didn't dare peek beneath. But it felt all right. As an afterthought she checked her face, relieved the welt and swelling across her eyes was diminished enough that she at least looked humanoid.

"Enough of that." She bundled up her discarded clothing, cleaned her teeth, and rejoined the others.

"You were fast. You look better. Ariam says we can all go and have lunch together!" Olvero bounced down from Ariam's arms. He clambered atop the rumpled bed to claim his previous position. No one else had moved. "Lieutenant Tickle!" Olvero said suddenly. "You know what? That's *your* new name!" His hands dove for Evetez's ribs.

"Oh, come on now." Even as he moved to defend himself, Evetez threw a hard glare toward Rett, the look promising retribution later. "Don't—"

"I like it," said Shannai, her hands going for the lieutenant's other side.

"Was that a screech I heard from him?" Ariam's eyes widened.

Rett crossed her arms over her chest and considered. "I think it was more of a squeal."

"Oh, like you didn't get pretty shrill yourself, Sergeant Kil—" Evetez's attempt at rebuttal ended in another explosive burst of uncontrolled laughter. "Yow! Hey, I thought we were on the same team! This is insubordination, you know!"

"Let's get Lieutenant Tickle," said Kallet, and Thalom nodded. Both boys joined the mayhem on the bed. The entire melee soon landed with a single loud thump on the floor on the opposite side.

Rett, Ariam, and Med, who still held Safkas, paused, ready to react to any sounds of distress. All they heard were giggles and Evetez's protests. Which, Rett supposed, counted as distress if she really wanted to get technical.

Not particularly.

Then she experienced a sharp moment of disorientation that sent her staggering into Ariam.

"Lieutenant Tickle is a much nicer name than Sergeant Killer," Safkas was saying, her voice echoing as if from far away.

Trust you to reenter with a bang!

~I'm back! Are you all right? Are the kids all right? What about Jessek? Did I miss anything?~ Pam asked.

It wasn't long this time. I'll catch you up later. But back down. Med's on me like a targeting scope, thought Rett urgently, for as her vision cleared she could see the warning implicit in Ariam's eyes.

"You are absolutely right, Safkas, Tickle is much nicer than Killer. So why don't you go tell him that?" Med set Safkas on the floor. "You, Sarge, over here." His alert gaze searched her face as she obeyed. "Time I looked at that ear."

Relief flooded Rett, and she plunged directly onto the very topic that would divert him. "Thanks for timing that intervention, Med." 457

"Sure. We've been getting some sticky questions, not only from 'our' group of kids, but also from some of the others. And Labonne was the one who suggested this squad of yours would benefit from some counseling, especially Shannai."

"Thalom said she was roughed up, but that was as much as Shannai let him say."

"She wasn't raped," Med confirmed. "Handled rudely enough, which is almost as bad, and came close to it at least once, from what I heard. Verbally terrified for sure."

"I wasn't too sure how far things went. I was hoping to get her alone for a talk. So Evetez beat me to it. He's very good."

"He is. He took a good deal of roughness from her edges. Your sister there, she helped in a big way, too."

Rett sent a grateful smile to Ariam.

"She wouldn't talk to me at all. And I was even being nice." Med made a face.

"Maybe that's why," Ariam dared to say, earning a hard glance from Med.

"One of the doctors here checked her over, though," Med said, turning back to Rett with a frown. "The trauma specialists coming in can safely deal with the rest."

Pam, thank all deities, sat quietly burning with curiosity while Rett patiently endured Med's examination of her eyes, neck, and throat. Both of them held on to that patience as he went on to having her twist, bend and flex the rest of her body. He nodded over the progress of the other wounds. "It'll match up in a couple days," Med assured her.

Rett snorted. "When have I worried about parts of me matching up in the past ten years?"

"Just saying."

"You did a good job, Med. Thanks."

He grunted. "Oh, I'm sure you'll blow it all to shit sometime in the next tenday."

Pam squirmed a bit, but held steady. Taking pity on her, Rett tried to send bits and flashes of what she remembered, but it didn't work as well for her to send them as it did for Pam to pick them out herself. And that she couldn't allow right now. *Later—and I promise.*

Next was a blood test—since Med was still tracking her chemical balances at regular intervals. Soon, Rett's patience, and the good feeling she'd had, eroded like an avalanche gaining momentum as the blood test was followed by whatever other trivial and insignificant test or procedure he thought of to drive her mad in the interim. She was aware the tickle fight had stopped. Six curious faces, seven counting Trebor's, well, eight, including Ariam, were waiting, their attention riveted on the tight, neat bandage covering the object of the most speculation at Complex 63.

Pam's frustration level peaked, almost causing Rett to echo it vocally. They both scrambled to dampen the reaction as Med grabbed Rett's chin in his hand and made her look him in the eyes.

"Something you wanted to tell me?" he asked.

"I'm hungry," she said.

"Good. As soon as I'm finished here." His fingers moved to her neck, thumbs against the back of her skull. Rett concentrated on mushrooms and on how hungry she was and how delicious a nice big mug of tea would taste. Her belly helped out of its own accord with a grumble loud enough to make all the kids giggle. "Hmm. I think another night of poulticing would be best, it'll take the last of the stiffness out of your neck," Med remarked, at last dropping his contact.

"Sure, Med." Another ten-hour shift wrapped from collarbone to ears in warm squishy stuff that turned into cold, squishy stuff that she didn't dare ask the ingredients of. And unlike the gelpacks, Med's poultice was not a very nice squishy. *Wonderful.*

"I'll get it ready."

His aura registered strong on her mind. Med enjoyed every minute, every second, of his spotlight. *He can give lessons in dramatic effect,* thought Rett sourly. She started to sigh with the deepest degree of resignation she could muster. Then she glanced in her sister's direction, then toward Lieutenant Evetez and the children.

Inspiration struck. And without the slightest help from an astonished Pam, who was stunned into mental inertia as Rett went into action.

Rett traded her building sigh for what she hoped was a seductive smile. Taking a lesson from Ariam, she tilted her head and sent Med a sideways glance through her eyelashes. Pitching her voice even lower than usual, she spoke. "Med?" As unmusical as she was normally, she managed to get at least three good notes into his name.

He froze midstep and turned to face her. She couldn't describe his expression, but she filed his reaction for future reference. Med cleared his throat. "Sergeant?"

She imagined her voice was as dark and sweet as spicebush root syrup. "Are you ticklish, Med?" Rett's still-sore throat and her effort to hold back giggles at how silly she must look and sound only added a husky purr to her voice.

Med was frozen in his tracks. She wasn't sure he was breathing.

Okay, this is working... let's go for the kill. All I have to lose is ten hours in a squishy poultice.

She let her smile grow, starting out slow and letting it spread. Whatever he had in his hands fell unnoticed to the floor.

"Well?" she drawled.

Med started to say something, swallowed, tried again. He picked up what he had dropped to get more time. He glanced at Lieutenant Evetez and the children, who wiggled their fingers at him, and then gave up gracefully. "I'll just take that bandage off now, shall I?"

"Whatever you want, Med," agreed Rett.

Ariam, gray eyes wide, sagged into a sitting position alongside Rett as if her knees had melted. Her hands were dramatically pressed over her heart. "Good deities, Rett. You did it. You absolutely did it. That shot hit dead center. We should have recorded this for training vids."

Pam, still astonished, managed to convey an enthusiastic, if bemused, congratulations.

"Like her passing out on demand the other day? I'd credit the threat of Lieutenant Tickle to my...discomfiture, thank you," said Med to Ariam.

"Credit whomever you like, Med. I know what I saw, and the end result is that you fell, and fell hard." Ariam laughed. "I will never, *ever* forget the expression on your face. Oh, and this is a good one, too." She laughed so hard she rolled to her back, the hands over her heart moving down to clutch her flat belly.

Med's dire frown reversed itself in the next second. Ariam's laughter was simply too infectious to resist. "All right, I was hit, good and solid. Never expected it. But don't expect to get away with something like that again." He glared at Rett, then let out a rueful chuckle. Swiping his hand through his sandy hair, Med shook his head and took a breath.

"No," Rett said, taking pity on him. Sort of. "I won't try it again. It'll ruin this memory." She had to bite the inside of her cheek in order to keep herself cool and nonchalant. Otherwise she'd be laughing her head off like Ariam.

"You'll be lucky if Evetez ever forgives you for his new name," Med said then. "The kids aren't going to let it go."

"I handled Killer for over six years, he can handle Tickle for however much longer he'll be in uniform." She straightened her back, tossed her head—not very hard, since her neck was still sore—and recrossed her arms. "Now, do I have something that looks like an ear over there? It never felt like anything was wrong with that part of me, you know."

Without further ado, Med removed the dressing from Rett's ear. His disagreeable face was back, his eyes narrowed as he leaned close. "Humph."

"Humph tells me a whole lot," Rett said.

"Well. Let's have a look." Sitting up, Ariam swiped the back of her hand across her shining eyes, then stood so she was better able to scrutinize what everyone saw except Rett. "I guess it's still there, but it's definitely dented, Rett. At least it's a perfectly symmetrical curve, with a nice matching mark over the top of your shoulder. Great shot, Trebor."

Pam couldn't help it. ~Trebor shot you? In the ear?~

No, Trebor shot Avok right through the left eye, returned Rett with inward satisfaction. *My ear and shoulder just happened to be in his path.*

"It's not quite symmetrical, Ariam, see here?" Lieutenant Evetez's hand was intercepted and nearly broken by Rett when he tried to point out the exact spot. "All right, I know when I'm not wanted," said Evetez with a wounded sniff.

Rett didn't trust him, especially when she saw him beckon to Safkas and Kallet, who followed him from the room.

"Going to hit me, too?" Trebor wanted to know.

"If you touch it, you're taking your chances."

A deep twinkle of amusement lurked just below the surface of her second's long golden eyes. Trebor regarded Rett for an extra moment before answering. "I won't touch your ear."

Then he put a firm hand on each of her shoulders and leaned close to seriously study his work. "Hmm. It was one of my better ones, but there's room for improvement. I think I might have gone a little too far to the right."

"Why don't I stand over there? You can make the other ear match." Rett sulked.

~Good grief, are you sure I was only gone a day or so on this end? You're just a regular pro all of a sudden!~

I've had good instruction. But I'm feeling a need for someone to take pity on me. First I get the shit squished out of me by Avok and company, next I get knocked from my bed and tickled to death, then Ariam calls me a big baby, Med tortures me with tests, and Trebor thinks he could have carved a better looking scar.

~Poor baby.~ Pam awarded Rett a soothing mental pat on the head. *And here's Olvero. Go deep again, okay?*

Pam obliged.

"Let me see it." Olvero climbed into Rett's lap. Very carefully, he knelt on her thighs and rose on his knees, taking her face in his chubby brown hands to make his own examination. "Does it hurt?"

"No," she said, her voice unhappy, her wounded pride grateful for his ready compassion.

"Don't listen to them. It doesn't look so bad. You can hardly see it. Don't worry, I still think you look very nice. Almost as pretty as my mom." He threw his arms around her neck—carefully—and planted a big smacking kiss on her cheek. "There! And one more to feel better." He did just that.

Rett hugged him. Maybe she had no business saying it to him without checking with his parents. But she couldn't deny a bond of some kind was between her and this particular child, one that was strong and deep. She couldn't keep what she felt inside any longer. "I love you, Olvero."

"That's wonderful, huh, Olvero?" Ariam plopped down alongside Rett again and leaned close, her smile pure joy. "Did you tell her yet?"

He covered his mouth, eyes widening. "I forgot. I'll tell her now." Fixing an earnest look on Rett, he started out by saying: "You know what?"

"What's that?"

"She's your sister." He pointed to Ariam. "And she's even a Special Forces like you. Did you know that?"

Rett swallowed back a laugh in order to return the serious intent Olvero was awarding her. Talented or not, he was still every bit a four-year-old. "Now I do. I'm glad you told me. Little sisters are always sneaking around without telling anyone what they're doing."

He giggled. "I didn't mean that."

"Then what?"

"She's my—what's that word again?" he asked Med, who whispered the answer in his ear. "Cousin."

"Ariam?"

He nodded. "And so are you."

"Me?"

"That's why I love you so much and you love me so much too."

"Cousin—? But...we don't—" Rett pushed her fingers through her hair, feeling extraordinarily stupid. "How is it possible? I mean..." Floundering again, she begged Ariam to help her out. "Dad's side is gone, Mother was from offworld. I know she had two sisters, but they both lived at GTC Central. We haven't heard from any of them since I was Olvero's age. So—"

"Don't try to figure it out, Rett. It's true. Don't tell me you can't feel Olvero in your mind just as you do me and P—" Ariam quickly reworded her statement, "—probably the same as you used to feel Tova. We went from zip to three. Enjoy it."

"When Med Rhozev started checking your bandage, Lieutenant Tickle let me message Mommy and Dad with his pcom." Olvero sounded proud of being so privileged. "And now they can see you because your ear's not shot off."

It took Rett a few seconds to understand exactly what Olvero meant. She covered her mouth with one hand to stifle her reaction. A snort still escaped, but she managed to turn it into a cough.

"And now you can see you look like my Mommy and she can see you look like her, too. You're *way* bigger than her, but you have the same eyes. You even have the same hair what's so slippery."

Serious now, Rett adjusted Olvero's position on her lap and eyed him. "You keep saying that. What do you mean?"

"Look. See? She's coming in now." Olvero pointed to the doorway, where two adults paused for a moment to greet Med before turning toward the group on and around Rett's bed.

Rett's breath caught in her throat with the same hard force it had under Avok's choke loop. The woman was slender, her skin dark, deep brown. Long, loose hair rippled in a black waterfall down her back, ending only a handspan above the backs of her knees. The frontmost sections were gathered into two glossy braids that hung over her shoulders.

The sergeant was glad she had Olvero on her knees, because if she'd been standing up she would have certainly lost her balance. Glad of

463

Pam, despite her own astonishment ready with the soothing mantra of *easy, easy, easy, breathe!* Glad of Ariam alongside, grounding her in reality.

Even so, she had to think, *Ariam would not be so cruel not to tell me before now.* And then she remembered: "We went from zip to three"... and that Olvero was her cousin, not her brother. No. No matter how hard she might have wished it, the woman coming toward her wasn't her mother, and Tovadan wasn't going to materialize from behind her. But this woman, even her hair worn in the same traditional style of her mother's homeworld, might have been Tonia's twin, and that left two possible choices for identity.

"Hello, Rett."

The voice decided it. She remembered her Aunt Valera's voice, a bit deeper than Tonia's had been, the offworld accent stronger with the lilting music of the watery planet that was her homeworld. "Valera." It came out as a whisper.

Her aunt smiled. "So you did inherit the same talent as Oonaugh— the one for voice recognition. It crops up every now and then among the people of my homeworld. Lords of brightness, look at you—you've grown at least a length and a half since I've seen you. Are you taller than your father now?"

Pam had to remind Rett to breathe again. *Valera.* She had visited them on Nyorfias for a while, long ago. But most of Rett's recollection of her was from the images her mother had showed them, the words spoken as Tonia lovingly described the family she'd left when she decided to make her home on Nyorfias. *"Most people mistakenly thought we were triplets. Except Val has my Dad's nose—like yours, Rett—and Oonaugh has brown hair."*

Tiny, colorful sparkles from the two braids hanging over the woman's shoulders caught and reflected the overhead lighting. *She's even wearing beads in her hair like Mother used to.* The tiny crystal chips danced and winked like stars as Valera bent to give Rett a warm hug around the shoulders. She didn't have to bend far. She was only half a head taller than Carakenne.

The physical contact broke Rett's trance and freed her voice. Clearing her throat, Rett tried again. "Aunt Valera. It's been a long time. Twenty…" *How old was I then? How old am I now?* It had been an eternity since Rett had even considered her own age. "…twenty-three years?"

"Yes. You were just turned five. Tovadan a toddler. Ariam a very tiny baby."

"Are you real? This isn't some weird aftereffect of Avok's drug?"

Valera sat alongside and took Rett's hands in hers. "Yes, I am," she said, simply, softly.

Rett stared at the contrast between her scarred, big hands and the darker fine-boned ones that, despite their fragility, gave the impression of strength.

Like Mother's.

"You know what? I'm going to be five," Olvero was saying. He stopped. "What's wrong, Rett? Did Mommy make you hurt inside?" He put a small hand over her heart, quick tears of sympathy brimming in his own eyes. "She didn't mean to hurt you. She thought you would be happy."

465

"I know that, sweetheart. And I am happy. I was just remembering my own mother." Rett glanced up at Ariam, then back at her aunt. "Another empath in the family," Rett said with a smile and a shaky laugh. "Should I be surprised? Aunt Valera, it's good to see you, but I'm in shock. Mother said you'd taken a permanent job as a translator with the GTC at the Core Station. Last I checked, that's a five-year trip from here."

"And I almost made it there, too. But I felt more strongly that I should come back here. Tonia and I had a connection between us…"

Rett and Ariam exchanged watery glances. They knew what that was like.

Valera did not miss their exchange. "With the precognitive talent I have, I simply knew something was going to happen to my sister. And that I wanted to reach her if I could.

"I was too late, of course, I knew she was gone, but by then, the ship was insystem and anyone entering Nyorfian space, who wasn't turned back or destroyed, was forced to land on Epnoce. I've been here ever since. And here I met Ulorath—Olvero's father." She held her hand out to draw the kind-faced man with whom she had arrived into the group.

"Ulorath, you met Ariam. This is Rett, my sister's firstborn."

Ulorath clasped Rett's offered hand with both of his, accepting her as family. She found his grip warm and strong.

"I'm glad to meet you," he said. "Thanks for taking care of our son."

"It was just about the other way around," Rett said with a short laugh.

Ulorath let that go with a small shake of his head. "Olvero has spoken of you and your resemblance to Valera—among other things—non-stop since coming back day before yesterday. We're proud to have you and Ariam in the family."

"I'm glad to meet you, too. Olvero didn't get to be wonderful from only his mother's side." Hands already occupied, she settled for giving him one of her best smiles.

Ulorath smiled back. "I know where you and Ariam got those smiles you use so well." The glance of loving affection he sent to his partner said so much more than words.

"I sent Dad a message," Ariam mentioned to Rett, who'd just wondered if Colonel Reve had any idea of Valera's existence. Even if she wasn't communicating with her father in any regular manner, this was something he had to know.

"And?"

"He'll try to get here for a day or so when he can."

"You have a dad?" asked Shannai. "I mean…of course you do, but is he around? What's his name?"

"Reve," Rett said.

"Wow," said Thalom. "Colonel Reve, from the 21st? He's your *dad?*"

Arms crossed, Ariam nudged Rett's leg with her foot, a very peculiar grin on her face and a daring gleam deep in her eyes. *You'd better swallow it for now, Rett,* said her sister's direct look loud and clear.

"He's Ariam's dad, too," Rett conceded gruffly.

"Oh! That's not what I meant, you logheaded idiot!" Ariam uncrossed her arms and swatted Rett on top of the head.

"I mean, yes, Colonel Reve is my dad."

"Better," Ariam said.

"Deities, Ariam, I've been knocked around enough. I don't need it from you." Rett shot her sister a glare.

Ariam just smiled.

"Colonel Reve's as famous as you are," said Shannai.

Olvero frowned. "But, Rett, why—"

Rett clamped down on her thoughts and laid a finger on Olvero's lips, stopping him. Dropping her head so her mouth was close to his ear, she whispered, "Olvero, that's something I don't discuss. One day I'll explain, but until then, we don't mention it. Please?"

"Promise to tell me when the war is over," he whispered back gravely.

"I promise."

"You and Ariam have so much of both of them," observed Valera after Rett hugged Olvero and lifted her head. "Well, except for that dent in the bottom of your ear," she added, her dark eyes teasing.

"At least it's almost perfectly symmetrical."

Valera changed the subject, earning Rett's eternal gratitude. "By the way, Olvero, who is this Lieutenant Tickle you mentioned?"

"You know him, Mommy. He's Rett and Ariam and Trebor and Tris and Atira and Mordell and Semage's lieutenant. He just went somewhere with the other kids—maybe to tickle someone else. We tickled Rett until she fell right out of bed." He sounded proud of the fact.

Rett chuckled. "It sounds as if you've met everyone in Easy Force in—what—less than two days? Or only the platoon leaders and seconds?"

"Oh, all of them I think. They're great fun, and you always slept so much longer than my naptime. But I came back to check you."

"He did," confirmed Med. "Faithfully."

Just then Evetez returned, somehow in the interim having quadrupled the number of children with which he departed. No doubt those four with hair color ranging from red-gold to russet were all related to Kallet, two of those obviously twins.

"Now this is going a bit over the top." The unusual affability Med had been displaying vanished into a threatening scowl. "A handful of kids roughhousing in here is one thing, but two handfuls?"

"We weren't going to do anything, Med, the kids just wanted to see the—" Evetez rapidly assessed the situation and brought his troops to an orderly halt just inside the room.

467

"How much are you charging them for admission?" Rett demanded peevishly. "I want a decent percentage."

But Evetez just shook his head. "I can see you're busy. We'll have to try later," he told the kids with him. They withdrew.

"See? That's Lieutenant Tickle, Mommy."

"I was unaware of his other name," Valera answered.

Rett's arms tightened around Olvero. "I didn't know I had any cousins, Olvero—but now that I do, you're exactly what I like the most about having one."

Olvero beamed and kissed her again, then settled back in her lap with a sigh, his sunny expression darkening, lower lip trembling.

"What is it, love?" Ariam asked. "Why are you sad?"

"I wish you both were little like me, so you didn't have to fight the bad people anymore and get hurt. Maybe get dead. You could come and live with us. I want sisters."

Rett buried her face in his neck for a minute. "Oh, Olvero. That would so nice. I'm sorry that we can't do it."

"I know. When I asked Mommy she s'plained it. But I still wish it could happen."

Ariam, already leaning into Rett's body, leaned in a bit more and bent her head toward Olvero. "I have something for you. A present."

"For me?"

A shiver went right up Rett's spine as Ariam's left hand went to her utility belt. She knew it went to the special pocket that never went into combat, but stayed safely behind. And she knew, too, what would come out of it.

As Ariam opened her closed fist, the bright lighting overhead caught and reflected in a storm of blue sparks covering every possible hue and range, from white-blue to blue-violet.

Those around them, who Rett had all but forgotten, gasped softly.

Olvero took the azurium crystal with both hands and cupped it gently. "This is for me?" His brown eyes shone, small blue lights flashing in them from the highly refractive crystal. "You loved him very much."

"Yes." Ariam sounded choked for a moment. "This belonged to our brother."

Rett couldn't say anything. She returned the pressure Ariam was leaning into her and tried to swallow past the fresh, sharp aches in her throat.

Olvero nodded. "What got killed with Mommy's sister."

"Tovadan gave it to me to take care of until he came back from Epnoce. I know he'd want his cousin to have it now."

"And you have the other piece?"

Reaching again into her belt pocket, Ariam produced hers.

Without hesitation, Olvero fitted the two halves together. "It's one again, see? Like our family."

"Yes," Ariam said softly. "And it always reminded me even if we're not one piece, we're still together."

Understanding what Ariam didn't say, Rett closed her eyes. She felt the warm pressure of her sister's fingers clasp her hand.

"I won't forget," Olvero said. "Thank you, Ariam." He lifted his arms to hug her. "I'll take good care of it. Just like you did for Tovadan. I still wish you can live with us."

"Excuse me—I know Evetez said there was a family reunion going on here, but timing is critical and I need to interrupt for a moment."

Rett startled exhale made Olvero's head turn to the doorway. He clung to her as she rose to her feet.

"Is he a bad man?" His whisper was very loud. "He doesn't look bad." Anyone standing within ten lengths heard that. "He's a Special Forces like you." Olvero cocked a confident eye at Yidnar's rangy form, not at all bothered by the stern expression on the officer's rugged face.

"I didn't expect you so soon, Major," said Med.

"I didn't come for a visit—that will have to wait for a while yet. Lieutenant? If any of those with you belonged to the original group, bring them in with you."

Evetez slipped inside with Safkas and Kallet, who both moved to be closer to Thalom and Shannai. The other kids crowded close to the door, but stayed in the corridor.

"I'm sorry to interrupt a personal moment, Rett. MainCommand and the Planetary Council have been persuaded to take a case under

469

advisement and they're waiting for me to finish my assessment—been working on that since I got in this morning, which is why I haven't been in to see you yet."

"Yes, sir. What's up?"

"I've been interviewing citizens concerning about a man named Branwud Labonne. He wants to stay here at Complex 63."

A storm of questions from the children inside the room greeted this statement.

"I thought he was just Labonne."

"He wants to be Nyorfian like us?"

"You mean he doesn't have to go away and be locked up somewhere?"

"He can stay and be the school warden like always?"

"He'll get to help my new baby brother get born?" asked Safkas, her eyes shining. "Like he did with me when Mommy had me after curfew and needed help, and they didn't let anyone go anywhere, not even to the hospital?"

Rett stepped closer to Trebor, letting her arm bump against his. "I'm gladder yet that you and the others held back from taking a shot at him."

Trebor moved his head in agreement. "I like him."

"He won't have to listen to the bad people any more? They made his head and tummy hurt a lot," said Olvero.

"Is that right?" Major Yidnar asked. "He won't ever have to deal with them again, that I can tell you right away."

The kids cheered.

"However..." The Major's word cut through the din without shouting or using That Voice. When they quieted, he went on. "The final decision rests on a majority agreement from the residents of this complex. I was told to talk personally with everyone before submitting my report. This is why I'm here. It seems five important people were missing from the school groups I just finished talking to."

"That's us. Me, Kallet, Shannai, Safkas, and Thalom. See? There's five. I can count up to one hundred, so I know how many five is." Olvero turned to Ariam and returned her half of the azurium crystal. He tucked his carefully into a deep cargo pocket on his jumpsuit.

Then he walked up to the Major and took his big hand. "We should go now anyway. That mean old Avok that Trebor killed dead when he shot off Rett's ear hurt her throat so it's sore. You know what? She laughed too much because we made her fall off her bed and now she needs to take a nap—but not until after lunch. I think Rett and Ariam and Mommy might want to have lunch by themselves now," he confided to Yidnar. "You know what? I broked my toe, but Med fixed it. Do you want to hear me count?"

"I would, but not right now." Yidnar glanced toward Rett. "When we get back here, Sergeant, I'll expect you to have started a more standardized report." A sharp look forestalled any comment from Med. "Since you're still on Medical disability—though I can't imagine why after hearing about what happened in here earlier—" his expressive eyebrows completely disappeared for a moment beneath his headband, "—Sergeant Trebor and Lieutenant Evetez will be more than happy to assist. Especially with those portions you were not present for. I advise you dismiss those extra visitors waiting outside, Lieutenant. At least until the report is finished."

"Yes, sir."

"Shall we go?" The Major offered his free hand to Safkas, who took it readily and added an engaging smile and a flutter of her curly eyelashes. The last of Yidnar's serious expression vanished as if it'd never appeared.

2.3.12 A PLACE OUT OF TIME

PHEASYCE DIDN'T HAVE A SOLID form, and couldn't remember if there was a time she actually had to breathe. But as the last of Xonomer's essence slipped away, it was as if a constriction on her entire being went with the dark entity.

Xonomer had said nothing. A bad sign. It didn't bode well for the final levels. Nothing would be held back.

The happy atmosphere surrounding her key Player at the moment filled her with hope, although she remained uneasy. Her focus on Rett and the children during the crisis just passed had brought her deepest doubt to the surface.

"Is it that you have made them dependent?"

The Speaker for her Order had joined her. Startled—and chagrined for not being aware of her mentor until that moment—Pheasyce didn't know how to respond.

"You are wondering why I—why none of us—have called you out on this?" Minos asked gently. "You are yet a neophyte, but ceased being a student when you began your testing phase; when you were given responsibility for this planetary system and these people. Faults can be assets. Assets can be faults. What will be, will be, and how you caused all things in this system to define themselves was entirely up to you."

"Connecting these people so strongly to this system and these worlds that they would choose to die as a race, instead of trying to start again elsewhere, is an asset?" Pheasyce turned away from the Speaker.

She must have appeared weak, for he reached out to infuse energy with her life essence, strengthening her.

"This doubt you feel has just cause, but it has been enhanced by Xonomer. I feel the dark influence in your life energy. Dismiss it. I cannot advise you on your Game, but I can give you personal advice. So take heed, Pheasyce. Do not overstep yourself. Release your concerns for any time but this one. Guardians, and the entities of Light and Dark, can step outside of Time, but none of us can change the past any more than we predict the future. Yet none of us must be so burdened either by doubt, or by faith, that we make each move blindly. This is where Tianorius failed with the Zetinorians."

Pheasyce winced. The Zetinorian Guardian had dissolved completely into the matrix of the universe after being convinced to let go any lingering grasp on his surviving Players. Those that were left were free to choose their destiny. The addition of the one named Labonne just a short while ago had filled Pheasyce with joy.

Then she looked at her key Player, her remembered joy fading. Would the one named Jaq choose to return? And choose to stay?

"Pheasyce. Do not concern yourself with what is not. Only with what is. This is what you must Balance within yourself if you are to be a worthy Guardian of Balance in this system. Every moment you spend doubting will be taken advantage of by Xonomer."

And with that, the Speaker was gone.

473

2.3.13 MEDICAL SECTION, COMPLEX 63
0535.13.26 (LOCAL RECKONING)

RETT WONDERED AT THE SHIFT in her aunt Valera's energy only seconds after the Major departed with the children.

Valera threw her and Ariam a wink, then turned to the other who still lingered. "Lieutenant Evetez, Sergeant Trebor. Maybe you two can get started on the report," she suggested. "You can bring it back with you in an hour or so. Better yet, we'll call when you can come back."

Rett clamped her teeth together and hoped her face didn't show her personal surprise at her aunt's tone and manner. Oh, it was pleasant, but definitely dismissive.

"The Major said—" Evetez stopped short when Valera held up a slender brown hand.

"Yes. I heard him. I'm so happy you're willing to help so we three can have some quality family time and a bite to eat while the children are elsewhere." Valera seated herself between Rett and Ariam, sliding an arm around each of them. "Dismissed. Go. Later. Thank you." And then she smiled.

Rett was quick to follow her lead, adding one of her very best smiles. From the corner of her eye, she saw Ariam light up with one of her own.

~Noted for future reference,~ said Pam.

"You're outgunned, Lieutenant." Ulorath offered a steadying hand to Evetez, who had the goofiest expression on his face and seemed to have been stricken with some strange paralysis. "Close your mouth, there, sport. Come on, I'll help you."

"Me, too," said Med, warily sidling toward the door. "I'll...have some lunch sent in. And make sure he gets the medical details straight."

~Man, she's good. Rett—I'm so happy for you. You found a cousin, an aunt, an uncle. I'm sorry I was gone earlier and couldn't help, but I'm happy I'm here to share this.~

Thanks, Pam.

A half-smile on his fierce face, Trebor gave Valera a nod of respect and without another word turned and followed the others out of the room.

474

"Slick move, Aunt Valera," complimented Ariam with pure admiration.

"As much as I like Labonne and want him to stay with us, having time with you both is more important. We have to grab and take what we can get in these times." Valera sat back down, keeping her arms around them. She gave Rett a very penetrating look.

~Oh my God.~ Pam was stunned, a sensation that spread into Rett as understanding dawned. ~She knows I'm here.~

"Yes I do," Valera said. "How very interesting."

How? And she went right past me to you without me—

~Apparently. And she even knows my name. You were worried about Olvero? Well...~

Rett swallowed. "Valera, I—"

Valera shook her head. "You don't need to explain. Or worry that I'll give away your secret. Just as I always knew it wasn't a good time for others to know the level of my Talent, I understand it's not a good time for others to know to know of your ego-merge."

"You know about them?" Ariam leaned forward.

"Not much more than you probably do. But I'm glad you have such a friend, Rett—and I'm concerned, because these things always have a reason."

Rett hunched her shoulders and looked down at her knees for a moment. "You wouldn't happen to know what that is?"

"No, I don't. But now I know why I was so driven to study all that was available about the merges."

Rett scraped a hand through her hair. She knew two people in her mother's family were Adepts, but she'd never heard Valera's name mentioned as one of them. "You're a Master Adept. And the GTC never came looking for you when you didn't return?"

"The GTC doesn't own me. But they've been in contact since arriving to back up our fight. They'll be sending a few extra people here to help protect and teach Olvero. I'm glad of that. But let's talk about the two of you. I want to know everything." Valera tightened the arm she had around Rett. "I know Pam doesn't mind if we ignore her for a while to catch up."

-No. I'll just be right here, in my little corner. Listening.-

Valera kissed Ariam on the cheek, then Rett. "Tonia's daughters. My heart is full again."

Rett's attention was caught for a moment, when Ariam opened her hand and the azurium crystal she held flashed blue sparkles. Ariam looked over at her and smiled. "I've carried these for so long." She took Valera's right hand and nestled the crystal in her aunt's palm, placing her hand over the slender brown one firmly. "I want you to have mine, Aunt Valera."

And Rett reached over to close her hand over both of theirs.

-oOo-

END OF BOOK TWO

The Adventure Continues in

STRATAGEM
Journey to Nyorfias, Book 3

ABOUT. THE AUTHOR

TERRY (T.M.) ROY'S PRIMARY CAREER is as a book designer, writer, editor, and graphic artist. By any other time she's a fiction writer, artist, illustrator, and anything else life demands she must be.

In 2003, Roy's novel, *Discovery*, was a finalist in the 2003 EPIC Awards for Best Science Fiction Romance. She prefers to write adventure stories in sci-fi settings, some of which have been over twenty years in the making.

She was lost in a wormhole for a while and stranded in North Dakota for eight years, but found her way back through the event horizon into the Pacific Northwest. A random tesseract then transported her back to the Upper Midwest where she now resides in the Minneapolis-St. Paul metro area with an opinionated Quaker parrot named Apple and a Senegal parrot, Sir Hugo the Naked.

When she's not writing, formatting, or drawing, she is campaigning to save the honeybee, gardening, "putting up" food, and when she can afford it, flying small airplanes.

She likes hearing from her readers. Feel free to drop an email to tmroy@zapstone.com or visit her Facebook pages:

Author page: http://www.facebook.com/pages/
TM-Roy-Terran-Moffat/297327413694111
Blog: https://teryvisions.wordpress.com/

ACKNOWLEDGEMENTS

THROUGH THE YEARS AND MANY revisions of this book I'd like to thank my fabulous sisters (Cathy, Nancy, Sharon, Maria, and Laura), who either eagerly listened to me read the very earliest versions and/or gave a lot of their personal qualities to my characters; my good friend Sara V., whose enthusiasm encouraged me to bring this story to the public and patiently edited through several heavy revisions; Kimberly S., who did some heavy nuts and bolts editing at one time; the sparkling Karli K., who fell instantly in love with my characters and gave fresh perspective; the magnificent Mary N., who willingly plunged into editing although she wasn't at all sure she liked science fiction; and finally but most especially to my friend and final editor, the indomitable and fiercely talented Cathy Wiley, without whom I would have never—again—found the will or courage to revise and complete this epic adventure.

www.ingramcontent.com/pod-product-compliance
Lightning Source LLC
Chambersburg PA
CBHW030910050726
47498CB00003BA/670